Reviews for *Love Me If You Can*

"Marie-Nicole Ryan has done it again in *Love Me If You Can* from beginning to the end." Black Ravens Reviews

"This is a mature and complex love story much like real life with ups downs and in-betweens...I highly recommend this well-written romantic suspense. I know it's one I will definitely reread." The Romance Studio

"Great pacing and mystery keep the reader at the edge of their seat..." Siren Book Reviews

"*Love Me If You Can* is a fast-paced read that will keep your attention until the last page. It is the perfect book for both romance and mystery lovers." Melissa's Sizzling Hot Reviews

"...a good, solid story with believable characters and a plot that keeps you on your toes..." Happily Ever After Reviews

"*Love Me If You Can* is a quick-paced race to catch a killer and maybe even a happily ever after that will keep your attention." Manic Readers

"**...**suspense plot is fast-moving and keeps the reader guessing until the surprising climax." *Romantic Times Magazine*

LOVE ME IF YOU CAN

Marie-Nicole Ryan

RYANDALE PUBLISHING

Romantic Suspense Novel

LOVE ME IF YOU CAN

Revised & Re-edited 3rd EDITION

Copyright 2010, Mary Varble
Cover Art, Mary Varble
All rights reserved, Ryandale Publishing

3nd Edition:
ISBN 10: 139358541
ISBN 13: 978139358541

Published in the United States of America
Library of Congress Registration: TX 7-385-764

DEDICATION

To my sister Sherry and my niece Emily because they always encourage and inspire me.

ACKNOWLEDGMENTS

I discovered, when I set out to write a book based in the town where I lived, it required even more research than a book in a fictional location where I could build the world I wanted.

Much appreciation goes to Danny Agan, Investigator and former Homicide Detective of Atlanta Metropolitan Police Department, for his input on what the job is really like for a homicide detective.

Also, to News Channel Five morning anchor Steve Hayslip, for giving me the inside scoop on what it's like to be a morning news anchor and general background on the profession. In no way does he resemble the morning anchor I created for this story.

As always, for anything I get right, the credit goes to these individuals. All mistakes and foul-ups are my own or are intentional for the sake of the story.

Chapter One

Scott parked his car in the lot and glanced at his watch. His first appointment wasn't for another twenty minutes. Just enough time to duck into Starbuck's for his morning jolt of java.

Great. Only one customer ahead of him.

The *one* was a spectacular redhead with a killer body, wearing a light tan jacket and a brown skirt just short enough to show off a great set of wheels. Not that he paid attention to a woman's body. Now, the mind... Hell, who was he trying to fool?

"Arabian Mocha Sanani. Double grande, skim— no, whole—no, skim." Her voice was low and pleasant, but did she have to waffle over what kind of milk?

Her head bobbed from side to side while she considered. "Skim, definitely skim."

Enough already. "Could you just make up your mind? Some of us have to go to work."

She whirled and glared. Her wide gray eyes, with flecks of darker gray, flashed with anger. "I just did." She turned back to the clerk. "Definitely whole."

There was something familiar about her. Maybe they'd met before? Gone to school together? He glanced at his watch and started tapping his foot. "Sometime this century, Red."

This time she whipped around and flashed a badge. "One more word and I'll arrest you for being a public nuisance."

A Metro Nashville gold shield. Yeah, one of the O'Malleys. "You'll arrest me?" Unable to resist, he grinned. "How about I make a citizen's arrest because you're a—"

Her fair cheeks flushed an angry red as she interrupted him, "Careful, you are so close to—"

So, she had the typical redhead's temper. Hell, she was too cute to alienate. Besides, what woman didn't love it when a man admitted he was wrong? "All right. I'm a nuisance—one Scott Holt. I admit it. Why don't you let me buy your coffee, and then I could apologize over dinner?"

Nothing ventured, nothing gained.

A flicker of something sparked, then died in her gaze. "Hmph. Is that your idea of a smooth come-on?"

He tried a smile. Maybe his charm alone would soften her attitude. "It's the best I can do on short notice."

Her hardened expression softened. Her lips twitched. "I'll pass."

"Now here I thought you were softening toward me. You know you almost smiled. I'm very observant."

She glanced at her watch. A self-satisfied smile lifted the corners of her luscious mouth. "Thought you had to get to work?"

He shrugged. "I'm the boss."

"Well, I'm *not* the boss, and I *do* have to get to work."

Without another word, she paid for her java, took a sip, and then sailed by him. His chin dropped. She left the store and headed down Fifth. He smiled. Nice hitch in her get-along. Oh, yeah.

"Hey, buddy," the barista said, interrupting Scott's train of thought. "You gonna order or stare at the scenery?"

Scott laughed. The redhead had him dazzled all right.

And dazzled was rare.

Scott tugged open the oak door to the Market Street office building. He loved the old building, always had. He gazed up at the foot-thick oak beams running up the inside of the historic building and visualized the massive oaks from which they'd been cut over a century earlier. The family business had occupied the same building for twenty years, ten before his father's death and the ten since. If he'd grown up in a different family, he might've chosen architecture as a field of study, instead of law school—make that law school dropout turned private investigator.

He entered the elevator and hit the button for the second floor. When the elevator doors opened, Scott stepped out. Holt Investigations occupied half the second floor while the other half belonged to a law firm. Except for the expansion last year, it was pretty much the same as when his father left the police force and opened the business.

Through the glass walls, he saw his stepsister Carrie already hard at work. As he entered, she stopped long enough to frown her disapproval.

So, he was late. So, what.

"How the hell did you get here before me? I left home first."

She wrinkled her nose and gave him a smug smile. "I don't have to make a run to Starbuck's for my morning coffee…unlike someone else, I could mention." Her fingers flew over the keyboard. Carrie had been his right hand since their parents died.

"The traffic coming down Church was murder and—"

"—there was a long line at Starbuck's. Yeah, I've heard your excuses before."

"It wasn't a long line. You see, there was this one redhead who couldn't make up her mind whether she wanted fat-free or whole milk."

Carrie raised a skeptical eyebrow. "I trust you waited like the polite and patient man you are."

He grinned. Polite, usually. Patient, never. "I'll have you know I made the simplest protest and the lady threatened to arrest me for being a public nuisance."

"*Arrest* you?"

"Yeah. I kept thinking I knew her, but when she flashed her gold shield, I remembered she was one of the O'Malleys."

She shot him a quick knowing grin. "And, of course, she's hot. Sounds promising."

"Not so much. Something tells me she's high maintenance…best admired from afar."

She let out a peal of laughter and nodded. "Shot you down. Didn't she?"

"Busted." He pulled together what dignity he had left and nodded. "I'm glad I've provided you with a dose of amusement."

"Don't go stuffy on me. You need to get out once in a while."

"I'm not stuffy. But like you said, she shot me down."

"Will wonders never cease?" She shrugged. "So, what's up for today?"

"Not much. Couple appointments." He shuffled through the mail in his inbox. "Bosley ever pay off his account?"

Carrie nodded. "Yeah, just in time too. I was ready to turn him over to collections."

He stopped and perched on the corner of her desk. "Why is it the slowest to pay are the ones with the most money?"

Carrie shrugged. "Fact of life." His sister sighed, then said in her clipped tone, "Anyway, your nine o'clock called. She can't make it until one, so I rescheduled her." She pushed her rimless glasses higher on the bridge of her nose.

"Anything else?"

"Justin's researching deep background for the Riley case and Tamsyn has back-to-back appointments. Word gets around." She smiled up at him as if daring him to object. Hell yes, he objected—not that either Carrie or Tamsyn listened to a word he said—so much for being the titular head of their family-run business.

"It borders on sleazy, Carrie." True, Tamsyn's services were in high demand. She was a knockout, and female clients would hire her to see if their fiancé or husband could be tempted to cheat. If he could she delivered the evidence back to her clients.

"Maybe, but it keeps a healthy flow of cash. Something this agency requires in abundance— something I shouldn't have to remind you."

"Doesn't mean I have to like it." He eased off the desk.

"You know, as well as I do, Tamsyn could leave and open her own agency if we didn't back her."

He shook his head. "It's dangerous…and more than a little unsavory." The idea of his sister pandering to men's baser instincts made him feel about one step above a pimp.

"She's careful and her instincts are excellent. Plus, she has Justin for backup."

"Which means it takes two operatives for each assignment and costs more time-wise. I can't believe you, of all people, support her efforts in this."

Carrie removed her glasses and rubbed the bridge of her nose. "This is an old argument, and since Justin's on salary like the rest of us..." She shrugged and turned her attention back to her keyboard.

"I still don't have to like it."

Something suspiciously like a groan emitted from his sister. "You're wasting my time."

"All right, I'll get out of your hair. You're the money person."

"And don't you forget it either." She flashed him a hungry shark's kind of smile.

Lucky for him, the phone rang. While she reached to answer, he escaped into his office and walked over to the tall windows overlooking First Avenue. Nice view of the Cumberland. The gray-green river flowed smoothly. Down on the waterfront, colorful flags flapped in the July morning's breeze.

Carrie had done the office decorating and saved the firm a ton of money. Simple brocade drapes framed the long windows. The oak bookshelves came from one of the antique shops on Third Avenue. She'd arranged plants and family photos on some of the shelves. His old books from law school filled the rest, a poignant reminder of what he'd given up.

Still, he'd never regretted his decision to leave law school. Maybe on occasion, when he heard a classmate's name mentioned on TV in regard to a newsworthy case, there was a twinge of regret. Just proved he was human.

A man did what a man had to do. His father always had, and Scott couldn't do any less.

He sat at the antique, leather-topped desk and leaned back in the modern—make that comfortable and ergonomic—leather chair. With his nine o'clock canceled, he had time to do a little skip-tracing on their youngest sister, Kim, who'd run away four years after their parents died. Any of his spare time went toward finding a new lead...one which wouldn't be months old and lead to another dead-end.

Still, the image of a certain detective with fiery red hair teased his mind's eye, no matter how he tried to concentrate on finding his sister.

Three hours later, her Starbuck's coffee was a memory and the squad room's version bore no resemblance to its superior counterpart. This was strong and thick and tasted as if someone had laced it with acid, but Detective Tess O'Malley sucked down the brew as if it were mother's milk.

She needed to get busy on background for the Brennerman case, but she couldn't help the quick flash of memory to the obnoxious guy behind her at the Starbuck's—admittedly a damn hot guy.

A shadow shifted in her peripheral vision. She glanced up in irritation and watched her partner, Detective Sergeant Denton Kozinsky shuffle into the squad room and set a cold case file box on her desk.

"What the hell is that?"

"Just what it looks like, toots."

"A cold case? We don't have time. We've got—"

"Hold on. While you were paying a small fortune for your morning cup of Joe, the powers that be had a powwow. We're off Brennerman."

Her stomach clenched and her temper threatened to boil over. "Why? Just because we haven't made any progress. It's early days in the case. There's a ton of background—"

Kozinsky cleared his throat. "Just in. They found the kid's body."

A rush of nausea hit her, but she swallowed the bitterness. "When? Where? Why weren't we informed? We're the primaries."

"I was just informed, and you're being informed right now. We *were* the primaries. As for this cold case, I was the primary back in the day. Check the name."

She read the side of the file box.

"Mason?" She shook her head. "I don't recall a Mason case." Then her brain made the connection to one of the more sensational murder cases in Nashville history. "I got it. Fourteen years ago, a kid from camp. His body was found a week later. Strangled and buried under a pile of leaves." Now, fast-forward to the present. "Todd Brennerman also went missing from the same camp."

"Bingo! Give the lady a cup of Joe."

"So, you were the primary on that one. I had no idea. I was sixteen and glued to the TV when he was found. There has to be a connection between the two—right?"

Kozinsky nodded. "Oh, yeah. Same camp. Whether or not it's the same M.O. remains to be seen."

Dreading what she'd find, Tess lifted the file box lid anyway. "Let's get busy."

Her hand paused as she reached the crime scene photos. Richard Mason looked even younger than his stated age of sixteen. His nude body had been placed in a fetal position. A T-shirt covered his face and head with his jeans folded neatly beside him. One of his tennis shoes was found in the shallow grave. Only one.

"The killer took a souvenir?"

"That's what we figured at the time." Her partner rubbed his chin. "The missing shoe was our holdback—at least until someone leaked it to the press."

A thousand possibilities raced through her mind. "We need to have another look at everyone connected with the camp. See if anyone from that time was there this time. How many are we talking about?"

Kozinsky rubbed a hand through his wiry gray, brush-cut hair. "It's all in the file, but best I remember off the top of my head, there were four counselors. Several teachers, too. Total of thirty-six students at the camp the year in question—half of them girls—guess we can eliminate them, or we'd be up to our asses in suspects."

"We already are." The morgue photos were even worse than the shots taken at the crime scene, clearly showing the bruises on his neck and wrists. "He was strangled, but not before he'd been bound and uh…" She shivered as she read the rest of the details.

"One sick bastard did that."

Tess stood. "Come on. Let's go. I want to see the scene where they found Brennerman. Maybe we can clear both cases."

"Ain't gonna happen. We've been ordered to step back and focus on the cold case."

"We're actually being sidelined for the cold case. How come?" Dammit. Just when her career was about to skip another rung up the ladder. Finding Brennerman's killer could make her career. Making captain by forty would've been a cinch. Sidelined for the cold case—even if the two cases were related—man, that sucked. Probably the good-old-boy system at work again.

"The Brennerman case is high profile. *We're* not high enough up the food chain. The lieutenant's handling this one…personally."

She shot her partner a twisted smile. "Of course, he is. Can't miss an opportunity to get his mug on the evening news."

"He's not so bad. Looks out for the squad." Kozinsky shrugged his burly shoulders. "Can't blame him for being on the fast track."

More than one could play the fast track game. "I can blame him if I want to. He's a pompous ass who owes his position to his uncle being the police commissioner."

"That's the way it goes." He slipped on his reading glasses and shot her a pointed look. "Not like you don't have some pull in the family department yourself."

"Not true!" She shook her head. "My father did everything he could to keep me off the force. And you made my life a living hell."

"Promised 'im I'd make it hard on you." A broad smile spread across his rugged face. "But you hung in there. Showed us all."

She took a sip of the bitter brew and swallowed with a grimace. "You don't know how many times I wanted to give up." Her brothers and her father, the captain, set the bar pretty high. They always had, but dammit, she was just as good a cop as her brothers. Better. And she'd certainly been a better student. Yet, on the job, she still had to prove herself every time she was assigned a new case. So, if the lieutenant wanted her to clear a cold case, she'd do it. "Okay, how many of these suspects do you figure are still in town?"

"Most of 'em." Kozinsky pulled out his chair and sat with a thud.

A snigger erupted, in spite of her best efforts to hold it back. "You gotta lay off the thick crust pizza. I swear your chair just groaned."

"Did not." He tossed his crumpled coffee cup at her.

She swatted it back, knowing full well she couldn't win an argument with her partner of three years. "If it's the same guy, why fourteen years between? Where's he been? Prison? Out of state?"

"Good questions. I expect you and your nimble fingers will find the answer on that danged computer." He sniffed as if above depending on a high-tech source. "As for me, I'll…"

"I know. I know. Dogged footwork. That's the ticket."

"Yep. Dogged determination and footwork."

"But with these *danged* computers, we'll eliminate some of the footwork and spend more time on the ones we like."

It was a familiar argument, and another one she wouldn't win with her fifty-five-year-old-partner. But she could push his buttons. "Say, aren't you ready for retirement yet? I hear there's a bar for sale down on Second. I wouldn't mind a new watering hole."

Her partner let out a chuckle. "I'll retire when pigs fly or when they stop making rounds for my service weapon."

Tess spent the next thirty minutes going over the interviews from the Mason case. She entered the names into the system. Kozinsky was right—no surprise. Most were still living in Davidson County. One name struck her as freakishly familiar. Holt, Andrew Scott—yeah, the Starbuck's guy. "You know this one? Andrew Scott Holt."

"He's a PI. Office is over on Market Street—Holt Investigations. His folks died 'bout ten years ago—drunk driver. Anyway, Holt left law school to take over the family business and put the rest of the kids through school."

"Quite an undertaking. How many were there?"

"Been a while. Let's see if my memory bank's working today…five or six."

"Hm. Matter of fact, I met him this morning at Starbuck's. Now I think about it, one of my brothers might've played football with him in high school."

"Why don't you start with him then? Trot over to his office. It's not that far." Kozinsky winked.

"Good idea. Think I will." She winked back. "See—I'm not afraid of a little footwork."

***

Scott ushered his one o'clock from the office. The client's inquiry was a routine one. She wanted the agency to run a background check on a financial counselor before she invested. Smart lady. Before he could fire up his computer and email Justin with the request, the intercom buzzed. "Yeah?"

"There's a Detective O'Malley to see you." Carrie's tone was amused, but he wasn't. What could the detective possibly want? Had she changed her mind about dinner? Or was she going to cite him for being a public nuisance, after all?

Chapter Two

Tess eyed the office of Holt Investigations. A historic building, brick interior walls built about the same time as the First Avenue warehouse where she lived in a converted condo. And her condo was a mere block away. Dammit. They were neighbors.

The receptionist was close to Tess' age, early thirties, slender, well-dressed and attractive with dark blond hair cut in a sleek bob and wide green eyes behind a pair of rimless glasses. She shoved the glasses up on her nose and grinned. "I hope you're not here to arrest my brother. I'm Caroline Lackey, the office manager."

Correction noted. Not the receptionist. "Any reason I should?"

"Oh," Ms. Lackey drawled, "he might've mentioned meeting you this morning."

Again, the playful grin. "This is business—not personal."

Ms. Lackey's eyebrows rose. "Straight back, Detective."

Tess nodded and kept her tone businesslike and neutral. How odd that today, of all days, she'd have a run-in with one of the suspects in a cold case before she'd even been assigned the case. In spite of Davidson County's over half-million residents, Nashville still felt like a small town. On any day, no matter where you went, you could count on running into someone you knew.

Ms. Lackey shot Tess an amused sort of smile and went back to her work. So, he'd mentioned their meeting? Didn't matter. Tess had Scott Holt's number. He was tall, dark and delicious with smoldering brown eyes; he was exactly the kind of man she normally avoided. In other words, he was bad news...even if he wasn't already a figure in her cold case.

Approaching Holt's office, she hesitated before knocking. The question remained—was the man who'd given up law school to support his siblings the same one who might've sodomized and strangled a teenage boy?

Jumping to conclusions was never a good idea. He'd only been questioned in the cold case because he was one of the four camp counselors. Which meant a mere twenty-five percent chance he was her suspect in the Mason case—not great odds. But not too bad, either.

She tapped on the door.

"Come in, Detective," she heard him say through the door. His voice was warm and resonant. The richness of his tone kicked her heart into a higher range and left her a little too breathless.

Opening the door, she found Holt on his feet, his hand outstretched to greet her. She crossed the wide-planked, heart-of-pine floors and took his hand. The warmth and strength of his handshake disturbed her on a deeper level. What was she doing? Cops didn't shake hands with suspects.

"Have a seat, Detective O'Malley." He gestured to one of two Hunter-green, Mission-style leather chairs. She perched on the edge of her seat while he walked around the desk, sat and leaned back. Clearly, the man was comfortable in his territory and on his terms.

Drat, he was every bit as hot as she remembered. A bit over six feet tall, Holt was lean and broad-shouldered. He smiled with good humor, crinkling the skin around his eyes. His dark hair was cut GQ short, but the front lay in unruly wisps on his forehead like a child's. His suit was charcoal gray and obviously expensive. Instead of a starched shirt and tie, he wore a gray V-necked T-shirt.

Business casual. Definitely at ease with himself.

He scratched his head as if puzzled. "How can I help you, Detective? Or have you come to take me away to the slammer for having the temerity to ask you out to dinner?"

His tone was soft and playful...seductive. Well, she'd bring him down in a hurry.

"Mr. Holt, I've been assigned a cold case. You might remember it— the Richard Mason case? His murder was never solved."

Holt's smile faded as he sat forward and leaned his elbows on the desk. "I'm not likely to forget Rich Mason—not as long as I live. I was questioned about it then. Now you're back for another go-round." His gaze traveled to the windows, then back to her. "I heard on Channel Nine they found the Brennerman kid today. Stands to reason you'd want to talk to me since the deaths involved the same camp. Go ahead. Ask your questions."

She pulled out a notepad, then settled back in the chair. "Tell me what you remember about the summer Rich Mason was murdered." Pen poised, she kept her gaze on him for a reaction.

His expression grew pensive as if he traveled back to that summer. "I was twenty and I'd completed my sophomore year at Vanderbilt. Actually, I was a semester ahead. My father and stepmother were still alive, so life was good."

She held up her hand. "More specifically, tell me about the gifted camp."

"I was getting to it. Fourteen years is a long time so I'm just trying to set the scene in my mind. Don't want to leave anything out. If anything I remember can help…" He closed his eyes for a moment before opening them to look at her again. "Believe me, I want to help."

"Go on. Do it your way." Likely he did everything his way.

"I hadn't planned on doing the camp gig again, but my dad said it was my duty to go. I'd been a student at Camp Einstein when I was younger. It was expected I would go back and offer my services as a counselor every summer while I was still in school."

"Why didn't you want to go?"

He flashed a wry grin. "I'd had a rough two years, carrying a hellacious caseload at Vandy so I could finish in three years instead of four. Plus, I still had law school ahead of me, and then after passing the bar, I'd be working to establish my career. I just wanted to have a good time that final summer—no responsibilities." He shrugged. "But I manned up and went."

"Tell me what happened at the camp."

"It was held in July." Holt steepled his fingers, but his forefingers tapped as if he were nervous. "Thirty-six students—the crème de la crème of Tennessee's high school students. They ranged from fifteen to seventeen. Good old Camp Einstein—better known as Camp Nerd—had the usual arts, math, science studies, but the owner added swimming and horseback riding. Kids were bright and focused. No serious problems with any of the campers until Rich disappeared."

"When was he last seen?" She scribbled as fast as she could. Hopefully, she'd be able to make out her chicken scratches later.

"The other counselors and I had done bed check at nine. Rich was in his cabin with five other boys. We had eighteen male students in three cabins. When it came time for roll call the next morning, he was nowhere to be found. His bed hadn't been slept in, either. We reasoned he might've snuck out to see one of the girls, but they were all accounted for. We combed the woods looking for him—nothing."

Scott shrugged. "Then Ned Forbes, the camp owner, called the authorities and Rich's folks—all our folks, in fact. The police came with search dogs, and the water recovery team came out to drag the lake. There wasn't a sign of him anywhere—not that first day."

"Were you still at the camp when they found his body?"

Holt rubbed his chin. "No, my dad came and made me leave. I didn't want to, but none of us were given a choice. Rightly so, since we were in the way of the investigation. Possibly in danger as well."

Damn straight. "What was Rich Mason like?"

"It was his first year at camp. He was your basic computer geek. Couldn't drag him away from his computer for any kind of physical activity. One of the principles of the camp was to develop well-rounded gifted students. Ned felt it was one of the things which set the camp apart from others like it. Rich's dad had passed away the winter before with cancer. We liked the kid, so we cut him some slack. It was good for him to get away from home and be with a bunch of guys—at least until someone killed him."

"Tell me about the other counselors in your cabin."

"We bunked in one cabin. We didn't have lights-out until ten, so we horsed around. Played some cards. Couldn't do too much. The cabins didn't have TV or radio."

"What about alcohol?"

"We were under twenty-one. That would have been illegal," Holt said, giving her a half-grin.

Probably had been some alcohol there. Maybe someone got out of control and it led to Mason's death.

"The other counselors?" she reminded Holt. Why couldn't he just answer her questions the way she asked them? Was he avoiding telling her the truth or was it because he'd planned on being an attorney?

Again, Holt leaned back, apparently growing more comfortable under her questioning. "Drew Wilson, he was a running back for UT. Heisman Trophy contender his senior year. He came from humble roots. Father worked for either the electric or gas company. Anyway, Drew's your real success story. He's an investment banker now, still living in Nashville."

"Who else?"

Holt frowned. "You probably already have all this somewhere in the file."

"I do, but I want to hear it fresh from someone who was there."

As if resigned to her controlling the questioning, his eyebrows twitched for a second, then he continued. "Okay. Then there was Tyler Jamison; it was his first year as a counselor. He was probably twenty-one then and had another year of college—MTSU. Basically, he was learning the ropes of being a counselor. Now, he's a news reporter for Channel Nine. That's about it for him."

Tess nodded for Holt to continue.

He leaned forward. "Are you getting all this, Detective? Not going too fast, am I?"

She glared at him. Jerk. If he was aiming to piss her off, he was succeeding. "You're fine. Go on."

"The last one is Bob "Dakota" Taylor. He's an offensive lineman for the Columbus Jackals. His team's a sure bet for the Super Bowl this year, Detective. I'd put money on it."

Holt's tone made it clear he thought she was the dimmest bulb in the package. "Taylor was still at the camp when Mason was murdered?"

"But he's not the one who took the Governor's grandson—*none* of these guys are. That is…if you think the two cases are related?"

Hell, yeah, she did. "Brennerman's not my case. I'm assigned to the Mason case."

His gaze narrowed. "But you think they're related, don't you?"

Damn the man. He wanted an answer. She straightened and pulled at her jacket. "What I think is of no concern to you, Mr. Holt."

Her suspect trotted out his best grin. "Come on, we're on the same side. Call me Scott."

Not gonna work on me, buddy. She stuffed her notebook back in her pocket, then stood. "That's it for now, but I may have more questions later."

"So, don't leave town?"

"Right." Even though they both knew she didn't have the authority to issue such an order.

Holt stood and flashed a killer smile. "Don't go off all mad. I used to play football against your brother Ryan. Our schools were archrivals. Consider me a suspect if you want, but I'm not your killer."

Was that so? She checked his left hand. No wedding ring. Man his age was usually married or gay. But surely, he wouldn't have asked her out if he was gay. "You're not married? Are you seeing anyone?"

"I've been engaged twice. Does that count?" he asked her with a cheeky grin.

"What happened?"

"My first fiancée dumped me like a pair of knockoff shoes. She wasn't interested in my plan to take care of my brother and four sisters. Said she didn't do ready-made in clothes…or families."

"Oh." Damn her quick tongue. She'd come off like an insensitive idiot. "And the second?"

His gaze darkened. "I was engaged again, but my fiancée died of cancer. Couple of years ago." He stood and gave her a full wattage, knee-weakening smile. "But it would certainly raise my spirits if you'd accept my dinner invitation."

Worse than an insensitive idiot. So, the man had bad luck with women. She didn't buy it. Damn his brash, then shy, seductive charm. It was hard not to like him, but she wasn't about to mix business with pleasure. Not a trap she'd fall into if she could help it.

She wrinkled her nose. "You're not my type, Holt."

"Just my luck." Still smiling, he bit his bottom lip. "For curiosity's sake, what *is* your type?"

"I don't have a type, but if I did, he wouldn't be someone I'm investigating as a possible person of interest in a cold case."

"Thanks for adding *possible*. Almost makes me feel better."

In spite of herself, she smiled. The man was picture-book handsome. And his not being her type was a lie. He was exactly her type if all she was looking for was a quick roll in the hay. "Maybe we could work on this together…under the department radar, of course."

His eyes widened. "You generally make a habit of working with PIs?"

"Seldom. But the sooner I clear you, the better. You might be of assistance with the other suspects." Heresy. Most detectives looked down on PIs unless they'd been on the job. What was the matter with her?

"I don't work cheap," he said with a knowing expression in his warm eyes.

"Didn't figure you would with such a big family to feed."

A broad grin showed Holt's even, white teeth. "We're self-supporting now and work for the family business, except for Allison—she's a nurse."

"Family renegade—huh?" she asked with a grin.

Holt grinned and shook his head. "Yeah, she never wanted to be anything else. The family pitched in and made her dream come true."

"Commendable."

"We like to think so. Like the Three Musketeers—all for one and you know how it goes."

"And literary too. A perfect family." Ouch. That came out snarkier than she intended.

"We do our best." Holt's cheeks flushed. "I don't like your tone, Detective. Frankly, you're starting to piss me off."

Tough. "Then I guess the dinner invitation is withdrawn?"

Holt stood, then walked from behind his desk. "I'll do whatever I can to assist in your investigation."

What was with the bum's rush? "Then you won't mind providing a DNA sample?"

He folded his arms across his chest and sat on the edge of his desk. "Go right ahead. Swab away. I hope you find the bastard who killed the Mason kid, but it wasn't me."

Secretly, she hoped he was telling the truth. She pulled the swab kit from her jacket pocket. Holt opened his mouth and allowed her to swab thoroughly. "I know my questions are intrusive, but with your background, you must understand they're necessary."

"Was there an apology in there somewhere, Detective?" A slight smile played at the corner of his mouth. "Anything else?"

Tess shook her head. "That's it...for now. Here's my card." She handed it to him and took his in return. "If you remember anything..."

He gave a quick nod.

She turned. He walked her to the door and opened it. A gentleman to the end, but she'd seen his temper flare. Had Rich Mason been unlucky enough to anger Holt, or was she completely off-base? Hell's bells. Off base or not—Scott Holt was totally hot.

Chapter Three

Scott waited until the sexy-as-sin detective had sashayed from his office, then ambled out to meet Carrie's no-nonsense gaze.

"So?" She stopped typing, her fingers poised mid-air over the keyboard while she peered over her glasses. "What did she want?"

He sat gingerly on the corner of her desk, taking great care not to disturb the precarious stacks of files and endure her never-ending wrath. "She's been assigned a cold case. Care to hazard a guess which one?"

"Mason? After all this time? But it's a perfect fit. The governor's grandson disappeared from the same camp."

"Not a great leap, is it?"

"Maybe not, but," she huffed, "it's ridiculous for anyone to think you were involved in Rich Mason's death, much less the governor's grandson."

"She doesn't know me, sis, but I'm fixing to change that. Says I might be able to give her a handle on the other counselors."

She nodded and gave him a knowing smile. "Oh, you *like* her. Don't you?"

He drummed his fingers on the desk. "Busted. She's smart—too smart to get involved with me, for now. But she won't stop me from doing a little investigating on my own." He eased off the desk and headed back to his office.

"Careful, Scott. You're talking about a real killer, not some unfaithful husband. Whoever's responsible isn't going to be thrilled to have you, or that hot detective, nosing around in his business."

He stopped at the door and winked at his sister. "Don't worry. I won't do anything crazy."

"Yeah, right."

He shut the door behind him. Carrie was right, but the thought of actually solving a cold case had boosted his energy and sent his excitement meter off the chart. The majority of cases handled by their agency were domestic ones, cut and dried for the most part. They paid the bills, covering the overhead and salaries for four of the family. Allison made a decent wage as a case manager at Parklane and tended any minor bumps and bruises they incurred along the way.

Heaven only knew how Kim managed. Several occupations came to mind and none of them were pleasant. Still, the family would welcome her home...no matter what.

He sat at the desk, read his email, and finished by firing off a message to Justin about checking on the investment banker for his one o'clock. That task out of the way, he couldn't resist starting to dig up histories on his fellow counselors.

One of the counselors, Drew Wilson, worked for Eidelman-West Investments. Good old Drew was a VP in the firm. Maybe it was time to make an investment or two. The last fourteen years had been busy ones. Drew spent only a year playing pro football for the Colts before a busted knee and a back injury ended his career. The banker then married a Miss Tennessee. One daughter, age five.

Tyler Jamison was the morning news anchor on Channel Nine. He married his college sweetheart, and they had two boys—ages five and seven—both on the soccer team Scott coached.

As for Dakota Taylor, he was still in Ohio and playing for the Jackals. At six-five, Dakota's massive physique had been made for pro football. A real player with the girls, too. That probably hadn't changed since he was divorced and managed to remain single after divorce number two.

Fast forward to early July. Todd Brennerman, who was a gifted artist, disappeared from Camp Einstein. Again, he was present at bed check and missing the next morning.

And now, his body had been located. Scott turned on the TV and left the volume on low. Maybe there'd be another news update with more information than the earlier broadcast.

He grimaced. Nothing but a soap opera—for Pete's sake. That's all he needed after the run-in with Detective Her Hotness O'Malley. Still, love in the afternoon didn't sound too bad.

Even though she wore a conservative pair of three-inch heels, Tess couldn't help wishing she hadn't picked today to do some of Kozinsky's highly vaunted footwork. Once back in the car, she kicked off the offenders and rubbed her feet before easing them into a pair of clogs and driving back to the Criminal Justice Center.

When she entered the squad room, everyone was buzzing with the news about Brennerman. Even though the autopsy wouldn't be completed until late afternoon, the rumor was the Medical Examiner already reported he was strangled and sodomized. Two more things which coincided with her cold case.

What about the victim's shoe?

She sat, toed off the clogs and wiggled her toes, then leaned toward Kozinsky and whispered, "I have to know. Was Brennerman found with both his shoes?"

Kozinsky zipped his lip. "The lieutenant's keeping mum on that particular point."

"Sure would help our case if we knew for certain." She tapped her nails against the desk. "What's the official line?"

"Official line is the autopsy report is pending. Period."

From the smug expression on Kozinsky's face, she'd bet her last chocolate-covered doughnut he knew something. She leaned closer. "Come on. Give me the 411."

"Forget it." Kozinsky frowned and shook his head. "What did you find out from Scott Holt?"

She took a deep breath. "Background stuff mostly." She grinned and held up the swab kit. "He let me take a DNA swab."

"Really? Nice." He drew out the word into two syllables. "Charmed him, did you?"

Since she wasn't particularly known for her charm, she wrinkled her nose at her partner's comment. "No, he was extremely forthcoming. I don't figure him for our suspect."

"Oh, I get it." Her partner leaned back and nodded knowingly. "You think he's hot."

Holt was hot all right, but she'd be damned if she'd give Kozinsky the satisfaction of knowing he'd hit the bull's eye. "Don't go there. He's still a material witness."

"Never hurts to be on good terms with a reputable PI."

She blew a lock of hair away from her forehead. "You think he's reputable?"

"His father was on the job. Bob Holt and his partner, Dan Shannon, put in for retirement and formed the agency."

"I thought the agency belonged to Scott Holt."

"I'm getting to that. His dad's first wife died of cancer and left him with two kids, Scott and a girl— can't think of her name. Couple or three years later, he met Jan Lackey at a widowed support group. Her husband was in Narcotics and killed in the line of duty. Left her with four kids."

"Sort of like The Brady Bunch," she suggested with a grin.

"Yeah, they moved into her house on Richland."

"Pricey address." She'd taken one of the Richland Avenue home tours. Early twentieth-century houses, mostly Victorian and Craftsman style. They took a lot of money to maintain. Where had the money come from? Had her late husband been on the take?

Kozinsky was already reading her mind. "Nothing hinky. There was some money on her father's side of the family. She was an only child, so she inherited it. It had just enough room for a couple more kids. Everything was good for about ten years. For some reason, Scott's dad bought out Shannon, and two days later, Tom and Jan were killed."

"Drunk driver, right?"

"Right. Anyways, Scott was in his last year of law school, so he dropped out to run the family business. Never heard a word of scandal attached to him. Makes him a standup guy in my book."

"But he was questioned in the Mason case." Just because the guy was hot, she couldn't overlook his possible involvement.

"Yeah, everyone connected with Camp Einstein was interviewed six times over. Not that it did any good." Kozinsky scratched his chin, a five o'clock shadow already darkening his cheeks. "Gonna run the DNA against what we have in our case file?"

She shot him a quick grin. "Is a school bus yellow? I'm heading to

Forensics with this." She held up the sample. "He offered to give me more background on the other counselors. Figure the sooner I clear him the better."

Her partner pasted a broad smile across his face. "Right."

She headed down the hall to the elevator. Dammit. What Kozinsky thought didn't matter one iota. She was thirty and old enough to think for herself. On occasion, her partner still treated her like a daughter or little sister. Good to know she had a partner who watched her back, but he didn't know squat about her personal life.

Personal life? She jabbed the DOWN button three times and waited.

What personal life? She didn't have one, not much of one anyway since she and her fiancé, ADA Kevin MacKaye, had broken it off after one too many arguments about the legal justice system and how the DA's office was more interested in politics than putting away bad guys.

Their last fight wasn't one of her finest moments. But when the DA's office refused to hold a low-life wife beater more than forty-eight hours after his wife refused to press charges, she'd gone ballistic. He'd called her "pig-headed and reactionary."

So be it. Her career, her duty to protect and serve, was more important than any relationship. Her father had made captain by the age of forty, and her brothers were well on their way. Little sister wasn't going to be left behind.

No way. No how.

Tess left the stationhouse and drove over to the TBI Crime Lab. Once inside, she slipped through the doors, then turned left. Her high heels clattered against the tile, and again, she wished she hadn't changed back from the clogs. She pushed through the doors to Forensics and smiled. Unlike TV shows with ideal personnel and equipment situations, this was the reality. Nashville was better than most but less than perfect. Depending on the TBI Crime Lab for forensics results meant no fifteen-second turnaround on DNA.

"Hi, Dani." She waved the DNA swab kit in the air. "I've brought you a prezzie."

The technologist was carefully filling pipettes with what appeared to be DNA evidence. She was tall, thin with dark brown hair and wore the ubiquitous lab coat.

"Take a number." The technician scowled over her glasses. "Don't bother to take a seat. I'm working with the Brennerman evidence. If that swab's not connected, don't even speak to me for a week."

"Look who's a grouchy girl today." Tess leaned her elbows on the slate worktop. "This could be connected. It's from a cold case—Mason. Similar M.O. to the Brennerman case. Swab's from one of the counselors who was at the camp when Mason disappeared." She leaned closer to Dani. "Besides, what I really want to know is did they find both of Brennerman's shoes?"

Her friend sniffed, and rolled her eyes, but kept working. "That's a definite need-to-know."

"Well, hon, I need to know in the worst way." Tess slid onto an empty stool across from Dani's workstation.

Dani ignored the cajoling and pointed at the IN tray. "Sign it in. I'll get to it when I can."

"How about a little bribe? Tell me about the shoe, or I'll tell Jack why you really called in sick last Monday." Tess's foot tapped. She wanted that info—now.

"That's not a bribe." Dani's cheeks flushed. "That's extortion. A bribe is supposed to give me something *I* want—just in case you care to try again."

"Yeah, like you want to keep your job." Tess gave the criminalist a wide grin.

"Tess O'Malley, if we weren't sorority sisters, I'd—"

"Just trying to solve a case—my case."

"Okay." Dani leaned in close. "Brennerman—only one shoe found in his shallow grave."

"Any DNA from the anal swabs?"

"That's two questions. I already answered one." Dani cast a long slow glance around the lab, then lowered her voice. "No DNA whatsoever. Must've used a condom."

"He's gotten smarter than he was the first time. Damn. Where do you think he's been for the last fourteen years?"

Dani shrugged. "In jail for something else. Or maybe he moved out of state."

Out of state meant she ought to be checking ViCAP, shorthand for the FBI's Violent Criminal Apprehension Program database. "I need to get busy and see if I can identify any similar patterns elsewhere."

A smile flitted across Dani's face. "Does that mean you're going to leave me alone for a while?"

Tess smiled back. "You win. Kozinsky and I are going to get this guy. When we do, we're going to find out where the bastard's been all this time and just what other ugliness he's been up to."

"You go, girl. I can almost hear the William Tell Overture playing." Dani waved, then turned back to her work.

Damn. The two cases were related which meant Nashville had a serial killer on its hands. The lieutenant would have to put her and Kozinsky back on the case before the killer struck again.

Scott hit the button on the remote and turned off the small flat-screen TV he kept in the office. Crap. Nothing new on the Brennerman murder. How long would it take to get some decent intel? Maybe Tyler Jamison had something the media hadn't released yet. Of course, the chances of that were slim to none. If the media knew anything, keeping a lid on it wasn't a normal part of their game plan.

But what would it hurt to try?

Tyler answered on the second ring. After hashing over the results of the last Sounds game, Scott came to the point. "What've you got on Brennerman?"

"Not much. Metro's keeping it close to the vest on this one. Why?"

"Brings back memories…Rich Mason." Silence.

"Ty, you still there?"

"Hey, man. That what a bad time. Didn't much like being interrogated over and over about that kid's murder. Made me feel guilty, when all the time, I knew I wasn't."

"Hell, none of us liked it." No more than he liked his interview with

Detective O'Malley today. "Metro detective came to see me today. Mason's cold case has landed on her desk."

"Man, I don't know if I can go through all that crap again."

Yeah? If Tyler was innocent, he shouldn't have anything to worry about. "She asked for my general impressions and a DNA swab. Suspect she'll be headed your way soon."

"Thanks for the warning. Listen, if I hear anything on the Brennerman kid, I'll give you a buzz."

Tyler broke the connection. Something about his responses set off alarm bells in Scott's gut—something just this side of off in Tyler's tone.

Next, he called Drew Wilson's office and was put on terminal hold. He was ready to hang up when Drew answered and asked if he was ready to set up a mutual fund with the firm.

Scott laughed. "Maybe soon, but that's not why I called. A Detective O'Malley came to see me today. Figure they're going to interview all of us again. Thought I'd give you a head's up."

"The sooner that case is closed—what's it been ten...no, fourteen years—the better off we'll all be. Let 'em have at it. That's what I say."

Drew's tone and mood didn't alter. Sign of an innocent man? Maybe not.

"Took a DNA swab too." Scott listened for any changes in old friend's tone.

"Yeah? Guess I'd better get ready for him then."

"Her," Scott corrected. "O'Malley's a dishy redhead with long legs."

"So's my Irish setter." Drew laughed, and to Scott, it sounded genuine. "Thanks for the warning." His tone grew sober. "Sorry about Carly."

"Yeah. It was rough." Rough didn't even begin to describe what he'd gone through. He and Carly had been engaged three months and were into full wedding planning mode when she was diagnosed with inflammatory breast cancer. She'd broken their engagement and called off the wedding, even though he'd begged her not to. The next two years were filled with chemo, surgery, radiation treatments, and a brief remission, followed by a swift decline and her death at the age of twenty-seven. He'd remained at her side through the pain, the vomiting, and the hair loss—all of it.

"Say, how about meeting me for a drink this afternoon?" Scott named a local watering hole, also known to be one where local law enforcement liked to hang.

"Not tonight. My daughter has a ballet recital and her proud daddy has to be there."

"Some other time then." He couldn't help but wonder if things had been different, would he and Carly have had kids by now? He couldn't help but imagine watching his little girl dance on tippy-toes and twirl around in her tights or maybe watching his son out on the baseball diamond or soccer field.

The other camp counselors had found time to marry and have kids. If fate had been kinder, he would've too. The agency was doing well enough he could take on another associate or two. Not that he'd ever give up control of the business. He'd worked way too hard to pull it kicking and screaming out of near bankruptcy, but a little free time wouldn't hurt.

His father and stepmother had been a true love match, even with the complications of a blended family of six kids. These days, the house on Richland was too quiet. They all took turns cooking or ordering dinner, but Tamsyn was usually out on one of her assignments and missed more dinners than she cooked or ate.

After dinner, he and Justin would head to the study and watch a game. They weren't picky. Whatever sport was in season was fine. Carrie and Allison would clear the kitchen. Carrie would head to her room to watch a chick flick or read, and Allison would be off to some do-gooder meeting. She had more causes than the United Way—prevention of animal cruelty, a cancer support group, and numerous charity walks to raise money for research of one sort or another.

Yeah, the house was too damn quiet.

He leaned back and watched *Bad News Bares*, starring two nubile youths who cavorted on the baseball diamond in the altogether. Lovely firm bodies. He leaned back and rubbed his crotch. He was careful to never download any of his naughty files directly onto the computer's hard drive. Instead, he had innocuous pictures of scenery from the many trips he'd taken and embedded within those files were his hidden stego files. To find them, one would have to know what one was looking for and how to find them.

So, they'd found his latest choice. Such a nice one, too. All things considered, it had taken very little effort to seduce the governor's grandson. He'd been a neglected child, not in the material side of things, but emotionally. The son of long-divorced parents, the older teen had needed a father figure to look up to and that's exactly the persona he'd projected.

Friendly. Positive. Encouraging…until it was too late.

Chapter Four

Tess sat at her desk and reread all the reports, then cataloged the material from the cold case file into a spreadsheet. There was evidence of DNA at the scene, but whether or not it matched any of the Camp Einstein counselors was the real question.

Scott Holt had offered up his DNA without hesitation. Good sign. She pegged him as too smart to think his DNA wouldn't match if he were guilty. Besides, Holt was a serious hunk. Not that it should matter. But somehow it did.

For Pete's sake, the man was a soccer coach and the mainstay of his family. In no way did he fit the profile of a sadistic, homosexual signature killer. Where was the lieutenant? Would he call in the FBI profilers or give the department a chance to find the killer first? She glanced over her shoulder and smiled. The lieutenant was in his office.

Maybe it was time for a little discussion about combining the cold case with Brennerman's and allowing her and Kozinsky back on the Brennerman investigation.

Kozinsky was on the phone and keeping it so quiet, she couldn't hear a word he said. Wonder what he was up to? She scooted back her chair, then stood. She stretched and moved her head from side to side to loosen the kinks.

No point in putting it off. She trudged over to the lieutenant's door and tapped on the glass. He scowled over his glasses but motioned for her to enter.

Lieutenant Dale Woods was forty-five and on the fast track for Chief, if not Commissioner. He was tall, well-built and had silver-gray hair complimented by frosty blue eyes. No doubt about it, the man looked good on camera and took advantage of every opportunity to represent his squad with the media.

"Lou?"

"The answer is *no*, O'Malley."

"But I haven't asked my question yet."

"My answer won't change. You see vague similarities between the Mason and Brennerman cases and you want back in."

"Not just me, Kozinsky too. Until this morning, Brennerman was our case."

Woods smiled. "You're a valuable part of my squad, O'Malley. That's why I want you and Kozinsky working on the cold case, specifically because of the similarities to Brennerman. With you two working on Mason, it leaves me free to concentrate on the Brennerman investigation. You will, of course, keep me updated on any areas where evidence might intersect."

"And you'll do the same for us…of course?" What would he say? Her right thigh jittered with the effort it took to remain calm while she waited for his answer.

Woods inclined his head once. A bare nod. Good. Even though she knew the answer, she couldn't resist asking for a second and official confirmation, "Speaking of evidence intersecting, was Brennerman found with both his shoes?"

The lieutenant lowered his eyelids a fraction. A cagey expression flickered across his perfect-for-TV face, then he uttered the single word she wanted to hear, "No."

She tamped down the urge to squeal and pump her fist in the air and managed to ask calmly, "Were there any other areas of similarity?"

If she wasn't mistaken, the lieutenant clenched his jaw before he answered, "Same victimology, M.O., and camp. Body found in the same general area in a shallow grave. What do you think?"

"If you'll pardon me for saying so, the cold case and this one should be considered as one." She shifted her stance from one foot to the other. Damn the boss for being so obtuse. "Any new evidence, in this case, might help solve the old one and vice versa. If we're working it as two separate cases, something could get lost in the shuffle."

"You're not going to let this go, are you?" He rubbed his chin, a good sign he was considering her argument.

"Letting go, when my gut tells me we have a signature serial killer on our hands, isn't part of my DNA, Lieutenant."

Dammit, say yes.

"All right. You and Kozinsky are back on the Brennerman investigation squad, but not as leads."

"Understood and appreciated, Lieutenant." Let him claim the limelight on this one. Her chance would come. Catching this particular unsub was more important.

"Now get out of my hair." His tone was gruff but there was a decided softness to his facial expression. Maybe Kozinsky was right and the lieutenant wasn't so bad.

She managed to beat a hasty retreat and not dance a jig of delight—but just barely. She eased over to her partner's desk where he was still on the phone. "Kozinsky?"

He waved her away, and reluctantly, she scrammed back to her desk. What the hell was going on with him? Casually, she leaned in his direction, hoping to hear his conversation. Okay, so she was nosy, but anything affecting her partner could, in the long run, affect her as well.

"Come on, Estelle," she heard him say with an aggrieved tone. So, he was talking to his wife. Marital problems—not good. Kozinsky's wife Estelle had been anything but thrilled with his having a young female partner, but over the last three years and with great effort, Tess had managed to win the older woman's approval.

One thing for sure, Kozinsky and his wife weren't arguing over her.

She headed over to the coffee maker and poured two cups, then carried them back to her desk. She took a sip from one—not bad. Reasonably fresh. Waiting for Kozinsky to complete his call, she watched him carefully. His face was red, and he shook his head as he talked. Finally, he hung up the phone.

"Problems at home?" she asked and handed him the other cup of coffee.

"Same old, same old. Nothing new." Kozinsky shrugged. "I'm over thirty years on the job and Estelle wants me to put in for retirement."

"No one would blame you if you did, not that I want a new partner."
Hell no. With his years of experience and street smarts and her energy and
tech-savvy, they made a damn fine team.

"I'm just not ready to call it a day. It's in my blood." He leaned back
and eyed her. "So, what were you talking to the lieutenant about—as if I
don't know? He shoot you down again?"

She shot a quick grin at her partner. "Matter of fact, this is a
celebration." She held her cup up to toast him. "The lieutenant's changed
his mind. We can work on the Brennerman case. He's still the lead, but he
agrees both cases involve the same suspect."

Kozinsky's green eyes lit up. "That definitely calls for a celebration."
He held his cup up to hers and toasted. "Clear the Brennerman and Mason
cases both, then I could think about retiring with a clear conscience."

She leaned back and eyeballed her partner. "Mason has bugged you
all this time, hasn't it?"

"Yeah." He nodded. "Figured we missed something right in our faces.
Never felt good about the Mason case going cold."

"You have another chance. I have a feeling we're going to…" She
laughed. "We're gonna put the lieutenant's face on TV one more time. But
what the heck? As long as we find this creep, who cares whose face is seen
on the evening news? Right?"

Having the lieutenant in charge of the case wouldn't help her career,
but at least, she was on the team and still had time to make captain by
forty.

"Right, kiddo." Kozinsky winked, then downed his coffee.

"Geez, Louise. You have to stop calling me kiddo. Ruins my cred."

Kozinsky broke out into a genuine belly laugh. "Can't have that, can
we?"

She smiled at his remark, but already her brain was teeming with
ideas for the investigation. "I've got some leads I intend to run with. I plan
to interview the other three Camp Einstein counselors, and I want to
interview anyone connected with the camp this summer as well."

Kozinsky nodded. "Clear it with the lieutenant. He may have already
done some of those interviews. No need to backtrack."

"I disagree." Excited and ready for the chase, she stood, then paced the small path between her and Kozinsky's desks. "This is the perfect time to interview them and jog their memories again. One of them might remember something new, especially now since the Brennerman kid's body has been found."

"Calm down, Dirty Harriet. Let's plan our strategy before we go off half-cocked."

Tess grinned. After the movie *Elektra, Dirty Harry* ran a close second in her all-time faves. "All right, I'm sitting and taking a deep breath." She sat and demonstrated her intentions, then pulled out her keyboard to access the witness list for the Brennerman case.

Holt had already told her, Camp Einstein wasn't just a camp for the gifted, it was a camp devoted to encouraging all-around excellence. After the first disappearance and murder, enrollment suffered for three years, but gradually, the camp rebuilt its reputation and thrived with financial support from some of the major corporations and wealthiest families in Nashville.

Unfortunately, Todd Brennerman, the governor's grandson and a talented young artist, had ended up dead.

Since Drew declined his invitation for an after-work drink, Scott worked even later than usual. He prepared surveillance reports for two new clients— both of whom had unfaithful spouses—and made return appointments in order to reveal the results, for which they'd paid handsomely.

At least one—maybe both—of the couples would end up in the divorce court, and their lives would never be the same. Why would a man or a woman cheat on someone they supposedly loved? Human nature? The grass is always greener syndrome? Lack of character?

He had no real answers. More and more, he realized the miracle of love his father and stepmother shared for the years they were together. It was damn special and rare. The chances he'd ever experience anything like it were even rarer.

"Scott?"

He glanced toward the door. His sister Tamsyn stood in the doorway decked out in one of her seduction outfits. Black suit with a short skirt, red stilettos, and a low-cut blouse. Her long dark brown hair was worn loose across her shoulders. Her dark brown eyes smoldered with intensity along with her dark tan. She carried a large leather shoulder bag which probably cost more than his single Armani suit.

"Aren't you going home tonight, bro?"

"I'm almost through." He frowned. "I see you have an appointment tonight."

"Ye-es." She drawled the word and fluttered her dark lashes. "I wondered if maybe my big brother wanted to cover my back. Justin's busy giving a speech at the computer geek society."

"Dammit, Tam. You left it a little late to ask. I might have other plans myself."

"Yeah, sure you do." She flounced into the office and perched on the corner of his desk, crossed her legs and wiggled one foot back and forth. "It shouldn't take long. The guy will either bite or he won't."

"You don't have to dress like a hooker to attract men. You could dress in anything and—"

"Come on." She opened the snap on her purse and pulled out a mirror to check her hair and makeup. "I know you don't like this part of the business, but I've seen the books. My cash flow and billable hours help out a lot." Apparently satisfied with her appearance, she dropped the mirror inside her purse. "I'm ready. So how 'bout it?"

"Dammit." No way he'd let Tamsyn barhop and attempt entrapment without backup. "Okay, kid. But get it over with quick—okay?"

She flashed him a wide smile. "The quicker the better. Suits me just fine."

Scott shut his computer down for the night, then followed his sister. "Where're we going and who's the unlucky fellow?"

"We're going to the Blue Mood. My client informs me her husband has been cruising the bar on a weekly basis. I verified his presence on two consecutive Thursday nights, his poker night. Guess we know what—if not who—he's probably poking. Anyway, my assignment is to record whether or not he's true blue."

"That's a cop hangout. Your client's a cop?"

"No, my client's husband is."

"Dammit. You're asking for trouble." Scott shook his head. He'd had enough of cops for one day. "All right. Not that you're giving me a choice."

She flashed him a quick smile, hopped off the desk and vamped her way to the door. "Let's go, big brother."

"Never could say no to you." Besides the quicker they left, the quicker he could get to the Y and then home to watch a game.

They walked down Market Street; the nightlife was beginning to rev up. Throngs of tourists and locals alike wandered the sidewalks. Tamsyn informed Scott of his role in her charade. They would enter the bar separately. He was to sit quietly and nurse his drink, keeping an eye on her back. At any sign of trouble, he was to pull her out of the situation by claiming to be her irate husband.

"How often do you have trouble?"

"Not very often," she said with a grin, "but Justin's acting is pretty good. He makes a very believable angry husband."

"I can do angry husband." Oh, yeah. Busting some guy's chops for hitting on his little sister would be a pleasure. But a cop in a cop hangout? Now that was begging for trouble.

She glanced up at him and dropped her tone.

"Just don't kill anyone, okay? There's no need for a fight to the death."

"You wound me." Damn, but she knew him too well.

"I've gotten to be pretty good at reading facial expressions and yours was pure Danger Man to the rescue."

"Always were too smart for your own good," he muttered.

Scott sat at one end of the darkly lit bar and watched Tamsyn do her number. There were at least six police officers between him, his sister and the object of her investigation. Starting a fight in a cop bar was a good way to get his ass hauled off to jail. Not how he wanted to spend the rest of his night.

She was already making headway. Even through the dim ambiance of the restaurant and bar, Scott could make out the getting-lucky-tonight expression on her subject's face. *Not if I can help it, buddy.*

"What the hell are you doing here? Are you stalking me?" The voice came from behind him, the woman's tone low and terse.

He jerked around. "Detective O'Malley?" He purposefully kept his tone low as well. "Have a seat." He gestured to the empty stool and leaned forward. "Keep quiet and I'll explain."

"Explain away, Holt. I'm listening."

"My sister's here on an assignment. That's Tamsyn at the end of the bar. I'm nursing my scotch rocks and making sure she doesn't get in over her head."

"What kind of assignment?"

"Uh, well..."

"Spit it out. I'm losing patience."

"Client confidentiality. I can't reveal what she's doing."

O'Malley leaned back and watched Tamsyn for a minute or so. "Looks to me like she's either a hooker or a PI paid to seduce some sucker to see if he can be seduced."

"Good guess. Must be why you're paid the big bucks, Detective."

O'Malley's upper lip lifted in a sneer. "And here I thought it was the PI who made the big bucks."

The bartender came over to take O'Malley's drink order.

"Coffee, leaded, cream and sugar," she said. The bartender nodded and left.

"No quibbling about skim or whole tonight?"

"I've had a long day." She rolled her eyes. "I just want what I want."

The bartender returned and poured her a large cup of the fragrant brew. She added the cream and six packs of sugar and stirred. "Before you can say it, yes, sometimes I prefer a little coffee with my sugar."

"I wasn't going to say a word." O'Malley's showing up was a distraction, albeit a pleasant one. He leaned his elbow on the bar. Down at the far end, Tamsyn was giggling and touching her subject's shoulder. Shouldn't be too long and Scott could blow the joint.

"So, how's the investigation, Detective?"

She frowned as if considering whether to tell him how it was going or take a hike. She took a sip of coffee, then finally said, "My partner and I are following both Brennerman and the cold case now."

"So, they're related?"

She eyed him skeptically. "What's your need to know, Holt?"

"I was there. I'd like to see the Mason case closed. I still do the occasional presentation at the camp. It's a good institution, and I'd hate to see it fall by the wayside because some weird-ass psycho killer has targeted one of the campers again."

Her brows rose. "You're still involved with the camp?"

"Yes, as are dozens of upstanding Nashville citizens."

"Interesting." She gazed down at her coffee, then took another long sip. "I'll bear it in mind."

"Detective, for the record, I didn't kill Rich Mason or Todd Brennerman." From the corner of his eye, he saw Tamsyn and her subject stand and start walking toward the door. The subject's hand gripped his sister's arm above the elbow, a little too tightly for Scott's liking.

"Hold on. I've got to rescue my sister."

By now, Tamsyn, her eyes wide with alarm, had walked by him and O'Malley.

"Harris!" O'Malley yelled. "What the fuck are you doing? Your wife is going to kick your ass."

Officer Harris stopped and glared at O'Malley, but he released Tamsyn's arm and walked back to his seat at the bar while she scampered out the door and up the street.

O'Malley leaned forward with a smile. "You don't know it, but you were about to get an ass-whuppin' from half the guys in here. In the future, I'd advise your sister to stay out of cop hangouts."

"Consider her warned." Scott grinned. "And thanks for saving my ass."

He left a twenty on the bar, stood and strolled from the bar, but his mind was on O'Malley. What a woman. She could hold her own with anyone.

His sister was half a block ahead of him. "Hey! Wait up." His long strides ate up the distance between them. "That was too damn close. What the hell were you thinking?"

"Officer Harris wasn't taking no for an answer, but your girlfriend saved the day—no thanks to you, I might add." Tamsyn flashed him a quick grin and patted her purse. "I have Harris on record. Say, you and the detective were looking pretty cozy there for a minute. What's with that?"

He shook his head. "Nothing. Detective O'Malley's on the Brennerman case and she's following a cold case as well."

Her mouth formed an O. "She's investigating you?"

"Something like that. When she first saw me in the Blue Mood, she accused me of stalking her."

"Ouch." His sister stopped at the parking lot entrance. "My car's here. See you at home?"

"Yeah. Sure." He waited until she entered her car and locked the door before hoofing it to his own spot. He opened the car door and hopped inside, then glanced at his watch. Damn. Too late for a workout at the Y.

Not when another kind of workout was on his mind.

Tess O'Malley, yes, indeed. She was all woman. Hard as nails when the job called for it, she could give as good as she got, but he sensed in the right man's arms she'd surrender. Soft and warm and sweet as a dish of melting ice cream, he couldn't wait to taste her.

Chapter Five

July nights in Nashville were sweltering hot and sticky humid. Part and parcel of the Music City, USA experience, Market Street teemed with tourists all year round, but during the summer, they came out in droves. Nighttime was no different. They were seeking good music, good food, and most of all, a good time.

Wiping perspiration from her forehead, Tess took the elevator to her tiny loft apartment. Eight-hundred- and four-square feet of pure privacy close to her stationhouse, and it was all hers. She'd had her eye on the downtown lofts ever since they started converting them into condos. When she graduated from the academy, her father had given her the money for a down payment. Without hesitating, she toured and picked one out within twenty-four hours.

She unlocked, then shoved open the massive metal door and stepped inside her haven from all the wrongs of the world. Here she had complete control. Over time, she'd furnished it with an eclectic assortment of furnishings. On the blank canvas of the once empty warehouse loft, she'd formed an entryway by placing a bank of two open bookcases to her right. A dummy wall that went only nine feet high was on her left and acted to isolate her bedroom from the rest of the open space.

Straight ahead was the streamlined kitchen with stainless appliances, polished concrete countertops, and a stackable washer/dryer combo. Her dining room was a peninsula with two stools. Wide-planked, original heart-of-pine floors ran throughout, except in the tumbled marble-tiled bathroom. Around the corner from the bookcases was her living room. Two tall windows looked out over the Cumberland River which snaked through the city, dividing it into east and west.

A high-definition TV/DVD player along the far brick wall. A deep green sofa and ottoman/coffee table along with two occasional chairs covered in taupe micro-fiber furnished the rest of her living room in easy comfort.

Large colorful canvases painted by her mother occupied the spaces over the TV and sofa. Overhead, in addition to the open heating tubes and vents, modern flexible lighting wove its way through the loft and revealed a homey, if eclectic, living space.

Home. She let out a sigh, shut the door behind her, walked over to the kitchen and set her purse on the counter. She kicked off her shoes, then carried them into the bedroom. Behind the dummy wall was a nine-foot closet. Her bed and a single wall-hung nightstand with a lamp were her only bedroom furniture. To her right was the small bath. It was large enough for a shower, but no tub. She quickly stripped off the rest of her clothes, then opened one of the closet doors. The handy shelves organized all her shoes and foldable clothes. There was even a hamper on the bottom rack. On the other side of the closet was a rack for hanging clothes.

Her tiny condo was perfect. She'd loved the space from the first moment she saw it. Then, with a little help from one of her mother's architect friends, the loft was transformed from a cobwebby mouse house into what it was today. Everything had its place, and everything was in its place.

She hung up her skirt and jacket, then threw the blouse and undies into the hamper. The hardwood was cool to the soles of her feet, and after the heat of the day, a pleasant relief. She opened one of the drawers and selected a clean cotton nightshirt, inhaling its laundry-fresh scent and sighed. No woman ever had it so good.

She padded into the living room and turned on her favorite country radio station before heading into the kitchen. Definitely too late for more coffee, so she opened the fridge and glanced inside. Pretty barren. Just some Chinese takeout and bottled water. She removed one of the bottles, opened it and took a long swig.

Her stomach growled, reminding her she hadn't eaten much all day. She opened the carton of cashew chicken and sniffed. Only a couple of days old. She set it in the microwave, set the timer, and then reached up into a cabinet for a plate. Life would truly be perfect if she just had someone to cook for her.

Does Scott Holt cook?

Now, why should she even care if he cooked? He was a complication.

Because he's hot, has yummy lips and dark eyes that set you on fire, doofus.

She didn't need a man. She already had a perfect life. With no responsibilities, except to the job and her partner, she could come and go and decorate however the hell she pleased.

Because you haven't had sex in six months.

Well, there was that.

Ding.

Tess opened the microwave and pulled out the cashew chicken and rice. Damn. No egg rolls or duck sauce left. She dumped the carton's contents onto the plate, then carried it into the living room. The spices in the chicken dish made her mouth water.

Geez, Louise. She'd forgotten the chopsticks. Famished, she ran into the kitchen and snatched a pair off the counter.

Settling on the sofa, she dug into her leftovers and then grabbed the remote to turn off the music and turn on the news. Gobbling the cashew chicken and rice, she nearly choked when she saw the lieutenant's face on the screen. Turning up the volume, she leaned forward to hear.

"Lieutenant Woods, we hear an arrest has been made in the Brennerman case."

Her boss nodded. "True."

True? Her mouth opened. What the hell? How come she was the last to know? Hadn't Woods just promised her and Kozinsky they could be a part of the case?

"We have arrested Edward Forbes, the founder and owner of Camp Einstein. We have eyewitness testimony linking Forbes to the victim and crime scene. He fits the profile of a homosexual sadistic killer."

"Agh!" She clicked off the television and threw the remote across the room. No wonder the lieutenant was so agreeable earlier. No, too quick and too easy. The body was just located this morning. How could they have a sudden eyewitness to give evidence so quickly? No way. The lieutenant was lying through his pearly white veneers.

She grabbed her cell phone and hit the speed dial for Kozinsky. She waited for him to answer. Crap. He sounded as if he'd been asleep. "Sorry, I know it's past your bedtime, old man."

"No shit." Her partner yawned. "See you in the morning."

"No, wait! Have you seen the ten o'clock news? Woods arrested someone."

"Okay." Without another word, her partner hung up. Apparently, he didn't expect or want a response.

Damn the boss for a sneaky rat. One thing for sure, he'd get a piece of her mind in the morning.

Her phone rang. Kozinsky must've woken up and realized what she'd told him. She answered, "Kozinsky?"

"No, darling, it's your mother." Her mother's tone was pained and tense.

"What's wrong?"

"Someone I serve with on a committee has been arrested. You remember Ned Forbes?"

"I just saw it on the news, but I didn't know he was anyone you knew."

"I know Ned couldn't have killed anyone, much less the way that poor Brennerman boy was killed. You have to do something."

"I'll do what I can, but the lieutenant is driving this case. My hands are sort of tied." She thought for a moment. "What about a PI?" She paused. "I…uh, know a reputable one."

"You think that's the way to go?"

"Yes, because if the lieutenant has made up his mind, he's not going to listen to anyone, and definitely not in a high-profile murder case like this one. The governor must be calling him twenty times a day."

"Give me the PI's name then. I've a pen and paper. Go ahead."

That was her mother. Always prepared, whether hiring an interior designer or a private eye.

"Hold on. I have to find his card." She got to her feet, walked over to the counter, then fumbled through her purse. "Okay, here we go." She read off Scott Holt's office number.

"Thank you so much. I'll call and give Ned's partner the number right away."

Her mother disconnected quickly.

Hmm. Maybe she and Scott really could work together…unofficially. It wouldn't be the first time a homicide detective used all available resources. And Holt was an attractive resource.

Several miles west, Scott watched the news and shook his head in disbelief. They'd arrested Ned Forbes. What the fuck was Metro PD thinking? Edward Forbes was a humanitarian and all-around good guy. Yes, Forbes was gay and just about anyone who knew him socially was aware of his long-term relationship with a stockbroker. Poor guy must be frantic.

He reached for the phone to call Ned's partner, Paul Whitten.

No answer. He left a message offering his assistance on Whitten's voice mail.

Stretched out on the sofa in the study, Scott fought sleep during the sports report. When his cell phone rang, he jumped awake and saw Letterman was well into his monologue. Grabbing for the cell with one hand, he hit the TV mute button with the other.

"Scott Holt."

"Oh, thank you for calling. The phone has simply been ringing off the hook since the news aired. Everyone is so upset, but you're the only one who's offered to help. I can't imagine why the police would arrest Ned. They took him away in handcuffs—like a common criminal."

Clearly rattled, Paul paused long enough to take a breath.

"Have you called his attorney?"

"Yes, first thing."

"Good. Now, how can I help?"

"I want you to investigate this on your own. The police have already made up their minds Ned's guilty."

The sad fact was if the department powers decided on one suspect, they developed tunnel vision when it came to finding another.

"I'll see what I can do. Come into my office in the morning and I'll clear some time for you."

"Thank you. Thank you so much."

No sooner had he hung up from Paul than his phone rang again, but he didn't recognize the number or the name—Regina Storm.

"Scott Holt."

"Regina Storm here." Her accent was well-educated southern. "My daughter, Tess, gave me your number. An acquaintance of mine, someone I serve on a committee with, has been arrested and I've been unable to reach his partner. Tess says you've got a good reputation and—"

"Tess is your daughter? Detective O'Malley?"

"Yes, I've always used my maiden name professionally. Anyway, I've been trying to reach his partner, Paul Whitten, but his line's busy. I thought I'd call you on his behalf."

Only in Nashville could something like this happen.

"Perhaps you could come to my office in the morning. I'll clear some time for you, too."

"Yes," she said, hesitating. "You'll clear some time for me *too*? I'm afraid I don't understand."

"Let's just say I've known Ned Forbes of Camp Einstein for a long time. I'm also acquainted with Paul. Because of client confidentiality, I can't say more."

"I see. Excellent. Will you be able to help him?"

"I'll do my best. It's obvious Metro has jumped to the simplest solution because Todd Brennerman was the governor's grandson."

"I rather like your attitude, Mr. Holt."

"I'll see you in the morning?"

"Yes, indeed. I'm sure poor Paul will need some reassurance."

"That's a pretty fair assessment of his mental state. I'm sure he'll appreciate your presence."

"Thank you for taking my call so late in the evening."

"No problem. PIs are used to late hours."

"I wonder why my daughter hasn't bothered to mention you to me before."

"We just met today."

"Then you must be impressive. I look forward to meeting you."

Damn. If he wasn't mistaken, this was a match-making mother on the prowl. "Office opens at eight-thirty. Why don't you and Paul come in at nine-thirty or ten?"

"Ten will be perfect."

Regina Storm broke the connection and not a moment too soon. Her mellifluous tone made him nervous. Husband material he wasn't. No matter what Ms. Storm thought about it, her daughter would have the last word, and it wouldn't be yes.

Never had he imagined marrying a cop, no matter how seductive her figure or gray her eyes or soft her lips. That flaming red hair and Irish name said temperamental, high-maintenance and way too much trouble for a simple PI. But intelligent—no doubt about it.

Who was he fooling? Tess might be temperamental and high maintenance, but those were the very qualities drawing him like a bee to honey. Something about her scored on a primal level. Down to her very being, she was a woman who possessed the go-the-distance determination of a marathoner. She wouldn't give up until a case was solved, and once she committed to a lover, she wouldn't give up on a relationship, either.

He watched the newscast and laughed to himself. The cops were so incredibly stupid, and their lieutenant was one dumb motherfucker. They'd arrested that pansy Ned Forbes. How rich. And so satisfying.

No one could stop him. He was too smart to get caught. Since his first kill, he'd done research on crime and the science of forensics. He knew better than to leave any trace evidence behind. His only mistake happened the first time when he'd left his DNA in the surprise and exhilaration of the moment. Now, he knew better.

Chapter Six

The next morning was hot and humid. Scott's shirt had already stuck to his back from the drive to the office. Walking into the office, he carried a cup of coffee in one hand and a briefcase in his other along with a stack of files under his arm. Carrie was already at her desk, sipping on the first of her many Diet Cokes. He stopped at her desk, set down the files, then restacked them before picking them up again. "I have anything at ten?"

She set her drink aside, removed her glasses and looked up at him. "Nope. Why?"

"Good. Pencil in Regina Storm and Paul Whitten. They'll come together…probably."

She gave him her *you are such a dunce* smile. "You do know this is done on the computer, don't you? No pencil required."

"You know what I mean."

"I see you stopped for coffee again." She gave him a knowing smile. "So?"

"Nothing. Just making an idle comment." Her green eyes sparkled, but she put on her glasses and went back to her work as if he weren't there.

Big deal. Yeah, so he stopped at Starbuck's again. He hoped he'd run into the detective. Pathetic. His X-rated dreams last night about a redheaded witch, who served him up on a platter, had him tossing and turning most of the night, had left him bleary-eyed this morning. A little high-powered espresso was just what he needed to kick-start his day.

He eased by his sister's desk and into his office. No mean feat, but he managed to set down his coffee, the briefcase and the stack of files without a minor catastrophic occurrence. He sat, signed onto his computer, leaned back and took a sip of the piping hot brew.

What other appointments did he have today? His brother Justin might be the computer guru, but Scott could still manage the basics like checking his appointment calendar.

After Paul Whitten, Scott's next appointment was at eleven, then another at twelve, followed by back-to-backs from two until five. Baseball practice was at six with his team of six and eight-year-olds, the Bellevue Beatles, which wouldn't be much fun in this heat.

He took another sip of coffee. Damn. Just enough caffeine and he was buzzing around like a one-legged shortstop. No way could he sit back and calmly wait for Paul Whitten's appointment. Would O'Malley's mother really come along? And what was the hot Tess's mother like? Hot as her daughter? Or a Belle Meade grand dame?

More likely the latter.

His fingers drummed against the desktop. Another sign the caffeine was doing its job. He jumped up and started to pace. What difference did it make what O'Malley's mom looked like? It was O'Malley herself he was interested in.

Oh, yeah. The detective was hot, scorching hot, from her expensive shoes to her fiery red hair.

He walked over to the window. The flags along Riverside Park were still. No sign of a breeze and the sidewalks were already dazzling with waves of heat. Hottest July since they started keeping track, at least that's what the radio said, and he believed it. "Scott?"

"Yeah." He turned. "What's up?"

Justin rested his lanky body against the doorjamb. His longish blond hair was combed behind his ears. His stepbrother was an okay guy for a computer geek, although Justin preferred guru to geek. "Wanted to see if you received my text about the financial adviser?"

"Uh…" He pulled the cell phone from his pocket and frowned. "Haven't checked. Just tell me."

"He has a good rep. Couldn't find anything negative in his professional or personal history."

"Great, I'll let our client know to go ahead." Good—a phone call. Something to pass the time until ten. He headed back to his desk, then sat. He picked up the telephone, ready to make the call when he noticed Justin hadn't moved from his spot by the door. "What?"

"Just wanted to say thanks for covering with Tamsyn last night."

"No problem. Glad to do it. Say, your presentation go okay?"

Justin nodded and grinned. "Pissed off a couple of guys with my theories on the ultimate limitations of random-access memory. Made my night." He ran his hands through his hair.

"Glad to know you had a good time arguing about whatever the hell you just said."

"Whatever, dude." Justin shrugged and strolled back to his office.

Scott spent the next few minutes reassuring Mrs. Bailey her financial adviser wouldn't skip town with all her money.

He hung up and scratched his head. Most people thought PIs led exciting, even romantic lives solving crimes and knocking around bad guys. Far from the truth. Most of his time was spent behind his desk or doing surveillance from his car in the parking lots of sleazy motels.

While Tamsyn's specialty was enticing and catching men on the verge of cheating, his was catching them in the *act*. Romantic? Anything but.

He spent the next few minutes checking dates, times and already known facts about Brennerman's disappearance. The police weren't naming their eyewitness. Why hadn't the eyewitness intervened? Why hadn't he come forward before now?

The intercom buzzed. "Yes?"

"Paul Whitten and Regina Storm to see you. Are you ready for them?"

He glanced at his watch—twenty minutes early. Great. That meant they were anxious and ready to sign.

"Ready." He rose and walked to the door to greet his new clients. After introductions, he walked back to his desk and gestured for them to have a seat.

Paul Whitten was pale and clearly upset. His body showed he worked out regularly, and his dress was business casual consisting of khaki slacks with a knife-edge crease and a short sleeve light blue shirt. His nails were manicured. He wore a large gold signet ring on his left hand and a gold Rolex on his right wrist.

On the other hand, Regina Storm was oddly spectacular. Her red hair was somewhat dimmer than her daughter's and worn back from her striking face in a ponytail. Her eyes were blue, unlike Tess's silver-gray. Ms. Storm was trim and attractive and dressed in a peculiar outfit. She wore slender white pants which nipped in at the ankle, and over the pants, she wore some kind of flowered oriental silk thing which was split up the sides. Her flat-heeled shoes were black with flowers embroidered on the toes. All she needed was a coolie hat and a rickshaw. He gave himself a mental slap for being so un-PC.

The woman was an artist and clearly believed in expressing her individuality. After she'd made the appointment, he'd Googled her name and viewed several of her avant-garde paintings online. Not that he could fully understand them, but her use of color and form was dynamic.

Paul spoke first. "You must help Ned. He couldn't have killed anyone. I just know it."

"Mr. Holt," Regina Storm began, "I completely agree with Paul. You must help us prove Ned's innocence."

"As long as you understand, it's up to the state to prove Ned's guilt. It's a lot harder to prove a negative." Scott pulled up a document on the computer. "I've done some basic fact checking. Todd Brennerman disappeared from Camp Einstein on the fifth of July, sometime after bed check. His body was discovered yesterday in the woods, but quite some distance from the camp proper." He leveled his gaze at Paul. "So where was Ned on the evening of July fifth? If he has an alibi, we can get him released."

Paul shook his head, his face flushed. "I was out of town from the first of July until the ninth. Ned always had so much to see to when the camp was in session, I took the opportunity to attend a financial seminar in Atlanta."

"How much time does Ned typically spend at the camp?"

"He's usually there for the opening and closing ceremonies. Most of his involvement is during preparation for each year's camp. Then during the camp, he remains available for any kind of crisis control."

"Like a disappearance?"

"Well, certainly that's a crisis," Paul said, "but usually it's more along the lines of drug use or excessive fraternization between the male and female students. He always said even though they were highly intelligent, they still had teenage hormones and were highly creative when it came to finding ways to break the rules."

Scott grinned. "Oh, I remember. I spent a summer there myself, then returned later to do several stints as a counselor."

Regina Storm smiled. "So, you understand what the camp atmosphere is like."

"Yes. I was there the year Rich Mason was murdered."

"You've come full circle, Mr. Holt." One of her graceful eyebrows arched. "You're the perfect person to assist us. You have a prior connection with the camp, and you already believe Ned couldn't have committed this heinous crime."

"I don't. Now then, did you speak with Ned at any time while you were away?"

Paul paused, then answered. "Yes, I'm sure I must've. Whenever one of us is away, we normally speak every evening."

"I'll need to get your cell phone records. The police may already have done so. Have they spoken to you at all?"

"Have they interrogated me? No, not yet. But I'm to present myself at the Criminal Justice Center at one. I'm taking Ned's attorney with me…I mean, he's my attorney as well."

"When they arrested him yesterday evening, what did they take from your house?"

"Oh, my. They took our computers. I tried to explain I work from home and can't work without my computer, but they took it anyway. It has all my client information and brokerage work on it."

"Your attorney should be able to do something about that," Ms. Storm suggested. "They can't deprive him of his livelihood, can they?"

Scott frowned. "Whether or not they could remove Paul's computer would depend on how the warrant was phrased."

Paul's hands fluttered, then he struggled to collect himself, folding his hands in his lap. "I was so upset at the time I don't remember what the paper said. They flashed the search warrant and literally shoved me out of the way. We own the house jointly, but I don't know if it makes a difference or not."

"It would help if I could see the warrant. I'll also work on obtaining phone records for you and Ned. If the two of you were in contact during the time in question, his location could be triangulated from the GPS chip in his cell phone."

"Wonderful. Just like on TV," Paul said, rising from his seat.

"Not quite that easy. I'm private and there are some limitations to what I can accomplish…legally," Scott said and flashed a smile.

O'Malley's mother rose gracefully and extended her hand. "I'm sure you'll do whatever you can. Thank you so much for seeing us."

After Scott walked them to the door, he went back to his desk and made detailed notes of the meeting. He couldn't help but wonder how O'Malley's father and mother met. Captain O'Malley had the rep as a fierce guardian of law and order while Regina Storm was from old money and a flamboyant artist. Now that was some combo.

At the Criminal Justice Center, Tess's meeting with Lieutenant Woods tanked. He was too busy to give her even a moment. No, make that too busy basking in the limelight of his most recent arrest.

She was still on the team, and by damn, she was going to get her hands on the evidentiary reports, specifically the eyewitness's statement.

She stood, but before she could head down to Evidence, her phone rang. "O'Malley."

"Morning, darling. Your detective is very yummy in a dark and intense way. You've been holding out on me."

"I don't have time for this now. So, you saw him…that's good."

"Yes, we saw him this morning at ten. I'm very impressed, and I hope you'll give him any assistance you can."

"Paul?"

"No, the yummy Mr. Holt. If you help him, it'll help Paul and Ned, of course."

"I've done what I can by giving you Scott's number. The rest is up to your private detective. Apparently, the lieutenant has already made up his mind."

"Why don't you ask him to dinner?"

"Why would I want to ask the lieutenant to dinner?" she asked innocently, not having time for her mother's matchmaking. No indeed.

"Now, you're being purposely obtuse. You know exactly who I mean."

"No, Mother, please…stick to the subject at hand."

"You're thirty years old, and it's past time you married. Your eggs won't last forever."

That old argument again. "Oh, I think they'll stick around a few more years. This is the twenty-first century, and women don't get married right out of college the way they did in your day. I have a career. I know you understand having a career, don't you?"

"I don't think I appreciate your condescending tone."

"For someone who doesn't even use her husband's name, you should appreciate my spirit and the determination to make it on my own."

"It's always the mother's fault," her mother said, letting out a theatrical sigh. "I raised a rebel."

"That's right, but you know you love it."

"Of course, dear. Now when are you bringing him home?"

"Mom! Give me a break. I just met him yesterday."

"But he's the one."

"Isn't that up to me?"

"I suppose if you wish to be picky about it."

"Some things just aren't under your control, Mom."

"There was a time when a young woman's parents decided—"

"That," Tess interrupted, "was in the Middle Ages." God. She had to get her mother off the phone. She kicked her desk and when Kozinsky raised his head, she pointed at the phone. He smiled and punched in her extension.

She leaned forward to ensure her mother heard the buzz. "Have a call, Mom. Gotta go. Love you, bye." She hung up before her mother could get in another word.

"Thanks. I thought she would never shut up."

"Trying to marry you off, is she?"

"Like the worst modern-day matchmaker." She shook her head.

"She's concerned about the state of my eggs and wants me to invite a man home for dinner. For Pete's sake, I barely know him."

"What him?"

"The PI," she said as casually as she could manage. "You know—"

"Scott Holt?"

"Yeah, he's the one."

Kozinsky leaned forward and eyeballed her. "How does your mother know anything about him?"

"Stop it. You act like you're a detective or something." She turned and pretended to thumb through her files. She needed to get him off track. Her partner probably wouldn't approve of her involving a PI in a current case. "I might've mentioned him in passing. Anyway, that's my mother; she jumped on the idea of a PI in the family like a duck on a June bug."

"Why on earth would you mention the PI to your mother if you know how she is about assisting you down the aisle to marital bliss?" He rolled his eyes.

"Let's drop the subject. I want to go over all these Brennerman files."

"Why?"

"Because something tells me Edward Forbes didn't do it. Plus, I have a few questions about the eyewitness."

A big wide grin spread across her partner's face. "Would that be your woman's intuition or maybe your gut?"

"It's my gut. Besides my mother knows Forbes and—"

Kozinsky pointed a long finger at her. "Bingo! You recommended she call Holt. Finally, the fog begins to clear."

She quickly glanced around the squad room and zipped her lip. "Geez, Louise. I'm sure there's someone out front who didn't hear you."

"Your mother met him, and she likes him." He shot her a sly smirk.

"Apparently a little too much for my comfort level. Maybe I should let my father know he has competition." She averted her gaze, then giggled. "Mom's right though. He's a total hottie."

"Is the hottie your father or Scott Holt?"

She sucked in a breath and let out a loud huff. "Not you too. Holt is the hottie, okay." Inwardly, she cringed. Maybe she'd said that a little loud.

A giggle from her left confirmed it. She glanced over at Detective

Sara Kagen who fluttered her eyelashes. "Problem, Kagen?"

"Not at all. I happen to agree with you," Kagen replied. "He provided a good lead on an old case of mine. He's very cooperative with the force."

"Grr." She scooted her desk chair closer to Kagen's. "I'd better never hear a word of this from anyone. If I do, I'll know the source."

"Whatever." Kagen rolled her eyes. "Get a life, Tess. No one will think less of you if you do."

Tess scooted back to her desk. No point in arguing. Scott Holt might be a serious hunk of manliness, but warnings aside, she hadn't heard her biological clock tick once.

In order to get Ned and Paul's cell phone records, Scott called in a favor from a friend, his late fiancée's sister, Susan. She promised anytime he needed absolutely anything to let her know.

The time had come. Susan worked for the phone company.

"Suze, I hate to ask you this…might be a little illegal."

"A favor is a favor." The sound of her voice, so like Carly's, unnerved him. "What do you need, Scott? I assume it's for a client?"

"Yes, can't go into any details, but I need a list of calls made from July first until the ninth for these two cell numbers." He read her the two numbers. "And for the second number, I need to know the location of the towers."

"In other words, you need to triangulate the location?"

"Exactly."

"Hm. It looks like the DA's office has already subpoenaed this information—yesterday as a matter of fact. You still need it?"

"Yes."

"Well, you're right. It's illegal."

"I don't want to get you in trouble, but I really need this. It wouldn't be the first time the DA's office ignored exculpatory evidence in order to get a conviction."

"One overdue favor coming up. I'm emailing these lists to you right now."

"You're a great pal, Suze."

"You know the drill. Anytime I can give you a hand, I will."

"Not necessary. We're even."

"Not even close. You filled my sister's last days with love and support. You deserve a dad-blamed medal."

Scott blinked rapidly and tried not to give in to the emotions nearly choking him. "Th-thanks." He broke the connection. Dammit. Losing Carly had been tough on everyone. No sense in making it worse by breaking down and crying like a kid.

When his first fiancée dumped him, he was so busy dragging the agency out of the red and into the black, he barely noticed her absence.

Carly was different. The entire Holt-Lackey clan loved her almost as much as he had, and they suffered with him after she passed. What would he have done without them?

In spite of all his flirting with O'Malley, he still wasn't sure he was ready for a real relationship.

Chapter Seven

Tess watched the lieutenant interrogate Ned Forbes through the two-way mirror. Her foot tapped impatiently, and her shoulders twitched. A mistake. A heinous blunder. That's what it was. Edward Forbes was in for another lengthy round of questioning. Instead of listening to his lawyer's vehement instructions to keep his trap shut, Forbes insisted on trying to explain away the circumstantial evidence.

In spite of the lieutenant's big announcement on TV, the eyewitness statement wasn't in the case file. She'd combed the file and couldn't locate that document or the DNA report. True, Forbes was at the camp when the governor's grandson disappeared but what was his motive? Forbes being gay didn't make him a murderer. And what about means? Forbes's physique was on the doughboy side. Could he have overcome a youngster who was three inches taller and had youth and vitality on his side?

If Forbes was this sadistic serial killer, why the fourteen-year gap in murders? These were valid questions, and the lieutenant should've asked them before he rushed to judgment and made a highly publicized arrest.

If she questioned the lieutenant about her doubts, he'd blow her off. After all, in his mind, she was nothing more than a detective who'd had her gold badge a mere three years. Eight years on the job including five in uniform. Maybe it was time she paid Daddy a call and pitched him a hypothetical question or two. Technically, it wasn't going over her lieutenant's head because her father was a captain in the West Precinct while the lieutenant was assigned to Central.

"Give it up, Tess." Kozinsky tapped her on the shoulder. "Forbes ain't about to cop a plea or confess either."

She whirled on her partner. "Why should he if he's innocent?"

"You think he's innocent. The lieutenant thinks he's guilty." He shrugged. "Hm. Now, whose opinion carries the most weight around here?"

"I'm still going to talk to him. I won't let this go."

"Go on. It's your funeral."

"But if I'm right, I'll have saved the city the cost of an expensive trial."

"Only way that's gonna happen is if you find a better substitute…if there is one."

The doubt rang through in Kozinsky's tone. Dammit. Even her partner thought she was chasing shadows. Well, she'd show all of them. But first, she'd rattle the lieutenant's cage again.

Before calling her father for lunch, Tess tapped on the lieutenant's door.

"Enter." He gazed up at her, frowning as usual. "What now?"

"Just wondered about the eyewitness, Lieutenant. His statement isn't in the case file."

The lieutenant's brows drew together. His forehead furrowed and he jabbed his pen into the scarred wood of his desk. "Probably still in dictation. Hell, how should I know?"

"I'll check. Just wanted to give it a once over because I have a few questions. What was his name again?" Like she ever knew.

The lieutenant's eyes glazed over. Why was he being so secretive about the eyewitness? "Silvey," he finally said. "Doug Silvey. He was one of the instructors at the camp."

"Well, see. I have a problem. Just what did he see and why didn't he try to stop it? Why did he wait until now to come forward?"

"It's in the report." He glanced at the door. Clearly, he wanted to get rid of her. She nodded and got the hell out of there. If the truth was told, he'd probably prefer to get rid of all the women on the force. He might keep his chauvinism under a tight rein, but his dismissive attitude was clearly visible to any female on the job. None of the good-old-boy back-slapping or joking around. No, indeed.

Kozinsky—she'd lucked out with him. Damn straight. As long as she did her job, he didn't care if she were a man, woman or a spotted leopard with a purple tail.

As for Doug Silvey, she definitely needed to find out more. If she didn't find his statement soon, she knew a damned good PI who might do some footwork for her.

Her stomach growled, reminding her it was past time for lunch.

Tess met her dad at the Calypso Café on Elliston Place at noon. Given the time of day, every table was taken. The Caribbean music blasted over the noise of the lunch-goers and the aroma of savory roasted chicken filled the air.

"Sorry, I'm late." She spotted her dad and slid into a chair across from him. In his youthful photos, he'd resembled a movie star from the forties. Even now at fifty-five, he was still a handsome man with salt and pepper hair and bright blue eyes.

He reached over and patted her hand. "How's my favorite girl?"

"I'm fine, Daddy." She pursed her lips and considered how to pose her questions.

"Uh-oh. Something on your mind? Come on, spill it." His blue eyes twinkled. Damn. He knew her too well.

"What's bugging you?"

"Suppose…"

He grinned. "I see. You got a hypothetical problem you want to run by me?"

"You always could read my mind." She paused for a second, still not sure how to broach the subject. "Suppose…you thought your superior officer had rushed to judgment and made an arrest…someone you thought was innocent. What would you do?"

He frowned, took off his glasses and made a show of cleaning them with a napkin. "Depends. What do you want to do—hypothetically?" He put on his specs, then studied the menu, but the question hung in the air.

As luck would have it, she didn't have to answer right away. A waiter with dreadlocks threaded his way to their table and took their orders—

barbecued chicken, black beans and rice for her father while she opted for the Lucayan salad and fruit tea.

Her father raised an eyebrow and cocked his head to the side. "Well? Do I have to break out my rubber hose to make you talk?"

She chewed the inside of her lip. He wasn't going to like her next question. "Suppose…the hypothetical detective worked with a PI on his or her own time?"

His forehead furrowed in a frown. "That'd depend on how trustworthy the PI was. Who did you…um, the hypothetical detective have in mind?"

She straightened. "Me?"

"Been at this a long time, kiddo. Can't fool me. This about the Forbes' arrest?"

A little guilty, she nodded. "Yeah."

"I know he's one of your mother's pals and she's all fired up about it. So, she's pulled you into this mess, has she?" A grimace flickered across his face. "Wish she'd keep her aristocratic nose out of things that aren't any of her business."

She ignored her father's dig, unfolded her napkin and placed it in her lap. "I sort of recommended a PI to Mom—Scott Holt."

Her father straightened. "I wish you hadn't. Never pays to go against your lieutenant. You have a career to think about."

Did he have something against Scott? Or was his disapproval of a more general nature? "But Kozinsky says Scott's cool. I've met him and he seems like an upright guy. Besides, his father was on the job before he retired and opened the agency. How bad can he be?"

"Nothing personal against Holt. He's about as good as they come." Her father shook his head. "But Woods won't like it if he finds out. You could be shooting yourself in the foot by interfering."

Further conversation halted while the waiter served their food, but her mind was racing. Her father had a valid point. Her career was important, but was it more important than helping her mother's friend?

He leveled his gaze on her and frowned. "Said all I'm gonna say. You're stubborn like your mom which means you'll do whatever you want—always have." He dug into his barbecue chicken, then followed with a bite of *boja* muffin. He pointed his fork at her plate. "How's your green stuff?"

She glanced down at her plate of leaf lettuce, roasted chicken, mandarin oranges topped with toasted almonds and drizzled with a light vinaigrette. She took a quick bite. Sweet, sour and crunchy all at once. "Great. Just great. You oughta try green stuff once in a while."

He wrinkled his nose. "Sissy food. Good for rabbits." He chewed, then pointed his fork at her. "Wish you'd listen to your old man just once. Follow your lieutenant's lead. It's his case. You won't win any friends if you go behind his back and work with a PI."

"I don't see any harm in it since all I did was give Mom his office number." She kept her gaze steady.

He shook his head, then set his cold drink aside. "Hope this doesn't come back to bite you in the butt."

"It's *my* butt."

"No argument 'bout that."

"Thanks for your help, Daddy." She nibbled on her muffin. Even if she was ignoring his advice, she appreciated his input. Even with his being against her talking to Scott, she knew he would be proud as punch when she found the real killer.

Once she got back to the squad room, Tess cornered Kozinsky at the coffee machine. "Pour me one while you're at it." She added in a lower tone. "Need a little background info."

"Sure." Kozinsky shrugged, then lumbered back to his desk.

She nodded toward the door. "Let's take it outside. More private that way."

A puzzled expression flashed across his face, but all the same, he followed her until they were outside on the street in front of the Criminal Justice Center. The July sun beat down on her head and radiated from the brick courtyard in dizzying waves of heat.

Her partner walked beside her. "Okay, kid. What's up?"

"Got anything else on that PI, Scott Holt?"

"What?" He gave a snort. "You want his pedigree?"

She shrugged. "Know anything negative about him at all?"

"Something personal, since we already covered his professional rep.?"

"Of course." She laughed. "He's kinda cute. Y'know?"

"So, you're still jonesin' for the guy?" He shook his head. "You're smarter than that."

She winked at him. "Doesn't hurt to look once in a while—now does it?"

"Long as look is all you do."

"No more serious relationships for me. I'm looking for some fun." Even as the words escaped her mouth, she realized they were true. Scott Holt looked like he could seriously use some fun, and she was more than ready to have some too, as long as it didn't interfere with her investigation. Before she could relax and have fun with Scott, she'd better do some follow-up interviews on the cold case.

"Can we go back inside now? It's too damn hot to be walking around out here." Kozinsky wiped the perspiration from his forehead. "And you've got a dozen new freckles."

More freckles? Just what she needed. "Sure. Didn't mean to cook your goose."

"Not my goose I'm worried about. It's my brain."

She laughed and tugged on his forearm. "All right. Let's go. Your brain was fried long ago. I'd hate to see anything else happen to it."

Back inside the squad, the barely comfortable AC system whined, rattled, and protested having to work so hard. Tess sat at her desk and pulled out three interviews from the Mason file. Tyler Jamison, currently a TV news journalist, one of the talking heads on Channel Nine. She'd take him second.

Drew Wilson, the UT running back who was now an investment banker, seemed like a good bet for her first interview. She flipped through Dakota Taylor's file and wondered where the heck he was currently. She'd interview him last, provided the powers that be would give her leeway to go wherever he was or have him brought to Nashville for questioning.

She entered Wilson's name into the DMV system and came up with his address and home phone. After calling his home, Wilson's wife gave Tess his office phone and address but warned her to call for an appointment since his schedule was usually booked weeks in advance.

She set the phone back. Booked weeks in advance. Tough. She wasn't about to wait weeks, and official police business trumped whatever he might have planned. Still, might as well give him a head's up.

Chapter Eight

Drew Wilson's office was in the First American Center located on one of the highest points in the city. It was a tall, dark glass monstrosity but visitor parking was close to the entrance. She took the quick hike to the entrance and stopped at the security desk.

"Detective O'Malley to see Drew Wilson with Eidelman-West Investments," Tess said, then signed the visitors' log.

The guard's eyebrows rose an inch, but she nodded. "Go left. Elevators are at the end of the hall on your right. Tenth floor, suite 1002."

Tess nodded. Inside, the walls and floors were tiled in beige marble. The only thing of note was a man sitting on a bench working over his laptop.

On closer inspection, it wasn't a man but a bronze figure; the man, the bench, and the laptop were all bronze.

Cool.

After a few minutes' wait, she was ushered into Drew Wilson's office. He rose. He was several inches over six feet with the physique you'd expect of a former running back. In spite of the passage of time, he hadn't run to fat. His hair was already salt and pepper, his eyes blue and his complexion golf course tan. He held out his hand. "Drew Wilson. Detective O'Malley, I've been expecting to hear from you."

Really? She hadn't given him that much notice. "Why's that?"

"Scott Holt gave me a buzz after you saw him. I'm more than happy to help law enforcement any way I can." He motioned for her to have a seat.

Instead of being seated right away, she walked over to his window and glanced out. From his office, she could see all of downtown Nashville. "Great view," she said, then sat and pulled out her notebook. "I've been assigned a cold case. Rich Mason's murder was never solved."

"I'll tell you what little I know."

His smile was friendly, and his eyes shone with good humor. Obviously, being outgoing was an asset in his business, but was it merely a front to charm her like he charmed his clients? He appeared relaxed which, in itself, was unusual. Most people weren't at ease when questioned by the police, even those with nothing to hide.

"Tell me about Camp Einstein and the summer Rich Mason disappeared. Was there anyone or anything unusual? Something that stuck out in your mind?"

"Unusual? Man, most of the campers were unusual. They were gifted, and I don't mean just your average, everyday intelligent kids. They were artists and computer geeks, before we even knew the word in that context, with a few math scholars. One of the purposes of the camp was to give these outstanding students a taste of normalcy and foster independence. This was the very reason for the insistence on each camper participating in the physical activities, in addition to concentrating on their intellectual abilities."

His glib speech seemed rehearsed or memorized. "How were you involved with the camp?"

"I used to play football and was one of the PE counselors. I mean I did all right in school, but I wasn't on the same playing field with these kids…unless we actually were on a playing field."

"Was the Mason boy close to anyone in particular at the camp?"

Wilson leaned back, screwing his mouth to one side. "No. It was hard to get him away from his laptop. Big, bulky old thing it was."

"A laptop at camp?"

"Yes, there was a computer lab—rudimentary by today's standards— art studio, music rooms. Don't get me wrong. The camp didn't deprive them of anything, just tried to keep their bodies moving half as fast as their brains."

"What do you remember about the night he disappeared?"

"That night...something...can't quite remember what it was. There was something unusual. Something special." His gaze turned inward, then he smiled. "Oh...I know. There was a campfire that same night. A partial eclipse of the moon or was it a total? Anyway, it was going to happen late. If I remember correctly, around eleven."

"Did all the campers attend the campfire?"

"No. Lights out was at nine-thirty, but some of the campers wanted to stay up later. Mason might've been one of them. Honestly, it was so long ago... Sorry."

"Who was in charge of the campers who stayed up late?"

"Let me think." Wilson ran his hand back through his thick gray hair. "Scott Holt and Tyler Jamison volunteered if my memory serves me right."

So, Holt was in charge of the late-night eclipse-watching. Why hadn't he mentioned anything about it to her? What else was he holding back?

"I see." She checked her notebook. "Then you and Bob Taylor were in charge of the rest of the campers?"

"Yes, ma'am. Bob—everybody called him Dakota, even back then—Dakota's a pro-football player. You probably already knew that."

"Yes." She nodded and noted Wilson's information. A little clarification wouldn't hurt. "What time did you and Taylor turn in that night?"

"Around ten. We saw the boys, except for the ones staying up for the eclipse, turn in around nine-thirty. Dakota and I talked a while, then turned in ourselves."

"What time did Scott Holt and Tyler Jamison come back to your cabin?"

"Couldn't tell you. Once my head hit the pillow, I slept like a damn rock. Wish I could sleep like that now."

Had to wonder what kept him from sleeping now? "What about Dakota Taylor. He sleep like a rock, too?"

"Guess so. Anyway, what's to tell? He's this big, big guy. Played defensive tackle for the University of Florida on a full-ride scholarship. Out of school, he signed with the Baltimore Colts, then after a couple of years, he was traded to the Columbus Jackals."

"Do you remember when he changed teams?"

"Does it matter?" Wilson frowned, then shrugged. "Surely, you don't suspect him."

She smiled. Just because Taylor was a pro-football player, it didn't rule him out for the Mason kid's murder. "I need complete records for my timeline." She rose. "If I have any more questions, I'll give you a call."

Wilson stood and gave her his professional smile. "Anytime, Detective. I'm always happy to assist our city's finest."

She turned to leave. His smarmy smile and comment didn't sit well. In fact, her stomach churned a bit. No one was *that* nice and accommodating when it came to cops unless they were hiding something.

So, time to pull a Columbo. "Just one more thing," she said with a smile. "I need to obtain a DNA specimen. Just routine to eliminate you, of course."

His smile faded, but he nodded. "No problem, Detective."

So, he wasn't thrilled about providing a DNA sample. Tough. She produced the swab kit and swabbed the cavity between his jaw and cheek thoroughly. "That should do it, for now. Appreciate your cooperation, Mr. Wilson."

"Was there DNA found on Mason?"

His tone was a touch on the nervous side. "As a matter of fact, there was," she said with a smile, then turned and left his office. "Back then, we didn't have the facilities for testing we have now."

Chew on that.

Her next interview was Tyler Jamison. Geez, she loved her job.

After leaving the First American Center, Tess turned left on West End, then another left on Thirty-first to Charlotte. Straight down Charlotte, left on James Robertson Parkway to the Channel Nine Studios. She parked in one of the spaces reserved for visitors, then went through the security rigmarole to see Tyler Jamison.

Soon enough, she was ushered into Jamison's empty office.

"He'll be with you in a couple of minutes, Detective," the administrative assistant said with a smile. "Make yourself comfortable…if you can."

"Thanks." The morning news anchor's office was small and cluttered with sticky notes everywhere. A rack hung with his on-air suits was shoved in one corner.

A long counter with a flat panel monitor and a keyboard took up one side of the room. On the other side was a lumpy sofa with one end of it piled high with files. A bookcase was in the other corner filled with paperback books. She was too far away to determine his reading matter. Probably mysteries or spy thrillers.

A full-length mirror occupied the far end of the office along with a makeup chair. A plastic case with what had to be on-camera makeup was set on the counter. Tess stifled a giggle at the thought of a man wearing makeup.

Over the sofa was his wall of fame. Photos of a handsome Tyler Jamison shaking hands with anyone of note who passed through Nashville. Numerous framed awards for community service. Baseball coach for the Babe Ruth League. Eagle Scout leader. A Habitat for Humanity shot with one arm around former President Carter and the other around the shoulder of a teenage boy who looked a lot like the late Todd Brennerman.

Damn. Did Jamison have a thing for teenage boys?

"Detective O'Malley, I presume?"

At the sound of a well-modulated baritone, Tess whirled. Tyler Jamison was even better looking in person than on air. At least six-feet tall, he was slender and built more like a marathon runner than a football player. His gaze was direct and his eyes an icy blue which fit perfectly with his styled, wavy blond hair. Even his eyebrows were perfectly groomed.

"Y-yes. I am." She nodded, just a little taken back by his intense scrutiny. His gaze swept up and down her body. He had the "it" factor in abundance. He wouldn't be a morning news anchor long. No, he'd move up to the major leagues quickly, provided he wasn't a serial killer.

"How can I help you?" He motioned for her to have a seat on the sofa. "Or if you prefer..." He gestured toward the makeup chair, then perched on the counter and awarded her his TV perfect smile.

She chose the sofa and began, "I'm investigating a cold case."

Jamison nodded. "Right…Rich Mason from Camp Einstein. Such a long time ago. Scott Holt gave me a call and said you'd probably be around sooner or later."

Holt was really into communicating with his old pals, wasn't he? "Then you won't mind giving me a DNA sample? We might as well get it out of the way. Wouldn't want to forget and have to come back."

"No, we wouldn't want that." He smiled, but it didn't quite reach his cold blue gaze. "Considering the fact, I'm a public figure and this could have ramifications for the station, I believe I should consult Legal."

"It's just a simple swab, Mr. Jamison, to rule you out; unless, of course, you have something to hide. Scott Holt and Drew Wilson cooperated fully which only makes me wonder why you aren't as accommodating."

Damn. He was on the verge of lawyering up. "Now…" He raised his hands. "I haven't refused outright. I just need to make Legal aware of the situation before you proceed." His on-air smile was plastered across his face. He could've announced a beautiful baby contest winner or an imminent terrorist bombing with the same sort of charming, but false, demeanor.

"What about answering a few questions about your activities the night Rich Mason was murdered? I mean it was so long ago…" She smiled back, hoping it annoyed him as much as his smile annoyed her. "Or would Legal need to advise you about that too?"

"The station has so many regulations and I'd hate to upset the station executives."

"Is that a no?"

"For the time being, Detective." He stood. Clearly, he was ready for her to leave.

Dogged stubbornness was one of her best qualities. "What about verifying where some of the other counselors were the night Rich Mason disappeared? At least, you could help clear the other counselors…unless you think you need permission for that as well?"

"Let me see." The practiced smile never left his face, but the muscles in his jaw tensed. Obviously, it was quite an effort to keep up his on-air face.

Good.

"Scott was at the campfire. Drew and Dakota decided they weren't interested in staying up to view the eclipse."

Nothing new there, but she didn't miss Jamison's caginess by not saying where he was. Damn.

"Surely you can tell me what your function was at the camp."

"Counselor, friend, go-to guy for personal problems."

"And did any of the students have personal problems?"

Jamison shot a knowing glance at the door. "That's all you're getting from me today, Detective O'Malley."

Jerk.

"Thanks." For damn near next to nothing. "Give me a call after Legal has their say…and don't make me wait too long."

"Yes, of course. Nice meeting you."

She clenched her jaw. A more uncooperative man she never hoped to meet. While innocent folks might lie when they didn't have to, the guilty always did. She had him pegged for a possible suspect.

Chapter Nine

Disappointment wracked through Scott's gut. "Thanks." He snapped his phone shut. Susan, his contact at the local phone company, had confirmed Ned Forbes's cell phone was used in the area of the camp the night of the Brennerman boy's disappearance. However, she was unable to pinpoint the exact location, other than the towers used to make the call which were well within the area of the camp and the murder scene. That circumstance didn't bode well for his client, Paul Whitten, or his partner, who was still rotting in jail. He had to wonder if O'Malley had discovered anything new in her investigation.

Tess O'Malley. Just the image of the fiery detective sent a jolt of lust to his groin.

Maybe he should drop in at the Blue Mood. Maybe O'Malley would be in the mood for some dinner. And after dinner, some sharing of information about the case and…

Who knew what might happen later?

Scott opened the door to Blue Mood Bar and Grill and walked inside the off-duty hangout. The jukebox in the back was grinding one of those cheatin'-heart-somebody-done-somebody-wrong songs. He'd been too concerned about Tamsyn the last time he was here to take much note of the surroundings. Lots of wood paneling gave the bar a comfortable feeling, and there was a pool table in the back corner where three off-duty cops were playing a game of cut-throat. He surveyed the rest of the patrons.

Bingo. Just as he'd hoped, O'Malley was sitting at the bar and had never looked hotter, wearing a short skirt which thankfully revealed her long legs. Wet dream material, no less.

"Fancy meeting you here, Detective." He slid onto the barstool beside her and ordered a German beer from the bartender, a retired cop who owned the place. Normally, he was a scotch rocks kind of guy, but the heat outside rated a cold brew. Nothing else would do.

She curled her lip and gave him a long sideways glance. "This gonna be your new hangout, Holt?"

"Maybe." He grinned. "Come here often?"

Tess stirred her frozen drink—looked like a margarita—then took a sip from the tiny red straw. "Surely you can do better than that." She ran her tongue across her perfect Cupid's bow upper lip.

Damn. Wished he could taste her right now. "I'm not sure I can. Your beauty scrambles my brain and I can't come up with anything witty enough to charm you."

She gave a sniff. "Any luck on clearing Forbes?" The bartender set the frosty beer bug down in front of Scott. "You know I can't reveal that...client privilege and all." He took a long pull on his beer.

"Thirsty?"

"Haven't you heard? It's summer."

"Seems like I might've heard a rumor or two."

She grinned and the urge to lay his head in her lap or on her pillow hit him hard.

"This place has the best German beer in Nashville, or so I was told this morning."

Another sideways glance, this one a shade more skeptical than the first. "And this being a cop hangout has nothing to do with why you're here?" He took another long swallow. "Might."

"So, you're stalking me?" All wide-eyed and innocent, she asked, "Or will any female cop do?" Her mouth gave a half quirk as she swirled the straw in the slushy ice of her drink.

"No, ma'am. I'm pretty particular. I was looking for you."

Her shoulders straightened and her chin went up a notch. "May I ask why?"

"I wondered if you'd like to have dinner."

"There's this device. It's called a cell phone. Maybe you've heard of it?"

"Yes, and I have your number on the business card you left me, but I didn't want to risk your saying no."

She captured her bottom lip between her teeth, sending a jolt of electricity to his groin. "And I'm supposed to believe you have so little self-confidence you couldn't call and ask me to dinner?"

"More a matter of not being able to charm you over the phone as I can in person."

Not so great of a response on the fly. She probably thought he was an arrogant idiot.

He couldn't argue. Five minutes in her presence and he was tongue-tied and stupid.

Eyebrows arched, she leaned back from the bar. "And you think you're charming me now?"

"Aren't I?" he asked with his most innocent expression. Not going well. Not at all.

"No." Her tone was flat. Not encouraging.

"You're breaking my heart, but since I'm the manly type, I can't show it." He took another long pull from the icy bottle.

"And now, you're really pissing me off. I'm here to have a quiet drink before I go home...alone." She leaned forward. "You won't tell me anything about the case...never mind that I'm responsible for Paul Whitten's hiring you. So why are you really looking for me?"

"Like I said...dinner."

"But I'm not hungry." She removed the napkin from beneath her drink and played with the damn thing until it shredded.

"And *I* am." He covered her hand with his. Her hand tensed, but she didn't pull away. Good sign. Her hand was warm and strong under his. A jolt of need zapped to his groin. "I'd be happy to talk to you about the case over dinner."

"Bribery's against the law, especially where a police detective is concerned."

"Come on. You have to eat. I have to eat. You really don't dislike me; you've just had a bad day."

She gave a sigh of resignation. "Here's the deal. I'll share the pizza I've already ordered. You can tell me anything you've picked up about the case, and then I'll go home, kick off my shoes and watch TV."

"Now you're talking."

The bartender brought her pizza already boxed. "We'll eat it here, Phil." Her facial expression bland as store-bought white bread, she nodded toward an empty booth.

Scott gave a mental groan. So, the lady liked being in charge which was okay…for now.

Relieved she hadn't kicked his sorry ass to the curb, he followed her to the booth and eased into the bench seat opposite hers. The pizza was hot and spicy, like the woman herself. The object of his lust was in a more playful mood as evidenced by the way her tongue licked the stringy cheese from her lips.

"Anything new?" he asked, unable to take his eyes off her mouth.

She chewed, then swallowed. "You first." She cocked her head to the side and gave him a flirty glance.

Two could play that little game. He snagged a slice, bit, and chewed…carefully and slowly.

After he swallowed, he took a long drink of the icy-cold beer and then motioned for another round. "I might have something."

She gave him a not-so-gentle nudge under the table. "Come on. Spill."

"My contact at the phone company struck out. She could pinpoint the tower used for Ned's call to Paul the night the Brennerman kid disappeared, but not the exact location. The time of the call fits with Paul's statement, but it was still within the location where the body was found."

"I was afraid of something like that. So, the camp and dumpsite are within the area of the cell towers. That's it?" A measure of disgust registered on her pretty face. "I thought you were supposed to be this hotshot PI and able to solve anything."

"And leap tall buildings in a single bound, too? Sorry, my capes at the cleaners." He grinned, hoping she'd give him a break. "I've only been on the case a day or so." He leaned forward. "I'm more anxious to know what you've discovered."

"I've interviewed the other two counselors." She stopped and took the tiniest bite of pizza he'd ever seen anyone take, then chewed with a thoughtful expression. God. Her mouth was to die for. Lips full and a rich pink without a speck of lipstick.

Damn, but his mouth was as dry as the Mojave.

Get your mind back on the case, dumbass.

"First, I saw Drew Wilson at his office in the First American Center. He answered all my questions, provided his DNA…"

"But?"

Tess's brow furrowed slightly, then her lips pursed as if choosing her words before speaking. "He just seemed too cooperative, if you know what I mean."

"Man, you cops are never satisfied. Look, take it from me. Drew's an okay guy. He almost married my ex-fiancée."

"Sounds incestuous."

"Not really. She dumped me and set her sights on Drew, even though I warned him." Scott chuckled. It had been a close call for both.

A puzzled expression crossed Tess's face.

He laughed again and shook his head. "You wouldn't understand. It's a guy thing."

"No doubt." She snatched another piece of pizza just as he grabbed for the same slice. His hand covered hers. At the casual touch, a thousand-watt burst of electricity zapped from his hand up his arm. His jeans grew snug in the crotch.

Damn. If touching her hand could…

"Not so fast, lady. I had my eye on that slice."

She grinned and smacked his hand away. "My pizza. My choice."

"Can't argue with your logic." He smiled and chose another piece.

"Drew is happily married and has a little girl. I'd bet my life he's not your killer."

Her gaze narrowed as she cast him another one of those super skeptical glances. "You're that sure of him?"

"I am." He nodded for emphasis. "For what it's worth. You strike me as a woman who makes up her own mind about people, but at the same time, you have that cop's distrust thing going on."

She picked up her margarita and sipped. After setting down the glass, she nodded. "You're right. The first day on the job, my partner told me, 'Expect it. Everybody lies whether they need to or not'."

"Cynical, but"—he admitted with a grin— "it's true. Same in my business. Very seldom does a client tell me everything." He took a bite from the rich, cheesy pizza. "Mm. If I'd known how good their pizza was, I would've been here sooner. What about Tyler Jamison?"

Tess crossed her eyes and huffed. "He plastered on his news anchor smile and said he'd have to check with Legal." She gave a snarl. "In other words, not cooperative at all."

"Really? Want me to have another word with him? I coach his kids' soccer team."

She shook her head. "I'll handle him. You're a coach? Yeah, you mentioned that before." Her brows rose and he could just hear her brain whirling.

"What? You think everyone who's single and coaches soccer or baseball is a pedophile?"

She ignored his protest and continued. "Your friend Jamison seems to be involved in a lot of activities with teenage boys. I saw the photos on the bragging wall in his office."

"Now hold on. I know where you're headed."

She leaned forward, her expression intense and focused. "Then why was he stonewalling me?"

"Dammit. He's the morning news anchor, a public figure. The station has a lot invested in him and you have to respect his position. He has a lot to lose if it became common knowledge he was a suspect in your cold case or the Brennerman boy's case."

"I don't care who he is or who'd like to cover it up. This is a murder investigation." She hit the table with her fist.

Scott could feel heads turn in their direction. Any second, he'd be surrounded by a bar full of cops. "Hold on. I'm on your turf and not looking for an ass-whuppin'."

She smiled at him over her drink. "There's something else you could check out if you were of a mind to."

Something new? "I'm listening."

"There's this eyewitness, a Doug Silvey spelled S-Sam, I-Idaho, L-Lima, V-Victor, E-Echo, Y-yellow. I need you to check him out on the QT."

"What's the deal?"

"I want to know if he's on the up and up. I had to pry his name out of the lieutenant, and his statement is missing from the case files. There's something fishy going on. The boss says it's in dictation, but I'm not of a mind to wait around. I've already checked the databases and couldn't find anything on him. Not even a Tennessee driver's license. Appears to be clean, but you never know."

She took another bite of pizza, her silver gaze never leaving his. "You going to help me out or not? Forbes is *your* client, after all." Her voice rose and, again, heads turned in their direction.

"Calm down. I'd like to live long enough to walk you home…and maybe get a goodnight kiss."

Taking a deep breath, she leaned back and signaled everything was cool. "You want to walk me home and kiss me goodnight? How sweet." Her soft tone mocked him, but he didn't care.

"Like we're high school sweethearts." She wrinkled her nose, but her eyes shone with moderate good humor.

"Would you rather I said what I was really thinking?"

Her lashes fluttered briefly, then she eyeballed him directly. "Maybe. Depends on what you were really thinking."

He lowered his tone a notch. "About pressing you up against the wall and having my way with you."

For a second, her gray eyes flashed silver. Damn. He was a goner—as in, he'd gone too far. Said too much. Too soon.

She leaned forward. "I'll have you know I don't engage in up-against-the-wall, wild animal sex on the first date, not that this is even a date." Her tone was matter of fact, but her cheeks flushed a pretty pink. Maybe he could still pull his nuts out of the fire before they went up in smoke.

"A guy can always hope," he said, without a chance in the world she wouldn't kick him to the curb. Or have one of her fellow officers do the honors.

"A *guy* can hold his breath…until he turns purple."

"I can see I've put my foot in it. I'm sorry, but damn, the sight of your mouth…your skin. Your eyes. Dammit. You're driving me up a wall."

"Another reference to the wall? Would that be the same wall?"

"Bad choice of words. Sorry again."

"So many apologies in such a short span of time." She gave a haughty sniff. "Most guys don't ever apologize for anything."

"I'll have you know I have four sisters and they've educated me—extensively—on proper behavior."

Her expression morphed from intense to playful. The corner of her lovely mouth twitched. "Glad to hear it. Maybe there's hope for you." She shot a meaningful glance at her glass, then at him.

Body language he knew. She was ready for another drink. He signaled a passing waitress. "Another round."

"Right back," the waitress said with a nod.

"Hm." Tess grinned. "You have been educated properly. For example, you didn't give our waitress the slow once over most guys would have."

"I didn't? That's a good thing, right?"

"Yes, women hate that in a man, even if it's instinctual to your half of the species."

"That didn't sound so good. Since I didn't, you're implying I don't have manly instincts. Not sure how I feel about that."

A low rumble of laughter erupted into an out and out giggle. "Your instincts are manly enough all right."

"Manly enough for *you*?" He covered her hand with his. Damn, if he wasn't on the receiving end of another zap of Tess's sensual electricity. He wanted her in the worst way, but was she tricky or just picky? Maybe some guy had treated her like crap. Some guy with shit for brains.

"Here ya go."

Scott glanced up at the waitress but kept his connection to Tess. The waitress set their drinks on the table and left. Thank God.

"I may be crazy…" Tess started, then stopped to chew her kissable bottom lip.

"You feel it too?" Scott shrugged. "Figured it was just me."

A small sigh escaped. The man was driving her nuts with his soulful brown eyes and warm glances. Not to mention his warm, rugged hand still holding hers. "No, not just you."

He glanced around, then took a long drink of his beer. "I'm not hungry."

"Neither am I," she admitted. *At least not for pizza.*

In her book, and anyone else's for that matter, the properly socialized Scott Holt was a keeper. Except the man didn't appear to be interested in anything more than getting her in bed. But would that be so bad? Come to think of it, it fit her agenda exactly. Fun and sport sex with a genuinely nice guy. Nothing more.

"May I at least walk you home? I'll behave."

Please, not on my account.

She took a deep breath, then slowly exhaled. "It's not far. Couple blocks."

Invite him in for coffee...or not?

The walk from Second Avenue down toward First was entirely too short as they wove their way through tourists and Friday night bar-hoppers. She stopped in front of one of the historic brick buildings. Ten years ago, it was a dilapidated warehouse, but now it was full of condos. "I'm on the third floor," she said, fluttering her lashes shyly.

Sheesh. Somehow, she'd turned into some kind of blushing maiden straight from a historical romance. This was the twenty-first century and if she wanted to have a man in for coffee, or whatever, it was no one's business but hers.

"May I at least see you to your door?" His devilish grin was anything but shy.

"Sure." Her heart ratcheted like a misfiring Uzi. *Get a grip, girl.*

He held the wrought iron and glass door open, then followed her into the discreet lobby. She nodded at the concierge who returned her nod and went back to reading his murder mystery. As she headed to the elevator, her heels clicked like castanets on the greenish-brown slate tile floor. Her heart seemed to match the rhythm as it kicked up a notch...or three.

"When I first moved in, we used the old freight elevator, but when they sold off the penthouse for a cool million, the new owner insisted on having something better installed. It came from an old demolished hotel." Her nerves had her sounding like some kind of demented tour guide.

"Never seen anything like it. Glad it was saved."

Truly, it was a stunning old elevator of steel and brass from the Art Deco period with a glowing sun and sunbeams of brass in the center against a field of glass. In each corner of the door were stylized depictions of crescent moons in shining steel along with a scattering of stars.

She jabbed the UP button and waited until the door opened. Scott entered right behind her and reached across to hit the button for her floor, then tugged the steel gate closed.

Growing more and more uncomfortable with his proximity, she considered her choices. Leave him at the door? Invite him in for coffee? Code-speak for you know what.

All too quickly, they reached her floor. Scott opened the antique gate and door and waited for her to exit. Such a gentleman.

A good sign or a bad one?

Good, she decided, since his manners seemed so natural.

Still undecided, she stopped at her door, turned, then gazed into his warm dark eyes. "You really didn't have to see me to the door...unless you want to come in for a cup of coffee?" There. She'd said it.

His brow furrowed.

Damn, why couldn't she just let it go? Let him make the first move. Why open her big mouth and invite the man in? Obviously, he wasn't as interested as she thought.

"I'd love a cup." He smiled down at her, sending her heart into orbit. "But my baseball team has a tournament starting tomorrow, and we have to be on the field, ready to go, at seven."

"I see. That's pretty early." Okay, as excuses go, it made perfect sense. He was a busy man, with commitments. Perfectly understandable. It wasn't a reflection on her—was it?

Before another inane thought could zap through her brain, Scott pulled her close and lowered his head. His kiss was soft, tender. Not demanding. Yet somehow more arousing and sensual than if he'd tried to swab her tonsils with his tongue. Her knees weakened and a wave of desire curled through her lower belly.

He ended the kiss…way too soon. A soft sigh escaped before she could call it back.

"Another night." His tone was low and full of regret. "Soon."

"Tomorrow?" Could she be any more eager? Damn.

His head went back with a bark of laughter. "Depends on how my baseball team does in the tournament."

"You coach both baseball and soccer?"

"Yep." He growled. "Look, kids need physical activities and good role models. We're not all perverts. Say, why don't you come to our game? The Bellevue Beatles can always use another fan in the stands." He placed a kiss on the tip of her nose. "And the coach could too."

Mm. She hadn't scared him away after all. He wanted her to come to his team's game. "Okay. Where?"

"Bellevue. Off McPherson Drive."

She grinned up at him. "All right. I'll see you there." She laughed. "Realistically, it might be a few minutes after seven."

"Just so you're there."

His soft low tone sent another sizzle of warmth to her core. More than anything she wanted his hands on her body. Her hands on his body. She shuddered and swallowed the knot forming in her throat.

"Lunch after the game?"

"Sure." Tess rested her head against his muscular chest. "That'll be nice." Comfortable and a touch antsy at the same time, she let out another small sigh.

He gave a low groan. "Gotta go or I'll never leave."

Full of reluctance and a measure of hope, she pulled back. "Tomorrow, then." She slipped her key in the first of two deadbolts and unlocked the door, then repeated the process.

"You bet." His gaze was full of warmth, as was his slow seductive smile. "Sleep tight…"

"Yeah, I know the rest."

She watched him mosey back to the elevator, then closed her door and locked the deadbolts. She leaned against the steel door and fanned her burning cheeks, as she tried to force her legs to move. Damn, that man was hot. And a good man. She could do worse.

For that matter, she already had.

His mood lighter than he could remember, Scott breezed into the house on Richland. He found his stepbrother in the den watching a ballgame. Scott swatted the back of his brother's head. "Got a little assignment for you."

Justin averted his gaze from the TV long enough to glare at Scott. "Friday night. I'm off duty."

"Background check on one Doug Silvey," he said, then spelled the surname.

"Can't it wait until Monday?"

"Nope. Possible eyewitness against our client. I need to know everything about him."

Justin turned back to the TV. "Damn! The game's over and you made me miss the winning run."

"TiVo, dude."

Fuck the cops. They'd already found his latest. And the itch had already returned. Why couldn't that special feeling last longer? Always present, the need to scratch the itch, but having to delay until he found the right one. The right opportunity. Whenever he thought the cops were getting too close, he held his breath and tried to cool it, but waiting was getting more and more difficult.

Contrary to popular belief, he didn't want anyone to make him stop. He damned sure didn't want to get caught, and making stupid mistakes wasn't a part of his game plan.

Not prison. He'd rather die on his own terms.

Chapter Ten

It was the top of the ninth inning. He hovered at the edge of the crowd of baseball parents. The next team scheduled to play would be older and more to his tastes. Even though the itch had returned stronger than ever, he'd take his time making his selection. In his rare free time, he'd scout his choice's home and scope his daily routine.

Choosing from campers was his preference, but it was getting dicey. Too routine. Too easy to get caught. Through the years, he'd varied his M.O. from his first special kill. It was more important to keep the authorities from pegging him as what he was, an extremely efficient and prolific serial killer.

Sometimes, he still couldn't resist obtaining a position as a trusted camp counselor. Away from home, teens could be extremely vulnerable and rash in what they perceived as the safe confines of a camp. That's where he'd made his mistake with the Brennerman boy. Too much publicity and heat. But he'd been ripe for the picking, so to speak.

Other times he posed as a cable installer looking for directions, a meter reader, or an electrician called to do a job. Locally, he kept a stash of disguises in a hidden cabin. How he loved his disguises, almost as much as he loved his choices, however briefly they were in his care.

He climbed the bleachers and spied a woman with red hair blazing in the sun. She was waving at someone on the field. He pulled his ball cap down to cover his face. Maybe his next choice should be a redhead. Not female—no, no. Not his type at all. But a young redheaded male nearing the peak of his sexual prime.

Perfect.

Now all he had to do was wait until he found one. And the itch would recede…for a while.

After the first game, he watched the home team players line up, and as if he'd put in a special order, there was a redhead on the team. His choice was tall, toned, but slender. Hadn't come into his full muscle growth, yet. Capable of fighting back, but unable to resist the tender advances of one so much stronger.

Perfect.

The game was nearly over when Scott sensed Tess's presence. A strong urge to turn and glance up at the stands coursed through him. There was a big turnout to see the little ones play. In his mind's eye, she was in the stands along with parents and grandparents who'd trooped out on a beautiful Saturday morning to see little Jack or Jill whack it out of the park…or at least give it a try.

Better if he kept his eyes on his team. He focused and waited until the teams changed positions on the field, then took off his ball cap and swiped the sweat from his forehead. Casually, he cut his gaze to the stands.

Hot damn. She'd come. If he wasn't mistaken, Tess was several rows up, wearing a short skirt and a bright blue-green top, shades and a white cap perched on her fiery red hair. He waved in her direction and was rewarded by her waving in return.

His team pulled through and won with an outright fluke of a triple play. Disbelief and sheer joy rocketed through him at the same time. "Way to go, team!"

The players gathered around him and tried to douse him with Gatorade, but he was onto their tricks. Besides, none of them was quite tall enough to pull it off.

"No way." He waved his hands and jumped back. "I'm having lunch with a pretty girl."

After a few "Coach has a girlfriend" quips from his players and "Good job" comments from the parents, he was finally free. He picked up his sports bag, hefted it over his shoulder, then walked around the fence to meet Tess who stood smiling and waiting for him.

"Looking good, Detective O'Malley." He gave a long, slow glance up and down her sexy self. Like most redheads, she didn't tan but her skin had a healthy glow. Her arms were firm and toned, her legs long and shapely.

God. He could already imagine those legs wrapped around his waist. *Sweet.*

She flashed him a wide smile, but her smoky gray gaze hinted at seduction. Could she read his mind? Probably. Some cops were like that.

"Why thank you, Mr. Holt, PI."

"What do you feel like eating?"

A smirk lifted the corner of her mouth and her eyes shone with mischief. Damn, what had he just said?

She chewed her bottom lip and adjusted her shoulder bag before cocking her head to the side. "I'm feeling sort of ethnic today."

"Mexican?"

Her smirk flashed into a full smile again. "Love it."

"Cancun's close. How about it?"

"Perfect. I have my car here. Want me to follow you?"

"Nope. I'll bring you back. Besides, you might change your mind about lunch and where would I be?"

An elegant russet brow arched. "Up that famous creek without a paddle?"

He laughed. "My thoughts exactly."

He ushered her into his fully restored, red 1965 Mustang convertible with white interior. His pride and joy. His only love—for now.

"Nice ride." Her expression agreed with her words.

"My guilty passion," he admitted with a grin. "Her name's Gloria."

She ran her hand over the immaculate dashboard. "You do the work yourself?"

"Of course"—he slid into the bucket seat beside her— "except for a couple of specialty items which, even with my superior intellect, I wouldn't risk botching."

"She's a beautiful vehicle. You should be proud." Damn, but this woman was perfect. She appreciated his car. Understood his passion. One of them anyway.

Cancun was busy with the Bellevue lunch crowd. The scents of Mexican spices and grilled meat filled the air. Tess's mouth watered, and with a low rumble, her stomach reminded her she'd skipped breakfast.

They were shown to a booth by the window. After she seated herself across from Scott, she shoved the menu aside and leaned forward. "Before this goes any further, there's something I have to know."

His forehead furrowed. "What? Pick one. A—lunch? B—the case? C—our relationship?"

She took a deep breath and let it out before speaking. "Um. B. Have you had a chance to check out the eyewitness yet?"

"My brother's working on it as we speak. By the way, I owe him big time since it's the weekend and all," Scott said with a grin. "But you really weren't going to say B, were you?"

Too smart. Ducking her head, she gave him a shy smile. "I should know better than try to fool a PI as observant as you. Yeah, I guess it would be C. I don't know where this is going, and it doesn't necessarily have to go anywhere..." She broke off. Damn. This wasn't going the way she expected.

Folded arms. Silence. Just great.

"First of all, my father isn't particularly thrilled I referred my mother to a PI." At least, she'd gotten that much out without biting off her tongue.

"Go on." His gaze was puzzled. Somewhat distant.

"I had lunch with him yesterday. He's afraid our connection might ruin my career chances."

"And your career's important to you. I understand." He leaned forward. "What are you saying? You don't want to see me after all?" Disbelief flashed across his handsome face and clouded his storm dark eyes.

"Now hold on." She reached across the table and covered his hands with hers to calm him. "I'm not saying I don't want to see you again. But..." Was she really about to tell this perfectly hunky man she only wanted him for sex? Was she that ballsy?

The waitress interrupted them to take their orders, then brought them a basket of chips, salsa and two glasses of ice water. After the waitress left, his gaze wary, he leaned back. "But…what?"

She lowered her tone. "I'm not looking for a relationship right now." She glanced around the room. Could anyone overhear them? "You're a great guy."

"Damn, if that's not a kiss-off, I've never heard one." He shook his head. "Talk about misreading signals." He glanced around as if looking for the nearest exit.

"No-no. You didn't misread my signals. I want to sleep with you. I do, but I don't want to get involved. It's just I've seen so many marriages break up because this job is all-consuming at times." No, she hadn't blurted out the M-word. She had.

His dark brows rose as if she'd just proposed something illegal. "Now wait a minute. Who said anything about marriage?"

"No one, except you seem like a family kind of guy, picket fence— all that. I just want to be clear about my goals and expectations. The job is everything to me. I worked my butt off to make detective by twenty-seven and I plan to make captain by forty. There are a lot of nights I won't be home for dinner, much less be waiting with your pipe and slippers." She scooped some salsa onto a chip. Maybe if her mouth was busy eating, there wouldn't be room for her foot.

Ah, just the right amount of heat and a hint of fresh cilantro, exactly the way she liked it.

"You don't know squat about me and what I want or expect. Right now, all I want from you is lunch and then maybe a quick hop in bed. There…" Scott jabbed a chip into the bowl of salsa. "Am I clear enough for you?"

Lunch and a quick hop in bed. Exactly what she wanted, why couldn't she have just said it without all the meandering and the M-word. "Then we're in agreement."

Hoping to defuse the situation, she said, "Tell me about your family."

His gaze leveled directly at her. "We don't dwell in the past. My mom died when I was six and Tamsyn was a toddler. Dad was on the force but somehow, he always had time for us. Our grandmother took care of us until Dad met Jan, our stepmom. After they married, it was a different life altogether."

"They were happy then?"

He took a drink of water, then nodded. "Dad was a forward-looking man. He had lots of plans. For the agency. For the family. Most of all, he wanted to write a book. Anytime he was home, he had a legal pad by his side, making notes of all his cases. All those plans were shot to hell when he and my stepmom died. The family—we dug in. Pulled together. Worked our tails off and kept the agency going. Since then, we haven't looked back."

What could she tell about the man sitting before her? There was a lot of love and pride in him, toward his family, but most of all, his father—it exuded from his very being. He might say he only wanted a quick hop, but *family* was his middle name.

His broad chest rose and fell, a sure sign of the emotional hold his family had on him. "You already know four of us work at the agency. My other sister's a nurse."

"Aren't there six of you?"

"Yeah." His expression grew grim as he fiddled with his silverware. "The youngest, Kim, she…uh, she ran away several years after our parents died. Sort of a continuation of our family tragedy."

"How long since you saw her?" She couldn't imagine how such a close-knit group coped when one of their members was missing.

"Seven years. She's twenty-three…if she's still alive."

"How horrible…not knowing."

"Our last lead's only a year old. Seems like we're always a step or two behind. She moves around a lot."

"Why'd she run away?"

"Hell, if I know." He shrugged. "Carrie blames herself. They had some kind of squabble and two days later, Kim was gone. No note. Nothing."

"Must be a nightmare."

The waitress cleared her throat. "Y'all ready to order?"

Scott grinned at the pretty, dark-haired waitress. "Another minute." He snatched his menu. Gave it a quick glance and shrugged. "Why bother?

I always order the same thing."

Tess grinned. "Me, too."

After the waitress left with their drink and food orders, Tess dipped a chip into the salsa and followed the hot bite with a swallow of ice water. The detective part of her brain kicked in. "What about the department? Did they ever do anything?"

"Hmph. The department? They did the minimal. Far as they were concerned, she was just another runaway."

"Was there any indication she might've been abducted? She didn't leave a note. My God. Maybe someone took her. Where was your last lead?" Her detective nature was coming out, but she couldn't help it.

"Outside Reno."

Land of divorcees? "Maybe she was getting a divorce?"

"Or working at some modern-day equivalent of the Mustang Ranch?"

"Geez. Hadn't thought of that."

"Don't get me wrong. I don't care what she's done to survive. I just wish she'd come home. We'd stand by her, no matter what."

"I believe you would. You seem to have a wonderful family." No exaggeration there. The more time she spent with Scott, the more she liked him. Respected him. "Anyway, my father has a wild hair up his ass when it comes to my career." She stopped. Her cheeks grew warm. "Sorry, I use too much cop-speak."

A half grin kicked up the corner of his mouth. "Not offended."

The waitress returned with a Corona for Scott and a frozen margarita for Tess. She took a sip through the tiny straw. The cocktail was so cold— brain freeze. "Mm. It's good. Now you know my passions—coffee and margaritas." She laughed.

His gaze darkened. His mouth grew playful. "Tell me your darkest secret."

She gasped. "What?"

"Surely you have a darker secret than being addicted to coffee and frozen girlie drinks."

She zipped her lips. "If I told you…"

His brown eyes danced with amusement, as he let out a bark of laughter. "You'd have to kill me? Surely you can come up with something better."

"You didn't let me finish. I was going to say," she batted her lashes flirtatiously, "you'll be so driven by curiosity, it would kill you."

"O-mi-god. You have a tattoo." He reached across the table and covered her hand with his warm one. "Come on. Tell me. What and where? I have to know." He let out a groan of mock despair.

"See already you're on the way to your death bed." She giggled. "I'm not admitting or denying anything." The spark of electricity she'd received from his mere touch had her too confused to think.

"A tatt—really?"

"Not admitting anything." She gave a shrug in a vain attempt to give her scattered brain cells time to recover.

"Let's see. You got drunk when you graduated from the academy and had a rose tattooed on your butt."

Still, she didn't pull her hand from his. The warmth surrounded and enveloped her.

"Not even close."

"If I'm right, you have to show me."

"Says who?"

"Come on." His voice took on a pleading tone. "You can't leave me here with my imagination running wild."

"Oh, yeah. I can...and will." *There challenge that.*

"I'll just wait."

"For hell to freeze over?"

"Until we make love."

What? Her heart kicked up, but she managed to give him a playful grin. "You sound awfully sure of yourself." Damn, but the man made her squirm in her seat. That wouldn't do at all.

"Ahem." The waitress smiled at Scott. "Let's see you had the beef chimichanga special." She turned to Tess. "And yours is the taco salad?"

"Yes." Tess nodded. "Salad's mine." Glad for the interruption and, more importantly, a defusing of the sexually charged banter, she picked at her salad, then sipped her margarita.

By the time she'd swallowed, she had a plan. "How about dinner on Monday night? My place?"

He grinned. "Better idea. Dinner tonight and breakfast tomorrow?"

She screwed her mouth into a frown. "Already have plans for Sunday with my family and it's not like we're in a time-to-meet-the-folks relationship."

"Then what's the problem? I think we have a chance at something special."

Something special? No. "I don't classify lunch and a quick hop in bed as something special. I was right you *are* a family kind of guy." Made sorting her thoughts out even more important.

She chewed her bottom lip, then forged ahead. "You see, we're a very close family. Blowing off the family's Sunday dinner would send the wrong signal. They might think we're serious, and special or not, they won't understand. My father and brothers have this Neanderthal idea I need protecting. You don't want them on your case, believe me. They don't understand the meaning of fun-sex when it comes to me."

"This is me backing off." He raised his hands in surrender. "I have sisters and I'm damned protective of them too." He frowned and took a bite of his meal.

"What's the rush? One dinner isn't going to make or break this thing we might have, but a major hassle with my family could."

He leaned back. "Okay. We'll do it your way."

"Good." She smiled. "Better get used to it."

"Doing it your way? O'Malley, I'll do you any way you want. Twice."

She chewed her bottom lip. Twice sounded good. Her imagination kicked into gear…the things he could to her at least twice. Mm.

He leaned forward; his warm gaze determined. "So, dinner Monday night?"

"Yes. That'll give me time to—"

"—to what?"

"Get ready, of course. Even a quick hop in the sack takes preparation if it's done right." She gave him what she hoped was a seductive grin to hide her confusion. Better keep it together or she'd never make captain by forty. More likely, she'd be baking cookies for the PTO.

He waited until his choice's team lost their game. The redhead's parents gathered around him and encouraged him with meaningless platitudes like "good game, son" and "better luck next time."

There'd be no next time if he had anything to say about it.

He followed them and noted the huge honking, gas-guzzling, black SUV they climbed into before climbing into his own slightly smaller guzzler. Fitting in with the neighborhood was a must. In his line of favorite pastimes, maintaining more than one vehicle was another necessity. Keeping a discreet distance, he followed them first to a fast food joint, then home to a McMansion with a yard the size of a postage stamp.

The sweet little family exited the fuel glutton, then trooped inside the house. He made note of the address. Tomorrow, the real reconnaissance would begin. He'd follow them to church if they even bothered to go. Then on Monday, it would be school and after-school activities.

He just needed the right moment. Because that's all it would take.

A moment.

Chapter Eleven

After lunch with Scott, Tess drove to West Meade and breezed into her folks' kitchen. Her mother was standing with her hands on her hips and shaking her head at a shiny new espresso machine. Cool. "Hi, Mom."

Her mother turned and gave Tess a puzzled smile. "I simply can't imagine why your father thought I wanted an espresso machine for my birthday when I gave up coffee five years ago."

Typical male. "Did you ask him?"

"I did. His answer was *we needed one*."

Even more typical. "Has he given up coffee?"

"No. Of course not. No matter," her mother said with a shrug. "I'm so glad you came by. I put on a pot of fresh coffee for your father not ten minutes ago. I can't figure out how to work this complicated espresso machine anyway. He'll just have to make his own." She fetched Tess's favorite Snoopy mug and brought it to the table. "So, what brings you by today? I can see by your clothes you're not working. Love the turquoise. Suits you."

"Thanks." She glanced down at her short skirt and T-shirt. "No, I'm not working. I've been to a little league baseball game and had lunch with…a friend." *Let it go, Mom.* The woman absolutely did not need to know every detail of her life.

She sat and rested her elbow on the table. "Had lunch with Dad yesterday. He's not happy I gave you Scott's number or that you're involved at all."

"Oh, I'm sure he was exaggerating. You know how he is." Her mother shrugged and sat down across from Tess. "Of course, he is a Taurus and they tend toward stubbornness." She patted Tess's hand. "Now tell me, how's the case going? Is Scott going to find some evidence to clear Ned of that ridiculous murder charge?"

"He hasn't made much progress, but it's early days yet." She took a sip of coffee.

Her mother smiled. "So...you really are working together? Wonderful."

"Yes, in fact, we just had lunch." Another sip of coffee and avoid her mom's eagle-eyed gaze.

"I knew you were being evasive for some reason. So, you had lunch with Scott—*lovely.*"

Her mother's show of innocence was wasted on Tess. "We're sharing information—that's all. If he uncovers anything, he'll let me know and I'll bring it to the department's attention," she said, then smiled and met her mother's gaze.

"You just want him to bring it to your attention first—right?"

"Damn straight. That's how cooperation works."

Her mother's eyes widened, then she gave a sniff of disapproval. "Darling, I do wish you wouldn't speak in such a manner. Sometimes, you're entirely too much like your father."

She let out a groan. "Mom, I'm a cop."

"Yes, and I did everything I could to steer you into a more ladylike pursuit, but with your brothers and father all being on the job..." She sighed and lifted her shoulders in an elegant shrug. "What more could I have done?"

Tess smiled and wrinkled her nose at her mother. "Not a precious thing. Sorry I couldn't be an artist like you."

"Well, you have an artist's eye for color and detail, but the talent..." Mom shook her head.

"The eye for detail serves me well. Thanks for that anyway."

Her mother leaned back and sipped her tea, but the speculation in her gaze was easy to read. "Tell me about your lunch. Are you seeing each other for reasons besides the case?"

Before she could answer, the home phone rang; her mother answered. Anxious to escape and avoid more of her mother's questions, she rose, but her mother held up her hand and motioned for Tess to wait.

After setting down the phone, her mother frowned, then let out the smallest of sighs. "The tile installer. He's coming for an estimate. We've had some water damage from a leaky pipe under the floor in the hall. Now there's a terrible squeak every time you walk down the hall. I believe we might have the hardwood removed and marble tile installed instead. What do you think?"

"Expensive, but okay…I guess." Tess glanced toward the hallway. "I dunno. Marble's cold. Personally, I prefer hardwood."

"But marble's so elegant. Anyway, it'll take forever to get anything done. Good tile workers are so hard to find." Her mother sighed. "I know you're in a hurry to get away and not answer any questions about your new relationship. Why don't you bring him with you when you come over for Sunday dinner?"

Tess shook her head. "Not such a great idea. We're not at the meeting the family stage."

"Really and what stage are you?"

"The getting on each others' nerves stage." Not quite true, but enough to keep her mother's questions at bay.

"Oh. I see. Go on, then." Her mother waved her toward the door. "Have a good rest of the day."

"Thanks, Mom." Tess gave her a quick kiss and headed for the door.

Yes, it was already a good day. The sizzling warmth between her and Scott was undeniable. Who cared where it led? It certainly was fun for the moment. On the way to her car, her cell phone chimed. She pulled it from her belt and checked the caller ID. Kozinsky.

"What's up?"

"They're arraigning Forbes today. Thought you might want to watch the fun."

"Wouldn't call arraigning an innocent man my kind of fun."

"Don't be so uptight. The lieutenant wants everyone on the team there for the proceedings."

"Why on earth would they call a special session to arraign him on a Saturday afternoon?"

"Now why do you think?"

"Governor's grandson. I get it. Maybe they'll set bail." She jerked open the car door and sat.

"You know better than that."

"You're right. I do." She slammed the car door. "I'm at my parents', but first I'll have to swing by my place and change clothes."

"Make it snappy," her partner said with a bit of a growl.

"Will do." She broke the connection and started the motor. No matter how gruff her partner pretended to be, he'd flip out if she showed up in court in a short skirt and T-shirt.

Scott parked in front of the large Craftsman-style bungalow on Richland. Not everyone was home, or he'd have to park in the alley behind the house. Five adults in one house meant five cars to park in a space meant for three.

Lunch with Tess left him a touch on the excited side of optimistic. He tamped down the giddy urge to skip up the sidewalk to the porch like a six-year-old kid. The less his family knew the better.

No point in rushing. Plenty of time to romance the detective with his brand of razzle-dazzle. Who was he kidding? He'd thought to have some fun. But who wanted to waste time just having fun? Life was too short. His father and stepmother thought they had the rest of their lives together. Just like he and Carly thought they would. Now they were gone.

He had to admit Tess was in a dangerous profession. He shook his head. If anything happened to her…

On the other hand, when the homicide detectives showed up, the shooting was already over, so her role wasn't quite as dangerous as that of a beat cop.

He opened the door, entered the house and sniffed. Someone had fired up the grill and was cooking burgers. Even though he'd just eaten, he moseyed though the house and peered through the French doors.

Tamsyn's silver sports car was the backyard and she was hosing it down while burgers sizzled and popped on the grill. He opened the door and walked out onto the deck.

"Hey! Making enough for me?"

His sister glanced up from her task, grinned, then sprayed him with the hose. "No way, Jose. Do I look like the cook?"

"You're asking for it, kid."

"Not me. Just minding my own business."

"You don't have a date tonight?"

She scrunched up her face and wrinkled her nose. "If I did, I wouldn't tell you."

He loped across the deck and down the steps. "That's it." He tackled her gently, grabbed the hose and sprayed her down. "See what you get for smarting off?"

She laughed, wriggled from his grasp, then managed to get control of the nozzle and direct it back at him. "See what you get for messing with your sister like a ten-year-old kid?"

"Who's a ten-year-old?"

"I may be younger, but you're still the kid in this family." She brushed the dark wet strands back from her face, glanced down at her short shorts and halter top. "You've ruined me. Besides, it's my turn to cook dinner. There's plenty for everyone."

Smiling broadly, he leaned back on his elbows in the wet grass. "All you had to do was tell me, and we'd both be dry now."

"Where's the fun in that?" Tam shrugged, then walked over to her car and rinsed off the last vestiges of soap. "Looks good, if I do say so myself."

"The way you carry on over your car, you must've been a guy in a previous life."

"Oh, yeah?" She whirled and aimed the spray at him again. "Insult me again, will ya?"

He jumped to his feet and took off running up the steps to the deck. Turning around, he leaned on the banister. "Just remember, sis. Revenge is sweet."

"Yeah," she taunted, as he slipped through the French doors. "Don't get mad. Get even."

He took off his shoes and tiptoed upstairs to his bedroom. Horsing around with Tam reminded him of the fun they'd had before the families blended. Coming from a family of two kids to a new one of six hadn't been easy. A new house—at least to Tam and him. A new stepmother. A new brother and three more sisters. It took a year of territorial skirmishes, but finally, they'd blended into a cohesive family. He wouldn't trade a single one of the nights, or fights, it took to get where they were now.

Dinner was a free-for-all affair. Scott stayed in and watched a baseball game after dinner. He had everything he needed. A bowl of chips, a cold beer, and the remote. Allison skipped dinner and headed out to meet three of her gal pals for a chick flick. Justin was in his room playing some online fantasy game where he was a half-elf warrior or some such creature. Tam cleaned up the kitchen and declared she was fed up with men and retired to her room with a book in hand.

Who knew she could ever sit still long enough? Carrie came into the den, plopped down on the sofa and put up her feet, then tossed a pillow at his head. "What's the matter? I thought you'd have a date tonight with your hot detective."

"She put me off until Monday night."

"Man, you are so dense." His sister laughed. "She's already got a date, and she just doesn't want you to know."

"Nah. She's pretty forthright. She had a family do for Sunday, and she's not ready for the meet the family rigmarole. Besides, I get the impression her father's pissed because she referred her mother to the agency."

She levered up on her elbow and snagged a handful of chips. "Her father doesn't like you? He oughta be thrilled to have a nice upstanding guy like you dating his daughter. What's his problem?"

He shrugged. "More to do with her chosen career path. She aims to make captain by forty and having dealings with a PI might tarnish her climb up the ladder. Hell, I don't know."

"Even so, he doesn't know you—why diss you?"

"Don't know. Had lunch with her today and she invited me to her place for dinner Monday night. Now you know as much as I do." He shrugged.

Carrie waggled her brows up and down. "Progress. Hang in there."

"And just when are you going to get back in the game?"

"A week after never." She shook her head. "I don't need the hassle. I have two brothers and two—no, three—sisters to look out for." Her expression grew somber and her eyes glistened with tears.

"Not a valid excuse. We're all capable of looking out for ourselves." He rubbed his chin and wished he could do something to pull her back into the world of dates and fun. "Heard anything from Remy?"

"Let's see." She batted her lashes and poked a finger in her check. "Nothing. And I'm more than happy to keep it that way."

And why not? Five years ago, her ex-fiancé called to say he was getting married to a sweet little Louisiana gal. Some interior designer. Her tone was flip, but the pain she hid behind the attitude was obvious.

"Nothing since?" Just as well, his sister didn't need the heartache.

"Drop it." Her tone grew testy. "For Pete's sake, Remy Boothe's ancient history. We've moved on."

"He has. I repeat, when are *you* going to?"

She wrinkled her nose. "Don't make me regret I came in here to keep my poor dateless brother company."

He smiled and handed her the bowl of chips. "Here—have another chip or two. Maybe you'll get so fat, no one will look twice. Would that be better?"

"Jerk!" She jumped off the sofa and stomped toward the door, stopped, turned, and dumped the bowl of chips in his lap, then stalked toward the door.

"All right. I deserved it." He stood. "Come on. I was just kidding."

She turned and flashed him an arch smile. "I know." She giggled. "But it's fun to watch you turn red."

Without another word, she sashayed from the den. He chuckled and brushed the chips from his hair. She was the best actress of the bunch. Tamsyn had nothing on Carrie who should've done something with her degree in theatre arts.

He couldn't imagine how they would've managed if she hadn't sacrificed her engagement and career plans to take on the role of mom, chief cook and bottle washer for their family.

Tess gazed out her window at the Cumberland. The river was a black velvet ribbon sparkling with the diamond-like lights of the riverboats as they moved slowly up and down the river. The night sky seemed to go on forever, intensifying from navy to deepest black and decorated by pinpoints of silvery stars.

Edward Forbes had been arraigned on murder charges and refused bond.

Running her hands through her tangle of curls, she sighed. Why hadn't she taken Scott up on his dinner invitation? She didn't have to be alone tonight.

Hell, Saturday night was date night. What was he doing? Probably called up the next number in his PDA. No, wait. He didn't strike her as the horn dog type. Her insecurities were showing.

She turned from the view and snagged the bottle of cold water she'd left next to the TV stand. A long drink of water was exactly what she needed.

After padding over to the sofa, she kicked off her shoes and lay down. The reason she'd given Scott for delaying their dinner date was bogus. No matter how her father felt about a PI damaging her career, she'd see Scott as much as she wanted. No, she just needed some time to get used to the idea of getting involved again. No matter what she'd thought in the beginning, this could evolve into a relationship—beyond a roll in the hay for fun. Images of his strong body clouded her mind's eye and sent a rush of warmth to her core.

Frankly, Monday night couldn't come soon enough.

No. No. No. She gave herself a mental slap. Career first. She couldn't have both, not if she wanted to make captain by forty.

Chapter Twelve

Sunday morning, he followed the choice and his family to mass at St. Henry's. So, they were Catholic; hopefully, he hadn't already been spoiled by the attentions of some pedophile priest. How deplorable. Inconceivable. Members of the clergy harming the children entrusted to them. If it were the case, it would truly be a disappointment. But he could always improvise.

He certainly wasn't anything like the pedophiles. No, he only chose those who could physically resist or welcome his attentions. Resist or welcome? Didn't matter. The outcome was always the same.

After church, the happy family piled into their vehicle. He followed a respectable distance behind them toward the old money section of town, Belle Meade, and turned into the driveway of an old two-story columned mansion. Probably for dinner with good old granny. Rich granny.

Dammit.

Since today was apparently an all family day, he might as well pick up his choice's trail in the morning. Better get back before he was noticed.

After taking an early morning run, Tess stopped at Starbuck's to caffeine load. She picked up the Sunday *Tennessean* and headed back home. A veggie pizza delivery made a quickie lunch and put the hunger monster at bay. Sunday dinner with the family wouldn't be until two or two-thirty.

She glanced at her watch. Plenty of time to go over her notes from the Drew Wilson and Tyler Jamison interviews. No doubt Kozinsky was sitting down to lunch with the fair Estelle. His twin sons were home for the summer from college, where they were both majoring in criminal justice at MTSU and would be seniors in the fall. One planned a law career and the other had some wild notion about joining the police force once he earned his degree.

Crazy kid.

She walked over to the bar and picked up her notebook. Might as well transcribe her uneven handwriting into a Word document. The original notes would remain in the case file, but the computer notes would be more in depth and include her thoughts and impressions as well as the subjects' body language in response to her questions.

She was almost through entering her notes when her cell rang. Kozinsky. "Yeah?"

"Multiple homicide at the fast food place on West End, across from Centennial Park. Close to thirty witnesses. Need all hands on deck."

"Across from the park?"

"That's the one."

"Be there in ten."

She broke the connection, then quickly changed into navy slacks, a white knit top and comfortable shoes. She checked her bag, belted on her service weapon, and clipped her badge to her waistband.

She'd enjoyed her time off, but duty called. This particular restaurant was always busy. Beside Vanderbilt Stadium, it was a prime location for students, tourists, and visitors to the park and the Parthenon.

When she reached the crime scene, there were at least fifteen squad cars with blue lights flashing and four ambulances. East-bound traffic was already being rerouted into the West-bound lanes of West End. Bystanders stood across the street and lined the park perimeter watching the action.

Nothing like blood and guts on a Sunday afternoon to draw a crowd.

She zipped her car into J. Alexander's lot next door, parked, slapped a police notice card on her dash, then hopped out and headed to the scene. She flashed her badge at the officer controlling perimeter, then ducked under the crime scene tape. "What do we have?" she asked the officer.

"Shooter came in and wasted his wife and sprayed the crowd. At least five DBs and more wounded. Already carried some of them to the hospital." He glanced down West End. "Good thing we're in hospital central."

His words were true enough, Parklane was a block away. Vanderbilt a couple of blocks and Baptist a couple more. "Got an ID on the suspect?"

The officer shook his head. "Got away."

"Seen Kozinsky?"

"Inside." He motioned with his thumb toward the fast food place.

She nodded her thanks. Pulling on a pair of latex gloves, she strode to the entrance and opened the door. The brackish smell of blood hit her. And there was enough of the stuff spilled to stock a small blood bank.

Kozinsky stood while an M.E. kneeled over one body and shook his head. "Dead."

"Really?" Tess' tone bordered on sarcastic. The female teen had no face. She assumed the victim was a teen because of her clothing and slender build. She counted five bodies. "Five total?"

Kozinsky came up behind her. "Yeah, but a couple more might not make it. Bastard used an AK-47."

"Just walked in with an assault rifle and laid waste?"

"Pretty much. First shot the assistant manager behind the counter, then turned and sprayed the rest of the place. Then ran out and hightailed it up Natchez Trace. Place was full."

"Must've been a madhouse." People scrambling. Screaming. Noise. Blood.

"No shit. About ten witnesses from out front who weren't injured, twelve who were. The worst injured are already on the way to the hospital."

She blocked out the images. "I'll start interviewing."

"Start with the first victim's co-workers." He jerked his head toward five uniformed workers behind the counter, their faces pale and eyes still wide with shock. "I'll start with the folks out here."

Tess nodded and walked down the hall to access the rear of the store. There was a tiny office she could use for the interviews. She walked over to the victim's coworkers who were huddled together, waiting. "I'm Detective O'Malley. I'll take you one at a time. First, I want the person closest to the assistant manager when this happened."

A pretty Hispanic woman timidly raised her hand. "Me. I was…right there." She pointed to a spot directly behind where the assistant manager had been shot. Close call.

"Your name?"

"Gia Lazlo." Her voice trembled and her dark brown eyes darted nervously around the room.

Tess noted her name and demographics. "This won't take long, then you can call your family and let them know you're all right. "

"*Gracias*. I happy answer your questions."

Tess led the woman back to the small office and sat her down. "Do you want some water or coffee?"

"No. No, I all right." Her Hispanic accent was faint and easy enough to understand.

"Do you know the man who killed your assistant manager?"

Lazlo nodded. "Her husband. He's been here before, yelling and screaming at her. Just yesterday he was here."

"His name?"

"Bud-dee Dawson. Bad man with big temper. Karen divorcing him. Took out restraint order. That why he so angry."

"What kind of car was he driving?"

"Red truck."

"I don't suppose you saw the license plate?"

"No." Tears brimmed in Lazlo's dark eyes.

"Were they still living together?"

"No."

"Did she move out or did he?"

"She move. She afraid of him. He couldn't find her new place…so he come here to see her. She file a restraining thing. You know what I mean."

Tess nodded she did. "Her previous address then?"

"On Nevada. I don't know exact address. Not far off Charlotte."

"Thank you. You've been very helpful."

Tess allowed Lazlo to leave, then headed back up front to see how Kozinsky was doing. "Husband is Buddy Dawson. Lives on Nevada Ave. Mrs. Dawson had moved out. Has a history of harassing her here at work.

She filed an RTO—not that it did any good."

"BOLO's already out on him."

"Good. I'll do a quick run-through with the rest of the employees. Getting anything else from the witnesses out here?"

Kozinsky shrugged. "Basic description of him and his truck. All we have to do is find him before he kills someone else."

"This ought to be a slam dunk." She glanced up at the video cameras. "We need to check the camera footage. Doesn't look like he bothered to shoot 'em out."

"Bastard oughta fry. He left one hell of a mess behind."

She headed back to the manager's office, completed the remaining employee interviews with nothing new resulting, except the sad news that Karen left behind three small children.

Five families devastated. And before the night was over, maybe more.

A grueling crime scene with five dead, including the suspect's wife, and twelve or more wounded. As far as Tess and Kozinsky could tell, their suspect had taken off for a healthier climate. He had a mother in Kentucky or maybe he was headed south. Anyone's guess.

When they stormed his apartment, it was a veritable armory of rifles and ammo. If he'd taken even half of what he'd left behind, he wouldn't go down without a fight.

It was after ten before she finished all the paperwork and made it home. The light was blinking on her landline voice mail. Wondering who'd called, she sleepily punched the numbers and retrieved the two messages.

She smiled. Both from Scott. One told her how he enjoyed lunch the day before and how much he looked forward to seeing her again on Monday. The second, his tone resonating with concern, asked her to call him no matter how late she got back home.

No doubt he'd heard about the shootings on the news and wanted to check on her. How did she feel about his checking what happened to her?

Warm and fuzzy...and frankly, a little freaked out.

She punched in Scott's number and waited.

He answered before the second ring. His voice was rough and deep as if he'd been asleep. "I'm glad you called. I saw you on the five o'clock news. Are you all right?"

"Yeah. Just got in. No reason to worry. By the time I'm on scene, the gunplay's usually over."

"Still...I don't know how you get used to things like that."

"You don't—or shouldn't." She sighed, then rolled her shoulders to relieve the cramping tension. "Look, it's late. I gotta get some sleep."

"Got it. We're still on for tomorrow night?"

"Yeah. Definitely."

"Just wanted to say goodnight then." His tender tone sent waves of heat to her lower belly and pooled between her thighs.

"Night."

She sighed and placed the phone back on the charger. Damn, he was definitely getting to her, and she was no closer to figuring out how to have her proverbial cake and eat it too.

In the meantime, her dilemma wouldn't keep her from having some fun. Yet deep down, Scott might be right when he'd said they had the potential for something special. Very special.

Damn. She'd forgotten to ask him if he'd dug up any information on the eyewitness.

That was the trouble with mixing business and pleasure. One always took precedence.

Chapter Thirteen

Monday morning, he parked in the cul-de-sac and sat waiting in the SUV, scoping out his choice's home. The father left at eight and the mother at eight-fifteen in her smaller edition SUV. Excellent. His choice was home alone with his little sister.

Of course, he couldn't just stroll up to the door, knock and drag him away to his lair for a round of fun and games.

A plan. He needed a plan.

Scott left for the office without breakfast. At seven, it was already eighty-five degrees. Today would be a scorcher.

When he arrived at the office, Justin was already putzing around the small kitchen preparing the first of several pots of coffee the agency would go through in a day's work.

"Morning," Scott growled. "You're here early."

"Wanted to complete the background on the Silvey guy. He's clean, but here's the kicker—until two years ago, he didn't exist."

Scott shrugged. "Keep digging. There's bound to be some sort of paper trail."

"Yeah, I'll keep at it." His brother brushed back his longish hair and grinned. His blue eyes shone with good humor. "And you're in a mighty glum mood…for someone who has a date tonight."

Justin tried to high-five, but Scott shook his head. "Grow up."

His sibling's eyes twinkled. "Testy? Getting frustrated?"

"It's not like that." *Liar.*

"Dude, who're you trying to fool? It's always like that." He flashed a wolfish smile, then poured water into the coffeemaker.

"Maybe you're the one needing a date, someone who isn't some kind of online elf princess. Heaven only knows what your online dates really look like."

"I'm a late bloomer. Give me time."

His brother was entirely too confident. "Dude, you'll grow old thinking that way."

"I haven't met the right woman. That's all."

"So? There's a lot of work to do before tonight."

Justin zipped his lip. "Maybe so. You oughta be dancing in here on twinkle toes, but your body language reads like the world is coming to an end."

"Not so." He opened an overhead cabinet and rummaged for one of his special cups. It was a Scooby-Doo kind of day.

"Where're you taking her?" Justin flicked the ON button, then leaned an elbow on the counter.

"None of your business." Scott paused, then shot his brother a smirk. No way was he admitting they were having dinner at her place. "You know all you need to. I have a date tonight…with a certain police detective who's obsessed with her career and making captain before she's forty."

"Dude, you're so fucked."

"Know what's crazy?" Scott laughed. "I know and don't care." Damn. What was he thinking? Why all the sharing? Wouldn't the coffee ever finish brewing?

"Holy shit. Tam was right. You're in love."

Scott shook his head. "Tam and her big mouth. Besides, too soon to call it love. More like lust."

Justin's teasing expression morphed to choirboy innocent. "She might've mentioned something the other night about a certain detective and the Blue Mood."

"Damned if I'm not going to move out. Privacy doesn't mean a damn thing in this family."

"Great! I get the master suite." Justin smiled with entirely too much satisfaction to suit Scott. "Have a fresh cup." He thrust the pot toward Scott.

"Thanks." He filled Scooby-Doo to the brim and turned. Too much work on his desk to waste time trying to one-up his younger brother.

"You can run, but you can't hide," Justin called after him.

In spite of himself, Scott grinned. It was gonna be a helluva day.

But the evening might make up for everything…as long as Tess could forget about her precious career for awhile.

Tess stumbled into the squad room a bare two minutes before her shift was supposed to start. All night long, she'd had scary and, at the same time, erotic dreams about—who else—Scott Holt. Dreams of running through the forest, being chased, then caught and made love to by a masked man revealed later as Scott. What did the mask symbolize? Was he hiding something? Or was she just plain running scared?

As a result, she'd overslept by thirty minutes and missed her morning jolt of java. She collapsed into her chair, glanced over at Kozinsky who was staring at her. She gasped, "Coff-eeeee."

He frowned and scratched his chin. "Never seen you without your morning fix, and I don't ever want to again. You're scary."

"What?" she barked.

"Your hair is wilder than usual. You have no eyebrows to speak of and I do believe you've used eye shadow on your lips…unless gray is their normal color."

"That bad?" She yanked open a desk drawer and fished out a small mirror. "O-mi-god!"

She jumped up and ran for the facilities. The haunted creature staring back from the mirror bore no resemblance to the person normally bearing the name Tess O'Malley.

Instead, it was some kind of otherworldly, zombie Tess. Her partner hadn't exaggerated one bit.

As quickly as she could, she repaired the damage to her normally pulled together image. Her hair was somewhat tamer, and her lips were no longer a sickly gray. Looking down at her outfit, she cringed. There wasn't a damn thing she could do about the red and green plaid top she'd pulled on to wear with a navy and white striped seersucker suit. More appropriate for a circus clown.

She walked back to her desk where a fresh cup of squad brew waited. She grabbed it like a junkie long overdue for a fix and gulped it down. Caffeinated, she turned and preened. "Any better?"

He gave her a skeptical once over, then shrugged. "Gotta tell Estelle about the newest in fashion. Plaids and stripes. Yeah, she's gonna want to know about that." He rubbed his chin and sniffed. "Still, have to wonder what happened that has the fashionista—isn't that the word you chicks use—of the department so rattled?"

She sent him a glance sharp enough to cut off his current tangent. "Didn't sleep well," she mumbled, hoping like hell her partner wouldn't bug her for details.

"What? Couldn't quite make out what you said." A wide grin split his face.

"Never mind." There was no way she'd share her erotic dreams of Scott Holt with her partner. No way in hell. But no matter. She had to leave on time today. There was too much repair work to be done on her hair. Her makeup. And her psyche.

Early afternoon, Tess checked for the eyewitness statement once more. Nothing. "Kozinsky, what do you know about the eyewitness, Doug Silvey?"

"What?" He scowled over his glasses. "Read the report. Statement's bound to be there."

"No. It's not. Have you actually seen it?"

"Can't say as I have." He leaned back and eyed her like a scolding mother. "I've been going over your interview with Drew Wilson. Pretty cut and dried."

"Almost too good, but Scott vouches for him."

"And just who is vouching for Scott?" he asked with a half-grin.

"I am. I trust him. He's one of the good guys." She'd bet her badge on it, but hopefully, it wouldn't come to that.

"Don't forget what you're doing. He was questioned in the Mason case which makes him a person of interest in the current case."

"He didn't do it. You said yourself he's a good PI."

"Doesn't rule him out," he said with a casual shrug.

"Doesn't rule him in, either," she snapped. Her partner was starting to piss her off. "Y'know, there's something fishy about this supposed eyewitness. Feel it in my gut."

"The lieutenant's the lead on this. If he wants to keep things close to the vest, it's his prerogative. They've probably got Silvey stashed somewhere in a safe house. You know how it goes." His gaze darted away from hers.

"But we're back on the case, and..." She reined in her temper as a thought hit. Kozinsky knew something and he was holding out on her. Why?

All right, she'd check with dictation. If they didn't know anything about the statement, then she'd just go to the lieutenant herself and demand— ever-so-politely—an explanation for being left out of the loop.

She reached for the phone and punched in the extension for dictation. After a ten-minute wait on terminal hold, Tess was told the report was "Eyes Only" and Lieutenant Woods had the only hard copy.

The lieutenant was holding out again—why? Hmm. Sally loved chocolate, even more than

Tess did. In her desk drawer, there was a specialty chocolate store gift card she'd never used. Time it did someone some good. A little bribery never hurt...as long as it involved chocolate.

Thirty minutes later, Tess had a photocopy of the eyewitness statement rolled up and slipped into her purse. Her skillful arguments contained references to the glass ceiling, the good-ole-boys' club, and the necessity of women sticking together. Sally refused to let her look at it in the department, even threatened Tess within an inch of her life if she ever revealed where she got it.

"I know people," she said, as she handed over the copy and snatched the gift card with one smooth motion. "And what's with the clown outfit today?"

Sally's insults were something Tess could handle, as long as she got the scoop on Silvey. "Just between us girls, it's a long story. And thanks."

A quick glance at her watch sent her heart into overdrive. Scott would be at her condo at seven and she was a freaking mess. She tugged her purse close to her side and headed back upstairs where she informed Kozinsky she was taking some personal time.

"Bye now," he said in an effeminate tone, then waggled his fingers. "Ta-ta. Have fun."

Before he could bust her chops any more, she beat it for the door. She managed to hold off pulling the eyewitness statement from her purse until she was inside her SUV. She scanned the document for details, but at the bottom was an addendum by Lieutenant Dale Woods stating the eyewitness was currently MIA.

Holy shit. They'd lost their eyewitness. No wonder the lieutenant didn't want anyone viewing the statement.

And now, if she didn't get her ass in gear, she was going to be late for a very important date.

Chapter Fourteen

Scott knocked and waited, drumming his fingers against his thigh. Finally, Tess answered the door. "Hi."

Her blazing red hair made a wonderful complement to her green dress. She turned and invited him in with a sultry glance. He entered and caught a whiff of her perfume. It was light and clean with an undernote of something very sexy. Curious to see just how she lived, he glanced around the unit. The condo was neat, colorful and suited her. "Cool digs."

"Thanks. It's small, but I don't need a lot of room," she said with a half smile and a glint of passion in her silver-gray eyes.

"No pesky roommates to come home and interrupt." And he was damned glad of it. Yes, the case could wait a few hours, but he couldn't. He loved that she allowed him inside her home, didn't imagine many saw her like this. Soft, feminine, and so vibrant and beautiful it hurt.

"Not a one." She gave him a wide smile, then gestured. "Living room, kitchen...bedroom on the other side of the wall. Compact. No more, but no less than I need." She walked straight ahead to the kitchen, then opened the fridge. "Beer, wine, bottled water, and Diet Coke. Have a preference?" She turned.

Her skin was like ivory silk, as long as he discounted the few fawn freckles dotting her shoulders. Her dress was made of some summery material with a skirt that floated around her shapely knees. Sheer need shot through his entire body. Her skin. Her eyes. Her lips. God. He wanted her bad.

"Would it be rude if I said I preferred you?"

She lowered her lashes and a pink flush spread up the ivory column of her neck. Her eyes darkened to slate. "Not at all."

He hardened in an instant and a shudder shook his entire body. He took a deep breath, stepped forward and pulled her into his arms.

"Detective, are you sure?" What he really meant was, Hold on. Are you ready for this?

"Extremely sure," she murmured against his neck, then reached behind her back and unzipped her dress. It fluttered to the floor in a shimmer of grass-green silk, leaving her clad only in a lacy bra and tiny panties the color of her skin.

She pressed her pelvis against his hard-on, then reached for his belt. "I want you. Right now." Playfully, she tugged him by his belt into her bedroom.

"Happy to oblige." He unfastened her bra and skimmed his hands underneath. Her breasts were firm and fuller than he expected. Her nipples tightened into small coral pebbles under the caress of his thumbs.

They fell back on the bed, legs tangling and hands pulling at their clothes.

A cell phone rang, actually played some female country-western group's song. "Not mine," he said. His cell had a classical ring tone.

"No," Tess groaned. "It's mine."

"I thought you weren't on call this evening. Don't answer it." He slid his hand between her legs where the crotch of her panties was already damp.

He massaged her mound with the heel of his palm.

She moaned, but managed, "Always subject to change at a moment's notice. This must be big." She reached over his shoulder and grabbed for the damned cell. "O'Malley."

He continued massaging her clitoris as she squirmed and tried to keep her tone businesslike. Her silken thighs trembled under his touch.

She shook her head at him, but he wouldn't stop playing. He slid one finger inside her panties and slipped it in her dewy slit. Eyes glazed, she moved against him and continued squirming.

"How long has he been missing?" she gasped, rolling her eyes and shaking her head at Scott.

He slid a second finger inside her warmth and moved both in and out. He nipped at her neck and massaged her clit with his thumb. She writhed under him as her body heated and tensed.

"No," she gasped. "I'm fine. Just fine." She bit her lip and ineffectually hit his shoulder with her fist. "On my way." She snapped the phone shut. "I should kill you for that."

"Want me to stop?" He had no intention of stopping until at least one of them came.

"I have to go. There's—" She shuddered and surrendered, melting into the bed, a tangle of arms and legs.

He ripped off the scrap of lace and bent down to kiss her honeyed sweetness. He circled her clit with his tongue and suckled.

"God, no." Her nails dug into his shoulders as she arched against his face and screamed with her climax.

He lifted his head and grinned up at her. "So, you're a screamer. Never would've guessed."

She gasped for breath, her breasts rising and falling with each ragged breath. "Didn't know myself. She reached for his dick, circled it with her hand and drew him to her. "Dammit. I don't have time for this."

"Baby, after all this, it won't take much time." He positioned himself over her and thrust into her wet core. He mined her warm depths to the hilt. She met him thrust for sweet thrust until his boys felt as if they'd explode. He came in quick hot jets. Her walls contracted around his length and she gasped his name as he groaned hers.

She dragged in a deep breath and tried to sit up. "O-mi-god, that was heavenly, but I have to go to work."

"Another homicide?"

She gave him the look, the unmistakable one that told him he was less than intelligent, and nodded. "That's what I do, Holt. Homicide. There's another kid missing. Seventeen."

"How long?"

"At least four hours. He was there at lunch when his sister left to go to a neighbor's." She shook her head. "Probably already dead. This unsub doesn't keep his victims alive long. If it's the same one."

He stepped into his jeans and zipped them.

"Not the same M.O. Taken from home. But he's the right age." She huffed and hurriedly refastened her bra. "I'm sorry. I have to go."

"I know." He leaned over and kissed the tip of her nose. "By the way, do you know you have a number tattooed on your ass?"

"Of course."

His expression grew puzzled. "Why a number? Why not a butterfly or a flower?"

"Long story." She gave a slight huff. "You had to be there."

With a bare backward glance, she redressed, this time in khakis and a pale blue knit shirt, grabbed her service weapon and purse, and ran out the door.

He laid back on her bed and let out a groan. The sheets were rife with the scent of their sex; he let out a groan. Her body, so responsive to his. Her every touch seemed programmed to make him want her more.

She was a hell of a woman and a cop. Let him not forget she was a cop first. Back to reality. He got to his feet and finished dressing. Time to earn his money. Snatched another kid—this time from his home? Damn. If it was the same SOB who killed the governor's grandson, the guy had big ones. He grabbed his cell and called Paul Whitten.

"Paul? Scott Holt. We've caught a break. A confidential source from Metro PD says another teenager's missing. Ned's attorney should petition to have him released right away."

"Thank you so much. How wonderful…not that—"

"Know what you mean. Call Ned's attorney and hang tight."

He disconnected.

Even if the M.O. was different, his gut said it was the same psycho who'd already killed at least two.

Tess pulled into the latest victim's subdivision. The streets were lined with vehicles. The local TV stations were represented with their video journalists and recording equipment. Closer to the scene were six patrol cars with flashing blue lights and a forensics van. She parked, flashed her badge at the officer who guarded the perimeter and ducked under the yellow crime scene tape.

"We gonna get 'im, this time, Detective?" The officer's gaze darted back and forth as he combed the crowd for suspicious characters.

"Sure as hell hope so." She spied Kozinsky standing in the victim's yard and hoofed it to his side. A little out of breath, Tess frowned at her partner. "How is it you beat me to every crime scene?"

He eyeballed her as if he knew what she'd been up to. "How come you're always late?"

She tugged at the collar of her knit shirt. Was it crooked? What had given her away? "If I told you, I'd have to kill you," she told him with a grin, then glanced down at her clothes. Sure, she'd dressed in a hurry, but nothing was showing that wasn't supposed to.

He smirked, but continued, "Seventeen-year-old kid, athlete. Here at eleven-thirty. Gone when the sister returned home from swimming at a friend's house. He's a good kid. Usually leaves a note if he's gonna be gone for any length of time. They called his cell phone but found it in the front yard when it started ringing. Parents and sister are inside. The mother's totally freaking out. Next door neighbor thinks she might've seen something. You take her statement, and I'll finish with the little sister and parents."

"Sure." A growing uneasiness swept over her, matching her new mood. "You know it's been over four hours. He's probably…"

Kozinsky frowned and kicked loose a divot of sod. "Yeah."

Tess entered the foyer. Her eye for detail noted the expensive bird's eye maple with walnut-inset floors. Stairs to the second floor on the left. Family huddled together on a sofa in the living room on the right. The mother short, slightly plump with red eyes and a blotchy face was collapsed against her husband's shoulder. He appeared mid-forties, tall, no excess weight, already losing his sandy red hair. Little sister was a miniature of the mother.

Another woman, blond and petite, flitted around the room, obviously too upset and anxious to sit. Before Tess could ask or even raise an eyebrow, Kozinsky introduced the blonde as Abby Smallwood, the next-door neighbor.

Tess half-gestured, half-pointed toward the kitchen. "If you'll come with me, Ms. Smallwood, we'll talk in the kitchen while Detective

Kozinsky stays with the family."

She followed the nervous neighbor into a kitchen all tricked out with the requisite granite counters and stainless-steel appliances. She pulled out a chair that slid easily on the polished hardwood. "Have a seat."

Would she ever get anything out of this ditzy blonde? The woman settled, but her blond head continued to bob like a canary on crack.

"Sorry. I'm so fidgety. I can't seem to sit still." Blinking rapidly, the woman wrung her hands over and over. Not that Tess could blame her. Who wouldn't be upset?

"It's all right." She dug in her purse and extracted her notebook. "Your full name and address?" Pen poised in mid-air, she waited.

"Abigail Louise Smallwood. I live next door. Thirty-seven Pinckney Place."

Tess jotted down the demographics. "Now just tell me, in your own words, what you saw and what time."

Smallwood nodded, then took a deep breath. "Three-thirty—that's what time I came home—I left work early with a headache," she explained. "There was a dark van, black—no, might've been navy blue—parked in the Hurley's driveway. Just like any repairman would drive…with a sign on the door."

"Can you remember what the sign said or maybe part of the phone number?"

The neighbor bit her bottom lip. "Handy…Home…Repairs. Something like that. Anyway, I couldn't make out the number. I'm not good at remembering numbers anyway."

"Just try." She kept her tone soft. Every bit of information the neighbor had stored in her brain was vital. "Think hard. Was it a local number with seven digits or was it longer with area code?"

The neighbor shut her eyes and frowned with the effort of concentrating. "Long-distance. Wasn't one of the toll-free numbers, either." Her lids popped open. "Wait. Three-oh-three." She shook her head. "Sorry, that's all I can remember."

An area code. Not much, but something. "That's excellent. You're doing extremely well. Now, what happened when you drove in the driveway? Did you see anyone at all?"

"I didn't see Danny if that's what you mean, but this man jumped from the back of the van, hopped inside and took off—rather quickly I thought at the time. If I'd only known—"

"How tall?"

"Quite tall. And with big shoulders, like one of those pro football players. Well over six feet. My husband's six-two and this guy is definitely taller."

"Hair?"

A furrow formed between Smallwood's brows. "Couldn't see his hair. He wore a baseball cap pulled down over his face. He wore a navy uniform, recently pressed because the creases were quite sharp. I'm sorry I notice stupid things like that instead of what he looked like. He had a badge clipped to his uniform, but I was too far away to read it. I wish I could be more help. Poor Danny—" She clapped her hand over her mouth.

"No, ma'am, you're doing great. License plate?"

"I wasn't paying attention. I really didn't think much about it, except Bob Hurley is such a do-it-your-selfer I wondered why the guy was there. I mean, Bob can handle just about anything, repair-wise, but I don't know how he'll handle something like this."

"And after the repairman drove off?"

"I went into the house and started supper. I didn't realize anything was wrong until Jeanette—that's Danny's mom—called and asked me if I'd seen him." She wrung her hands again. "If I'd just called the police when I saw the van…" She gave a sob. "Danny's probably already dead, isn't he?"

Although Tess personally agreed, she said, "You mustn't think that way. We're working very hard to find him. Everything you tell us is a great help to our investigation."

Smallwood wiped her eyes. "His mother is devastated. We all are. Danny was…is such a good kid. He doesn't deserve this."

"Ma'am, no one deserves something like this. No one." She swallowed back her emotions, reached into her jacket and pulled out a card, then handed it to the neighbor. "If you think of anything else, call my cell immediately, no matter how insignificant it might seem."

"Y-yes, I will." Smallwood pocketed the card. "C-can I go now?"

"Yes, ma'am. I'm going to distribute the description to the rest of the force and to the media. He made a mistake this time. We'll find him."

"This time? Do you think he's the one who took the governor's grandson?"

"Actually, too early to tell, Ms. Smallwood."

Hell yeah, he's the same one.

In the living room, Kozinsky sat on an ottoman and gently interviewed the Hurley boy's ten-year-old sister. "Sophie, what was Danny wearing when you left for your friend's house?"

The child rubbed the tears from her eyes and sniffed. "I should've stayed here with him. He'd be okay."

"This isn't your fault, hon. All by yourself—you couldn't do anything. You're just a little girl." He paused. He had to give the kid time to calm down, but time was a-wasting. "Do you remember what Danny was wearing?"

"Cut-offs and a purple and white Father Ryan T-shirt—he pulled it out of the dirty clothes. I told him Mama would be mad, but he said he didn't care. And his new running shoes."

Kozinsky's ears perked on the word *shoes*. The unsub typically kept one of his victims' shoes. "Tell me about his shoes, Sophie. What kind were they?"

"New Balance," she said with a sad little smile. "Danny really, really liked them. They were gray with white trim and a big *N* on each side. They cost over a hundred and fifty dollars," she said, beaming with obvious pride.

Mrs. Hurley blushed and reached for Sophie's hand. "That's not important, Sophie."

Kids. Got to love 'em, especially the young ones. "You're a good girl, honey. You got a good memory." He turned to Mrs. Hurley and kept his tone gentle. "Ma'am, if you'll just tell me what time you arrived home?"

She swallowed and started off in a shaky voice. "I didn't get home until six—I had to stop at Harris Teeters—you don't care about that, do you?"

"Everything's important, Ma'am. Go on."

"Anyway, Sophie was home and I could tell she was sunburned and hadn't used sunblock, so I was fussing about that. Then I asked her where Danny was—he has baseball practice tonight. Sophie told me he was gone when she came home at five. He hadn't left a note. I checked the den and his room both."

She ran a trembling hand back through her dark hair. "I started to get an uneasy feeling. A mother knows—we just *know*—when something's wrong. So, I called his cell to fuss at him for not leaving me a note. And th-then, I heard his cell phone. It was outside in the yard. He never goes anywhere without it."

She bowed her head and rubbed the forehead with her fingers. I can't believe I was going to fuss at him and then—"

"Yes, Ma'am. Please, go on. Everything's important."

"Then I thought about the governor's grandson and if someone could get him…" She buried her face in her hands and sobbed. After an uneasy moment or three, she composed herself and continued. "I called Abby next door to see if she saw Danny at all when she came home. She told me about the handyman's van in the driveway. That's when I freaked out and called my husband. He was already on his way home, and he told me to call the police right away." She fought tears, then shot a nervous glance at her daughter, then said in a low tone, "This isn't going to end well, is it, Detective?"

Not unless we can catch the rat bastard in the next ten minutes or so. Not something he could admit out loud. Instead, he offered them what he considered the most useless advice ever known to man. "You have to keep a positive attitude. We got on the case quickly. It may not be related to the other case you mentioned."

He forced his thigh muscles to relax. More than anything he wanted to get out there and find the creep. "Is there anything else? Have you noticed anyone in the neighborhood who didn't belong? Or at any of Danny's baseball games?"

Slowly she shook her head. "I can't think of anyone."

"What about recent photos? Sometimes a victim is stalked for several days or weeks to get an idea of their schedule. What about pictures taken at the ballpark?"

"Yes, my husband took some with his digital camera at the game on Saturday." She glanced over at her husband with a mother's undying hope in her eyes. "Didn't you, Bill?"

"I'll need your camera, Mr. Hurley."

"Certainly." Somewhat shaky, Bill Hurley stood. "I'll get it."

Kozinsky handed his card to Mrs. Hurley. "Anything at all. Call me. Day or night."

"You don't think this is kidnapping for ransom, do you?" Her eyes were shiny with more tears.

"No, Ma'am, but we're getting a warrant to tap your line just the same. There'll be a uniformed officer to stay here—just in case."

Hurley returned with the camera. He cleared his throat. "That's the last we have…"

"Don't worry. You'll get them back." *And if the angels are on his side, hopefully, your son, too.*

Tess returned to the living room just as Kozinsky stood and nodded at the family. He held a small digital camera in his big beefy hands.

"Don't worry," he told the family. "You'll get it back."

She gave the Hurleys what she hoped was an encouraging smile, then turned to her partner. "You through? I've a basic description of the driver and van the neighbor saw this afternoon. We need to get it out to the force and the media ASAP."

Kozinsky nodded his agreement. "Plenty of media types out there. Hand it over to the department spokesperson. He's bound to be on scene by now."

He jerked his head toward the door. "Mr. and Mrs. Hurley, we'll let you know of any developments." He handed his card to the boy's father. "Don't hesitate to call if you remember anything or have questions."

She waited until they were outside and away from the parents' earshot. "What did you learn from the boy's parents?"

"They didn't know shit." He shook his head and related the results of his interviews.

"What was he wearing?" Tess interjected.

"Oh—" He paused to check his case notes. "Wore cut-offs and a purple and white Father Ryan T-shirt. Expensive new running shoes, gray with white trim."

"What about the camera?"

"Photos in it from his last ballgame. Thought we ought to check 'em out. See if anyone looks out of place."

"Good idea. He might've stalked Danny before snatching him." She slipped under the crime scene tape and found the department spokesperson quickly enough. After giving him a brief description of Danny's attire, the handyman and van last seen in the area, she added the typical person of interest, possible witness BS.

With Kozinsky dogging her heels, she headed for the SUV. What a nightmare for the Hurley's and there was no telling what Danny'd endured.

She didn't care about psychological babble. She'd been on the job long enough, seen too much and knew some folks were just born evil. This bastard was one of the worst. Putting him, and people like him, behind bars was one of the reasons she'd become a cop.

"What did you hold back?" he asked close her ear.

"Let's get away from the cameras." She headed over to her vehicle. Her partner squeezed in on the passenger side.

"The neighbor thinks she remembers an area code from the side door signs. Three-zero-three. It's not a Tennessee area code. But it could give us a lead where this fellow's been for the last fourteen years."

"And where he was up to his same sick tricks." She nodded, then called Dispatch. "Find out where this area code is, please?"

"Sure thing, Detective. Hold on a sec."

She waited, growing more and more impatient. "Denver," came the melodious voice.

"As in Colorado?"

"You got it, Detective."

"That sure was easy," Kozinsky said with a wink. "I must not have a sexy voice."

"Pays to be nice." She smiled. "Now we check with ViCAP and look for similar M.O.s and victimology from Colorado and points between."

"Now you're talking, kid." Kozinsky pulled out his brand-new cell phone with the TV hook up. "You gotta get one of these babies. Let's see what our spokesperson is saying about the case."

She peered at the small screen. Damn, that was none other than suspect number three, Tyler Jamison of News Channel Nine, with his mic on camera asking the big question of the department's official spokesperson.

"Do you believe this case is related to the kidnapping and murder of the governor's grandson?"

"No, at this time, we do not believe this case is related to the kidnapping and murder of the governor's grandson. The method and time of day are all different. We have the alleged murderer of the governor's grandson already in custody. We're looking for someone entirely different. The only similarity is the young man who has disappeared is the same general age as the previous victim. This appears to be a crime of opportunity. Danny Hurley was in the wrong place at the wrong time."

"In his own home? Seems like the perpetrator was the one in the wrong place."

A perfectly coifed Jamison faced the camera. "Tyler Jamison, News Channel Nine reporting to you from the scene in Bellevue where today seventeen-year-old star athlete Danny Hurley was kidnapped from his home. Stay tuned to News Channel Nine for the latest details."

Tess banged the steering wheel with her fist. "Damn! I can't believe the official story is this is a different suspect. We have a serial killer on our hands, but it's business as usual with the department."

"That's the way it goes." Kozinsky shrugged his wide shoulders. "The Metro spokesperson made some valid points about the M.O."

"Come on. What's your gut say? Mine says they're related."

He flashed a wolfish smile. "And my gut's shaking hands with yours." He opened the door and hauled his large butt out of the car. "I'm heading back. See you there."

She shot him a two-fingered salute. "Beat ya."

Turning the key in the ignition, she checked for traffic, then pulled into the street and made a quick U-turn.

Time was running out for Danny Hurley. Maybe already had.

And what were the chances of Tyler Jamison's doing the interview? He was the morning anchor. Did he have a special interest in this particular story? Wouldn't hurt to check his whereabouts over the last fourteen years.

Dammit. The next-door neighbor bitch who pulled into her driveway and stopped him before he had his choice completely secured. Hands and mouth—yes. Feet and ankles—no. The teen was bigger and stronger than he expected, and it took more effort than usual to get him knocked out and loaded into the van. At last, though, he'd jerked the cell phone off his choice's waist and tossed it into the yard.

Still, drugged with chloroform, his choice should stay unconscious long enough to reach the cabin. He high-tailed it from the oppressive over-development of McMansions, stopping only long enough on a back road of Edwin Warner Park where he ripped off the handyman sign and tossed it in the back of the van. The choice hadn't moved. So far, so good.

Back in the van, he drove carefully through the streets of West Nashville until he hit the Interstate. His gaze flickered from the highway ahead to the review mirror, watching for any pursuing vehicles. With great concentration, he maintained the van at the speed limit.

The longer he drove, the more the itch increased. His entire body was consumed by prickles as if ants crawled over his arms, legs, back, face and groin…especially his groin. He was *so* ready. Time to stop and play games with his choice. Good thing his exit was coming up. He hit the turn signal and exited off I-65 South.

Danny woke up—his head fuzzy like he had a hangover or something. Even though it was dark, he knew he must be in the back of his kidnapper's van. He struggled against the duct tape until his wrists were raw.

Damn stuff. He'd never manage to break it. His butterfly knife was in his front pocket. Yes, the knives were illegal, but all his friends in karate class had ordered them so he had, too. It wouldn't do him much good though since the creep had bound his hands behind him.

He'd read the newspaper articles about the governor's grandson and what the killer had done to him before he died. Gross. He shivered. Man. That would have to hurt like hell…but the killing part— there wouldn't be any getting over that.

For some reason, the creep had stopped short of taping his feet. As soon as the back door opened, Danny was gonna book. He was an all-around athlete, dammit. Baseball, soccer, and track. A real hot shot—that's what the coaches called him. He excelled in the sprints as well as the longer distances. Give him just one chance, he'd be bolt like a jackrabbit and lope along until he got the fuck away from this one scary son of a bitch.

If only the bastard hadn't ripped off his cell phone. According to those TV cop shows, the police could've used it to track the pings from the cell towers.

No rescue coming from the cops. He had to rescue himself.

Underneath him, he felt the van bumping over uneven ground and slowing, rolling to a sudden stop. This would be his only chance.

Play dead. Wait…for the door…to open.

Chapter Fifteen

Scott hit the TV remote and sat riveted to the news reports all evening. Unbelievably, the police department spokesperson said the cases weren't connected.

"Stupid bastards!" He raised his arm to throw his empty beer can at the flat-screen TV but stopped just in time. Hell, destroying the plasma wouldn't accomplish anything, except maybe drive Justin to commit justifiable homicide.

His brother ambled into the den, plopped down on the leather sofa and propped his size twelves on the coffee table. "You were in a damned good mood and had a shit-eating grin when you came home. What happened?" his brother asked with a not-so-innocent smirk.

"Huh?" Scott glared and wished his brother weren't so damned observant.

"Got the old hard drive optimized, did ya?" Reality dawned. So he'd had a sappy smile.

Dead giveaway. "Is it that obvious?"

"Oh, yeah. But only to someone who hasn't..." Justin shrugged.

"Enough!" Scott covered his ears. "Too much information."

"Let me guess." His brother kept smirking. "Wouldn't be a certain Metro Homicide Detective, would it?"

He narrowed his gaze and stared back at his brother. Maybe that would shut him up.

"Now hold on a minute. We're brothers. Brothers share everything, not that I expect you to share..." Justin's fair skin heated up to a slight pink. "You know what I mean."

"Quit while you're ahead, dude."

Justin linked his fingers behind his head. "So are ya gonna tell me what had you ready to chuck a beer can at our precious high-def TV?"

"The MNPD has it all wrong. This kid who just disappeared today—he fits the same victim profile as the others. But Metro, in their greater wisdom, says it's unrelated to the Brennerman case."

"Maybe it is. Wasn't this new victim taken from home instead of a camp?"

"I'm sure all the camps are on their guard and have warned their campers not to wander off in the middle of the night with anyone. Besides, there's a fourteen-year gap since the last one. Maybe this guy's been out of state and he's versatile, not tied to any one M.O."

In Scott's mind, it ruled out Drew Wilson and Tyler Jamison, but who could be so brazen to snatch a nearly grown teenager from his home in broad daylight? Guy had balls. Big ones.

Justin abandoned his relaxed position and sat forward, eyes wide, his interest piqued. "Okay, so it's the victimology we need to research, not just the M.O." He wriggled his fingers as if he were already in front of his computer. "I can help with that."

"Metro just doesn't want to admit they made a mistake when they rushed to arrest Ned Forbes." Another news break and there was Tyler Jamison again. Same old party line. Scott hit the remote and turned off the TV. "I've heard the same BS too many times."

"At least they can't blame the newest one on our client."

"That's the only good thing about it. If, and when, the Hurley kid is found, the manner of death will either point to the same killer or not. If it does, Forbes' attorney can push for a dismissal of the charges."

"You think the Hurley kid's already a goner, don't ya?"

"'Fraid so."

"Then the sooner I hack into ViCAP, the better?" Justin shot Scott a puckish grin, the one he always gave when he was on the verge of doing something illegal.

"I did *not* hear you say you're going to hack ViCAP." The quicker they located the killer, the better. Worry about the fallout later.

"No, you didn't." Justin stood, raised his brows innocently and shoved his hands deep in his pockets. "Ya must've misunderstood me." He bolted for the door. "Guess it's time to have another go at Dragons and Faeries."

As soon as he reached the door, he skidded to a stop and turned. "One more thing. I've raked every database I can hack and Doug Silvey didn't exist until two years ago. No doubt about it. I found the birth and death records for one Richard Douglas Silvey. Born 1972 in Lancaster, PA. Record of death a mere two weeks later. Could be our eyewitness obtained the birth certificate and created a new identity." He shrugged. "Just a thought."

"Good point." Scott nodded. "I'll let Tess know. You focus on the victims."

An innocent man was rotting in jail for a crime he didn't commit. The sooner they found documentation of similar victims, the closer they'd come to find the real killer, and the incidental clearing of Drew and Tyler wouldn't hurt either. As for Dakota Taylor, he wasn't even in the state.

What would the agency do without Justin? Damn, but his brother was worth his weight in Twinkies.

Back in the CJC, Tess gulped down a cup of coffee as she entered the victimology parameters, then the manner of death, and the most telling item, the one missing shoe which the local unsub was apparently taking as a souvenir. Then she sat back and waited. "Well, ViCAP is working or so the computer tells me. How long's it gonna take?"

"Fifty states in the U.S. Might take all night." Kozinsky opened his mouth and gave a yawn so wide she could count his fillings. "Estelle's pissed because I blew off dinner again."

"She ought to be used to it by now."

"There must be something in the secret wives' decoder book which says after fifty missed dinners, stop cutting the guy any slack."

"Wouldn't know myself." She laced her tone with a good-natured bite of snark.

Kozinsky shook his grizzled head and said with a world-weary air, "Believe me, it exists. I've fallen short enough times to know."

She drummed her nails on the desktop, then stood and gave him an encouraging smile, more to hide what she was about to do than from any demonstration of goodwill. "Be right back. Gotta make a call...*personal.*"

He let out a whoop more appropriate for cranes' mating season and shoved his fist into the air. "I knew it. You're up to something. With someone. A certain PI perhaps?"

She shook her head and kept the smile plastered on her face. "Need to know only." Walking out to the hallway, she pulled the cell phone from her belt, leaned against the wall, and waited until no one was close enough to hear her before she punched in Scott's number.

He answered, his tone softer and sexier than any man ought to sound this time of day. "Hey there, Detective O'Malley. I was about to call you."

"I have something you might want to look into." She kept her tone low. "The neighbor gave me a three-zero-three area code on the truck signage. That's Denver. Thought you might want to concentrate your efforts up there. So why were you going to call?"

"Whoa. You're all business, aren't you? My call was going to be a touch more personal. I'm looking forward to seeing you again."

His tone was low and sexy and images of their quick encounter flashed through her mind, sending merry tingles to her naughty bits. The muscles in her thighs tightened.

"I enjoyed it, too." Back to business. No time for all this. "But we've got to find this kid—if it's not already too late."

"Understood, but there's one more thing on my mind."

"Yeah?"

"Your eyewitness didn't exist until two years ago, but there was a Richard Douglas Silvey born in Lancaster, PA, who only lived a couple of weeks, so—"

Someone tapped Tess' shoulder. Her breath caught in her throat. She whipped around. Kozinsky. Dammit. Had he heard her leaking info to Scott?

"Sorry. Gotta go." She disconnected, pretty sure she knew the rest of what he tried to tell her. The mystery witness was a fake. And who would most likely create a false identity and give false evidence—the killer.

"What's the big rush, Kozinsky?"

"You need to get back in here and see what your printer is spitting out."

She slipped the phone back on her belt and sped back to her desk. Disbelief settled heavily on her shoulders like a three-hundred-pound druggie high on PCP.

"Holy Mother." She flipped through the stack of pages and sank into her chair. "Basically, every metropolitan area in the U.S. has a smattering of victims who met the criteria I entered dating back to 1994 in Savannah, Georgia, where there were two victims. Both bodies recovered in shallow graves. One shoe missing."

"Sounds like our guy."

"Had to eliminate all who are the right age demographic but listed as missing, so they don't fall into the missing shoe category." She continued and the numbers kept mounting. "In 1996, he moved on to Newark, two more recovered and the shoe was missing. Chicago, 1997 was the next target of our unsub's presence with one body located with a missing shoe. You wouldn't believe how many kids in this demo are missing."

Kozinsky frowned and rubbed his chin, a sure sign he was considering all her info. "Maybe he's getting better at hiding the bodies."

"Maybe. One in Denver from 1999 was found dead with a single shoe missing. Six more missing in Denver in one year. Must've gotten pretty hot for him there. Apparently, he headed to Los Angeles where he hit an all-time career-high with four bodies in two years."

"Rapid progression of kills. Sounds like he's devolving."

She nodded. "Then nothing much from 2002 until now."

Kozinsky rubbed his chin. "Might've flown under the radar. I can think of a couple of places where the locals might've been too busy to miss a few teenage boys. Kansas City for one was pretty busy with BTK in 2002. And what about Louisiana in 2005? Who would've noticed?"

"Could've been in jail for something else. At any rate, he's our problem now. What brought him back? Homesick?" She tapped her pen on the desktop and counted. "Kozinsky, that's at least ten possible victims who fit the late male teen profile. Now we have to take this to the lieutenant. We need an FBI profiler to weigh in on this, or kids are going to keep dying."

Her partner frowned. "You know he isn't gonna ask the feds for help. You keep this up and you'll never get invited to the boss's annual barbeque, much less make captain."

"Don't care. Not interested in snagging an invite to the barbeque. I just want this guy off the streets." Making captain she cared about—barbeque not so much.

"Makes two of us. Just be careful about how you present it. You're good, but I don't want to see that hot temper of yours come back and bite you in the ass."

She buffed her nails on her blouse, then shot him her best sneer. "It's not easy being right all the time, and dammit, I know I'm right this time."

He let out a loud guffaw while she went back to working up the Smallwood woman's interview. With Scott and his computer genius brother also working the same lead, something had to give.

She desperately needed some time to delve into Tyler Jamison's background. Maybe he covered stories out of state before he landed the news anchor job? Did he have a secret life? Or were the missing eyewitness and the unsub the same person?

Afraid to move or even breathe, Danny stayed hunkered down behind an old oak. The sounds of psycho-freak crashing through the woods grew closer. His heart hammered as if he were on the verge of pitching a no-hitter. It was almost dark, but his head was clearing. Maybe his headlong rush through the woods had helped some. Good old adrenaline had done the rest.

His hands were still tied. His arms cramped like a son of a bitch, but as long as his legs worked, he could outrun this lumbering bastard.

"Danny. Oh, Danny boy, where are you? You've misunderstood my intentions. I thought you'd like playing my game, but since you don't, show yourself and I'll take you back home."

Yeah, right. Might've been stupid to get caught once, but not stupid enough to fall for the fucker's bullshit a second time. Still, he was in a helluva mess. Some freaking woods or park. Not a clue in the world where he was. And a flat-out freaking perv calling his name…to play games.

A beam of light splashed the undergrowth, not two feet from where Danny hid. He froze and held his breath. Fucker had a flashlight. Of course he did. He was prepared for his games. Playing fair wasn't in the scuzzball's rule book.

Track. Soccer. Baseball—they all had rules. Not this guy. He was big as the side of a house, strong as a powerlifter. Danny couldn't risk the bastard laying hands on him again. Lucked out with the drug wearing off.

No second chances.

All right, he'd made a mistake. His choice was taller, stronger and could run like a fucking racehorse at the Derby. The real mistake was the nosy neighbor bitch coming home before he could duct tape the kid's ankles together. His groin throbbed and ached but not from the itch this time. No, the little bastard had played possum and then kicked him in the balls. He'd pay for his treachery with a lot of pain before dying if he could just find him.

Failure wasn't an option.

He splayed the flashlight beam over the underbrush, moving slowly and deliberately. He knew these woods all too well. Because of his last bit of excitement, the campgrounds were closed, but he knew the back road entrance. He'd made his first choice right here fourteen years ago. How fitting to come full circle.

So many choices he'd made since the fateful first one. From each, he'd taken a souvenir. A shoe. And each one of them was a lovely reminder of the time he'd spent with them.

"I know you can hear me. Come out. It's time to go home. I'm getting tired of playing hide and seek."

He listened. Nothing other than a bird call or two. Not a whisper of wind blowing through the trees. Not a crackle in the undergrowth. He sniffed the air like a bloodhound sniffing for his missing prey. The fetid smell of a dead animal wafted through the humid and fecund forest. His nose wrinkled.

What a waste. He needed to find the damn kid almost as much as he needed to get back to his real life before he was missed.

Danny spent a miserable night crouched in one spot, afraid to move. Almost afraid to breathe. Might be summer, but the night was cool. His cut-offs and T-shirt didn't help much. The perv had left for what seemed like hours. Then just as he'd decided the creep was gone for good, he came back, crashing around and swearing. Bastard just wouldn't give up. Eyelids heavy, Danny fought sleep. He could sleep when he got back home.

Or when he was dead.

At the moment, dead seemed a lot more likely than ever seeing his parents or sister again. Mom would be totally ape-shit by now. As for the old man, he never showed much emotion so who knew how he was reacting to all of this. Probably be mad as hell because Danny'd let his guard down.

His dad had warned him. No strangers. Yeah. Just never thought of a handyman as a stranger. Maybe even recognized the guy from somewhere. Yet the friendly handyman hadn't seemed so strange— nothing like a freaked-out perv killer ought to look until the funky-smelling cloth was shoved in his face.

Yeah, that was the first clue—duh!

Chapter Sixteen

Mighty pleased with himself, Scott shuffled quickly downstairs the next morning and headed to the front door. Pleased because, for once, he'd gotten up early enough for a workout at the Y before office hours. Doubly pleased because, in spite of Tess's abruptly terminated phone conversation, she'd entrusted him with information known only to her and her partner.

Justin must've gotten up even earlier and headed to the office. The office computer system kicked ass and any additional hacking incursions into the Feds' database could be masked and hidden behind a multitude of dead-end firewalls. At least that was the gist of his brother's explanation.

Scott downed the dregs of his coffee and grimaced, then looked up as his brother rushed in with a stack of reports. Justin's smile was one degree short of a shit-eating grin.

"Hey man. You gotta see this. Denver had one missing male teen, aged fifteen to seventeen, in ninety-nine and a bunch more missing. Get this, the body was found…with one missing shoe. Same scenario. Boy Scout Camp, Band Camp, you name it." Justin handed Scott a printout on the cases.

"Wow." He took the printout and motioned his brother to have a seat.

"Save your wows for this." He handed Scott longer printout. "There's more. All over the U.S. from 1994 forward. Savannah, Newark, Chicago, LA. Just concentrating on the ones who've been found and were missing one shoe. And get this. They're not all missing from camps and campgrounds. Looks like he got creative in L.A. Now among those still missing, there are reports of abductions from the victim's homes. Reports of a handyman type van in four of the abductions, but each one reported a different color van. Black, gray, white, dark blue. He's either renting vans or changing the paint colors. Smart guy."

"Bingo! That fits the last M.O. here." Scott jumped to his feet. "I'm calling Ned's lawyer. The MNPD is trying to say this last one isn't related and they won't release him." He held the papers aloft. "This ought to help change their minds."

Too many things on his plate at once and all of them vital. Ned Forbes. The mystery witness. The missing teens from all over the U.S. But first he'd better put in a call to Tess or better yet see her so she couldn't give him the bum's rush like she had on the phone.

Tess rubbed her eyes. Pulling an all-nighter in college was one thing, but pulling one at the advanced age of thirty required a lot more caffeine than previous years. Per the tip line, there'd been a multitude of reported sightings of dark blue vans. So far, they'd all been ruled out. According to the rest of the neighborhood canvass, Abby Smallwood was the only neighbor who saw anything.

Damn.

The department was spinning its wheels tracking down all the leads, but they couldn't afford to overlook anything, no matter how insignificant it appeared. While no one in the department would admit it to the public, the general consensus was Danny Hurley was already dead.

She studied the photo provided by his mother and copied for all of law enforcement. Redhead, freckles, gray eyes. Hell, he could've been her little brother, but in reality, he was Sophie Hurley's big brother. What would that little girl go through growing up knowing her brother had been kidnapped and brutally murdered?

Was? Had been? Yes, she figured him for a goner, too.

Later that afternoon, Tess glanced up at the shadow filling the doorway of the squad room. She smiled. Her pleasure at seeing him so unexpectedly set her heart tripping the light fantastic.

"What brings you here, Mr. Holt?" She ignored the giggle from Kagen at the next desk. It was a damn good thing Kozinsky was having lunch with his wife. At least he wouldn't be around to tease her.

Scott ambled over to her desk and perched on the corner. He smiled down at her, his dark gaze more serious than his smile. "Need a favor."

She grinned, then teased him with, "I'll have you know I'm not in the business of doing favors for just any PI who happens to stroll in here." She motioned for him to have a seat, so they could have a more private conversation beyond the big ears of a certain other female detective.

He eased into the chair and leaned forward. His tone was low and intimate. "I thought since you and I were so rudely interrupted last evening, you might cut me a little slack."

She grinned at the memory. "Normally, it would be the case, but now I have to ascertain if said brief encounter was an attempt to bribe this detective or if it was sincere?"

"Oh, sincere, definitely."

His deep, sexy tone sent a thrill through her body. Heat pooled between her thighs and her inner muscles clenched in response. Squirming in her chair, she did her best to banish the impulse to rake everything off the desk and have her way with him—again and again.

She swallowed the lump in her throat and heat suffused her cheeks. Dammit. Her face was probably lit up like a house afire.

"Then…" She paused unable to continue her train of thought. God, what was wrong with her. One passionate quickie and she was ready to do the deed on her desk and forget all about the reason they'd been interrupted. Poor Danny Hurley.

"It's not that big a favor, darlin'." His warm gaze caressed her like a lover's touch. "Something's come up. I'd like to share what Justin found."

A little deflated, she said, "And I thought you were here to reschedule a repeat of our last moment in time."

"Put it on the agenda—as long as we can compare notes too."

She fluttered her lashes. "Tonight? Hm, I need to check my PDA." She made a show of checking, then smiled up at him. "You're in luck. I happen to have an opening—my place, say seven? Besides, I have something to share I think you'll love." From his wide smile reaction, he probably figured something a little naughty. Well, it was, but not the way he obviously expected. Actually, sharing a witness statement with someone other than Ned Forbes' attorney was more than naughty. It was illegal.

"Seven's good." He leaned forward and kissed her forehead. "See you then." He stood, then strode to the door. She watched him stop, turn and snap a two-fingered salute.

More giggles from Kagen. "That guy's totally hot. Please tell me he has a twin brother."

"You're out of luck, Kagen. He has a house full of sisters though," she said, ignoring the fact he had a brother, just not a twin. No way was she giving Kagen any kind of way to get at Scott. He was all hers. All six feet plus of sexy male animal.

Slow down, hon. You're not into forever after. Yours, for now, that's all.

"Hmph. Not into girls," Kagen said, then sighed.

"Like I said, S-O-L." Tess ignored the detective's open mouth. Some sexy new underwear was in order. Hell, why bother? He'd rip it off seconds after he got there. Maybe a power nap. Wouldn't do to fall asleep while they made love.

As if...

Back at his office, Scott walked over to the window and stared at the murky green waters of the Cumberland. There was a tap on his door. He turned and saw his sister Carrie. "Hey. What's up?"

She shot him a level gaze over her glasses. "That's what I came to ask you. You've been in such a good mood. When I asked Justin what was going on, he just laughed. Allison said she didn't have a clue. Tamsyn just grinned and shrugged." She paused for breath. "So...spill."

He grinned. "And you need to know...why?"

"Hmph." She placed her hands on her hips and eyed him skeptically. "Maybe you've started something with a certain police detective?"

"A gentleman never—" He shrugged. "—you know."

Her green eyes brightened. "Cool! When are you bringing her home to meet the family? Find out what she likes to eat, and we'll have a big shindig. I know—a barbeque outside on the deck." She rubbed her hands together, clearly delighted at the prospect.

"Hold on now, sis. You're rushing things a bit."

"Come on, now. I know my brother. You're not a player, so it must be serious."

He rubbed his forehead. "Dammit. Keep your voice down. You want the whole office to know my business? Do we have to talk about this stuff? Whatever happened to boundaries?"

His sister laughed so hard her shoulders shook. "Yeah, the whole office is your family. And we already know you and Tess O'Malley are sizzling like steaks on a grill."

"Close the door," he said. "I need some advice." She frowned but did as he asked. She folded her arms across her chest. "Okay, big brother, what is it?"

"I—I, hell, never mind. I don't do personal stuff." No man did, not willingly.

"Chicken. None of your manly parts will fall off if you ask for advice...or directions."

"I—uh, think she's more interested in her career than having a family."

"So? This isn't the fifties. Tess is a modern woman. Why shouldn't she feel that way? Are you such an old-fashioned guy you can't accept her the way she is?"

Busted. He sat at the desk and fiddled with his pen, flipping it from one end to the other. "Is that your not so subtle way of calling me a male chauvinist pig?"

"Well, your desk is looking more and more like a feeding trough to me."

He snorted. Come to think of it, his desk was a mess just like his life. He picked up a stack of files and straightened them. Here he was getting involved with a woman who had no intention of settling down and having a family. Wasn't that what he wanted in the long run? Maybe he ought to call and cancel.

Nah. Besides a woman could always change her mind.

"Hello! I'm still here." His sister was waving her hands to get his attention. "Where'd you go?"

He snapped to attention. What was the matter with him, losing focus like a teenage boy with a boner? "Nowhere. Forget I said anything."

Clearly irritated with him, Carrie rolled her eyes. "Whatever."

He watched his sister sashay from his office, but she stopped at the door and glanced at him over her shoulder. "I'm always available…anytime you're ready to talk."

Tess sat at her desk, going through the ViCAP printouts. She glanced up when Kozinsky returned from lunch.

Poor guy. His expression was glum. His bulky body slumped as he trudged into the squad room. He flopped in his chair, then hunched over his desk and stared at the wall. "She says I gotta choose—her or the job."

Crap, she didn't want to break in a new partner. No, that was selfish on her part. "What can I do? Better yet, what're you going to do?"

He shook his head. Poor guy almost had tears in his eyes. "Hell, if I know."

"She's got a point. You've got your thirty years and can retire with a decent pension. Maybe you've put some aside as well?" She pointed at him. "She's stuck with you all this time. Got to be a record of some sort."

"Yeah, but she's not thinking straight. Our boys have another year of college. One wants to be a lawyer. In case you haven't checked tuition rates for law schools, it takes money. Another five years and the pension will be a lot better, and they should both be out of school and on their own." He shot her an expression of dread. "But then, what'll I do? I don' want to be one of those ex-cops who sits around the house all day or in a bar, reliving the good old days."

Man, the guy was really in a funk. "Okay, look at the bright side. You and Estelle could travel. Hell, she deserves a damn reward for putting up with you all these years." She leaned back and grinned at her partner.

"You trying to get rid of me?" he growled. "You want a younger partner? Damn traitor—that's what you are."

"No." She shook her head and shrugged. "Frankly, I'd just as soon keep you. I mean, there's nobody who belches the Star-Spangled Banner like you. Where would I find someone else like that?"

"Yeah?" he said, twisting his lip up in a sneer. "And who do you think will stop and let you buy a new pair of shoes on the way to a crime scene?"

"Right." She nodded, then his words registered. "Hey! I never—."

"Only 'cause you know I wouldn't do it."

She gave the desk a light thump with her fist. "We're both your partners, Estelle and me. But, fella, she's got to be your priority. You know all those vows and things you said in front of the priest."

"That was a long time ago." He cut her a sideways glance. "I'm not sure I remember exactly what we said." Then he grinned. "I know you're right. I just hate to turn in my papers. I never was a quitter."

"You've done your duty. You've given Metro thirty years of service. You're not a quitter—not in my book or anyone else's." She set down the printouts. They could wait. Scott and his brother could do the grunt work for a change.

"Thanks, kid. I'm gonna miss you—hell, I'm gonna miss all this."

"You might be surprised. You might like retirement more than you think. Besides, what is all this? Bad coffee, a grouchy partner on her good days, and flat feet."

He shook his head. "Guess I'll give it a shot—in another five or so. Say, did Estelle bribe you to say all this?"

Tess laughed. "No, but if she wants to send me a lei from Hawaii or some fancy perfume from Paris, I wouldn't turn it down."

"Or some *shoes* from Italy?"

She pointed her forefinger like a gun and took aim. "Now you're talking."

But honest to Pete, she'd miss the big guy. Still, he'd paid his dues and he deserved to have a better life with the faithful Estelle. Okay maybe she was rushing him a bit. If she had to lay down some hard cash, she'd bet on his staying another five years, no matter what his wife said.

Chapter Seventeen

Fresh flowers, enough candles to burn Chicago down all over again, and Chinese food. What more could a man want? Besides her, that is. She'd made sure she was perfect too, down to the bits of taupe lace she wore under a short coral sundress. Strappy coral sandals made up the rest of her ensemble for seduction—part deux.

Fresh sheets on the bed—assuming they'd end up in bed again. If she had anything to say about it, they would.

A knock at the door jumpstarted her. One last glance around the loft—everything was perfect. She rushed and opened the door. She managed not to sigh—just barely—at the sight of his sweet, hunky self as he stood in the doorway with a jacket casually thrown over his shoulder. A pale blue shirt opened at the collar set off his dark tan. His dark hair was combed back and sleek. Damn, but he would've made a great GQ cover model.

"You gonna stand there staring or let me in?"

She grinned sheepishly and jumped back. "Well, come in, of course. I hope Chinese is okay?" Honestly, did he have to stare? His knowing gaze undressed her with every sweep up and down as if he could see right through her dress to the naughty lacy bits underneath.

He ambled inside and glanced around. "Love it. Smells great too."

"Cool," she blathered like a teenage girl on her first date. Scott was everything she'd ever wanted in a man. More than handsome and sexy, he was a good man. A family kind of man.

Sheesh. There was that word family again. Not exactly what she was looking for. Still, a hormone surge hit and left her warm and aching to take him on the spot. No man had ever had this effect on her. Not a single one.

He put his arm around her and pulled her close, kissing her lightly on the mouth. "You smell good, too."

Her legs weakened as if the bones had morphed into flimsy rubber bands. Unable to move from the spot, she watched him prowl around the small loft like a wolf patrolling his turf. Not once did he so much as glance toward the bedroom, even though he knew it well enough. What she really wanted was to rip off his shirt and her dress and get down to some serious lovemaking.

But no, he came for dinner.

First things first. After all, she had self-control. Of course, she did.

She grabbed the divider to steady herself, then managed to follow him into the loft. "You want dinner first or would you rather discuss the ViCAP findings?"

Why was this meeting so awkward? Last night, they'd made love. Yes, it was a quickie by necessity, but the sex had been hot, hot, hot…before she'd had to drag herself away to respond to a crime scene.

Actually, she was the one who was awkward, not he. Oh, no. He seemed perfectly at ease.

He turned. The intensity of his gaze shot through her to her core. Her inner muscles contracted. Oh, God. She wanted him now.

Calm down. Take a deep breath.

"I'm hungry." He waggled his eyebrows up and down.

What a silly, but sweet expression. "Dinner's ready then." She giggled and quickly turned away to attend to the food.

He threw down his jacket, took her by the wrist and pulled her close to his muscled chest. "Not so fast. I need another kiss. I've thought about you— and us—all day long. Couldn't get a damn thing done."

Shakily, she gazed up at him. "Is that so?"

Her heart rate spiked then settled into a ragged staccato rhythm. She took a deep breath. Damn the man—he smelled so good. Coffee and a hint of sandalwood aftershave. "I thought you wanted a kiss?"

He grinned like a naughty boy with his hand in the cookie jar. "Mm. I like a woman who's in a hurry. Don't worry. It's gonna be good. Guaranteed."

"Uh-huh. Sounds like all talk and no action to me."

He slanted his lips across hers, tenderly at first. She opened her mouth to his questing tongue. He pressed her up against the counter, his erection shoved firmly against her belly. So, she wasn't the only one ready for another go-round. She reached for his belt.

"Hold on, hon." He winked. "Dinner first."

She rubbed her pelvis against his erection. "This tells me you'd rather have me first."

"I would, but I'm on a mission. I'm not here to take advantage of you."

Confused by his comment, she pulled back. Dammit, he wanted her. There was visible, physical proof of it jabbing her belly. What had she done to turn him off? "It's business first then?"

"Duty first. You're familiar with the concept—no?"

Smarting a little from his rebuff, she nodded and eased from his embrace. "Here." She handed him the bottle of wine. "If you'll open it, I'll fix our plates. Then we can eat."

He set the wine bottle on the concrete counter and leaned back. Apparently, he wasn't quite ready to let things remain unsettled. "Don't be pissed. There's no need to rush. Let's take our time, with no interruptions. Plus, I sure don't want to be thinking about ViCAP files, when I'm going down—"

"You won't be going anywhere if you don't shape up. You definitely won't be going down—" she said, adding some major snark to her tone.

"Is waiting such a bad thing? I'm not here for a quick roll in the hay. I want it all, Tess. I want dinner with you across the table from me. I want— no need—to go over those cases using your crackerjack detective's brain. And finally, I want to love you like no one's ever loved you."

"Oh." She swallowed the hard lump in her throat. The man certainly had a way with words. Even if they sounded way too serious.

He grinned, his dark brown eyes glittering with desire as he watched her confusion. "But I can't help but be flattered you're anxious for another encounter, as you called it."

"You arrogant dope." She gave a huff and tossed a chopstick in his direction. He ducked and the damn thing clattered to the floor. She ran around the bar and scooped it up.

With an expression as serious as a heart attack, he stepped forward and held out his hand.

The oven timer beeped. She glanced at the stove. "Sorry. The dessert."

Thankful for the oven timer's giving him a brief reprieve, Scott took a deep breath. She raced around the bar to the kitchen, then bent over and opened the oven. Her flirty, short summer dress hiked up and gave him a view of slender thighs and a little bit of lace that didn't begin to cover the smooth, rounded cheeks of her ass.

Damn. He was hard as a brick and ready to be laid. He stepped behind the bar to hide his body's response and took a deep breath. Maybe counting backward?

Shut your eyes, fool.

"What's in the oven?" Better distraction than self-destruction.

She closed the oven door, straightened and smiled. "Dessert, but it's not done…yet."

He laughed. If she only knew. "As it so happens, dessert was on my mind as well."

She slanted him a sultry sideways glance. "I bet I know what's on your mind."

His mouth grew dry. He leaned his elbows on the counter and grinned. "You'd probably win that bet."

Her cheeks turned a pretty pink. Was he the reason for her blushes? Or was it the heat from the oven?

A little shyly, she fluttered her dark red lashes. "Maybe we'd better talk about something else?" As if he'd made her nervous, she proceeded to straighten the silverware, which was already straight, and refold the napkins.

Maybe? "How's the Hurley case going?" he asked. "Any more leads you want to share?"

Her expression grew serious. "Lots of leads. Nothing's panned out."

"He's dead by now?" The death of a young person never failed to sadden him and remind him of his parents' death and his missing sister.

How would the Hurley's manage to go on? Like everyone else who lost a family member too soon—and it was always too soon—they would manage somehow.

"Unless there's a miracle."

"Not many of those around nowadays." Still distracted, he picked up the wine and proceeded to open it. The cork popped slightly as he removed it.

"No." Tess held out her glass for him to fill. "You know, I've seen more death in my years on the job than most people see in a lifetime, but other than my grandparents, I've never lost any of my immediate family. Not like you have." She took a tiny sip from her glass, then licked the wine from her lips.

The sight of her tongue sent a bolt of lust to his groin. Keeping track of the conversation wasn't easy with a woman like Tess in the room. But he tried. "When it's sudden and totally unexpected, it's a sucker punch to the gut and the heart. So much to take in at once. Too much. Incomprehensible pain. With my folks, I wondered if they saw the car coming. If they suffered for even a few seconds? What were their last thoughts?"

She came over and put her arms around him. "I'm so sorry."

He cupped her ass and pulled her closer, inclined his head and kissed her, an easy gentle kiss which rapidly grew longer and deeper. His cock hardened until he was ready to explode. She opened her mouth to his and yanked his shirt from his pants. He loosened his hold on her long enough to whip the shirt over his head. Her slender long fingers splayed over his chest, then tweaked his nipples.

She slipped her dress straps over her shoulders and bared her breasts. He weighed them in his palms. Lush. Firm. Coral-tipped. Passion welled up in his chest and nearly choked him. "My God, you're beautiful."

"Make love to me. I don't want to wait."

He picked her up and carried her into the bedroom and laid her gently on the bed. Somehow, he managed to shuck his slacks and briefs, shoes and socks. He raised the skirt of her flirty dress and eased down her lacy panties. The crisp red curls at the apex of her thighs were already damp. Her thighs jittered at his touch and opened to him.

He inhaled her feminine musk, tempted to bring her to climax with his mouth alone. But no, she wanted more. She reached for his rigid shaft and cupped his balls.

"Wait." She reached into the bedside table and withdrew a condom. She opened the pack and sheathed his cock, then lightly caressed his balls. His entire body jerked in response to her touch.

"Now."

"No, not yet." He pulled the dress over her head, leaving her lush body to his unobstructed view. He centered his body over hers but resisted driving into her warmth. Starting at her neck, he left a trail of kisses, then sucked each tightly budded nipple. Underneath him, she writhed and twisted, clenching the bed linens in her fists and moaning her lust.

Mate of mine. She was his and had to be for all time. He could never give up this woman, no matter what. So generous with her touches, she had to feel the same.

He reached the core of her womanhood and flicked her clit, burying his nose in her musk. She tasted like a heaven he'd never known. She arched against him and moaned.

He slid a finger inside; her slick inner walls clutched at him, but he pulled out. "I have something better."

"Mm, please."

Feeling like a rampant stallion and close to losing it, he thrust deep. She took him fully, her inner walls adjusting to his size. Moved against him with slapping thrusts.

She met and matched his frantic pace. His mate in every way. Never could he desire another.

Her body gripped his and grew hot under him. The flame of desire centered in his groin; his breathing grew ragged. He tried to slow the pace, but she wouldn't stop clenching his cock, over and over with her rhythmic thrusts.

He rolled and flipped her over until she straddled his body. Her breasts bobbed in front of him. He levered onto his elbows and captured the budded nipple of one in his mouth. He nipped and raked the tender bud with his teeth.

She rode him. Hard.

Fast and furious, until his groin filled with sensations of passion and near pain. His body spasmed and pumped deep into hers. Above him, she cried his name and rode him until neither had the strength for more, then collapsed on his sweaty chest.

She felt so right in his arms, her soft breasts molded against his chest, her legs twined with his, her firm ass cupped in his palms, and the way their bodies fit together as one. He never wanted to leave her side.

"Tess O'Malley, I can see us spending our lives together like this. Just think our kids will have your red hair and my brown eyes. They'll be as beautiful as you are right now."

She stiffened in his arms and then pulled away. "Spending our lives together? Kids? Have you lost it?"

Desperate not to lose her, he straightened and sat up in bed. "What the fuck? I don't mean right this minute. Later...in a couple of years or so."

She swung her legs over the side of her bed. "I don't know what gave you the idea I was marriage material." Hands trembling, she started jerking on her clothes.

"But—"

"But nothing! This isn't a topic I wish to discuss...ever. I have a demanding career. Family and children aren't a part of my plans. What we're doing here is for fun and mutual enjoyment. That's all!"

He swung his feet to the cold floor, pulled on his slacks, fastened them and yanked up the zipper. "Excuse the hell outta me for wanting to spend my life with you. Never meant to insult you or ruin your life with my boring dreams." He jerked on his shirt, buttoned and tucked it inside his pants. He faced her once more. "Go ahead. Be a modern woman. See if I give a flying fuck what you do!"

"Get the hell out!" Tears shone in her eyes. Her face was red with emotion, her lithe body visibly shaking. Good thing she wasn't armed.

He turned, headed for the door, then stopped and turned. He sucked in a deep breath, still determined to make her see reason. "I'm sorry I upset you. I didn't mean...it was never my intention—"

"You know where that paved road goes. Just so we're clear. I never want to see you again. We're through."

"Fine." He'd rushed her and ruined a promising relationship to boot. *Way to go, dumbass.*

Without another word, he left her condo. Still, all things considered, she was so mad she could've shot him in the back. At least, he knew where she stood, but he wasn't a man who gave up easily. She might've won this skirmish, but he'd win the war and her heart along with it.

The heavy steel door slammed.

But the sound was nothing compared to the door slamming in Tess' heart.

Just when everything was going so well, he had to ruin it by demanding more than she could give.

Dammit.

Her fault entirely. Everything about the man and his life said *family.* Hell, he still lived with his brother and sisters. How five adults managed to live in one house and not trip all over each other was more than she could comprehend.

Space. Privacy. Career.

Those were the things she cherished. Words she lived by.

Yet if they were, why did she feel so empty and lost? As if all life had to offer had just stormed out the door.

No. Correction—as if she'd *shoved* all the good things life had to offer right out the door.

She raced back to the bedroom and collapsed on the bed, the sheets still warm from his body. Picking up the pillow, she inhaled his scent and began to sob.

Chapter Eighteen

The next morning, Tess breezed into the squad room and sat and stared at the dark computer screen. In the grand scheme of things, she'd barely known Scott Holt for a minute or two. He meant nothing. Just another pothole on the interstate of life. Wasn't denial a wonderful thing?

"Another bad night?" Kozinsky leaned over and tapped her shoulder. "You're looking a little freaky this morning."

She straightened. "Don't know what you mean. I'm dressed appropriately and coordinated. My makeup is flawless. My hair is always a trial, but that's a given."

"No. I mean your eyes. They're wild. Whirling around like a stripper's tassels. In different directions even." He tried to demonstrate with his fingers but failed.

"No such thing." She booted up her computer, slipped in a flash drive, then pulled up her interviews on the cold case. She'd distract Kozinsky with Jamison and let him continue thinking she didn't know shit from Shine-ola about the mystery witness.

"On the cold case, we need to buckle down. I figure Mason was our unsub's first kill. He was inexperienced. Maybe a little careless. Any clues he left behind will lead us to who he is today. Now this Tyler Jamison—"

"The TV news anchor?"

"Yes." She kept her tone crisp, like her manner. Relationships were a waste of time. Catching this unsub was a million times more important than a bust-up with some insignificant PI.

"I'm calling the station to get his résumé. I want to know where this joker's been from 1994 until the present day."

"You figure him for the doer?" Kozinsky scowled and shook his head.

"There's something not right with him. He refused a DNA swab. Wants an attorney. I figure his background could use a spotlight."

"It's plain to see you've got a bug up your ass this morning. Look, this Jamison guy is from around here. Appears our unsub has been all over the U.S. of A. What're the odds Jamison's been the same places and at the same time?"

"Well, we won't know until we do our homework, will we?" she snapped.

"Knock yourself out."

"Maybe it's a waste of time, but the sooner we get to it, the sooner we can eliminate him. If that's what we end up doing."

Kozinsky's phone rang. He answered and his voice rose with excitement. "You're sure it's Buddy Dawson. And he's there now?" She watched him scribble an address, then stand.

"Someone just dropped a dime on the Vandy fast food shooter. Says he's holed up at a cousin's house in Antioch. Let's go."

Scott walked into the office, nodded at Carrie, then headed for his brother's office. Naturally, Justin wasn't there.

"Where is he?"

Carried huffed and glared at him over her glasses. "Good morning to you, too."

"Sorry. Rough night."

"Oh, really?" Carrie smirked and her eyebrows rose. "Is he anyone I know?"

He waved his hands. No way was he sharing his pathetic love life with his sister. "No details."

Rough night indeed. After leaving Tess, he'd driven home and pored over the ViCAP case files for hours. The inability to get her off his mind had made most of those hours a waste. Why had he rushed things with her?

Why indeed?

He was overdue for a real relationship, and clearly, the lady in question wasn't interested.

Hell no, she wasn't.

"And you need Justin for what?" Carrie replaced her smirk with her business face, the one which, no matter what wild tale a client gave her, never varied. No shock. No humor. Polite interest at most.

He hesitated, then gave her the business face right back. "Some follow-up on an old case." Their brother's research skills made his involvement a given. "Notify me when he comes in."

"Sure, boss." Carrie flipped him the bird, a sure sign she thought he'd stepped over the arrogance line.

"Sorry." She'd every right to call him on his shitty attitude. After all, every member of their blended family was an equal partner in the agency, even if he was the nominal head.

His sister gave him another one of her eye rolls which pretty much said she'd overlook him one more time. He flashed a grateful grin in her direction and headed for his office.

Okay, gotta lighten up or everyone was gonna know Tess had dumped his ass.

Before Scott could finish checking his email, Justin rolled into the office. "You're a real jerk—you know?"

Startled, Scott glanced up. "What've I done to you?"

"My car gave up the ghost. And you...you passed right by me on West End. The least you could've done was stop and give me a ride. Hell no! You whizzed on by with your head in the clouds."

"Car? You dignify a 1954 Nash Metropolitan by calling it a car?" Scott grimaced. Honestly, he hadn't seen his brother. "It's a bile green lunchbox with wheels. The world's a better place without it."

"How could ya miss it?"

"Sorry." Damn, but he seemed to be saying sorry every time he turned around. "I didn't see you—no lie. How'd you get here?"

"Being the geeky type, I walked. Do you know how far—"

"Hold on. I've only been here ten minutes, so I know you didn't walk all the way."

His brother lounged in the doorway and laughed. "Nah. I caught a ride with a real doll on her way to work from Bellevue. By the way, she thought my car was cute and was so sorry for me she gave me her phone number. We have a date this weekend if I can get my motor running."

Scott snorted. "Your motor is always running—one way or another." He shrugged and shot his brother a thumbs up. "Good reason to get your hair cut."

Justin shook his head and ran his hands through his dark blond, sun-streaked, surfer-dude hair. "You'd be surprised how many like it this way."

"That's because of your vast research in the field of what women like?"

"Smartass. I don't see you spending too many nights away from home. Any-hoo—what's up? Carrie warned me you had a stick up your ass this morning."

"She didn't say that—not those exact words."

"No. That's what she implied." Justin grinned, then made a bow of obeisance. "How may I serve you, great master?"

Scott jerked his head toward the door. "Shut it." Justin's brow rose. He shut the door behind him, then ambled over and plopped down in a chair. "Secrets. What fun."

Unable to believe he was actually going to tell his brother what had happened, he paused. Ah, hell, might as well tell someone. "I—uh, screwed things up with Tess last night. She tossed me out on my ass."

"Must've been some screwup," Justin muttered and raised a brow.

"Afterwards...you know...I mentioned maybe having a family...someday."

His brother shook his head and screwed his face up like a little kid's. "What was the rush, dude?"

"Hell if I know. Then there was a big discussion—meaning she yelled, and I kept my damn mouth shut—about her career. Blah. Blah. Blah."

"Dude, keeping your mouth shut was the only thing you did right."

Scott shrugged. "Yeah, well..."

"Not that I'm an expert on career women, but give her some time to cool down. Can't hurt."

"Ya think?"

Tess was in his blood after a few hot minutes of the sweetest sex he'd ever had. And no chance of a repeat transfusion.

The Antioch neighborhood where the shooter was holed up ran along to I-24. Made up of hundreds of two and three-bedroom houses built back in the seventies, the crime rates in the subdivision had climbed steadily over the years as it became a hot spot of illegal immigrants and drug activity.

Buddy Dawson's cousin, wife, and two kids lived in a three-bedroom house on one of the shady streets, and Tess had a sneaking suspicion the cousin himself had dropped the dime just to get Dawson out of his house.

She pulled on her Kevlar vest with MNPD on back, then checked her service weapon. Full magazine and two extra in her belt. Houses were already evacuated on all sides of the target house. It was even money that Dawson was well-armed and not the least interested in conversation or giving up. SWAT was in position.

"Cover the back." Kozinsky nodded to two of the officers. He tugged on his vest. "Damn, if I'm not outgrowing this puppy."

"Told you. Too much of Estelle's good cooking and pizza," she joked, more to take the edge off her nerves than anything else. Her own vest fit snugly, but a vest was never a hundred percent. To relieve the escalating tension, she rolled her shoulders and looked from side-to-side. The flutters in her belly weren't about to go away. Not anytime soon.

Still, nerves kept you on your feet. Kept you sharp. Kept you alive.

A lieutenant from SWAT strode to where she stood with Kozinsky. "We've already checked the house with thermal imaging. There's only one person inside."

Kozinsky spoke first. "Then let's move. Door. Flashbang."

The south precinct commander came on the scene. "Let's give him a chance to surrender. Get him on the bullhorn."

"Hmph." Kozinsky curled his upper lip. "You didn't see the carnage he left behind at Wendy's. He's a shooter. Not exactly the conversational type."

"Well, the last thing we want is a suicide-by-cop situation," the precinct commander said. "Are we sure he doesn't have any hostages in there?"

"He's alone, Commander," Kozinsky insisted. "We're gonna need to storm the house."

Kozinsky was Tess' partner and had thirty years on the job. But did she agree?

No. But would she say so and contradict him in front of their fellow officers? Hell, no. Somehow, she had to urge caution. "Is the individual inside moving about?" she asked the SWAT commander.

"No."

"Suppose it's someone besides the shooter?" No need for a repeat of an incident like the one a couple of years earlier in a neighboring county. An assault team had invaded the wrong home, and the homeowner fearing a home invasion came out with his gun and was killed.

"Call him on the landline. If he doesn't answer, raise him on the bullhorn," the precinct commander ordered.

The SWAT negotiator called the number. Finally, after no response, he shook his head and disconnected. He raised the bullhorn. "Bud Dawson. This is the Metropolitan Police Department. You're surrounded. This doesn't have to turn nasty. Come on out with your hands in the air. You won't be harmed…if you do as instructed."

"Got movement on the thermal imaging. Heading to a window."

Further discussion was unnecessary.

The unmistakable sound of window glass breaking shattered the stillness of the hot, muggy summer afternoon. The spray of semi-automatic machine gun fire raked the front line of police vehicles.

She ducked for cover. "Damn," she muttered. "Guess he doesn't want to play nice."

A low growl emanated from her partner. "Didn't expect him to. Seeing as how he didn't play nice when he ordered a hamburger and then killed his wife and all those other folks."

Another burst of automatic fire. A grunt from her right.

Kozinsky.

"You're hit!"

"No shit." He frowned and swiped at the blood dripping from his ear.

"Just a graze."

"A half-inch to the left and your head would be sporting some serious ventilation. Ever hear the word duck?" Still, that was way too close.

Another burst of automatic fire. She peeked over the vehicle as SWAT launched a couple of flashbangs into the house. All around her, she could hear the rush of SWAT officers storming the house. "You going to be all right?"

"Reckon I could use a damn band-aid or two." Two paramedics ran forward with their gear.

"Got it."

Hungry. Thirsty. It must be mid-afternoon by now. He'd already pissed his pants twice, like a damn baby. Forced to lick a drop of water here and there from the leaves of a nearby bush.

Afraid to move. Danny's head said, *Run. He's gone.* But his gut instinct said, *Don't move. He's still out there. Waiting.*

But he'd have to make a move and soon. His shoulders were cramped from his hands being tied behind his back. His wrists rubbed raw to the bone. Leastways that's how it felt. Insects were investigating his wounds. He felt them crawling, biting. Legs nearly numb from being crouched all night and half the day.

Slow. Careful. Quiet. He managed to roll to his side and move his leaden legs out in front of him.

Stopped. Listened.

Nothing.

Would the feeling come back? Would he be able to run if it did?

Oh, God. Wave after throbbing wave of needles of pain as the feeling returned to his feet and legs. He bit his bottom lip to keep from squealing like a girl.

Finally, after what seemed like an eternity, the throbbing and pins and needles stopped. Over to his knees, he dug his shoes into the undergrowth and forced himself to his feet.

Waited. Listened.

Driving back and forth to the area where he'd let his choice get away was a bitch, but he couldn't afford to be missed. Somehow, he had to find that damn kid. No way could he risk leaving him alive.

His hand-held police scanner squawked. Nifty little thing. He'd bought it at Radio Rack Online for only four-hundred and nine-nine bucks. Kept him informed of all the latest police doings. He parked and turned on his mobile phone to check the news station.

"A shootout in Antioch. The Vandy fast food shooter is dead from a self-inflicted gunshot wound." At least this was one occurrence where they weren't focused on him and his present choice. Big city like Nashville. Crimes didn't come one at a time. There was the Metro spokesman telling all the viewers about the death of the shooter and the homicide detective who was wounded slightly in the melee. In the background footage, he made out the figure of the redheaded detective bending over her partner. Then the spokesman said she and her partner were both involved in the investigation of the death of young Todd Brennerman, the governor's grandson.

"Hmph." *Come and get me, Red. That'll be the day.*

Hold on. Was the rustling an animal or his choice? He eased open the door.

More noise. A twig snapped. The chase was on!

Chapter Nineteen

Except for the paperwork, the fast-food shooter was a closed case, but instead of completing the paperwork, she pulled out the sheaf of papers spit out from the ViCAP database.

Ten bodies recovered all with one shoe missing. If she could place Tyler Jamison at any of those locations in the timeframe of the murders, she'd be on her way to the Assistant DA for an arrest warrant. She grabbed the phone and punched in the news anchor's work number.

Voice mail. Damn. How late did a morning news person work anyway? Seems like they started the show at five, so they must have to be in bed pretty early to be so energetic and on air that early.

She tried his home number. Same deal. No answer. This time, she left a message to return her call. She glanced at her watch—already seven. God. Where had the day gone? Ready to Google Tyler Jamison's name and the locations, she first checked the bios on the station's website.

Ah ha. Jamison graduated from MTSU in 1994. Went to grad school in Miami, majoring in Broadcast Journalism. In 1996, he worked in Newark as a field reporter for a local station and then as the Denver morning news anchor in 1999. Back to Tennessee, in 2005, where he took over the anchor chair of News Channel Nine.

Some of the timeframes were right on, but there were a lot of holes in his website bio. Dammit. She needed to re-interview him in the worst way.

Before she could research further, her cell rang. Lo and behold. Tyler Jamison's name showed on the caller ID.

"Detective O'Malley. Thank you for returning my call so promptly, Mr. Jamison." She waited. Let him stew a few seconds.

"I—uh, talked with Legal here at the station. I'm ready to answer your questions."

"Great. Where and when?"

"Somewhere private. I'd rather not come down to the police station unless you insist." His tone was hushed, as if afraid of being overheard.

"Not necessary. I'll be happy to drop by your house." She couldn't blame him for wanting to keep his being questioned on the QT.

"That won't work for me either."

Come on. Quit playing around. "You name the place."

"Uh, I have a small rental apartment. Close to the station…I use it when I have to spend the night away from home."

Yeah, right. She could just imagine what went on in the apartment. "Okay, give me the address. I'll meet you there in fifteen minutes. Can you manage that?"

"Yes," he said softly, giving her the address, then adding, "I'll be there."

Fifteen minutes later, she pulled into the underground parking garage of the apartment building where Jamison's rental was located. She rode the elevator to the tenth floor and stepped out into a long, plain vanilla hallway. Verifying the room number he'd given her, she turned right and walked about halfway down the beige carpeted hall and knocked on apartment 1021.

The door opened immediately. "Did anyone see you?" Jamison asked, glancing up and down the hall. "Not a soul. Haven't observed anyone since entering the building."

"Good." He stepped back and allowed her to enter. The beige color scheme carried over into the living area of the studio apartment. A more drab and uninspiring place for a session of afternoon delight she'd never seen. "I'm going to record this. Won't bother you, will it?"

"No." He shook his head emphatically.

"Didn't figure it would," she said with a smile, "since you're around mics and recording equipment every day."

"Let's get it over with then." He motioned her to have a seat on the puffy beige sofa and seated himself on the matching side chair.

Tess sunk and settled on the cushy sofa, then pulled the small digital recorder from her purse. She turned it on and set it on the out-dated brass and glass coffee table. "First, I would like to just fill in your background. For example, where you've been since the Mason boy was killed back in 1994. I checked your bio on the station website, but there were a lot of holes time-wise."

His jaw tightened until she could plainly see the cords in his neck. "My assistant will be happy to provide you with an up-to-date CV."

"In the meantime, why don't you just bring me up to speed? Afterward, I'd like to talk about the night Rich Mason disappeared from Camp Einstein."

"I graduated from MTSU's broadcast journalism department in '94 or was it '95? No—'94." He nodded sharply as if certain of the year. "I did my graduate work at the University of Miami's School of Communication where I received my MA in Broadcast Journalism in 1996."

"Is that a good school?"

"One of the best." Jamison straightened and shot her an arrogant glance as if she should've known. "After I graduated, I moved to Newark, New Jersey and worked for a station there. In 1997, my wife and I moved to Chicago and spent two years there."

"When did you marry?"

"Right after I was awarded my master's degree."

"And after Chicago?"

"Denver."

His career path was right on track for the unsub's list of victims. Was it a matter of bad timing or was he her serial killer? "How did your wife feel about moving all over the country with your job?"

He frowned as if he didn't quite know where she was going with her line of questioning. He grimaced; his jaw muscles clenched. "She wasn't crazy about it. We separated for a time."

"While you were in Chicago?"

"No, when I was assigned to the L.A. market. She moved back to Nashville and took a position with a local PR firm."

Given the increase in the L.A. body count, the separation could have been a stressor. "How long were you separated?"

"Off and on for the two years I was there. I'd come back home. We'd reconcile for a day or two, but she wouldn't leave her job. I had a firm contract, so I couldn't leave mine, either. One of my trips home, she got pregnant, so we decided to stay together. My contract with the L.A. station was ready to expire in 2002. I tried to find something here in town, but Kansas City was as close as I could get. But in 2005, I was offered the morning anchor position here in Nashville and jumped at it."

"So, your wife was glad to have you home, I guess."

"You could say that." His tone was flat. His facial expression matched, except for his gaze which shifted quickly from side-to-side.

"How are you getting along now?"

Jamison's shoulders grew rigid. He scowled. "Where are you going with these questions, Detective?"

She shrugged casually but never took her gaze from his. The man was hiding something. Had to be. "This is just background stuff." She kept her tone reassuring to keep him calm and away from calling an attorney.

"This is regarding the cold case?" A certain degree of wariness flitted across his chiseled features. "Let's see if I can get this right. You've identified similar cases and you're trying to match my places of employment. How many more cases are there? Come on, Detective. I'm not stupid. I know how these things work. You're trying to pin this on me." He stood and began to pace back and forth in the small living area.

"You have something to hide?" She smiled, hoping to pull him from the ceiling. "For now, why don't we just focus on the Mason case?" She pulled out her notebook. "From our last meeting, you said Scott Holt was at the campfire, Drew Wilson and Dakota Taylor didn't attend the campfire. Where were you the night Rich Mason disappeared from Camp Einstein?" So far everything he'd said matched with Drew Wilson's memory of the night in question, as well as Scott's.

"Sorry to disappoint you, but I stayed at the campfire with Scott. We waited for a long time. Most of the kids grew bored and went back to their cabins before the eclipse ever started."

"You and Holt were together the entire time?"

"Yes, we waited until the eclipse was full, then we put out the fire and headed to our cabin."

"Who was there when you returned?"

"It was pitch-black…so I don't remember seeing anyone. We didn't turn on the lights, out of consideration for our fellow counselors."

How convenient. So, someone could've been absent, and no one would've noticed. "What was your relationship with Rich Mason?"

"No particular relationship. He was just another smarter-than-average kid at the camp. One of many. Made no real impression on me at all."

"None?"

"See here, Detective. It was a long time ago."

Okay, his face was flushed, and she could almost smell the stink of fear on him. "How did Legal react when you told them about the investigation?"

"They advised me to cooperate fully—hence, this meeting. They're supportive of me. We report the news without assigning guilt or innocence. As an employee, I'm afforded the same courtesy."

"How fortunate." For show, she consulted her notes again. "Tell me. In your office, wasn't there a photograph of you with Todd Brennerman, the governor's grandson?"

"I knew who Todd Brennerman was. He attended Camp Einstein, and I've acted as a professional consultant for the camp. Did presentations for career day—that sort of thing."

"You're involved in a lot of activities with young people—especially males in their late teens."

"Right. Again, I know where you're going," he said through clenched teeth.

"Do you? Why don't you tell me then?"

"You want to know if I'm in the closet, hiding my homosexuality behind my wife and children. Let me assure you…I'm not. I married my high school sweetheart. We've had our share of troubles, but we've managed to keep our family afloat."

"Where were you yesterday between twelve and seven?"

"I was on camera interviewing your department spokesperson from seven on."

"Yes, I caught your dog and pony show."

"You think I had something to do with Danny Hurley's disappearance? My God, you really think I'm guilty of something—don't you?"

"Remains to be seen. By the way, I need that DNA sample."

"Gladly, Detective. Swab away." He opened his mouth. His icy gaze sparked with a flash of heat for once.

Before he could change his mind or lawyer-up, she pawed through her purse for the DNA kit. On retrieving it, she swabbed his mouth thoroughly. "Thank you for your cooperation." She carefully sealed the DNA sample and labeled it. "And your whereabouts from noon until seven?"

Jamison scowled and pulled out his PDA. A few taps on the screen. "My schedule as follows. I co-hosted *Talk Around Town* from eleven-thirty to twelve-thirty. After that, I had lunch with my wife. You may verify that with her."

"Where and how long?"

"Ichabod's. She dropped me off at the station at two. I checked my messages and emails, scanned the incoming bulletins until three. I left then and got home at five. Was called out to the Hurley scene around six-forty-five."

"Isn't that unusual? Aren't you the morning guy? Why would you get called out in the evening?"

"It's summer, Detective. *Vacations*." He shot her an expression that clearly told her he thought she was too stupid for words. "And it was a missing teen-breaking news thing."

"If it bleeds, it leads?"

"Sad but true."

Funny. He didn't look sad. But she hadn't forgotten his schedule gap. "What about from three to five?"

"Traffic. I-65 was heavy. That's how long it took me to get home to Brentwood."

"At three? Not exactly rush hour, is it?"

He glanced around the room. Pulled at his collar. "I've nothing to add, Detective." He stood.

She rose. If he was through talking, he was through. "Thank you so much. If I come up with more questions, I'll give you a call."

"Fine." His fingers beat a tattoo against his thigh. "If you don't mind going ahead…"

"You'd rather not be seen leaving with me?" On her way to the door, she shot him a knowing smile. "Sure, no problem." So,he had the leaving separately routine down pat. Now, who was the supposedly happily-married news anchor fooling around with?

Chapter Twenty

Running. Running. Running.

A part of him was tempted to give up and let the perv do what he would.

No! Keep running.

Sweat ran down in his eyes. Burning. Blinding. Couldn't wipe it away.

His heart pounded so loud in his ears it was a wonder the perv couldn't hear it and find him that way. He gasped for air. What time was it? It was getting dark again. How long had he been running? Felt like a full marathon. Lying low for two nights and two days had sapped his strength. No water or food. Still, he could outrun that big lumbering freakazoid who was still out there just waiting to pop out and play his twisted games.

Not on this dude!

He'd read between the lines in the newspaper. Old Freako was a nasty piece of work.

Where the fuck was he, anyway? Damn woods. Damn big woods. He gasped as he ran. Didn't dare stop and listen. Couldn't risk it.

Never see his mom again or Sophie. Hell. Right now, he'd blubber like a baby if he could just see his dad one more time.

Branches scratched his face. Mosquitoes had dined on him like he was a super-size meal. God only knew what else had nibbled on him during the night. He itched but couldn't scratch. God. He wanted to scratch.

Maybe he should say the rosary or something. No. Couldn't spare the breath.

Never go camping again. Never. Ever.

Wait. Was that daylight ahead? Was he coming to the end of the woods? The end of shelter?

Daylight. But the sun was going down. He shuddered. Could he stand another night in the woods?

No. Water and food. His gut growled. Not the first time.

Reaching the perimeter of the forest, he slowed his pace. Wouldn't do to run right out and into Freako's arms.

Geez Louise, what a day of contrasts. One bad guy down. Another still out there somewhere. A teenager still missing. Over twenty-four hours. Most likely dead and buried.

Just like her budding relationship with Scott.

She turned on the television, and Danny Hurley's parents were on the ten o'clock news pleading for their son's return. Waste of time. In her gut, she knew it was the same unsub. No matter what the MNPD's official take was on his disappearance. In addition to being one sick SOB, this one was intelligent and organized. He didn't keep his victims alive for long.

First thing tomorrow, she'd present the lieutenant with a rundown on all the ViCAP case files of similar cases. He'd have to call in the Feds. This string of murders required a profiler. Too late for Danny Hurley and Todd Brennerman.

But please, let them be the last.

She padded over to the fridge and pulled out a bottle of water. After twisting off the cap, she aimed for the trash and tossed it.

Damn. Damn. Damn.

Scott wasn't worth the hassle. No man was.

A deep sob wrenched from her chest. Surprised as hell. Who knew she'd grown to care so much? What was it about the man that touched her so deeply? Intelligent. Funny when he wasn't being obtuse. A good man. Cared about his family. Just the kind of man most women wanted to settle down with.

But no! Their goals just didn't jive. He wanted a family—a wife and two-point-five kids. As the child of a career law enforcement officer, she knew the job and how much the partner had to put up with. Who knew if her parents' marriage would've survived if her mother hadn't been such a strong and independent woman with a career of her own?

Scott leaned back in his chair and yawned. He'd watched one of the popular forensic crime shows. Man-oh-man. Those were some dedicated CSIs. Wish the real world was more like television. DNA reports in less than an hour or even seconds, instead of days or weeks. Now that would be cool.

He picked up the remote, then set it back down. Might as well watch the local news and see if there were any new developments in the latest kidnapping. He heard the newscaster say, "Local authorities say no real leads in the kidnapping of Danny Hurley," and promptly dozed off.

He woke up during the sports spot. A familiar name? He hit the reverse button on the DVR and watched again.

"Dakota Taylor of the Columbus Jackals has been spotted out and about Music City. Are the Titans looking to hire him or is he angling for a new team closer to his old stomping grounds after all his years in Ohio?"

Good question. So, the gang was all in town. Now that was something Tess ought to know. He reached for his cell phone, then stopped. He doubted she'd welcome his call or that she'd had enough time to cool off.

"You're gonna want to see this, dude." Justin ambled in, carrying a pile of paper that resembled a manuscript gone wild more than anything else. He plopped it beside Scott's elbow on the side table. "You were busy with those two new clients this afternoon, so I brought the rest of it home."

Startled by the massive printout, he sat and stared. "What the hell?"

His brother perched on the arm of the couch and leaned forward, his eyes sparkling with excitement. "Like I told you. ViCAP reports on similar M.O.s and victims. From all over the place. Lots more still missing that fit the victimology." He leveled his gaze on Scott. "You know you've gotta take this to Tess."

"Not gonna happen." Scott shook his head. Metro's investigation wasn't his responsibility. His client was. "She has access to ViCAP. Hell, she's the one who pointed us in the right direction. What I'm gonna do is call our client and give him what we have so far. In turn, he'll notify Ned's attorney so we can turn our information over to him."

"But it would be a good way to see if she's calmed down a bit. Huh? Huh?" Justin grinned and nudged Scott's shoulder.

He snorted. "Calmed down? You kiddin' me? Probably shoot me on sight."

"Might've reconsidered." Justin slid off his perch onto the sofa, stretched out his legs and propped his feet on the coffee table.

"Doubt it. Metro's been pretty busy. Besides, she spelled out her views on career and marriage. Captain by forty says it all."

Before Justin could respond, Scott's cell phone sounded. "All work and no play," he grumbled and yanked the thing off his belt. Tyler Jamison, according to caller ID. Wonder what he wanted?

"Scott Holt."

"Hey, man. This is Ty Jamison."

"Yeah?"

"Gotta talk to you." The morning news anchor's tone certainly wasn't as resonant as the one he used on-air, slightly on edge. What was that about?

"Anytime tomorrow. I'll ask Carrie to work you in."

"No, like now."

"Look, dude, it's late."

"I wouldn't ask if I wasn't desperate."

Scott glanced at his brother, then shrugged. "All right. Come on." He snapped the phone shut.

Justin raised his brow. "What?"

"Beats me. Ty Jamison's on his way over here. Urgent. Couldn't wait 'til tomorrow." He shrugged as if he had no idea, but actually, he did. Ty was on Tess's suspect list for the cold case. She must've gotten around to rattling his cage.

And rattled it good.

When Scott let Jamison inside, the news anchor was shaky and flushed. Was he having a heart attack? Scott motioned for the news anchor to have a seat in the den, but instead of sitting, he shook his head and paced.

"Hold on. Are you trying to wear out the hardwood or are you going to get around to telling me why you're so agitated? Preferably, sometime tonight?" Hell, that didn't sound too hospitable, did it? "Want a beer? Something stronger?"

His guest sucked in a breath, then exhaled. "Stronger."

Scott stood, then walked over to the corner cabinet the family used as a makeshift bar. "Whiskey?"

"Fine."

He poured two fingers into a glass and handed it over. Jamison took it with two shaky hands and sucked it down like mother's milk. Might as well have given him turpentine for all the attention his late-night guest paid to the best whiskey Tennessee had to offer.

"You're making me nervous." Scott jerked his head toward the couch. "Go on. Have a seat." He stifled a yawn, then sat. "Suppose you start at the beginning."

"That detective—O'Malley. She thinks I'm some kind of sick monster."

Suddenly, sleep didn't seem like such a desirable option. He leaned forward. "What makes you think that?"

"She all but accused me of killing that Mason kid and the governor's grandson—and a whole bunch of others. She grilled me about where I'd worked and how long I'd spent each place. Hell. I've worked all over. Something tells me she's got a long list of other cases up her sleeve."

An image of Justin's stack of ViCAP cases filled his mind's eye. "So, you let her question you. Did she swab for DNA?"

"Yeah. Didn't want to, but Legal at the station said to do it, so I did." He shrugged as if to say, you know what they're like.

"So, what do you need with me?"

"I need to hire you. Find out what she has on me—not that there's anything. Not really."

Not really? That usually meant there was something. Maybe not murder, but something.

Scott shook his head. As much as his curiosity was piqued, he couldn't let Jamison continue. "Sorry. I can't represent you." Why did he have to be so ethical? Just once, why couldn't he take Jamison on long enough to find out what he was hiding? Against the rules in his PI handbook—page thirty-two, paragraph three.

"Come on. We go way back." The pleading sound of Jamison's voice twanged uncharacteristically for a news anchor. Sweat beaded on his forehead.

"It would be a conflict of interest…if I took your case."

"Someone else involved has already retained you?"

He nodded. "Can't say who though."

Jamison sprang from the couch and resumed pacing. "Man, I can*not* believe you won't help me. We've known each other for years."

"That's the way it goes. I can recommend someone—another agency. He's a good guy. You can trust him with whatever you're hiding."

"Hiding? What makes you think—?"

"Come on, Jamison. I'm a detective. Used to reading body language."

"You think I'm capable of doing what this killer's done?"

"No, but I can't handle two clients whose interests could be in conflict." He grabbed his PDA off the side table and opened it. "Paul Gendron. His office is in the same building as ours. I'll even give him a head's up to expect your call." He read off the number.

Jamison's hands trembled as he entered the number in his PDA. "Thanks." He replaced it and withdrew a handkerchief from his inner pocket, mopping his brow.

Scott stood, more than ready to get rid of his old acquaintance. Jamison's comment "Known each other for years" was a wild exaggeration. They'd had little contact except through the soccer league. "Go home. Call Paul tomorrow."

"Yeah." Jamison's gaze shifted back and forth. Shifty eyes—not good for a TV on-air news anchor.

"You okay to drive? We can watch a game or something if you're not."

"Yeah. I'm all right." Jamison held his arms out like a damn tight-rope walker and headed for the door. In spite of everything, his gait was steady and straight.

"I'm no State Trooper, but I guess you pass," Scott said, anxious to dig into the guy's work history and compare it with the ViCAP files, but he didn't want to risk anyone's life in the process.

He waited until his friend drove off, then walked over to the stairs leading to the second floor. "Justin!"

His brother emerged from his bedroom and leaned his head over the railing. "You bellowed?"

"Work to do. Bring down those case files, ASAP." He didn't wait for a response. Instead, he headed back to the den and cleared the newspapers and sports magazines from the coffee table.

The sound of Justin's shuffling downstairs reached him. Good. Another avenue for inquiry. Given the fact Metro still considered Ned their prime suspect, poor guy needed all the help he could get.

Laden with the stack of ViCAP printouts and a laptop, Justin ambled into the den. Scott quickly brought his brother up to date about Tyler Jamison's visit. "I had to turn him away, but he's given me an idea."

"Let me guess. Compare Jamison's work history with the case files?"

"Exactly. And another thing—just heard it tonight—Dakota Taylor's in town. His team has played in all the major cities. See if you can correlate his team's schedule with the other cases as well. Can we get that done by tomorrow morning?"

"Tomorrow morning? Are you nuts? You want me to go back over ten to twelve years of football schedules, too?" Justin eyeballed Scott and grinned. "I know. That's why you pay me the big bucks, bro."

"I'll help."

"Yeah, right. You know, if you hadn't rushed things with your detective, you could already have the intel."

"Too late now."

"Too late now," Justin mimicked somewhat wryly, then set his laptop on the coffee table. "Okay, Tyler Jamison, morning news anchor, let's see what you've been up to for the last fourteen years." His tone drifted lower into on-air news anchor depth. Scott watched as his brother's long fingers danced over the keyboard.

"Jamison won't take long," Justin said, then leaned back to watch. "We have ten definite bodies found with one shoe missing and a ton of missing guys in their late teens."

"Stick to the ones recovered with a missing shoe," Scott said. "We don't have time for the rest."

"Points, where the victims converge with dates Jamison was in the vicinity, coming right up."

"Like ordering a steak for dinner," Scott groused. He'd never understand how his brother managed everything.

"Only if you know what you're doing." His brother's cheeky reply was punctuated with a broad smile.

An hour later, Scott had nodded off.

"Wake up, sleepyhead." Justin prodded Scott's shoulder. "Here we go. Points of convergence include one in Miami, two outside Savannah. Then, Newark

1996 two victims; Chicago 1997 one victim; Denver

1999 one victim; L.A. 2000 four victims. Holy shit. Had a field day in la-la land. Good buddy Tyler Jamison was employed in all those markets at the times the victims disappeared and were found. As for Dakota, I'll work him up in the morning. The office computer's faster and it won't take as long."

Scott nodded and leaned back. Damn. The sheer numbers of male victims in their late teens, sodomized and strangled, stunned him. Why hadn't the FBI been notified? Why wasn't a federal profiler crawling all over this case?

A loud knock at the door shook Scott. He glanced at his watch. Five after one. He yawned, pulled his aching body from the chair and shuffled to the front door. Through the glass, he could make out the form of two men. Tall. Broad-shouldered. Dark suits and ties. At one in the morning.

Maybe his visitors could answer his questions if they were of a mind to. He held back his misgivings and opened the door for the Feds.

"Special Agent Michael Chase," the taller and older of the two said, then nodded at the younger agent, who was so scrubbed, polished, and earnest, it hurt Scott's eyes. "Special Agent Derek Havens." Both agents showed their badges. Scott read them carefully. Yeah, they were Feds all right.

"Nice badges, fellows." He tried for a little levity, but from the grim expressions across their faces, neither appeared to have anything resembling a sense of humor. Then again, they were the Feds. "Come on in. I'll put on the coffee."

"Not necessary."

"My brother and I were just about to turn in. What can we do for you?"

"For a start," Agent Chase began, "you will turn over the ViCAP files you obtained illegally. We'll go from there."

Fuck.

Chapter Twenty-One

The Feds followed Scott into the den. "My brother, Justin Lackey." He nodded once toward his brother. "Go on. Hand 'em over."

Justin complied, but from his crossed eyes, it was clearly not his preferred game plan.

"Have a seat, Agents." Chase and Havens declined. Hell, it was gonna be a long night. Stifling a yawn, Scott managed, "I'm glad to see you fellows—excuse me—agents on top of this case. My brother and I were wondering why you weren't tracking this creep."

The oh-so-earnest Agent Havens bristled and shot a stern expression in Scott's direction. Wonder if he practiced it before a mirror? Had to. It was an exact replica of Agent Chase's.

From Chase's clenched jaw, he was obviously pissed. He took a deep breath before speaking. "We *are* tracking him—"

"Yeah? Took you long enough to get here. Does Metro know you're here?"

"And your investigation ends, effective immediately," Chase said, ignoring Scott's question about Metro.

"No way." Scott shook his head. "I have a client who's been arrested for murder, and it's my responsibility to see he gets his money's worth." Okay technically his client, Paul Whitten, wasn't the one arrested for murder, but same diff.

Havens collected the pile of ViCAP reports, while Chase eyeballed Scott. "Holt, you get in our way? We'll hold you for obstruction of justice…not to mention unauthorized hacking into a federal database."

Hands behind his head, Justin leaned back on the sofa and propped his feet on the coffee table. "I don't suppose you wanna share some of your best guesses, do ya?"

"Justin," Scott warned. Dammit. His brother should know better than to piss off the Feds. But what he wouldn't give to know what they already knew.

"Guesses?" Agent Havens perfectly shaped eyebrow shot up. "You have no idea what you're dealing with."

"Talking about yourselves or the unsub?"

"Both."

"I disagree." Scott gestured for the agents to have a seat but neither agent took the hint. "From what we've found, the unknown subject is an organized, extremely intelligent, homosexual sadistic killer. His first kill was here, and I was at the camp when Rich Mason disappeared. I know what we're dealing with. He's killed young males in their late teens all over the country, and he takes one of their shoes as a souvenir. Now, he's come back where he started. How am I doing, so far?"

Agent Haven's gaze darted sideways to Agent Chase as if he didn't quite know what to make of Scott's lowdown on their case.

Agent Chase leveled his gaze on Scott. "You are to forget all of this. The fact he leaves a shoe behind is—"

"Was leaked to the local media back then. You forget, Nashville had his first kill and the last one was the governor's grandson. The department may be holding something back like an eyewitness, but evidently, everyone and their brother knew about the missing shoe."

"Eyewitness?" Chase's tone had no inflection, but his icy blue eyes blazed with interest. He sat on the edge of the coffee table. "You'd better tell us everything you know."

"Doug Silvey, supposed eyewitness, didn't exist until two years ago. My brother located a birth certificate—matter of public record—for a Richard Douglas Silvey, born 1975, Lancaster, PA, who died two weeks later."

The federal agents cast glances at each other. Must've hit a button with Silvey. Good to know.

"I've spoken with my client's attorney, and if I'm not mistaken, Ned Forbes hasn't been documented anywhere near half of those vicinities. I hope you're going to give me some good news like you'll order Metro to release him.'"

"We have taken over jurisdiction in this case, but it suits our purposes for Metro to keep Mr. Forbes in custody while we locate the unsub. We don't want him taking off again."

"There's another possible victim."

"We're aware." Agent Chase stood, nodded to Havens, then darted his gaze toward the door. "Federal Building. Ten a.m. We'll take your official statements then."

After watching the Feds walk out the door with their ViCAP files, Justin turned to Scott, then jumped. "Hot damn! We were onto something. Close. Man, we were close!"

"Go on. Get some sleep," Scott said. "I'm calling Paul right now. He needs to know we have good news at last."

Good news of a sort. The Feds weren't looking at Forbes as the killer, but whether or not they could find the killer before he acted again or high-tailed it out of town was another matter.

Hopelessly lost and disoriented, Danny skirted the perimeter of the woods until it grew so dark he was afraid to move. Nothing but fields and farmland as far as he could see. Couldn't bring himself to leave the cover and safety of the woods. He hunkered down for the night completely exhausted, his mouth dry as dirt and his arms numb from the shoulders down.

The only good thing—he hadn't heard the freako move around in hours and hours. Maybe he'd given up. Maybe he hadn't.

Tears trickled down his cheeks. In the morning, he promised. Try again. Sooner or later, he had to come across a house or a road. Roads went somewhere. Houses had phones.

If only the perv hadn't taken his cell phone away. Not that his hands were in any condition to use it.

In spite of tossing and turning all night, Tess eased into the office at seven. Last night, she'd been tempted to call Scott and give him another piece of her mind. But she couldn't risk it. Couldn't risk hearing his voice and falling under his sultry spell again. Instead, she developed her current game plan. Basically, she'd go over the photos from the Hurley's digital camera. There might be a clue there. Someone always present but maybe didn't belong. Then she would drop the ViCAP reports in the boss's lap and demand that he admit he'd arrested the wrong man.

That was the plan.

She unlocked her desk, opened the file drawer. Her mouth dropped open. No ViCAP reports, no case file. Every single thing related to her cold case and the Brennerman case was gone, including the mystery eyewitness' statement. Luckily, she still had the flash drive backup.

At that moment, Kagen drifted into the squad room with a cup of coffee in one hand and two donuts in the other. "You look like hell. Is it the case or the cute PI?"

Instead of answering, Tess stood and headed to the lieutenant's office. His door was closed. Dammit, she didn't care. She rapped twice and barged in. The lieutenant had guests.

Surprise. Surprise.

Two tall men in black suits. So, the Feds had finally arrived. How timely of them. Lieutenant Woods scowled at her and shook his head. "Not now, O'Malley."

"Aren't you going to introduce me?"

Woods did the minimum of intros. They were indeed Feds. Special Agent Chase was a choice specimen of federal manhood. Close to forty. Dark brown hair, icy blue eyes, square jaw—the whole nine yards. Now the young and juicy Agent Havens, he was another matter. He was more on the prime side than choice with wavy light brown hair and warm brown eyes. The mental image of two sides of beef sprung to her mind. With effort, she held back the giggle that wanted so much to erupt. They'd never appreciate her peculiar sense of humor…at their expense no less.

Hands on her hips, she said, "Just being a plain old detective and not a special government agent, I surmise my missing files are in your good hands. Would I be right?"

"Your assumption would be correct, Detective." This from the prime cut who gave her a flicker of a smile. Had to give him credit. His gaze warmed just a tad.

The choice cut ignored her and turned to the lieutenant. "A profiler is coming from D.C. He's already familiar with the previous case files which your detective was so astute in pulling from the ViCAP database. We'll bring him up to date on the two new local victims—"

"Now hold on a second." She glanced at Woods. "Sorry, boss, but my partner and I have done all the footwork."

"The FBI has jurisdiction in this case," the lieutenant said, giving her the fish-eye. "That's all I'm saying in the matter."

"Begging your pardon, sir. Being cut out of the case like this—it's not fair."

"Not being fair is someone stealing your dolly," Woods said. "These gentlemen are federal agents, and they happen to have jurisdiction. Now get out of here."

Agent Prime Cut Havens cast his gaze to the floor, while Agent Choice Cut Chase stared her down.

She lifted her shoulders in a casual shrug. "Had to try, didn't I?" Glancing from beneath her lashes, she was rewarded with a wider smile from Agent Havens.

Maybe she could work him to her advantage. No way was she staying off this case.

He sat at the desk for a while and considered what to do next. His choice had gotten away. Damned kid could give the police a description. If he was ever found.

Dammit. If things had gone as planned, his life would've gone on as usual. Only one thing left to do—bid Mommie-not-so-dear a fond farewell. It would have to make up for losing his choice.

Finally, he'd get even. Every time he'd misbehaved or dressed up in her clothes or tottered around in her special shoes, she'd locked him in the closet with all her shoes. Even now, he could smell the stink of all her shoes in that confined space.

Yes. It was time to say, 'Buh-bye' to her and to Nashville.

***

At a quarter to ten, Scott and Justin parked in front of the FBI field office on West End. He gave his brother the once over. He was on the pale side, more than usual. "You all right?"

"Yeah, sure. The Feds are getting ready to reformat our hard drives…or worse." He banged his fist against his knee. "I'm fucking fine."

"Shouldn't be that bad."

"Ri-ight." Justin drew out the word until it was two syllables and glanced over his shoulder. "Just hope they don't use electrical shock to make us forget whatever they think we know."

"Don't be so paranoid." He flashed his brother a wide smile. "They won't incarcerate us for more than ten to twenty years."

The color leached from Justin's face. "You're kiddin, right? I know you are."

"Yeah." He nodded, but he wasn't sure. They'd hacked into a federal database. Had to be a violation of at least a couple dozen federal laws. "Come on. Let's get it over with."

Justin shook his head in disbelief, but he couldn't hide the visible shiver that shook the rest of his body. "You're the boss."

"You can always take the fifth."

"Gee, that's the best you can offer? Didn't you almost finish law school?"

He grinned. Not that he blamed his brother. If he had to make an educated guess, the Feds were more interested in what he and Justin knew than in what they'd done.

A guy could hope—right?

They entered the building and gave their names. All too quickly, they were given visitor badges and escorted to Special Agents Chase and Havens. At least they weren't handcuffed on sight. Had to be a good sign.

The grim-faced agents split them up, and they were shown to two interview rooms. Justin went with Agent Havens, leaving Agent Chase for Scott's interview. He walked into the room. Dammit. Two-way mirror, A/V recording devices—the whole nine yards. Divide and conquer—the oldest interrogation tactic in the book.

Agent Chase sat, placed a folder on the table just out of Scott's reach and gave him a friendly smile. "Coffee? Water?"

Leaning back, Scott shook his head. More tactics. "Don't bother. My prints have been on file with the state since I earned my PI license, and my DNA sample is somewhere at the State Lab as we speak." He had O'Malley to thank for that. "So, what else can I do for you?"

Frowning, Agent Chase opened the file and pulled out a stack of photos. "These were taken at Danny Hurley's last two ballgames. I'd appreciate your taking a look. Is there anyone unfamiliar in the background or just seems out of place?"

Hot damn. They were more interested in what he knew. He nodded his willingness and the agent slid the photos across the table.

"Most of the people I know are parents. The teams play on different fields at different times. I understand Danny Hurley was on an older team, so I'm not necessarily familiar with all those folks. But I'll give it a shot." He scanned each enlarged photo, focusing on the faces in the background.

"Well?"

"These are a little blurry. Not very clear, are they?"

A low growl came from the agent's throat. "Depends on the definition of the camera at the time the photo's taken. The Agency appreciates any assistance you can give us."

Scott held back a smile. "Guess those forensics shows don't always get it right." He went through the entire stack of enlarged photos quickly, then again one at a time, much more slowly. Finally, he separated out two photos.

"Here…" he said, tapping a figure who appeared in both. "This guy is familiar. I might've seen him at one of my ballgames. He reminds me of someone."

"What makes him stand out from the others?"

"Some of them I actually know and others I've seen frequently, even if I don't know them by name. He's different. In the first, he isn't watching the game at all. He's staring up toward someone else in the bleachers. In the second, he's staring at someone on the field all right, but I can't tell who. Could I see the originals with the entire photo, maybe enlarged times two instead of these?"

Agent Chase nodded and passed over the originals. Scott flipped through them until he found the two photos. "This guy. He's staring up, appears to be watching that redhead in the stands. Looks like Detective O'Malley. Weird, but she's only attended one of my team's games. Yeah, that's definitely her. She was wearing a blue top and a white visor." Now, he had another reason to call her and trade intel.

Hell, any excuse to call her would do.

The agent's eyebrow rose a notch. "You're involved with Detective O'Malley?"

"Briefly." Scott shrugged. "It—uh, didn't work out."

"And in the other photo, where do you think he's focused?"

"Definitely at Danny Hurley. Whoever took the photo of Danny captured this guy. It's easy to get a better overall visual on him. He's big, taller than I am, but he's wearing a baseball cap, so the upper part of his face is in shadow."

"But he's still familiar?"

"Yes. It bothers me that I can't figure it out. If I come up with his name, I'll call you." He waited. Would the Feds let him go?

Chase collected the photos and rose, then fished in his pocket for a business card. "You're free to go. If his name or the location where you might've seen this individual before comes to mind...or anything else, please give me a call."

He took the card, rubbed his thumb across it, then placed it in his pocket. "My brother? He's free to go?"

Chase rubbed his chin. "I'll check. Wait here. Thank you for your cooperation. I know I don't need to tell you to treat anything we discussed as confidential."

"If you say so."

"I do." The agent's tone was as dead as the Grim Reaper's.

He waited until the agent left and resisted the urge to wipe the sweat from his brow. No doubt someone was still observing him through the mirror.

The door opened again and Agent Havens stuck his head inside. "You're both free to go."

Didn't have to be told twice. Over Havens' shoulder, Justin appeared all in one piece. They were escorted to the lobby. Breathing easier, he turned to Justin, whose eyes flashed with excitement. What was up? His hands were jittering at his thighs.

Scott waited until they were in the car. "What?" His brother slammed the passenger door, then let out a huge sigh. "Man. I thought our collective goose was cooked. Havens did his best to intimidate me—actually, he totally did—but I bluffed. He threatened twenty years in federal prison, then suggested I complete an application to join the FBI. Seems they can use good computer people like me. And no, I'm not shitting you."

His chin dropped. What had he expected the Feds to do? Not sure. But the last thing Scott expected was for them to try to steal his brother from the family agency for the big Agency—the one with a fucking capital A.

"Don't worry. I turned him down." Justin started laughing. "Man. I gotta upgrade our firewalls."

No shit.

Tess ran her hands through her hair and wished she could get her hands on Lieutenant Woods for just five minutes. Wringing his neck was one of the milder things she had in mind for him. Had he notified the Feds?

No, because he was certain he had his killer already in lockup. Had her ViCAP inquiry led them to Nashville? If so, she only had herself to blame.

What was she supposed to do? Twiddle her thumbs? Wait for someone to get killed and just go on to her next case? Kozinsky's desk was empty. Surely, he hadn't called in for a nicked ear lobe? She missed the old grump. Even though he'd probably held back the info on the supposed eyewitness, she'd trust him to cover her back, no matter what.

Her cell phone rang. When she saw Scott's name on the caller ID, she took a deep breath. What could he possibly want? They were so over. Were they? Curiosity got the better of her.

"O'Malley," she barked, not willing to give an inch.

"Nice to hear your charming voice, Detective. This is business. Few things you ought to know, so I'll make it quick. You've rattled Tyler

Jamison's cage. He's nervous as a long-tailed cat in a room full of rocking chairs. Dakota Taylor's in town. And the Feds came by last night and confiscated everything we had on the case."

"Tell me 'bout it. The Feds were here early this morning. Took everything I had, too." Almost. But that was her little secret.

"Bet you didn't have to present yourself at the local FBI office."

Her stomach lurched. "Sorry, I pulled you into this. Are you…?"

"No, we're not in custody."

"Thank heavens."

"There's more intel, but we need to work on this together—somewhere neutral. Don't worry. I'm not trying to worm my way back into your good graces."

"That was the last thing on my mind." *Liar.* "All right," she said. "I'll drop by your office when I get a chance. Maybe this afternoon. Have to see how my day goes." How her day went? Her major case was gone. Her slate wiped clean, so-to-speak.

Not counting the flash drive in her purse.

"Fine." He disconnected without saying goodbye or anything personal.

Before she could sink into a deeper depression, Kozinsky lumbered into the bullpen. She clenched her jaw. "We just had our biggest cases ripped off by the Feds—Brennerman, Mason, and Hurley since he's still missing. There's not a single piece of paperwork left on any of 'em. Feds took it all."

"Rat bastards. I don't suppose you stashed away a backup copy of anything?"

She crossed her arms over her chest. "And if I did?" Of course, she had. Did he think she was an idiot?

"We could still work the case, especially the Hurley kid. He could still be alive."

"Not unless he has the luck of the angels on his side."

"It wouldn't hurt…" Kozinsky smiled, "…and it would look damned good in our jackets to find the kid before the Feds."

"Want to retire on a high note, do you?"

"And someone wants to make sergeant pretty soon, doesn't she?"

Before she could respond, Tess's landline rang. "O'Malley."

Silence.

Great, now the MNPD was receiving crank calls.

"I-I know who k-killed the Brennerman boy."

The voice was female and elderly. Tess's heart rate soared and hammered. "Yes, ma'am. Go on." Not wanting to scare off her informant, Tess tried to keep her tone calm and relaxed. "I'd certainly like to talk to you. Will you give me your name?"

"When I talk to you, I'll explain everything."

"Will you come downtown to the precinct?"

"Oh, no. I don't drive in downtown traffic. I do my own errands around here in Brentwood, but not downtown."

"That's not a problem. I'm happy to come to you. What's your address?"

The woman gave an address on Heather Lane and Tess wrote it down on a notepad. "Thank you. My partner and I will see you in about thirty minutes." She replaced the receiver and glanced at her partner.

Kozinsky's bushy brows were raised. "Was that what I think?"

"Well, it wasn't Daddy calling to take us to lunch." She grabbed her car keys. "Let's go."

Chapter Twenty-Two

Finally.

When Danny saw the farmhouse from the perimeter of the trees, he didn't trust his eyes. Had to be one of those hallucinations like a waterhole in the desert. But there it was—the first sign of civilization. A house meant a driveway. And a driveway was always connected to a road.

He was gonna make it. Dammit. He was gonna go home to his mom and dad and little sister. For the rest of his life, he would never give them another moment's worry. Emotions bubbled to the surface, but he was too dehydrated for tears. He wanted to laugh and cry at the same time, but fear kept him from both.

One last time, he stopped and listened. Birds chirping. Insects buzzing. Nothing else. First one foot, then the other, he stepped into the open field bordering the woods.

Focused on the farmhouse, he ran like hell. Stumbling once or twice, he quickly regained his balance and kept running until he clambered up the front steps.

He kicked the door. No one. He turned and tried to use his hands to turn the doorknob. Hands like dead lumps of raw meat. No good. He kicked the door again.

And again.

The doorframe splintered and he staggered inside the trashed farmhouse. A phone? No way could he manage a phone, if he could even find one. Something to cut the duct tape. Energy flagging, he weaved back and forth to the rear of the house, hoping to find the kitchen.

No luck. The kitchen was empty. No knives. No nothing.

He stumbled out the back door. There—an outbuilding, the size of a small barn. Tools. Maybe.

He cracked his knee on something. A water trough. Brackish water with bird droppings. But it was still water. He bent down and drank his fill, then collapsed on the dirt floor. Just needed a little more time. Get his energy back. Find something to free his hands. His eyelids grew heavy and closed.

Safe…at least for now.

As the junior member of the team, Tess drove. Maneuvering her way through downtown traffic, she seethed. When she stopped for a red light at Ninth and Broad, she darted her gaze to Kozinsky who had an enormous bandage on his ear. Making a bid for sympathy? Or had Estelle done the honors herself?

The light changed to green and she gunned it through the intersection. "Kozinsky, you and I are a good team, but your getting hit yesterday made me think maybe Estelle's right. Maybe you should retire before something bad really happens."

"Stereo nags singing the same tune. Don't know if I can handle both of you."

"Just think about it." She merged onto the inner loop, the quickest route to I-65 and Brentwood. Her cell phone rang. She pulled it from her belt and saw Scott's office number on the screen. "What now, Holt?"

"I forgot to tell you. They had me look at the pictures from the Hurley's camera. Thought you'd be interested."

Damn. Damn. Damn. She hadn't seen those. No fair that he had. "As I said, I'm off the case."

"Meet me at the Blue Mood for lunch. I'll tell all."

"Can't make it. I'm on a…a new case."

"After your shift then. I'll buy you a margarita."

Sweet. He remembered her favorite drink. Wait. She gave herself a mental slap. He was off limits, along with all the other family-oriented men in Nashville. "No thanks."

"Tess, please? Your mother's friend is still in the slammer, and Metro doesn't intend to let him out until the real killer's arrested."

She hung a left and merged into the Interstate traffic flow. "Don't have time for this…"

Okay, more than anything, she wanted to see Scott again. The warmth of his tone reminded her of his warm body against hers, making her squirm in her seat. But if he had valuable information… "Okay."

"See you after your shift." He disconnected and a sense of loss ripped through her body, a bubbling of emotion and confusion.

"Who was that?"

"Personal," she said, keeping her tone even. "What was that address again?"

A buzz of lust shot through Scott as he set the receiver back on the phone set. Tess was still mad at him—that much was obvious. But she'd agreed to meet him for a drink. Had to mean something.

So, only six hours or so until the end of her shift. He could wait that long. He shifted in his seat as the events of the night before and this morning ran through his mind. As much as he anticipated seeing her again, something else nagged at the back of his mind. The man in the photo was so familiar. The one which showed him staring up into the stands—guy had to be six-four or five. Not just tall, he was bulky like a defensive lineman.

Bingo. Dakota Taylor was a tackle, and according to last night's news, he was in town.

Scott settled back in his chair. Something else, his mother and father still lived in the area. He pulled out the phone book. What was his father's name? Allen. Albert. Yes, there it was. Brentwood number and address. He grabbed the phone and punched in the number.

A woman with the quivery voice of an elderly woman answered. "H-hello?"

"This is Scott Holt of Holt Investigations. I wonder if I might speak to your husband."

"He passed away earlier this summer. What is this about?"

"Are you Dakota Taylor's mother? He and I were camp counselors a long time ago. I was thinking of offering him a job in my agency."

"That won't be possible." Her tone was amused, verging on sarcastic. "He's still playing professional football."

"I realize that, but he's back in town. I wonder if I could come by and talk to you about old times." Okay, he was grasping at straws.

"No, I don't think so. The other detective should be here soon."

Be here soon? Was she referring to Tess? Was Tess already ahead of him? "Do you remember the detective's name?"

"It was Irish. Let me think—O'Malley. Yes, she's on her way, so I don't think you coming over would be a good idea."

He heard the sound of a doorbell through the phone.

"Just a moment," she said. "That's probably her now."

He waited and listened for the sound of Tess's voice. Was that a scuffle? A whimper? Then the definite click of the call being disconnected. Someone hung up the damn phone. Not Tess. Had Taylor come home to tie up a loose end? No matter, Tess was heading into a trap. He tried calling her back but his call rolled to voice mail.

Stubborn.

When Tess turned onto Heather Lane, she noticed a car in the driveway. The dented white 1990 sedan just didn't fit the profile of a Brentwood resident. Most of them drove SUVs of one brand or another. Taking into consideration the age of her caller, it was more likely she drove a luxury vehicle.

"Looks like she has company," Kozinsky said.

"Probably her cleaner," Tess suggested. She drove past the house to circle around the cul-de-sac and park in front of the house, incidentally blocking the drive. "Nice neighborhood. Homes worth half a million easy."

"Glad you keep up on the real estate values, O'Malley."

"In this town, it pays to know who you're dealing with."

"Yeah. Yeah. All right. If you can quit assessing the houses, we have a possible witness to interview." He opened his door and jumped out. "

Not to be left behind, she did the same.

His long strides up the brick walk forced her to rush to catch up with him. Taking the initiative and control, she slid under his outstretched arm and rapped on the door herself.

No answer.

"Ma'am, it's Detective O'Malley. We talked on the phone. Ma'am?" She knocked again. This time the door opened a bare inch with a chain keeping it from opening any further. Through the opening, she could make out a diminutive white-haired woman in what appeared to be a pink vintage Chanel suit.

"You've made a mistake. I didn't call anyone." Her voice wavered. Clearly terrified, the woman's teary gaze darted all over the place.

"I recognize your voice from the call. We're here to help. Won't you let us inside? You wanted to tell us something. Something about the Brennerman boy's murder and the kidnapping?"

The woman emitted a tiny yelp of pain.

"Ma'am, are you alone?" Her partner yelled through the door. "Is someone hurting you?"

"No-no. That was m-my cat. He scratched my ankle."

If she wasn't mistaken, someone was menacing this old woman. She wasn't about to leave the woman in the clutches of a possible killer. "But you called and gave us this address. We really need to discuss whatever it was you wanted to tell us."

"No, you've made a mistake. I didn't call you." Tears rolled down the woman's face.

Could they pretend to leave? Would they have time or would whoever was threatening her kill her before they could return on foot?

"All right, ma'am. We'll take your word for it. Sorry to have bothered you," Kozinsky said. He must've had the same thoughts. He motioned for her to move the car and indicated he would cover the back of the house. She nodded her understanding.

Reluctance wove through her gut and set it roiling. He pretended to enter the driver's side and Tess the passenger side, but he crouched down outside the vehicle and Tess slid over to the driver's side. As she pulled away, Kozinsky kept his head down until the car reached the edge of the property, then sprinted for cover while she called for backup. Four houses down, she parked in the driveway. She pulled her service weapon and checked the magazine.

Full. Another magazine on her belt. She grabbed her walkie-talkie and exited the vehicle. Cutting through the neighbors' backyards, she'd just reached the next-door neighbor's yard when she heard gunfire. *Pop. Pop. Pop.*

She eased from the cover of a large magnolia. Her partner was lying face down on the back patio. "Officer down. Repeat. Officer down." She rattled off the address into her walkie-talkie.

A bullet whizzed over her head. She ducked behind the old tree. "Kozinsky!"

Nothing.

"Hold on. Help's on the way." She picked up a handful of gravel and threw it toward the patio. Another shot.

"Gotcha," she muttered. He was firing from a first-floor window. The patio led out from walkout basement. She laid a round of shots at the raised window, then scrambled for the patio. She tugged on Kozinsky's body. "Better have your vest on."

He groaned, a low gut-wrenching sound. "It's on."

No time for niceties. "Drag your sorry ass under the deck before you get us both killed."

Another shot slammed into the ground between them, missing by fractions. Kozinsky levered up to his knees and crawled his way to safety beneath the upper deck. Just in time. Another bullet pinged on the flag pavers, scattering stone fragments. One flew up and nicked Tess's cheek; she swiped away the blood with the back of her hand.

"We've gotta get in that house. No telling what he's done."

"Can't move. Wait for back-up." He rubbed his chest and groaned.

"Can't wait. There's a hostage."

"Which is why we wait for backup and a hostage negotiator."

Her partner rubbed his chest. "Bastard got the vest right over my heart. Damned good shot. Think one of my ribs is broken."

No way was she losing her partner this way. "Stay here. I'm going in."

"That's your plan? You're gonna storm the place like Dirty Harriett?"

"You got a better one?" She ejected the magazine. Two rounds. One more mag in her belt.

Another round from the shooter drove into a deck post. She aimed at the window and emptied her weapon. She dropped back, ejected the empty mag, pulled the full one from her belt and jammed it into the butt of her weapon.

"Wait," he called. "Just heard a vehicle pull up out front. Back-up's here. Just wait."

"No sirens."

Movement in the periphery of her vision. She whirled and aimed.

What the fuck? Only Scott ducking for cover behind the same magnolia she'd used earlier. "Holt? What the hell are you doing here?"

"Don't shoot. Dammit, I came to help."

Just how and where he knew to come were questions for later.

"I don't need your damn help."

"How was I to know you didn't need my help? I have to say he's not looking too good from my point of view."

The sound of a car motor, gunning and taking off, interrupted what he was saying. A sickly expression crossed Scott's face.

Shit. "Left the keys in your vehicle, didn't you?"

"I was in a hurry to help you."

He ran for the front yard and Tess followed. "How'd you end up here?"

"Dakota Taylor, the pro ball player—the photos I tried to tell you about—this is his mother's house." Not quite making the connection, she shrugged.

Again, how he knew to come here was a question for later.

On reaching the front yard, Scott bellowed, "No!" When she rounded the house, she found him jumping up and down like a two-year-old in the throes of a temper tantrum. "He stole my car."

"Serves you right." She shook her head. What kind of dumbass left his car keys handy for the suspect to take off with?

With more important things on her agenda— like the welfare of her informant—she went to the front door. "Ma'am, are you all right?"

"In here," came the woman's feeble reply.

Before she could enter the house, sirens pierced the air. Four Metro squad cars, an ambulance and a Brentwood squad car all screeched up at once. "My partner's behind the house. He took one in the vest, thinks his ribs are broken. Possible injured elderly woman inside the house," she said to the EMTs. To one of the patrol officers, she said, "Our shooter got away. Need a BOLO on a 1965 red Mustang convertible. Tag number…" She glanced at Scott.

He came over and gave his tag number to the officer while Tess headed back inside the house. She found the woman crumpled on the floor, and indeed Scott was correct. She was Millicent Taylor, mother of the pro football player. Other than nearly being scared to death and on the receiving end of some very nasty bruises, she was in pretty good shape. She assisted the woman to her feet. Another EMT came inside and applied an ice pack to the woman's poor bruised face.

"Who did this to you?" Tess asked, even though she was sure of the answer.

"My son…Bobby." Her head nodded as if palsied. "He was going to kill me."

"What did you call to tell me?"

"He killed that Mason boy and the governor's grandson, too."

Her pen poised over her case notes, Tess asked, "How long have you suspected your son?"

"Ever since my husband committed suicide. I thought it was because of his cancer, but no. All these years, he knew about our son and hid the truth. I believed my son was as normal as anyone. He's a football star. I never quite understood why he never came home but guessed he was just too busy."

"What did your husband's suicide have to do with finding out about your son?"

"He left two suicide notes. One for the authorities and one for me." The woman's face grew tight; the stringy cords in her throat bulged as she swallowed. "That note spelled out all the nasty details of what our Bobby had been up to for the last fourteen years." Her body visibly shuddered. "It was the shoe thing."

The holdback clue. Tess leaned forward. "Do you still have your husband's second note?"

"Yes. It's in my Bible."

Tess closed her eyes for a second. Murder evidence against her son hidden in the Bible. What a fucked-up family.

An EMT brought a second gurney into the house. "She's gonna need X-rays."

Tess held up her hand. "Hold on a sec. We need that note, ma'am."

As soon as she had the note in hand, she bagged and tagged it, then allowed the EMT to bundle the woman onto the stretcher.

Time to check on her partner. She followed the EMT and hopped into the back of the ambulance. "So, are you gonna live?"

"Hmph." Kozinsky groaned and cradled his chest. "O'Malley, I knew you were trying to get me to retire, but I didn't think you'd get me sidelined so quickly. Damn, but you're efficient."

"I'm not the one who got in the way of a bullet and it wasn't from my weapon. Get over it. you sit on desk duty for a couple of weeks. The worst that can happen to you there is a paper cut or getting your dick jammed in a drawer."

The EMTs and the ambulance driver whooped with laughter. Her partner tried to laugh but instead cradled his chest and grimaced with pain. "You and Estelle are in cahoots."

"Don't whine. It's not becoming."

Her duty to her partner done, she smiled at the EMTs, jumped from the ambulance and spoke to one of the officers. "Mrs. Taylor needs a police guard at all times. We don't know where her son is, but he might try to finish the job."

What was Holt up to? She glanced around and found him being grilled by the commander of the Brentwood Police Department. True, Scott came to assist, but—and it was a very big but—he left his keys in his vehicle and allowed Taylor to escape. Whatever happened to his little red Mustang, it wouldn't be pretty.

Taylor would be frantic to get out of state, but he'd have to steal or carjack a couple more vehicles before he could get away clean. Still, they knew who they were looking for, although he'd be touted as a person of interest for the media broadcasts.

She caught Scott's attention and strolled toward him. His expression was grim and she had to tamp down the rush of tenderness. More than anything, she wanted to put her arms around him and lose herself in his warmth. Instead, she told the commander, "He'll come down and file a stolen vehicle report at your stationhouse, but first, I have a few questions for him related to this case."

The commander, a red-faced, burly man with watery blue eyes and a tendency to posture, scowled back. "All right, but I got some of my own." He nudged up the bill of his cap with his nightstick. "See that you get down there this afternoon or first thing in the morning, Holt."

Scott nodded. The commander seemed to find something else to occupy his attention and walked away, giving his shoulders an arrogant swagger. "Thanks. He wanted to clap me in his pokey, for sure."

"Not such a bad idea. Thought about it myself once or twice." She glanced over at her vehicle, then back at Scott. "I suppose you need a ride."

His eyes widened as if surprised by her offer, then shook his head. "Nah. I'll call someone at the office."

"Get in the car. Ride with me to the hospital. They can pick you up there. In the meantime, you need to answer some questions."

"Sure." He grinned.

Yeah, the grin that was supposed to charm him back into her good graces. It wasn't working. No matter how glad she'd been to see him, she wasn't about to risk getting involved again.

He gestured toward her vehicle. "Back seat or front?"

She hesitated, fumbling with her cuffs for show. Let him sweat. "Front," she said finally, then motioned for him to get inside.

Once Scott and Tess were inside the SUV, she faced him. Her gray eyes flashed with anger. Not exactly a comforting expression. She was still pissed and nowhere ready to consider the truth. "Now, Tess—" he began.

"I didn't say you could talk. What were you thinking? Just fly to my rescue like you're some grade B comic book superhero."

"They're called graphic novels now," he said with a smirk. Any other time, he might use his skills of persuasion to bring her over to his side of the argument, but he had the feeling she'd do more than bust his chops.

She ignored his correction and continued, "How the hell did you know to come to the Taylor's? She refused to leave her name when she called the squad, and I didn't take time to do a reverse look-up."

He leaned back, determined to appear at ease, even if he was anything but. "The Feds. I told you Justin and I spent some time with them this morning. One of the agents showed me the pictures from the Hurley's camera to see if I noticed anyone out of place in the background shots."

"Did you?" She jammed the key into the ignition and the motor roared to life.

"What I noticed was some guy who was familiar. It kept bugging me until I figured out who he reminded me of. Dakota Taylor's been seen about town—I heard it on the news, so I put two and two together."

He quickly ran through the rest of the details and his thought processes which led him to call Millicent Taylor in the first place. "She said she didn't have time to talk to me. A Detective O'Malley was coming over to ask her some questions. Then her doorbell rang, and I heard what sounded like a scuffle. Then someone hung up the phone. I figured you were heading into a trap. Tried to call you back, but it went to voice mail."

"Yeah, sorry about that." She kept her gaze on the street and maneuvered her way through the other police vehicles.

"How's your partner?"

"You take a direct hit to the chest with only a Kevlar vest between you and a .45 caliber slug and see how you feel." She made an effort to temper her tone. "It's akin to being hit with a baseball bat at the very least. He's probably got a broken rib or two."

"Ouch. Sorry." And he was sorry…yet relieved it wasn't Tess who was hit. Broken ribs hurt like the devil on speed, but her partner would live.

A broken heart was trickier to mend.

Broken heart? What the fuck was he thinking? He didn't have anything like that. Broken hearts were for broads. He and Tess had barely gotten to know each other. Still, their brief lovemaking sessions were imprinted on his brain like X-rated movies.

"What's so funny?" Her curt tone snapped him back to the present like a bailiff calling the court to order.

He shook his head. "Nothing."

Why did his mind always go there when she was around? Because they were a perfect match with close families and cops for fathers, even if she wasn't interested in marriage. It wasn't just the great sex, but she was smart, tough, and never let anyone intimidate her. Her passion for her job...for justice...briefly for him—all of those qualities pulled him in better than a subpoena.

"Hmph."

One more try. "Tess," he began softly, "I miss you. Can we still have that drink later?"

"Nope." She glared over at him. Typical afternoon traffic on Harding Road slowed the SUV's progress to a crawl. "I only agreed to meet you for a drink for an exchange of information. That's already been accomplished."

"Dammit." All right he was about to ruin everything. "Can't we start over? No expectations."

"It's not that simple and you know it." She stretched to see what the traffic holdup was. "Geez, Louise. Looks like a wreck at the entrance to Saint T." She reached under the seat and pulled out her emergency light, then slapped it on the dashboard and hit the siren.

Bumper to bumper with five lanes of traffic packed as solid as his law library bookshelves. "Where are they going? There's no room to pull over."

She shot him a steely-eyed glare. "They'll move." Slowly, the cars ahead crept over as far as they could. A couple took advantage of the Woodmont Boulevard cross street and turned right.

Farther ahead, cars turned up Kenner, leaving room for Tess to work her way through to the accident. Two SUVs with minimal damage sat sideways obstructing all the westbound lanes, causing maximum delay.

Two patrol officers were already on scene directing traffic and rerouting the outbound lanes into the incoming ones.

"Looks like the ambulance with your partner and Mrs. Taylor just missed the accident."

"Yeah." She pulled over into the left-hand lane and was waved around the wreck, into the hospital entrance by the patrol officer. "Losing

Taylor's mother is the very last thing this case needs."

"Any leads on the Hurley kid?"

"Nope." Tess shook her head. "The tip line was crazy the first couple of days, but nothing panned out." She pulled into the ER lot and parked. "Let's see how bad her injuries really are and what else she has to say."

Surprised she hadn't already kicked his ass to the curb, he nodded.

No point in pushing his luck.

Now that they knew who the serial killer was, maybe no others would have to die. Still, it sickened him to know Danny Hurley hadn't been so lucky.

Sooner or later, his body would be found and the Hurleys would have whatever passed for closure.

Or like so many others, maybe it would never be found and the Hurleys would never know for sure.

Chapter Twenty-Three

Danny shook himself awake. Confused for a second, he glanced around. Right…the old barn. He looked over his shoulder at the trough and couldn't believe he drank the water.

Gross.

His mouth was still dry, but his head was clearer now. There was something he needed—right. Find something to cut his hands loose. He rolled to his knees, then managed to get to his feet. His head swam. He steadied himself against a splintered post and waited until his head cleared again, his eyes focused.

Had to be all sorts of crap in this place.

It wasn't that big of a barn, nothing like the one Granddad Hurley used to have before he retired to a condo in Johnson City.

Used to have horses here. Several old leather harnesses hung from wooden pegs. Looked rotten, like maybe they would disintegrate if touched. Over in one corner of the building was a pile of wood shavings and a sawhorse. Someone did a lot of woodwork in here, too. He kicked the pile of shavings. Maybe there was an old file or an ax.

He looked upward through the motes of dust in a broadband of sunlight streaming through a hole in the roof. Sticking out from the loft was the wooden handle of something. Whatever it was, maybe he could use it…if he could get up there. A rickety ladder led to the loft, but could he climb it without the use of his hands?

Might as well find out.

Doing his best to keep a low profile, Scott followed Tess as she strode confidently into the emergency room. It wasn't his nature to play shrinking violet, but whatever it took to keep the ER staff from tossing him out on his ass, he'd do. One of his sisters was a nurse, and she was damned formidable when it came to protecting her patients. He expected no less from the nurses at Saint Thomas.

Tess flashed her badge at a short, stocky nurse with chocolate brown eyes whose ID badge said simply, 'Debbie, RN,' and inquired about her partner. After being assured he was stable, she insisted on speaking to Taylor's mother. "ASAP."

The nurse pursed her mouth, nodded, then cast a fishy stare in his direction. "Who's he?"

"Someone crucial to my investigation. He won't get in anyone's way. I'll kick him out myself"—a wintry gray stare was cast his way, this time from Tess— "if he even thinks about giving any trouble."

"That's me." He pointed to his chest. "Crucial to the investigation and No Trouble is my middle name." He smiled for good measure.

Nurse Debbie flashed him a wide smile and batted her lashes expressively as if she'd seen one too many of his kind, then relented and directed them to the exam room where Taylor's mother lay on a gurney.

When he and Tess walked in, a doctor type— intern, resident or whatever—leaned over the woman's fragile body and was checking her reflexes.

"Detective O'Malley," Tess said and showed her badge again. "I need to take Mrs. Taylor's statement as soon as possible."

"I'm Dr. Frields. Mrs. Taylor's alert and oriented. Neuro checks and reflexes are normal. She needs a couple of skull films and a head CT, but they're backed up in Imaging, so you can have her until they're ready."

She thanked the doctor, who turned and left them alone with Taylor's mother.

Scott looked at the woman and realized she wasn't as old and elderly as he'd thought. True she was fashionably thin and her hair was snowy white, but he doubted she was a day over sixty. Wasn't sixty the new forty or some such?

Millicent Taylor had a large bruise on the right side of her face as if she'd been backhanded by someone much stronger than herself. Her right eye was puffy, and she'd have an awesome shiner before the day was over.

"How are you, Mrs. Taylor?" he asked, without thinking Tess might want to take his head off. If his stepmother had lived, she'd be about the same age. He could easily imagine how he'd feel to see her in the same position.

"I'll be all right." The woman grabbed Tess's hand. "If you hadn't come when you did…" Her voice faded and tears filled her eyes.

Finishing her sentence wasn't necessary. All three of them knew what could've happened.

"Just sorry I didn't get there before he hurt you, ma'am." Tess extricated her hand from Mrs. Taylor's, then pulled out her notebook. "I need to ask you some questions."

"But I already told you everything."

"I just need to get it down officially and make sure we haven't missed anything. You did say it was your son…Bobby Taylor…who was responsible for Richard Mason's murder and that of the governor's grandson?"

"Yes." The woman went into great detail about her husband's second suicide note. "I didn't know until then. He killed himself because he found out there were a lot of victims all over the United States."

"And yet you didn't call us until now?"

"No. I didn't want to turn him in. What kind of mother turns in her son as a murder suspect? That's what I kept asking myself, but my answer was always it was the kind who didn't want any more mothers' sons to die."

"Go on. Is there more?"

Taylor's mother nodded, reached a scrawny hand for her water cup, then took a sip before she continued. "When the governor's grandson was found in the woods at Camp Einstein, I was afraid he'd come back. I guess he thought with his father dead no one else knew he killed that Mason boy. I tried to be a good mother. How could he have done all those horrible things?"

Tess shook her head. "No one knows, ma'am." She wrung her hands. "When Bobby was a child, he was so sweet—most of the time. The only problem I had was when he dressed up in my clothes and shoes." She glanced from Tess to Scott, her eyes wide with a plea for their understanding. "You understand I had to punish him for that. That's a mother's right and duty. If I'd known how sick he really was, I never would've let him out of my closet."

So, she was in the habit of locking him in her closet? Wonder what else she did?

"I know I should've called you sooner. Maybe that other boy would've been saved."

From a corner of the exam room, he leaned against the wall and listened as Dakota's mother went over the details. It was the first he'd heard of the two suicide notes. It sickened him—all of it. Dakota Taylor, the big stud football star and his father hiding the real truth for years. How many lives had he taken? They'd probably never know for sure.

As for Tess, except for an occasional show of emotion in her eyes, her expression remained a frightening neutral mask. Frightening because she had to be as horrified as he. He schooled his expression to match hers. He wasn't here to judge the woman. He couldn't help but think again of the Hurley family who were grieving, and at the same time, hoping for the best outcome possible.

Tess had just closed her notebook when the door to the exam room opened. "Imaging's ready for her," a transporter said.

Scott waited until the transporter rolled Dakota's mother into the hall and headed for the elevator before he followed Tess into the hall.

Tess turned to him, her expression still a mask. "I'm going to check on my partner," she said with a slight shrug, "and you can call whoever."

"You're through with me...just like that?" He leaned in close. "In case you've forgotten, I saved your life today."

"In whose world?"

"All right. But you have to agree my timely arrival distracted him from shooting you and your partner."

"Your *arrival* allowed him the time and mode of transportation to get away."

"Guilty as charged, Detective." He dropped his tone even lower. "But I'm glad you're all right. No serious damage to mar your beautiful body."

She clenched her jaw, trying to look away from him. Did he imagine it or did her gaze soften just a bit?

"Call your ride, Holt."

"I give up." He held up his hands in a gesture of surrender. Maybe he'd said the words, but had he really given up? Could he?

No way.

She huffed, then turned and left him standing alone. All around him the noises of the ER invaded his consciousness. They seemed like one ongoing turmoil, but he could distinguish the squeak of a nurse's rubber-soled shoes against the tile, the rattle of a cart, the overwhelming buzz of conversation from triage and a baby's crying.

He was a fool to hope. He pulled a cell phone from his belt, then punched in his home number. Someone would be there by now. While he listened to the phone ring, he watched Tess stride off, her shoulders squared.

What a great ass.

After speaking with one of the nurses, Tess eased behind the curtained cubicle where her partner lay on a gurney. "Hey, there, Kozinsky."

He scowled up at her and winced with obvious pain. "Haven't forgiven you yet."

"Forgiven me?"

"You called me a whiner. I'll have you know I have *two* broken ribs." He tried to smile but grimaced instead. "It really hurts."

"Too bad you're not in the army. They'd give you a purple heart."

"A little sympathy—that's too much to ask from my partner?"

"I came to see if there was anything I could do. Want me to call Estelle?"

He shook his head. "Already called her. She'd have a duck fit if someone else called. Scared I'd bought the farm."

"Yeah, I know." She shrugged. If his wife was lucky, she'd never know how close she'd come to being a widow. "Anything else?"

"I guess you're on your own for a couple of days. After two injuries, doubt anyone's brave enough to take my place."

"Just a little run of bad luck," she insisted. "No reason to give me such a hard time."

"A little bad luck is a couple of flat tires. Letting your partner get wounded twice in two days is more than a little bad luck. You and Estelle have conspired against me."

She laughed. "Starting to look forward to retirement, are you?"

He tried to laugh again and clutched his chest with the effort. "I can hardly wait until I'm cleared for desk duty."

"Just be careful of the desk drawers. You might really pinch your memb—uh, fingers in one of them." She winked, then turned and left him trying to laugh and cry at the same time.

She suppressed a giggle and headed down the hall to the exit. Unable to stop herself, she glanced around. No sign of Scott. Someone from his family had probably picked him up. A mixture of relief and disappointment shot through her. She walked outside in time to see him jump into a Toyota Camry driven by a cute strawberry blonde. A frisson of jealousy buzzed in the back of her brain.

Maybe it was one of his sisters. Of course, it was. Besides, what difference did it make if the woman wasn't a sister? She and Scott were through.

Over. Kaput. Fini.

Like yesterday's news.

Dakota Taylor, aka Doug Silvey, stopped at Old Hickory Boulevard, ready to turn right and head for I-65. The faster he blew town the better. No, wait. Better idea. Avoid the interstate and meander through the pricy residential neighborhoods.

And find another car. The red Mustang was handy, but it wasn't the best vehicle if he wanted to avoid attention. He turned right on Old Hickory and then passed through the Franklin Road intersection, following it all the way to Granny White Pike before turning toward town. Even though he wanted to drive like a bat out of hell, he maintained a cautious speed, but it was an effort all the same.

Finally, there it was. David Lipscomb University. Summer school.

Cars. Summer sports program—a baseball game was in progress. He eased into the parking lot and parked. He shoved his police scanner in his hip pocket and looped the headphones around his neck. No way was he leaving that stuff behind. Exiting the Mustang, he left the car keys in the ignition for whoever found it. A sweet ride it was, but not what he needed right now.

Casually, he walked past the line of cars watching for one with the keys in the ignition. He could always hotwire it but a set of keys would make his life so much easier.

Bingo—a silver Buick sedan. Not too splashy. Much less recognizable. And with the keys in the ignition. Slowly, he opened the door and heaved his body inside. He turned the key and the motor purred to life. He eased from the parking space and considered his options.

Rush hour in Nashville. The interstates would be packed. Bumper-to-bumper was no way to get outta Dodge. What he needed was a temporary hideout with a garage. It wasn't long before he found what he wanted. A duplex with a FOR SALE sign in front and a driveway that circled around the back of the building. He whipped into the drive and drove around back, parking under the double carport. No one could see him from the street and thick bushes surrounded the backyard. Nosy neighbors couldn't see him either.

It only took a minute to break out the backdoor glass to one of the units and open the deadbolt.

Inside, it was a flashback to the sixties. Yellow Formica countertops and old wallpaper with tea kettles. Seventies beige vinyl covered the floor. He wandered into the living room. The dark green matted carpet had seen better days. Two small bedrooms and a single bath with girly flowered wallpaper.

Good enough for an afternoon's hideout. Once it was dark, he'd return to his cabin, pick up his souvenirs and say adios to Nashville. He walked into the cleaner of the two bedrooms, sat and leaned against the wall, setting his hand-held police scanner down on the carpet beside him. He settled the headphones on his head. If he dozed off, its squawking would alert him of any possible sightings.

Not that he was worried anyone would find him.

Chapter Twenty-Four

"Mmph!" Danny rolled over on his side and tried to keep from crying. Dammit. He'd fallen four times and every muscle in his body ached and throbbed. Last time, he'd made it halfway up the ladder before it cracked and collapsed. He hit the floor and the upper half of the ladder fell on top of him, whacking his head.

His stomach gurgled and churned. Big surprise. No food since Monday. The nasty stuff he'd drunk earlier would probably kill him anyway. He was just gonna lie on the floor of an old barn, die and rot down to nothing but a nasty mess. Someday, someone would find his bones and then the CSI guys would have to figure out who he was and what had happened to him.

In the meantime, his mom would go crazy, his dad would drink too much, and his sister would be smothered by his parents trying to keep something from happening to her.

If he didn't get off his ass.

He could almost hear his coach calling him a sissy girl for lying in the dirt and thinking negative.

"Well, coach." His voice croaked from disuse and dehydration. "I'm getting off my ass." He sat and got to his feet. More and more difficult. Time to find his way home. "And I'll be there for the next game."

Okay. He headed around the front of the house and found the dusty overgrown driveway. More path than a driveway, but hell—it had to head somewhere.

Might as well get a move on.

***

On her way back to the precinct, Tess observed the tree leaves were upturned. A hint of rain in the air. Maybe it would cool the temperature to something approaching comfortable.

Back at her desk, she worked on incident reports and wondered where poor Danny Hurley's body was. Paperwork completed and ready for a bite of dinner, she stood.

"Hey, O'Malley," said one of her fellow detectives. "Check it out! Nashville's made the national news. WNN Headline News' Felicity Pace is featuring Danny Hurley's disappearance."

She cut her gaze to the TV in the corner of the squad room. Sure enough, the blond ex-D.A. was breaking the news.

"We go to Nashville, Tennessee, where seventeen-year-old high school baseball star Danny Hurley was apparently taken right from his own front yard. Confidential sources reveal the suspect is a sadistic serial killer. We have Metro Nashville Police Department spokesperson, Mark Barron. Mr. Barron, is Danny Hurley's disappearance related to the kidnapping and murder of the Governor's grandson, Todd Brennerman?"

"No, Felicity. We don't believe it is. We already have a suspect in jail for Brennerman's kidnapping and murder."

The former prosecutor frowned. "Hm. Same victimology. Elizabeth, can you show the pictures of Todd Brennerman and Danny Hurley. Both are young males in their late teens. Any chance you have the wrong man?"

"No, our evidence, which includes eyewitness testimony, is very strong. These cases are very different."

"Have the Hurleys submitted to lie detector tests?"

"Yes, both of them have solid alibis, but they volunteered for the tests anyway. They are definitely cleared as suspects in their son's disappearance."

"Thank you, Mr. Barron. At least that's something."

Felicity quickly recapped the details of Brennerman's disappearance and murder. "After this break, we'll speak with Danny Hurley's parents who are joining us from Nashville."

While Felicity Pace did a lot of good by profiling missing children and adults and bringing attention to the cases, too often, their bodies were found too late. Once in a while, there was a success which was a wonderful moment for the families when a missing family member was found, safe and sound. In the face of the odds against them, how those same families managed to keep hopeful Tess couldn't fathom.

Somewhere, right now, young Danny Hurley was no doubt lying buried in some remote spot. Sooner or later, a hunter and his dog would stumble over what was left of the teenager's body. The Hurleys would grieve all over again. For the rest of their lives, nothing would ever be the same.

"I'm heading out," she said to no one in particular. A missing Danny Hurley weighed heavily on her mind. As did Scott Holt. It'd be a long time before she forgot either one.

Scott pulled a beer from the fridge, then popped the top. Instead of taking a drink, he set it on the island and wandered over to the French doors. He walked out onto the deck and watched the descending sun paint the sky red, then purple through the old oaks growing on the west side of the property. Purple and white butterfly bushes were massed across the east side of the backyard, so many of them he could smell their sweet scent fifteen feet away. The humidity was high and breathing the air felt as if he'd been smacked in the face with a wet T-shirt.

Danny Hurley was somewhere out there. Whatever the heat and bugs had done to his body wouldn't be any worse than what his killer had done. Sooner rather than later, he hoped someone would find the teenager's body and end his parents' questions and nightmares.

Not knowing might even be worse than knowing what happened. Certainly, Kim's running away had affected all of their family. Never knowing if she was safe or had enough to eat. Most of all, never knowing why she ran away…or what she did to survive.

Whine. The sting of a mosquito bite. He slapped the side of his neck. Time to head inside. Once he was back in the house, he snatched his beer from the island and headed to the study. Without turning on a light, he grabbed the TV remote, turned it on and settled into his favorite chair.

Damn, but it was good to see Tess again, even if his screw-up had given Taylor the means to get away. She was a pro when she interviewed

Taylor's mother. Firm, but never judgmental, no matter what she thought about how long it took the woman to turn in her only son. Gentle because it couldn't be easy for any mother, no matter how horrific the crime.

He took a long drink and pondered what might've been. Tess—the woman was tailor-made for a family like the Holt-Lackeys. Perfect fit for him, too. Passionate and smart. He could almost feel the soft texture of her skin, taste the sweetness of her honeyed lips. How her eyes sparkled with passion when they made love. Except she disagreed with everything he wanted out of life.

Justin whacked the top of Scott's head with a rolled-up magazine. "What's the score?"

Startled, Scott glanced up at his brother. "Huh?"

"The ballgame—what's the score?" Justin laughed. "What's up? You're sitting here in the dark, drinking, and you aren't paying attention to the game."

Rather than confess who was really on his mind, he shrugged. "By the way, what was Doug Silvey up to the last two years? Any way we can connect him to Dakota Taylor?"

"Dude, talk about changing the subject."

"Wasn't aware there was any subject being discussed."

Justin brushed the hair from his eyes. "You attorney types—always splitting hairs." He sat on the edge of the coffee table and leaned forward, his facial expression demonstrating his intent on worming something from Scott. Something he wasn't ready to discuss.

"I was discussing your attitude, and ya changed the subject to something else entirely."

"Not tonight. Just get me some information that'll tie these two together."

"Well, if ya spent more time in the office instead of playing superhero, you'd have this intel on your desk. Doug Silvey was hired as a fitness coach for Camp Einstein earlier this summer. Whatcha think of that?"

Now that was tying them together. "You wouldn't happen to have a picture of him?"

"According to his Pennsylvania driver's license stats, he's six-five, weighs 250, has light brown hair and blue eyes, plus he's an organ donor. Big sucker, isn't he? And here ya go straight from his driver's license." Justin shoved the photo in Scott's face. "Recognize him?"

He flicked on the lamp beside his chair and peered at the picture. "Height and weight, coloring match. Features are coarser. Still, he's fourteen years older, but I'd put money on it—Silvey and Taylor are the same guy. What I can't understand is why someone at the camp didn't recognize him as Dakota Taylor?" He shook his head. "Guess defensive tackles don't receive the amount of press a quarterback does."

"So, did you get a good look at Taylor as he drove off into the sunset in your shiny red Mustang?"

He glared at his brother. "Just the back of the bastard's head."

"Kid like Danny Hurley wouldn't have a chance with a bruiser like that." Justin shook his head. "For that matter, neither would I."

"Nope." The very idea of what Taylor had done sickened him, and he knew in his gut Taylor was the serial killer. If they could catch him before he blew town, there wouldn't be any more victims. Let it stop here where it began.

The problem was MNPD wouldn't acknowledge Taylor as the suspect. All they had on Taylor was an assault on a police officer, his mother, and a stolen vehicle charge. Ned Forbes was still locked up.

Scott reached for the phone and punched in the number for Ned's attorney. Without taking time for the niceties, Scott told Raul Palermo what was going on. Specifically, he shared that the MNPD was holding a man they now knew was innocent and the real killer was Dakota Taylor, aka Doug Silvey.

Satisfied, Scott hung up from the call. What a day.

In the distance, he heard the low rumble of thunder. Outside lightning flashed.

One foot in front of the other.

Danny stumbled over a rock and went down to his knees, then struggled to get back on his feet.

Each time he fell, it was harder to get up. No more hunger pains. Must be bad. He hadn't eaten since Monday afternoon. What day was it, anyway?

Getting dark in the middle of nowhere. No streetlights. So tired.

A flash of lightning streaked across the sky. Maybe it'd rain. If it did, he'd just lie down, open his mouth and drink it in. So dry, he couldn't piss or break a sweat. Water. He needed water.

Keep going. One foot in front of the other.

What was that? He shook his head and blinked his eyes. Was that a light in the distance? Somebody was home.

One foot in front of the other.

He began to run.

From her window on First Avenue South, Tess watched the twinkling lights of boats on the river and then across to East Nashville, even to Madison. In the distance, she heard the unmistakable roll of thunder. Heat lightning brightened the sky a few moments later. Maybe it would rain soon and end the drought.

Alone. She didn't have to be, but she'd chosen a different path. She'd chosen to follow in her father's footsteps. Granted, there were times when she almost regretted it.

Like now.

Her cell phone sang. What now? She yanked it off her belt and answered. "O'Malley."

The desk sergeant called to tell her Scott's Mustang had been found in a parking lot at David Lipscomb University and was in perfect condition. He also told her another car had been stolen from the same lot. Taylor was likely in a silver Buick sedan and the BOLO was already updated to reflect the new information. She thanked the sergeant and disconnected.

Now she had to call Scott. As much as she dreaded hearing his soft sultry tones, calling him was the right thing to do.

After a single ring, he answered. "You must be a mind reader. I was about to call you—"

"Really? I don't think—"

"Will you just shut up and listen for once? Dakota Taylor and your eyewitness, Doug Silvey, are the same person. Silvey didn't exist until two years ago and he was hired as a fitness coach at Camp Einstein this summer."

"Interesting. Now for the reason, I called. Your car's been located."

A low groan reached her through the phone. "Wrecked, stripped or totaled?"

"Cherry condition."

"No shit?"

His response was so real and unguarded, she forced herself to hold back a giggle. A giggle would only encourage him. "No shit," she said, careful to keep her tone flat.

"Thanks. When and where can I pick it up?"

"When? After we're through dusting it for prints. Where? Metro Impound lot. They'll let you know."

"Thanks, Tess. I—uh, appreciate your calling."

"Just doing my job." Why had Scott paused? What else did he want to say? "Thought you'd want to know," she finished, sounding as lame as she felt.

"Duly noted."

She paused, wanting to say more, but couldn't come up with anything she hadn't already said.

"G'night." His voice sounded thick with emotion. "Night." Somehow, she managed to keep her tone crisp and businesslike. Knees weakening, she clicked the OFF button and flopped on the couch. She missed sparring with him. In spite of his mistaken ideas about her, he was a good man. A caring man.

One day he'd make someone a good husband—just not her.

The dial tone whined in Scott's ear like a blind date with a bad attitude. An intense urge to toss the cell phone across the study grew in his chest, but he clenched his fists and resisted. Instead, he stood, snagged his beer from the side table and started pacing.

Dammit. He'd handed Tess the direct connection between the serial killer and the eyewitness against Ned Forbes. Couldn't she at least be grateful? Not that he expected fireworks and a band, but stiff and formal didn't fit his favorite redhead…the one he'd made such hot, sweet love to.

So warm and willing, responsive to his touch. Skin softer than a well-seasoned catcher's mitt. Legs long enough to run all the bases…and then some.

He sank back into the overstuffed recliner and banged his fist on the table. Dammit. How could he just give up on his first chance at a real relationship in the last two years? True, his initial thoughts leaned more toward having some fun with the fiery redhead, but fun quickly turned into something more. At least it had for him.

Since he wasn't the stalker type, he wasn't about to go chasing after her. Not this time. The next move in their little game was hers.

Grabbing the remote, he turned on the TV just as his brother ambled into the study and stretched out on the couch. "What's on?"

Scott shrugged. "Beats me."

"What's the matter with you? Someone take a whiz in your cereal bowl?"

"Nothing. Nothing at all." He crossed his arms across his chest and huffed. "It's over."

Justin shot Scott a skeptical glance. "The game? Looks like it's just starting."

Could his brother be any more obtuse? "No, Tess and me. We're done."

"Too bad, dude. She was smoking hot."

"You got that right." Scott picked up his beer and killed it. For once, he could've cared less the Sounds were playing.

A sound.

Dakota startled awake. He hadn't planned on a long nap, but the week's fruitless business had taken its toll. What the hell? Had Metro found him already? No, it sounded like someone coming in the front door. Faintly, he heard the sound of a woman's voice—no, two women.

"I really appreciate you showing me this place so late."

"I don't usually show property after it gets dark, but this is a nice neighborhood."

A real estate agent—fuck!

He pulled his weapon from the waist of his pants, checked the magazine, and jammed it back into the butt end of the gun. Carefully, he pulled back on the slide and chambered a round with a loud snick that echoed in the empty house.

From the living room, one of the women said, "Did you hear that?"

"Is someone here?" The other women's voice quivered.

Yeah, lady, the big bad wolf. Silently, he rose to his feet and held his breath.

"You see why I don't like showing properties at night?"

"Maybe we should leave and come back in the daytime."

Thunder crashed. Both women squealed like pigs for slaughter.

"Let's get out of here," one of them screeched.

Good idea, ladies. Then I'll be long gone. He held his breath. *Go on. Get your Yuppie asses outta here.*

Step. Step. Another shuffling step. Each one an effort. Feet must weigh a ton each. He bit his cracked lips and tasted the salty tang of his own blood. His tongue so dry and caked, he couldn't summon enough spit to lick his lips.

If he didn't get some water soon, he'd die of dehydration. What he wouldn't give for a gallon of a sports drink, any drink.

Lightning flashed overhead and thunder cracked loud and sharp. Too close. Danny jumped, glanced upward, then stumbled and fell for the umpteenth time only five yards from the front porch—the light where he'd aimed his depleted body for what seemed like hours. He rolled to his side and whimpered. Almost there. Almost wasn't good enough. Don't give up.

No, he wasn't a sissy girl. He scrabbled in the rocky driveway, trying to get to his knees. The sharp stones dug into his knees and he collapsed, sobbing.

"Holy Mary, Mother…"

The flashes of lightning bloomed, and then the sky faded to black.

Chapter Twenty-Five

After the ten o'clock news, Tess pondered Scott's intel while she showered, then dressed for bed in a short nightshirt. At the very moment she was ready to slip between the fresh cool sheets, her cell phone rang. She growled, then answered, "You've reached Detective O'Malley's voice mail. Please leave a message and she'll return your call after she's had a good night's sleep."

"You can't fool me," said Detective Sara Kagen, who happened to be pulling a rare nightshift. "Something interesting for you. Might be related to your case."

All thoughts of sleep quickly evaporated. "Yeah? Go on."

"West precinct had a call from a real estate agent who was showing a house earlier this evening—a duplex on Granny White. She and her customer heard a noise, got scared and high-tailed it. When they circled the property, they saw a late model silver vehicle parked behind; the duplex is supposed to be empty. So, when patrol got around to checking it out, the car was long gone, but one of the apartments had been broken into. Since the car matched the general description of the one stolen from Lipscomb, forensics is there checking for any possible DNA or fingerprint evidence."

Tess nodded. "Could be Taylor hid out there until it got dark. Thanks, Sara. Appreciate the heads up."

"Thought you might."

After Kagen hung up, Tess hurriedly redressed.

Taylor, aka Doug Silvey, was a former Nashville resident, and as such, he'd know a hundred ways to get out of town. Putting a roadblock around a city like Nashville was impossible. No doubt he'd already taken any one of those hundred ways to leave town.

Wouldn't hurt to check out the duplex. Not that it would help Todd Brennerman or Danny Hurley, but it might give her a lead on where Taylor was headed next.

Inside the duplex, there wasn't much to see. It was empty and her trip was probably a major waste of time. She walked into the front bedroom and shined a flashlight around the room. "Looks like a greasy spot on the wall. Maybe he sat there and leaned back while he waited for nightfall. Check the area for hair and skin cells. Check the toilet, too. He's bound to have taken a piss."

Remembering the car parked under the carport, she said, "Check for tire marks. If you find any, make impressions and check them against the tire database to see if they're consistent with the vehicle stolen earlier tonight at Lipscomb."

She wandered back into the living room. The realtor and her client were two very lucky women. Good thing they'd beat it before Taylor got hold of them, or there'd be a bloodbath instead of just ratty old green carpet.

Reaching for her cell phone, she put her hand into her pocket, then stopped. Dammit. The impulse to call Scott and give him an update was entirely too strong. She'd gotten used to sharing info with him.

So what? He could just get his updates on the news like all the other citizens.

Crack! A flash of lightning dazzled her eyes.

Holy shit, that was close. She ducked instinctively at the sharp sound and headed outside for the shelter of her SUV. Before she could reach it, the skies opened and drenched her to the skin.

Once inside, she wiped the water from her arms, brushed the wet tangles from her hair and pulled it back with a band she found in the glove box.

Where would Taylor go next? Most likely, he'd rip off another vehicle and head out of town. How would they ever catch him? They'd missed their best chance while he was holed up just down the street from where he'd stolen the Buick.

The women had no doubt seen his car when they circled the duplex, so now it was a liability.

Where was his young redhead? Little bastard. No one had ever gotten away from him before. His size and strength had overcome all of his other choices. Must be slipping. The kid would probably die from dehydration or starvation before anyone found him. Serve him right.

Fat drops of rain started smacking against his windshield; he reached and turned on the wipers.

Fuck it. He hated driving in the rain, especially at night.

All his souvenirs were back at his cabin. No way he could leave town without them. Each and every one of the shoes was a dear memory.

He was too recognizable now. Surely, the police would put out a bulletin on him. So much for his football career.

Maybe it was time he called in his backup. He hit the speed dial.

Damn. Voice mail.

He grinned as he left a cryptic message, one his friend would understand yet would seem innocuous to anyone else. "It's your old buddy. I'm in town for a while. Thought we ought to get together...at our old place."

"Hey there."

Danny's eyes opened. Night. A flicker of lightning. Rain in his face. He blinked. Throat dry as cotton. Opened his mouth. Nothing.

"'Sokay," a woman yelled at him over the sound of crashing thunder. "Gotta get you inside. Can you get up?"

He tried to nod, then pulled up his knees, rolled over on his stomach and managed to kneel. Gravel embedded in his knees. He moaned.

Somehow, the woman pulled him to his feet, and with her arm around his waist, managed to drag him up the porch and inside. It took fucking forever.

"Just a few more steps, hon." Her tone was kind. An angel couldn't have sounded any sweeter.

She turned him around and nudged him back into a recliner. His lids fluttered. "Thanks—"

And he was out.

The next thing he knew…cold. His entire body shivered and shook like a wet dog's.

"Here you go." She wrapped a towel around his head and set to rubbing all the skin from his arms and shoulders. "You'll warm up in a bit. Gotta take care of those hands of yours." She started loosening the duct tape.

Pain. "Ow!"

"Sorry. You gotta hold still so I don't cut you."

He held as still as he could, trying not to flinch. His lips were dry and caked. "Water," he croaked.

"Of course. What was I thinking?" She bustled away and came back with a cup of water. "I got you some soda pop, too. Wish I had some of those whatchamacallit sports drinks. One of those would perk you up just fine."

He gulped from the cup she had to hold for him. "Slow down or it'll make you puke."

"M-more," he managed to gasp.

"What's your name, son?"

He licked his cracked lips. "D-Dan…Dan…ny."

"What happened to you?"

"A…man…he…"

"Good granny grunt. You're the boy what disappeared from Bellevue. They've all but given you up for dead, son."

He pulled his mouth into a smile. "Me…too." So tired. He tried to open his eyes wider, but they were too heavy.

A nap. He just needed one so bad.

Danny awakened and struggled. Where the hell was he? His hands were wrapped in bandages and he was trapped in some kind of cushy recliner. He blinked from the bright morning sunlight shining directly in his eyes. Guess the storm had passed all right. As the smell of frying bacon reached his nose, he grinned.

Food. His stomach rumbled. "Hello!"

"Hold on, Danny boy, I'm a-coming."

Who was coming? He searched through his memory. Right. A little old lady found him and brought him inside. He kicked at the chair's footrest. "Kick down on the footrest. That lever hasn't worked in years."

With some effort, he managed the footrest. With the woman's help, he stood, his head spinning like an out of balance top.

The woman placed her hand on his shoulder and steadied him. "Take a second, son. Get your legs under you."

"Gotta pee."

"Praise be. That's a good sign."

He held his hands in front of him. "They're numb."

"No matter, son. I'll give you a hand."

He gulped. "Uh—no."

"Uh—yes, 'cause you can't stand here and whiz on my carpet. The john's back in the hall, and then we'll get you a bath and some clean clothes."

"No!" He shook his head. "Those police and forensics shows. They should see me like I am. DNA and clues—all that stuff."

The woman nodded. "Didn't think about that. You're one smart kid."

He glanced at the cordless phone on the side table. "Call my parents?"

"Can't. Phone's out, Danny boy. Now get a move on. Have a pee. Then I'm taking you to Williamson Medical Center. We'll call 'em from there."

He nodded. "I'm sorry you have to do this, ma'am. Please don't tell anybody."

"Cross my heart and hope to die. Nobody but you and me are ever gonna know you needed this old woman's help to pee."

He let her nudge him toward the hallway. Danny winced, then asked, "Where am I anyway?"

"You're in Williamson County between Franklin and Columbia. You look like you've been in the woods for days."

"Feels like it. What day is it?"

"Friday. Go on now. I'll tell you all I know on the way to the hospital."

"Yes, ma'am." He stopped in the doorway to the bathroom and turned to face her. "Thank you."

Didn't take long. She slid down his stinky shorts. "Might be easier if you sat down."

The teenager turned and scowled. "Not gonna sit and pee like a girl. No way."

"All right. Guess you'll just have to—uh, dangle over the commode. Don't worry I can't see a thing. The sooner you pee, the sooner we'll get somewhere there's a phone that works."

He couldn't help but giggle. This was one part of the story he'd never tell his friends.

Never. Ever.

Dakota pulled into the cabin's driveway in a maroon two-door with plates stolen from a car in a hospital parking lot. Since returning for his father's funeral in May, the cabin had served as his base of operations for the entire summer. Just like his old man to rat his son out to the cops once he himself was beyond the long arm of the law which unfortunately didn't reach all the way to Hell.

When he entered the cabin, he first cast a quick glance around the room. Nothing out of place as far as he could tell. He walked over to the storage cubby where he'd set a large khaki duffel bag and assured the lock remained intact.

His souvenirs. Each one of them special in its own way.

While he waited for his backup to arrive, he might as well watch a little TV. He didn't have cable but he could still pick up the local stations with an on-air digital antenna.

He grabbed the remote and turned to the local news. Watching, he chuckled at the report of two women who had the scare of their lives when they went to view a property for sale in the Green Hills area. They identified a stolen car, stolen by a thief in the area. Any information…

What bullshit.

The news segued to storm damage and the electrical power outages in rural Williamson County. That's where he'd let his last choice get away from him. Dammit.

As if the local anchor could read his mind, the news segued again, this time to the still missing Danny Hurley.

Blah. Blah. Blah. Just a rehash.

Kid oughta be dead by now from dehydration and exposure. Or struck by lightning. Too bad. So sad. Little red-headed bastard could've had a quicker, if not easier, time of it if he hadn't run away.

Hold on. They were showing another red-head, Detective O'Malley. He'd seen her on TV before. Looked like the TV reporter caught her as she was going in to work. Had a big old coffee cup in her hand, so she stopped and asked the public to call with any information. Search parties had turned up nothing as yet.

Blah. Blah. Blah.

Dream on, bitch. You'll never find his sorry carcass.

Damn. On the other hand. Was the kid really dead? What if he'd found shelter and someone—nah! If he'd found help, someone would've already called the police. Maybe the thinks-she's-so-hot detective would like a clue to his general whereabouts? He hated to miss all the fuss and bother of searchers combing through the weeds, chiggers, and ticks. After making note of the tip line number, he scratched his arm and shivered. Damn ticks. His pants had been crawling with the tiny little buggers when he finally gave up on tracking the kid.

He reached for one of the disposable cell phones he'd bought from a street hustler. It was likely stolen and definitely untraceable.

Here we go. Gonna have a little fun.

"I need to speak to Detective O'Malley. Got some information she might like to have."

Whoever answered tried to get his name. "No names. Get me O'Malley." But the tip line was serving up nothing but delay. Trying to trace his call, no doubt about it. Wouldn't do 'em any good. "What time does she come in? Does she want to know about that missing kid or not?"

He heard a commotion in the background, then...

"O'Malley. What do you know about Danny Hurley?"

"I'd rather tell you in person."

"Fine. Then come on down to the Criminal Justice Center and make an official report. Know it?"

"I thought this tip line was supposed to be confidential."

"It is but if you have information on Danny's whereabouts, you need to spit it out right now."

"Civil War battle fought close by." He chuckled then snapped the phone shut.

Figure that one out, Detective Smarty Pants. Time to lose the phone.

Chapter Twenty-Six

"Dammit!" Tess turned to Kagen who tried to get a trace going on the tip line. "He's gone. Anything?"

Kagen shook her head. "Cell phone, most likely disposable. Best we can do is see where it pinged." The detective's fingers flew over the keyboard. "Crap. Closest we can get is south of town. Wasn't on long enough to triangulate a solid location."

"I'd bet my badge it was Taylor. What was it he said? 'Civil War battle fought close by.' Hell! That's most of Nashville and Franklin." All right. Eliminate Nashville. There weren't enough places to hide the body without running the risk of being seen. Williamson County had more than its share of bloodshed during the Civil War, and it wasn't as thickly populated as Nashville. There were plenty of places to hide the kid's body.

Why was he suddenly contacting the police? Not enough media attention? The department's official stance was the two kidnappings weren't related. What would he do if he didn't get the publicity he wanted? Take another kid?

God no, not that.

She jumped up and strode to the lieutenant's office, knocked and watched frustration sweep over his face. All the same, he nodded for her to enter. "We just got something on the Hurley tip line." Giving him the short and sweet version of the conversation, she finished with, "Now what?"

The frown lines deepened at the corners of the lieutenant's mouth. He didn't bother to look up from his paperwork. "Pass it on to the FBI. They're handling this case."

"No! This is my lead. The caller asked for me by name. He wants something—publicity, credit— whatever. We have to act."

Then the lieutenant shot his evil-eyed gaze in her direction. "You want to go scrubbing through all the woods and fields in Williamson County, be my guest." He paused, but it wasn't reassuring. "Just turn in your badge first. If you can't follow department policies and procedures, you're of no use."

What a load of crap. "Come on. You don't mean that. We know who he is. We need to alert the entire middle Tennessee area. God knows what he'll do next. We've already seen what he's capable of."

"The Brennerman and Hurley cases are under the purview of the FBI. It's their call."

"You want me..." She broke off and tried to regain a semblance of control. "You want this department to just stand back and sit on our hands while this killer is running free to do whatever he wants. And you don't want to let the media know what's really going on. Edward Forbes is stashed away in isolation because the Feds don't want to admit he's innocent in hopes the killer will strike again. Well, he did. He took Danny Hurley."

He pushed back in his chair and gave her the fish-eye. "You're on a slippery slope to insubordination. I've heard enough."

"No, you haven't...and neither has anyone else. I'm taking this to the media."

At the word *media*, his mouth tightened until she couldn't see his lips at all. "And he'll run before the Feds can catch him. Then what happens? He moves on to another city. Then more teenagers go missing and bodies keep piling up. How're you going to feel then, O'Malley? You want to follow the rules or charge off like Donna Quixote?"

"Nice literary reference, boss, but we already have BOLOs out for the stolen cars. Can't I follow up on that, at least?"

Woods shrugged. "Give the information from the tip line to Special Agent Chase. You run with the stolen car angle." The lieutenant leaned forward, his gaze drilling into hers. "But, hear me on this, O'Malley; if I hear a single word of this in the media...I mean, if I even hear it whispered in my ear by a mosquito, your ass is fired. Got it?"

The silly urge to snap a salute hit her, but she clenched her fists and resisted. "Got it."

She turned and left Woods to his paperwork. Seated back at her desk, she let out a groan.

Kagen sniggered. "Looks like you had a major ass-chewing in there."

Tess stood, glanced over her shoulder, then shrugged. "Nothing's missing, but it was a close call."

Another snigger from Kagen.

"Enough already. Say, want to give me a hand with this stolen car deal? Might be related to our killer." She picked up a pencil and waited.

Kagen's eyes widened as she looked askance. "You want me for a partner? Do I look like I fell off the truck last night? You're kinda hard on your partners, O'Malley. I'll pass."

"Yeah, yeah. Whatever." Back to tracing Taylor's whereabouts from the time he left his mother's. A few minutes later, her landline rang.

"O'Malley."

"I like you, Detective. I'll show you where I left the Hurley boy, but you have to meet me alone."

Again she motioned for Kagen to trace her call.

"Yeah, right. Like I'm stupid enough to fall for that."

"Don't you think his parents would like to know where he is? Closure—isn't that the word?"

"We'll find him." Might take months, but sooner or later, they'd find Hurley.

"But will you find him *in time*?"

"In time?" *Omigod.* Her heart sped up double time. Was there a chance he was still alive? Even a tiny one?

"I didn't kill him. He's still out there."

"Come on, tell me, Taylor. We know who you are—"

"Later, Detective."

Dial tone.

"Dammit!" Furious, she slammed down the phone, then glanced at Kagen. "Well?"

"Nothing. Same general area, sorry."

Tess drummed her nails on the desktop. What to do? Tell Woods or not? Not. She stood and grabbed her purse.

"Where're you going?" Kagen asked. "Are you about to shoot yourself in the foot...or worse?"

No way was she sharing her plan with Kagen. Best lie like a rug. "Nah. Need some fresh coffee."

She'd have some coffee all right. Without a doubt, Taylor would call again until she agreed to meet him. She had to be ready with back-up and no way would the lieutenant sign off on her plan. She headed out into the hallway and pulled out her cell, hesitating because it could mean the end of her career if she screwed things up. If everything went as planned, she'd be hailed a hero. Who couldn't buy into that? Besides, it would show her father and brothers she was as good a cop as they were.

All right. Nothing ventured. Nothing gained.

In spite of the fear Scott wouldn't give her a hand—not after the way she'd treated him—his sister answered and put Tess straight through.

"Good morning, Detective O'Malley. Is it really you, or did my sister have a caffeine-withdrawal hallucination?"

His tone was as smooth and rich as premium milk chocolate, sending a warm thrill to her nether regions. Not that it mattered.

"Yes. It's me," she finally managed to say. This wasn't going to be easy. But she needed him...professionally.

"I'm really glad you—"

"Just shut up and listen. This isn't about anything personal between us. It's business."

"Business? Can't say I can do business with you." He gave a little chuckle. "Conflict of interest and all that."

"Glad to know you're so ethical, Holt." No, he wasn't going to make it easy. "Look, I need someone to back me up...if a certain person calls back. You're the only one I trust. The lieutenant has already threatened to fire me once today if I don't keep my nose out of the case and let the Feds handle it."

"Back-up? I can certainly arrange that. My brother's available."

Justin, the computer nerd? Now Scott was playing with her. Had to be. "No, it has to be you. I said it's a matter of trust."

"My brother is a fully qualified and licensed PI. I wouldn't propose him if he weren't trustworthy. What's this about anyway?"

She could hear the unmistakable hint of amusement in his tone. Dammit. "All right! Someone—I'm sure it was Taylor—called me twice this morning. Woods expects me to turn all the info over to the Feds. But listen to this, Taylor hinted the Hurley kid might not be dead yet. Gave me this stupid clue— 'Civil War battle fought here.' That kind of crap. I'm sure he'll get in touch with me again, and when he does…" Still undecided, she paused. Was she really going to ask Scott to back her up off profile?

"You want me to go along as back-up?"

"He's a big bruiser. I'm small and I'm quick, but I'm not stupid. If he gets hold of me—"

"No, we wouldn't want that."

Again, the tone of barely suppressed humor was coming through and it was getting on her last nerve. "There's no 'we' in this situation, Scott. I *know* it's a trap, but I trust you to cover my backside and recognize Taylor when you see him."

"Strictly business?"

"Exactly."

"You'll need to come by the office, pay a thousand-dollar retainer and sign a contract. My daily fee for personal services, which includes being at your personal beck and call twenty-four/seven, is five-hundred plus expenses."

Ouch. Hopefully, she wouldn't need him for more than a couple of days. "Fine."

She hung up without another word, walked back into the squad room and let the department A.A. know she was taking a personal hour.

Make that two.

Amused and damned hopeful, Scott set the receiver down and leaned back. So, Tess was on her way over to sign a contract for his personal services. Could lead to something even more personal; if he had anything to say about it, it would. At least, she wasn't going to try taking down Taylor on her own. By the time it was all over, she might actually get the lowdown on where the Hurley kid's body was buried. No matter what Taylor hinted, Scott didn't believe for one moment the teenager was still alive.

The boy's family would be scarred forever. The little sister would grow up under a cloud of fear and uncertainty. The parents would kick into over-protective mode and she'd probably rebel. Scott knew loss. First his mother, then his father and stepmother. The loss of a child had to be even worse. Still he'd survived, and hopefully, Danny Hurley's parents and little sister would, too.

It wasn't long before Carrie let him know Tess had arrived. "Send her in." He stood, then walked to the door and opened it.

Holy hotness personified. She wore a light tan suit, a cream silky/slip type thing under it. Her wavy red hair was pulled back and piled on top of her head, but curls had escaped along the nape of her neck and in front of her ears, softening the severe businesslike expression on her face. A tan leather shoulder bag completed the detective's wardrobe. Still, he'd rather see her in nothing at all.

Dream on.

"Seen enough?"

"Can't blame me for looking." He grinned down at her. Talk about a woman in a pissy mood, one who didn't like asking for help. "It's a guy thing." He motioned for her to take a seat while he perched on the corner of the desk.

"So," she gave a shrug, "where's the contract?"

"Carrie'll have it ready in a minute. You're looking good this morning."

"As opposed to when?"

Strike one.

"Just a general comment, Tess. No aspersions on your appearance at any other time were intended."

She sat on the edge of the chair, as if ready to sprint for the door at the slightest hint of anything personal. "You still talk like a lawyer."

"Almost was." He abandoned his perch, walked behind his desk and sat.

Just business—hell, he could do business. He drummed his fingers against the desktop. Where was Carrie with that contract?

As if summoned by his psychic energies, his sister tapped on the door and entered with the contract. She gave Tess a somewhat tentative smile and a brief nod.

Tess pulled a pen from her shoulder bag. "Where do I sign?"

"As an almost attorney, I'd advise you to read it first. You might be signing away your firstborn."

Her mouth drew into a fake smile. "Right. Do PIs normally ask for that?"

He grinned back, hoping she'd lighten up a little. "Hardly any I know."

She scanned it for a moment, then scrawled her name with a grand flourish across the bottom. Catching his gaze for a second, she slid it across the desk. "There. I'll call you as soon as I hear from him again." Clearly, having had enough of his company, she popped up from the chair like a puppet on strings.

He stood, ready to see her to the door. Should he try again? "I look forward to hearing from you…soon." He stopped, then forged ahead. "You really think Taylor was telling the truth about Hurley being alive?"

She shook her head, causing a couple of longer curls to escape. As much as he might want, he didn't dare brush them back or kiss her.

Strike two.

"Can't take the chance though," she said. "He might be telling the truth."

"If he's alive, why hasn't he shown up somewhere? Think about it, Tess. I hate for you to get your hopes up and be disappointed."

"This is about the case. Not about my hopes or disappointments. Just see you're available when, and if, I call."

Strike three. You're out!

"Yes, ma'am. Message received." He moved around the desk.

"No need. I'll see myself out." Slinging her bag over her shoulder, she strode from his office without as much as a backward glance.

Scott hunched his shoulders and sat.

Game over.

Chapter Twenty-Seven

It was hot as Hades outside. The concrete sidewalk was certainly hot enough to fry the proverbial egg, but Tess was shivering by the time she left Scott's office. Good thing her SUV had automatic key locks. Her hands were shaking too hard to be of any use.

Inside the car, she started the motor and waited for the air conditioning to cool things off. Dammit. Scott still possessed an overabundance of power to affect her in more ways than she could count. During their brief meeting, it'd taken every ounce of self-control to keep from jumping his bones. His warm gaze, gliding greedily up and down her body, unnerved her until she could barely form a coherent thought, much less actual sentences.

Not fair. Not at all.

She'd made her choice. Done the right thing. Terminated a going-nowhere relationship.

Still, seeing him hurt her more than she expected. How telling was it she trusted him, and only him, to cover her back? But if there was even the smallest possibility Danny Hurley was alive, she had to follow up on it. Scott's presence would help even the odds. A strategic move—that was all.

Stop lying to yourself.

Great. Now she was reduced to talking to herself. If she wasn't careful, she'd be answering too. Thanks a lot. Kozinsky was right. She'd spend the rest of her life alone if she didn't let someone in. But she had and it wasn't going to work. It couldn't.

Speaking of Kozinksy, she hadn't heard from him since the night in the hospital. She pulled the cell phone from her belt and punched in the

Kozinskys' number. Estelle answered and said he was on his way into the CJC.

"Brave man."

Estelle snorted and said he was already such a pain in her behind she wasn't so anxious to have him home fulltime anymore. "In fact, maybe he ought to go for forty years instead of his thirty."

Tess laughed and let Estelle go. So, he was coming in. Damn. All she needed was her partner putting the kibosh on her plan.

After his phone call to the detective, Taylor called in his marker, then took a long hot shower and redressed. The all too familiar itch was on him full force.

Wouldn't have happened if he hadn't lost his choice in that miserable wooded area outside Chapel Hill.

Not the time to be reckless. The authorities knew who he was. Can't risk finding another one now.

Research took too much time. Time he didn't have. Time to get the hell out of Dodge.

But he did have time for one more trip downtown and some fun with a certain police detective. Back in the day, before he'd discovered his true calling, he'd been attracted to girls like the detective...or thought he was. His worldview had flipped 180 degrees the first time he touched young Richie Mason.

Of course, he hadn't been the only one to touch Richie that night. In fact, it hadn't even been his idea to take the boy out in the woods. Even so, the experience had been a revelation and he hadn't been the one who puked when all was said and done.

Wouldn't it be fun to whack the smartass detective and leave her body displayed prominently for the slut she surely was? Trying to be a man. In a man's job. Believing she was as smart or strong as any man.

He'd show her a real man.

But first, there were a couple of people he needed to take care of. That's where his back-up would give him a hand.

Time to go. He stopped at the door and looked around the snug cabin.

It had served its purpose.

Back in the squad room, Tess found Kozinsky back at his desk. "So you managed to come to work today? Aren't you the brave soldier? How're the ribs?"

"So sore I can barely breathe. Thanks for asking. Anyway, old Estelle's mad as hell. Putting up with you is preferable to when she's in one of her moods."

She gave him her most insincere smile. "Aw, you have such a way with compliments."

"Not really." One of his bushy brows arched. "It just so happens you're the lesser of two evils."

"How's Taylor's mother?" he asked. "She go back home?"

"Nope. According to the Feds, she's leaving the hospital today, but she'll go into protective custody until Taylor's caught."

He leaned forward and said with a grim smile, "Good. I'd hate to see him have another go at her. Might not be so lucky next time."

"Right." Tess arranged and rearranged the files on her desk. When would Taylor call her again? He hadn't identified himself, but he wasn't fooling her. She drummed her fingers on the desktop. Should she apprise her partner of her new plan?

No way. An injured partner would be of no use as back-up, and being protective as hell, he'd most likely interfere or rat her out to the lieutenant. Besides after Kozinsky, she had the best back-up in town. Someone who cared about her, even if he made her sign a contract and pay his retainer in advance. True, he cared a little too much, but as long as she kept her head and emotions entirely separate, it was purely a business arrangement.

Her partner glared over his monitor. "You're antsy today. What gives?"

Another minor adjustment to the pile of files. Okay, so she was acting like someone with OCD. Better stop futzing around before he got a real bug up his ass. "Nothing." She pulled her hands away from the files and proceeded to pull up the DMV records. Dammit. Why didn't Taylor call?

Leaning back in his chair, her partner laughed, then winced and grabbed his ribs. "Right. Known you too long. You're up to something."

"Nah. Just restless. Ready for some action." She curled her lip, then glanced around the squad. "Never knew a Friday morning to be so quiet."

"Never a good murder when you need one?" He gave another laugh. "What's the matter? Worried about job security?"

"No." She shrugged, keeping it as casual as possible.

"Any sightings on the last car he stole?"

"Aren't we leaving this up to the Feds?" she asked, hoping to divert him from the case altogether. Opening her desk drawer, she started to rummage for a nail file. Anything to keep her hands busy.

"I don't get it." He sent her a puzzled scowl. "Lieutenant Woods said he'd given you approval to follow-up on the stolen car angle. Wouldn't look bad in either of our jackets to bring this guy in ourselves."

"Personally, I don't think you have any business chasing down stolen cars." For emphasis, she slammed the drawer shut.

Her partner's bushy brows arched. "What—" Before he could finish, her landline rang. "Gotta get this."

Against her better judgment, she ordered, "Put a trace on." Snatching the receiver, she answered, "O'Malley." Procedure was procedure, no matter what her partner thought or how he might screw up her plans.

"You sound so businesslike, Detective. Here I thought you might be a little nicer when I called back."

Same voice. Taylor. "Did you leave him alive or not? That's all I really need to know."

"Don't you want to know where he might be? Alive or dead—that's valuable information. Worthy of some accommodation, I'd say."

"Can't offer the killer a reward these days for information on the whereabouts of his victim. For some strange reason, the public doesn't take kindly to the department's doing things like that."

"Not even to save his poor parents' suffering?"

"I'm not authorized to make deals."

"I'd like to take you to him, Detective. Or at least where I saw him last."

"Was he alive?" A low rumble of laughter came through the phone. A shiver shook her body and a chill zapped its way up her spine. Playing games. This guy really liked them. "I'll meet you. Just tell me where."

Another laugh, more sick and evil sounding than the first. "Come alone." He laughed again. "Or the deal's off."

"We don't have a deal." She bit her bottom lip and glanced at her puzzled partner. "I get Hurley's location and you get what?"

"I go free, of course."

"We can talk about it, but I have a real problem with letting a sadistic serial killer go free to run amok wherever the hell he likes."

"Detective, name-calling isn't terribly PC."

She glanced over her monitor at Kozinsky. 'Are you getting this?' she mouthed. His affirmative nod reassured her. She had to keep Taylor talking. "And killing teenage boys is?"

"Unfortunately, it's what I do. Sorry, running out of time." With that, he terminated the call.

"Dammit! Did we get his location?"

Kozinsky nodded. "Interesting. He's downtown."

"Close then." A chill the size of an iceberg zapped up her spine. Close. She could go out and eyeball him on the street somewhere.

Bait—that's what she was. He didn't want to meet her and take her to the Hurley's last known location. No, he'd fixated on her for some sick reason known only to him. Again, it all came back to bait.

Bait—works for me.

Dakota Taylor chuckled as he ended the call.

If she knew just how close I am.

He perched on the concrete barrier outside the Criminal Justice Center. His disguise was good— great even. With the addition of several layers of clothes, he'd added fifty pounds to his bulk. Hunched over, he ambled along, pushing a stolen grocery cart loaded with some homeless person's junk. While he kept an eye on the police personnel parking lot, he was a typical homeless person to the casual observer. His personal vehicle was nearby and handy…or maybe he would grab the detective and force her into her own vehicle.

Sweat dripped down his chest and between his shoulder blades. Damn it was hot. Nashville always was an oven in the summertime, and this summer was no exception. After making sure no one was paying him any attention, he chucked the cell phone into the planter. No matter. He never used the same one twice.

He didn't have long to wait. The redheaded detective soon emerged from the building just as he thought she would. She surveyed the street, then headed for a black SUV.

An electric thrill ran through him. It wasn't the same kind of excitement he experienced when he'd chosen one of his male victims to honor with his special brand of love. No, this would be fun…for him at least. The chase was on.

Scott hung up from Tess's call. Adrenaline was already surging through his body, his heart rate intensifying. She'd set herself up as bait on purpose and was depending on him to cover her gorgeous ass and keep her alive while she led Taylor on a wild goose chase.

What's more, he was supposed to accomplish all of this without tipping off Taylor he was being followed. As luck would have it, he had driven the agency car he used for stakeouts, a silver Camry with a souped-up engine. Had to be a hundred thousand silver cars in Nashville. Just about as nondescript as one could get.

"I'll be out of the office the rest of the day," he told Carrie cryptically as he strode past her. Didn't wait for a response. Didn't have time. Tess gave him ten whole minutes before she headed out of the police station which was a big gamble. The cell phone pings had pinned his location downtown, and she bet Taylor had positioned himself where he could see her leave the building. Scott had to be in place to spot Taylor when he made his move.

Whether Taylor would follow her in his own vehicle or if he'd strong-arm his way into her SUV, now that was the question.

***

The midmorning heat was dizzying, radiating from the concrete sidewalk in waves. On the way to her SUV, Tess checked her watch. Eleven minutes since she'd called Scott. Okay, he'd better be somewhere close. Driving a silver Camry. Not a bad choice for a surveillance vehicle. In her book, something a little less shiny would've been even better.

She glanced up and down the street, looking for a man in the range of six-foot-five—that would be Taylor. Where was Scott? She'd left her partner behind in the throes of a near-stroke when he heard what she planned. He'd gone to report her, but she ducked out and hid in the public restroom until the ten minutes she'd given Scott to get in position had passed.

An obese homeless man lounged on one of the concrete planters. He was certainly tall enough to be Taylor, but at least fifty to sixty pounds over her target's weight. Still, easier to add weight than take it off.

Several cars down the block she spotted the vehicle she hoped was Scott's. Good. She couldn't see the driver but her gut said it was Scott. Still, the adrenaline rush had already started. With her Glock 22 service weapon and a back-up piece in her back waistband, she was armed, dangerous and more than ready to take Taylor out. No stilettos for this operation. She wore comfortable, sensible shoes— black leather Adidas— in case she had to run.

Taylor wouldn't come unprepared, either.

Maybe it was her imagination, but she felt his gaze as surely as an arrow aimed at her back. She twitched her shoulders to release the tension. Not that it did any good.

No. Jumpy and twitchy was good. Her reflexes were honing up for a fight.

Scott. You'd better be in place, old friend. I've a feeling I'm going to need you.

From his vantage point, Scott watched, his fingers drumming against the steering wheel and his feet tapping. There she was. Stopped. Looking up and down the street, her movements twitchy and nervous. Now heading to the police department car lot.

Gigantic homeless guy following. Taylor in a disguise? Difficult to tell his height since he was hunched over pushing a cart of filled garbage bags. Homeless guy on the move. In her direction.

Dammit. Wish there'd been time to wire her up. He gave a quick glance around. Traffic moving

in a normal fashion. Homeless guy paused and looked around. Rocking back and forth in his seat, Scott hit the steering wheel with his fist. "Come on. Somebody, do something!"

Tess had already unlocked her car when her cell phone sang. She snatched it off her belt and saw her partner's name on the caller I.D. "What do you want?" she snapped. "Already tattled to the lieutenant, have you?"

"No. Zip it for once and just listen. The Hurley kid's been found alive. There's no need to set yourself up as bait. Come back in."

"That's—"

Before she could finish, she was grabbed around the waist and hauled off her feet. The cell phone went flying across the hood and landed on the sidewalk with a clatter.

Her captor shoved a gun under her chin. "Okay, Red. Get in and drive."

Chapter Twenty-Eight

"Do you honestly think you're going to get away with taking me hostage?" Damn! Who knew a three-hundred-pound homeless man could move so fast? A moment's distraction. Just long enough.

Damn Kozinsky for bugging her anyway. Still, he gave her exactly what she needed for the upper hand—knowledge the sweating slob didn't have.

"Already have," he reminded her by jabbing his weapon in her ribs. "Now drive."

"You don't think someone has already reported this?" She fastened her seat belt. "You weren't exactly subtle."

"Head for the interstate."

She shook her head. "Uh-uh. Smarter to stick to city streets if you want to evade pursuers," she told him, hoping to give Scott time to catch up. "Too easy to spot us on the interstate. The choppers would have a clear view."

The last thing she wanted was a high-speed chase that would endanger citizens. A nice quiet street where she could wreck the SUV and gain the advantage over Taylor, now that would be ideal.

Okay, not a great plan, but the best she could do on short notice. Improvising had always been one of her strong suits. She checked the rearview mirror, noting Scott was two cars behind them. She'd better figure out something fast.

Or her captor would.

"All right then. Head for Granny White," he ordered, his hand brushing over her breast. "Gotta meet someone in Maryland Farms."

"Watch it!" She shivered at his touch. "Thought you preferred teenage boys, Taylor."

"Going for your gun, Detective—not your tit." He jerked the service weapon from her shoulder holster.

One down, but she still had her back-up piece.

She headed for Twelfth Avenue South which would turn into Granny White. Too many schools at first, but much more residential the farther out it went. If Scott didn't come up with something before they reached the outskirts, that's where she'd make her move.

She passed David Lipscomb University and a middle school on the right...as well as the duplex where Taylor'd hidden after he dumped Scott's precious Mustang.

Should she tell her captor Danny Hurley'd been found alive? Not a good idea. Playing dumb was her best bet. "Where are we headed?"

"Told you I'd show you the kid's last location."

"And then you'll just leave me just like you left him—raped, strangled, and dead like all your other victims. I don't believe for one instant he's still alive."

His upper lip curled. "You're not my type, Detective."

"Oh, how lucky I feel." She drove, keeping her eyes peeled for just the right spot.

Taylor shrugged. "Damn kid got away from me."

"I will, too," she said in her most matter-of-fact tone.

"Like I said, I prefer teenage boys. Why would I sully my hands by touching you?"

"Beats the hell out of me." No oncoming traffic. Nice little cul-de-sac coming up.

Now.

She whipped the steering wheel into a three-sixty turn.

"Crazy fucking bitch!"

The SUV skidded and crashed the passenger side into a telephone pole.

Taylor was thrown toward her, then back, bashing his head against the passenger side window. His weapon flew into the backseat. Her elbow jammed against the door and her head hit the side glass. The seatbelt tightened, nearly choking her.

***

Scott called Tess's abduction to 911, then continued to follow her past the housing project on Twelfth to Granny White. What the hell was she up to? Why was she taking that route? Precious little traffic now. The only car between them turned off, leaving him no way to conceal his presence behind them any longer. He eased off the accelerator and dropped back a bit, hoping like hell he wouldn't tip off Taylor.

He followed her SUV for miles, then without warning, her SUV spun, skidded hard, and crashed into a telephone pole. Passenger side-impact, but he could tell Tess was thrown about some too.

He slammed on his brakes and stopped. Leaving the motor running, he pulled his weapon, chambered a round, then jumped from the car. He ran to the SUV and jerked open her door. "You all right?" Taylor appeared dazed; his eyes rolled back. His chin lolled. Wreck must've been her plan B.

"Where were you heading anyway?"

Still a little stunned, she shook her head as if to clear it. "Yeah—uh, he said he was supposed to meet someone at Maryland Farms. Go figure." She glanced over at Taylor and shrugged. "Guess he should've worn his seat belt."

She rubbed her elbow and winced. "Gotta call it in. He's going to need a bus." Somewhat gingerly, she eased from the SUV.

The distant wail of a siren grew closer. "I already did. Are you really all right?"

"Bruised, a little battered," she said with a grin, "but no blood. In my book, that's okay."

"You did good, detective." He pulled her into his arms, and surprisingly, she didn't resist. Instead, she molded her body to his and rested her head on his chest. "I'm glad you're safe. That's all that counts."

She smiled up at him, kicking his heart into an erratic rhythm. "By the way, that was my partner on the phone when Taylor grabbed me. Danny Hurley's been found alive."

He grinned. "No shit?"

"I shit thee not. He's in Williamson Medical Center right now, in reasonably good condition."

"It's over." Elation rushed through him. The Feds would release Ned Forbes, and there'd be no more victims…at least not attributable to this sorry piece of slime who'd started to come around and groan.

He released her as six squad cars and two ambulances made their appearance. She morphed into detective mode and gave her statement to the on-scene officer, as did Scott. Taylor received treatment from the EMTs in the form of oxygen and I.V. fluids, then was bundled into the back of the ambulance. Whether he lived or died, Scott could've cared less.

No. Wait. Croaking from a head injury was too good for the bastard. Yeah, he ought to live and be imprisoned for the rest of his life. However, considering Tennessee was a death penalty state, and one of Taylor's victims was the governor's grandson, it didn't bode well for a long sojourn on death row.

Naturally, Tess refused transport to the ER. "I'm fine," she insisted while watching her sweet SUV hauled away by the wrecker. Total loss. Oh, well, that was why she paid those high insurance premiums. She darted a quick glance in Scott's direction and remembered, with a flush of heat to her cheeks, just how good his arms felt around her.

And that good feeling must've been the reason her next words came too quick to call them back. "Give a girl a ride?"

His wide grin and the warmth in his dark brown eyes zapped a blaze of heat to her lower belly. Oh, no. Why had she even asked? *Back off. Back off.*

"Anytime, anywhere, Detective."

She couldn't hold back the smile tugging at her lips. He possessed so many of the qualities she wanted in a man. Funny. Great back-up. And so sexy it ought to be a felony.

No. It would never work. She wouldn't—no, couldn't—give up her career.

"You know, never mind." She shook her head. "One of the unis will give me a ride to the station. There are a couple of reports I need to file.

Sign my official statement. That sort of thing."

His mouth tightened and his gaze averted for a second, then back with his anger displayed by a clenched jaw and flaring nostrils. "You're blowing me off for paperwork?"

"Can't be helped. Duty calls." She shrugged and flashed him a tight smile.

Get your head out of your ass, O'Malley. It'll never work.

"Every time you and I seem to be back on the right track"—he shook his head—"you stop and back off. I see it in your expression as plain as day. You've hardened your heart against me, time after time. Just like you are now."

Her body tensed. Was she that obvious? Fine.

"This was business. You earned your fee. We're over."

"Over? Never really got started." His tone was low. Intimate. Made her want to fall into his arms and tell him how wrong she was. Thankfully, none of her fellow officers could hear him.

"Tess..."

Fists clenched at her side, she steeled her resolve. "You never listen. I told you I'm not looking for a family and two point five kids. I have a career I love. That's a real issue, and it's not going away no matter how my body responds to yours or how much I might want to see where it could lead."

Whoops, was she a little loud on that last bit? Now she was the recipient of some curious stares from the first patrol officers who answered the call.

Time to shelve the discussion.

Turning from Scott, she called, "Officer Terry, how about a ride back to the stationhouse?" Terry motioned come on and she made tracks for his patrol car. Even though it felt as if she were leaving her heart behind, she didn't have the courage to give Scott a backward glance.

Scott watched Tess hop in the patrol car without so much as a wave goodbye. He'd served his purpose by covering her ass, and now he was expendable. What was he thinking? That she'd be grateful? No—still too hung up on making captain by the time she was forty just like her father.

Dumped. Dissed. And right in front of her fellow officers, too. What could be more final?

Stee-rike.

The air grew suffocating and stifling as he tried to breathe. For the first time, he took stock of his surroundings. Crepe myrtles in pink and white dotted the large front yards of the cul-de-sac while soaring oaks and maples provided a bit of shade. The smell of newly cut grass and the acrid odor of fresh mulch assailed his nostrils.

About time he accepted the truth.

Game over. No trip to the playoffs.

Chapter Twenty-Nine

Since her SUV was out of commission, Tess called the police garage and requisitioned an unmarked car to make a quick trip to Williamson Medical Center. She checked on Danny Hurley and found his parents on cloud nine. They had their son back again, safe and mostly sound. He definitely identified Dakota Taylor in the photo lineup as his kidnapper. The doctors were optimistic his hands could be saved. As for the elderly woman who'd rescued him, she deserved a blooming medal for her timely discovery and care through the stormy night. She would personally see to it that Trish Henley claimed the reward—no matter how much the dear lady protested she'd only done her duty to a fellow human being.

Back in the office, Tess spent the rest of the afternoon finalizing the case files on Dakota Taylor. Drew Wilson cleared. Check. Tyler Jamison cleared of murder and kidnapping. Check. Still, she knew he'd been up to something. Hopefully, it wasn't illegal and didn't involve anything more than screwing his assistant or being spanked for being a very naughty boy.

Bob "Dakota" Taylor, aka Dean Silvey, was in custody, and at present, in the Neuro ICU at Vanderbilt with a closed head injury. Best of all, he was expected to recover and stand trial for the two murders and one kidnapping with attempted murder right here in Nashville. The other states could wait in line. Tennessee had him and they'd keep him.

Something Taylor said kept nagging her. What was it? Oh, yeah, he was supposed to meet someone at Maryland Farms. Most likely, they'd never know who. If Taylor was smart, he wouldn't give up the time of day, much less the name of his accomplice.

A call to her mother was in order as well. She'd want to know her friend was officially and publicly cleared of any wrongdoing and, as of four p.m., a free man.

"I knew you and your yummy detective friend would pull it off," her mother purred.

"He sort of helped," Tess admitted. Yeah, he covered her ass and did a damn good job of it, too. "But, Mom, we're not together. It'll never work."

"Are you sure?" Her mother's tone was wistful. Probably counting on those grandkids already.

Tough. "It's kind of difficult to explain. There are…issues."

"Aren't there always issues, Pumpkin?"

Major eye roll. Mom hadn't called her Pumpkin in years. "These are big."

"Nothing ventured, nothing gained."

"Could you be any more trite?" The snarky comment escaped before she could stop it. "Sorry."

The department A.A. waved and told her she had another call. "Gotta go."

"Come by for dinner…soon. We never see you anymore."

"Soon. I promise."

Instead of a much-desired dinner to celebrate with Tess, Scott headed for the Y and the weight bench. Sweat dripped off his brow and ran back in his ears. He shook his head and inhaled, lifted the two-hundred-pound weight, lowered it slowly while exhaling, then pressed up. Five more reps to go.

Hell, fifty more reps wouldn't erase Tess from his mind or his heart. After the accident, she'd been on the verge of surrender. He'd seen it in the softness of her expression and felt her yearning when he held her close. Then just as quickly she stiffened, pulled away, and dumped his ass like a has-been pitcher on the skids.

Inhale. Lift. Lower, exhaling. Press.

It wouldn't matter how much he loved her or thought they belonged together. The woman had a one-track mind and it was focused on career advancement. Not that he expected dinner on the table at six every night and a wife who met him at the door with his pipe and slippers. In the Holt-Lackey family where the women outnumbered the men, he was certainly no chauvinist.

If today was any example, the woman he loved was an adrenaline junkie. No matter what she said about the shooting being over when the detectives arrived on scene, it hadn't kept her partner from getting injured. How could he risk losing her?

Inhale. Lift. Lower, exhaling. Press.

Yes, he wanted a family. He'd been raised in one, a big one after his father remarried. It was only natural to want that kind of happiness for himself.

Inhale. Lift. Lower, exhaling. Press.

Tess. Intelligent gray eyes. Damn, her gaze could pierce body armor. And her bullshit meter was phenomenal. The way her wavy red hair fell across her lightly freckled shoulders and tickled his chest— unforgettable.

Inhale. Lift. Lower, exhaling. Press.

Her breasts were full and rose-tipped, any teenage boy's wet dream. Her slim and yet curvy ass, her long shapely legs.

God, she was all woman. And what a woman!

Inhale. Lift. Lower, exhaling. Press up!

Scott left the YMCA and sat in the car trying to sort out the nagging questions that lingered and refused easy answers. Something about the case was just too tidy. Granted, his client was a free man and back home. Yes, the case was tied up nice and neat with football hero Dakota Taylor at the center.

But who was he going to meet at Maryland Farms? Did he have an accomplice after all? It might be rare, but it wasn't unheard of for a sexual predator to work with a partner. Given the nature of his crimes, the partner was most likely male.

Now if he could just wrangle his way past the uniformed guard and into Neuro ICU, he'd ask Dakota who he was supposed to meet in Maryland Farms and who his partner-in-crime was.

Hell, what if he was still unconscious? Scott banged the steering wheel with his first.

Dammit.

He reached for his cell. Tess would come a lot closer to seeing Taylor than he could. Should he call her? She'd just get all up in arms and emotional again about how they had no future. How many times did he need to hear that?

But if there was still someone out there who was involved, the sooner he was found the better for everyone.

He punched in her number.

The moon shone through the tall windows in streams of light and spread in a wash of silver across the hardwood floors. An hour earlier, Tess had turned off the TV after listening to the news report of Taylor's capture. She'd seen his image so many times she finally declared no more.

True, it wouldn't be the last time. Taylor wasn't just big news in Nashville. Oh, no. WNN's Felicity Pace had already done a breaking news update that very evening. The feisty, former prosecutor was a victims' rights advocate and would certainly keep her viewers informed about Taylor's trial as it progressed.

Tess walked to the window and gazed out at the lights across the river. Every Fourth of July, there was a gigantic music festival and fireworks display, and every year since buying the condo, she'd had a front-row seat.

Alone. Not necessarily lonely, mind you. The AC kicked on and sent a blast of cold air. She rubbed the goosebumps on her upper arms, then hugged her body and rested her chin on the back of her hand.

Memories of Scott's passionate and gentle touch flooded through her mind...and body. Why did he need so much from her? Her father and mother, married forty years, loved each other, she was sure of it. But they had carved out separate lives. Somehow, they managed it.

Still, it was a lot to ask of a man like Scott, so family oriented.

No police officer, even a detective, was safe on the job. Could she tie herself down to home and hearth, have his children, knowing each time she left home, she ran the risk of never returning?

The answer was, for now, and forever, no.

Her cell phone sang. When she read Scott's name on the caller ID, she clenched her jaw. What could he want now?

"You're wasting your time," she growled.

"Hello to you, too. It's about the case. Something you said right after the accident has bugged me all evening."

"Yeah? Go on." She listened while Scott explained his theory of an accomplice and the need to question Taylor further. Dammit. The same thing bugged her, too. Scott was good…too good.

"Call it a night. I'll question him, but not tonight. He's unconscious." Not wanting to encourage him further, she kept her tone brusque, but the sound of his deep voice never failed to send curls of desire eddying through her entire body.

"You're sure?"

"Yeah, I'm sure." Get the man off the phone before she weakened, turned into a puddle of need, and asked him to come over to discuss the matter some more. "Thanks for the tip."

"Let me know?"

The man would not give up. "You can read about it in the paper, okay?" She ended the call before he could ask another question. Where he was concerned, her defenses were fragile—as in they might crash and burn if she listened to him for another five seconds.

It was close to midnight when Tess pulled into the driveway of her parents' Hillwood home and parked. A single light was on. Maybe the folks were already in bed. Still intrigued by Scott's tip, she jumped from her car and ran up the sidewalk to the porch to unlock the door. She opened it and walked inside.

"Mom? Daddy?" she called. Surely, someone was home at this time of night. Her mother might be at some affair, but her father was usually in his study watching ESPN on his high-def TV. Probably had it turned up so loud, he couldn't hear anything less than a full-out assault.

A single beam of light spilled from the kitchen into the hall then came the sound of her mother's voice. "In the kitchen, darling. What's going on?"

Relief flooded through her. Maybe her mom could help make sense of it all. She poked her head into the kitchen and found her mother was sitting at the bar, sipping a cup of tea. Her hair was pulled back in a ponytail, her shirt sleeves rolled above her elbows.

"You've been working late, haven't you?"

"I'm not the only one, I see." A wide smile flashed across her mother's face. "You know how I forget the time when I'm working on something new. I've started a new series of oils...views of the Cumberland."

"Sounds great." She chewed her bottom lip, then said, "I'm glad you're still up. I was afraid you might be in bed or out for the evening."

Regina rose and pulled another cup from the cupboard, poured a cup of coffee, then slid it over with a reassuring smile. "Now tell me what brings you home this late on a Friday night?"

Warmth and acceptance radiated from her mother. Tess blinked back the misery, the knot of lonely nights forming in her throat. "Oh, Mom, everything is such a mess. I don't know what I'm gonna do."

Her mother leaned forward, her eyes widening with concern. "Tell me all about it, pumpkin."

"It's Scott. He's so...family...oriented."

Her mother straightened, an expression of mock surprise flickering across her face. "A family-oriented man? Such a tragedy. What's the world coming to?"

"I'm serious. He wants more than I can give. Family. Children."

"Imagine that." Her mother's smirk and elevated eyebrow didn't hold the reassurance Tess needed.

"But my career. It's no secret I plan to make captain before I'm forty. A family would absolutely interfere."

"Yes, it might, but would you be any less successful if you reached your goal a few years later and still had the love and support of a good man and a couple of children? More importantly, will your rank keep you warm at night?"

Tess drew up. "That's not the point, Mother."

"It's exactly the point," her mother said with a huff, then eyeballed Tess. "While I admire your ambition, this goal of yours is about winning your father's approval and proving you're just as good, if not better than your brothers. When you were growing up, it was the same thing. It didn't matter if you had straight As. I just thank God they didn't have a girl's football team, or you would've tried out for that too."

"But—"

"But nothing. You've shown everyone you're as smart as your older brothers and just as tough. You can have a full family life and still devote yourself to your job. Heaven knows I've done it. Just remember, your life is yours to live—not your brothers."

"Mother!" All right, her exasperation was showing. She took a deep breath to calm down. "You're an artist. You're not out dodging bullets and bringing down serial killers instead of attending PTO meetings. What if something happened to me?"

"What you really mean is what if having children lessens your edge. Made you a little less ready to jump into harm's way? Then I say, good. From what I saw on the news tonight, you take too many chances as it is. Your father says you're already in trouble for taking off to meet that killer on your own without back-up."

"I had back-up—Scott."

"Exactly. Neither of you have conventional jobs. If Scott loves you, he'll support your career as your father has mine. If you love *him*, you'll find a way to make your lives together work."

Denial and anger bubbled and warred within Tess. No one understood—not even her mother. Coming here was a waste of time. She should've stayed home. "We're too different."

Her mother shook her head. "No, you're not any more different than any other two people who fall in love and have to come to terms with who they are, how they're alike or different, and how they'll live their lives."

Groaning, she shoved her coffee cup away from the edge of the bar and stood. "I need a solution, not platitudes."

"No, you need to make a decision which only you can make. First of all, you need to decide if you love Scott and if being a captain by forty is more important to your happiness than he is."

"That simple, is it?" She clenched her jaw as if afraid of losing her teeth. "Easy for you to say. You've already done it."

"Simple, yes. Easy, no." Her mother reached across the counter and patted Tess's hand. "Give it some time. He's not going anywhere, is he?"

"No."

But *she* was going crazy. Tess swallowed back the hurt. What happened to the independent woman she'd always thought she was? Here she was floundering around and unable to make up her mind. Could she make a one-eighty, turn her back on her long-held goals and rush into Scott's arms like some heroine in a romance novel?

Chapter Thirty

Groggy and dizzy, Scott opened his eyes. His head ached like a son-of-a-bitch as he tried to look around. Damn. Oxygen mask over his face. IVs in his arm. Monitors filling the room. Tubes up the who-ha. Hell, he was in some kind of hospital room.

Then the memories returned in a flash. A gas leak. At home. Allison and Justin made it downstairs okay. Tam wasn't home. He'd dragged an unconscious Carrie off the sofa.

Carrie?

He yanked down the mask. "Hey! Where's my sister?"

No one answered. Through bleary eyes, he could just make out the figure of a nurse at the desk. "Hey! I'm awake. What about the rest of my family?"

The nurse looked up, scowled and bustled to his bedside. "Put that mask back on. It's one-hundred percent oxygen, and it needs to go in your lungs, not out here."

Damn thing fit tight too. He tried to mumble.

The nurse shook her head. "Breathe. Quit trying to talk while I check your CO level." She frowned at one of the contraptions he was connected to and nodded. "Good. CO level's coming down. O-two's coming up. Not where we want it yet, and until it is, that mask stays on your face."

Tried to mumble again.

"As for your family, they're okay, better than you—except for one of your sisters. Right now, she's in a hyperbaric oxygen chamber, but the doctor thinks she'll be all right."

He loosened the corner of the mask.

The nurse's eyes bugged. "Keep that mask on your face before I have it welded in place."

He scanned her expansive body and determined expression. The woman was clearly big enough—not to mention determined enough—to do the job.

Barely holding herself together, Tess waited while Lieutenant Woods read her report of Taylor's capture. Pretty much single-handed, she'd caught the serial killer. What was the worst she could expect from Woods? A reprimand? A few days' suspension for not following procedure?

Surely, he wouldn't ask for her resignation. Hell no. She was the fucking hero of the hour. Even so, she clenched her fists to keep them from shaking. No matter what the lieutenant decided, she'd take her punishment. Taking Taylor down was worth every disgusting moment she'd spent in his creepy-ass company.

Would she do it all over again? Hell, yes.

Woods scowled over his glasses. "I ought to ask for your shield and service weapon."

She swallowed hard, then nodded. "Yes, sir."

"Detective, today you showed abysmal judgment. Instead of informing me, as procedure demands, and setting up a police trap, you grandstanded and put yourself and citizens at risk."

"Yes, sir." Her heart slammed loud enough the lieutenant could probably hear it.

"I don't take insubordination lightly."

Insubordination? He was going to fire her, after all.

He cleared his throat. "Given the circumstances and the publicity surrounding the case, you'll keep your job, but I'm placing a letter of reprimand in your jacket. See you don't repeat this offense, O'Malley."

"Yes, sir." She held her breath, afraid to believe her ears. Was that it? A lousy letter of reprimand. Not a suspension. Slid by, by the skin of her ass.

"Dismissed."

Not needing a second invitation to get the hell out, she left and waited until the door shut behind her before heaving a sigh of pure relief.

She found her partner leaning back in his chair and grinning. "I see you still have a job."

"Yeah." She sat, still a little shaken from the ordeal.

"Surely, you knew he wouldn't fire you." Kozinsky rubbed the five o'clock shadow already on his chin.

"Did *you* know?"

He nodded once. "I did."

"Why didn't you tell me all I'd get was a letter in my jacket?"

"Figured it wouldn't hurt you to sweat it for a while."

"Gee, thanks a whole hell of a lot…partner."

Kozinsky's left eye twitched. She'd never seen him so nervous. Twitch. Twitch.

Her gut clenched. Something was off. "What the hell's the matter with you?"

Twitch. Twitch. He ran a finger around the inside of his collar.

Damn. Her partner's unease was infectious. Her shoulders tightened. "What?"

He swallowed. "I'm sorry, Tess…you need to know."

"Know what?"

"Scott Holt and one of his sisters. Some kind of gas leak at their house. Carbon monoxide poisoning."

She staggered and grabbed the edge of the desk, then collapsed into her chair. Kozinsky called her name, but the sound of his words came from far away. Time slowed. Blood pulsed in her ears, slower and louder than physically possible. With a sickening rush, time fast-forwarded. Her breath rushed back in ragged gasps. Finally, her mouth formed the words, "Is he…"

Her partner shook his head. "No, he's in the ICU. His sister's in guarded condition, but they should both recover."

"I have to get over there. Which hospital?" She forced her rubbery legs into action, sprang from her chair and raced for the door.

"Parklane," he yelled after her.

***

All the way, she raced while images of the cherry-faced bodies she'd come across in her career loomed in her mind. At least Kozinsky hadn't said anything about an explosion. Thank God. She shook her head. She hung a right and pulled under the portico of the doctor's building and parked. She rushed through the granite-floored lobby and into the medical center, heading up to the fifth floor ICU.

She entered the unit, showing her badge to the charge nurse. "I'm here to investigate the circumstances behind the gas leak victims, Scott Holt...I'm not sure which of his sisters was involved."

The heavy-set nurse raised an eyebrow. "You think it was foul play, Detective?"

"Need to rule it out. May I see Mr. Holt?"

"You can see him all you want...after his doctor says it's okay."

She leveled her no-bullshit gaze at the nurse. "Now."

"He's asleep," the nurse said, not backing down.

Tess took a deep breath, then nodded. "Fine. I'll wait." She glanced over at Scott who was snoozing away or giving a very good imitation of it. "Mr. Holt and his family, are they going to be okay?"

"Officially, I'll tell you this much. Two of the family were treated and released. If he continues to improve, Mr. Holt will probably be moved to the floor today and released sometime tomorrow. His sister"—the nurse glanced at a round carousel of charts—"Caroline Lackey, had significant exposure—she was closer to the leak—and is spending some time in a hyperbaric oxygen chamber. She's not talking to anyone. Condition is guarded, but her prognosis is optimistic."

Memories of the tall blonde who ran Scott's office came to the fore with a sickening rush. "Close call, then."

"Yes, very. She's lucky her brother launched a midnight raid for a PB and J. He found her already unconscious. Got her and the rest of the family out of the house."

"What about after-effects?"

"They vary from one patient to another. Depends on the length of exposure," the nurse said, slipping into teacher mode. "Just a few are diminished verbal and written communication skills. Short-term memory loss. Long-term memory loss. Nausea, poor appetite, headaches, drowsiness, apathy, ambivalence, bladder control problems. Diminished balance control. Impulsive need to count things. Honey, the list is long.

There's just no telling how she'll be affected."

"Omigod."

The nurse nodded emphatically, then glanced over her shoulder. "I hear their doctor now. He'll give you a better report than I can."

"Yes, ma'am," she said, but in her book, the nurse had done a damn good job and doubted the doctor would take the time to be so concise.

He strode into Scott's glass-walled cubicle. He was a six-footer with the build of an ex-football player gone to seed around his middle. His dark hair was streaked with swipes of white along each temple. His eyes were gray and thoughtful behind stylish glasses. Jared Silverhill, M.D., Pulmonology Associates was embroidered in cursive across the left pocket of a white lab coat so crisply starched she could almost hear it crackle.

He awakened Scott and looked askance at her. She flashed her badge, introducing herself. He nodded, then shined a light in Scott's eyes, listened to his heart and lungs, and checked his reflexes. When through with the examination, he made notes in the chart incredibly slowly, so damn slowly he could've written half a novel.

"I don't see any signs of after-effects. You can be moved down to a medical floor as soon as there's a bed available, and I'll re-evaluate you in the morning," Silverhill told Scott.

"Need to get outta here now." He struggled to sit. Failed. Gave up. "Well, maybe one more day."

Tess smiled to herself. That was Scott and he was definitely all right.

"I don't think you'll have any permanent effects from this," Silverhill said, "but I'd like to see you in a week or so just as a precaution."

"Do I have to stay here? Man, these beeping monitors are driving me crazy."

Silverhill grinned. "As I said, you'll move to the floor today and we'll get you off the monitors so you can get up and move around a bit. Home tomorrow."

Scott nodded and his gaze traveled in her direction. She shot him a quick grin.

"I believe the detective has some questions for you." The doctor shut the chart, nodded, and left to see another patient.

"I thought you were going to sleep all day," she said, trying to keep the concern from her tone. What if he hadn't needed that midnight snack? God, what if he'd died? How could she live through that? So much time wasted over her vain desire to reach captain before she was forty. Her mother was right. It was about winning Daddy's approval and showing everyone she was as good, or better than her older brothers.

"Lucky I didn't go to sleep early last night."

"Yeah," she managed, then swallowed the lump in her throat. "I need to do some follow-up on that gas leak. Have you had any recent work done or had it checked?"

"I don't think so, but Carrie would know for sure. She schedules all the household maintenance stuff. Besides, it's summer. We don't use the gas, except in the winter—no, there's a gas water heater."

"She's a little indisposed, right now." She chewed the inside of her lip, then said, "Tell you what...I'm going to send the gas company to check it and see what gives."

"Sure. Say, have you interviewed Dakota yet? Is he awake?"

She shook her head. "He's my next stop."

"So I was just the first bullet point on your agenda today?"

She flashed a smile. "No, the lieutenant had that singular honor."

His gaze was warm and full of mischief. "You get in big trouble for yesterday?"

Mindful to keep matters between them casual, she shrugged. "Letter of reprimand."

"What did you expect? You're the hero of the hour." His eyes flickered with amusement, followed by the shy grin guaran-damn-teed to soften her oh-so-determined heart. "Y'think that letter will keep you from making captain by forty?"

"Maybe. Who knows?" He wasn't going to forget that, was he? "Maybe it doesn't matter as much...as other things."

The nurse trudged into Scott's cubicle, a no-nonsense expression on her round face. She stopped, set her hands on Texas-wide hips and cleared her throat. "Sorry to interrupt, Detective, but we're moving this hunk to the floor. Gotta get him ready."

"Fine. I'll be back...later." Tess nodded at Scott and made her escape. His soft words and glances sent waves of need curling through her body.

Why did she have to react to him every single time she saw him?

Why?

Because she was in love with him.

In the hallway outside ICU, she leaned against the wall and waited until her heart stopped racing, then punched in the number for Nashville Gas and arranged for a repairmen to be sent to the Holt-Lackeys' house. One task accomplished. Next, she called Vanderbilt's Neuro ICU and spoke with the charge nurse. Taylor's brain CT was better than expected. His Glasgow Coma Scale improving. Not capable of answering questions, but he could awaken anytime.

Dammit.

Someone else was still out there.

Chapter Thirty-One

Tess headed up Twenty-first toward Vandy. The university medical center was massive and spread over several city blocks, but her target was in the main hospital building. After parking, she strode into the brick building and headed straight for the Neuro ICU. It wasn't her first trip to interview a patient, or a suspect, for that matter.

No matter how she tried to focus on her upcoming interview with Taylor, Scott and his close brush with death kept popping up in her thoughts. He could've *died* and what would she do, if he had? Want to die along with him.

It only went to prove no one was safe anywhere. Not on the job or in a secure family home. Was her mother right, after all? Was making captain by forty supposed to be the be-all and end-all of her life? Her father loved and respected her, and that wouldn't change if she tweaked her plans a bit.

No, she couldn't give up her dream of making captain for making babies. Maybe she just needed a more inclusive, bigger dream. Could she have it all? Scott, children, and a successful career?

Modern women made the same type of decisions every day. Why was she any different? Of course, her change in plans presupposed Scott would accept her as is.

No returns. No refund. No kidding.

Tess stopped outside the double doors and turned off her phone before entering the ICU. Mentally, she crossed her fingers and hoped like hell that scum-ball Taylor was awake enough for questioning.

She walked to the nurses' desk and showed her ID to the unit assistant. "How's Taylor doing? I need to question him if he's awake."

"Bed four," the assistant said. "His nurse is Beth Barker. She's with him now."

Wondering where the uniformed officer who was supposed to be guarding Taylor was, she frowned and entered the cubicle. Taylor's eyes were open. He had two IVs, a heart monitor, and oxygen running, but that was about it for fancy equipment. Per regulations, he was handcuffed to the side rails.

Barker was young. Tall, thin and blond, she looked more like a supermodel than a nurse.

"I'm Detective O'Malley." Tess flashed her badge. "Where's the uniformed officer?"

"He went to the waiting room for coffee." The nurse nodded at Taylor. "He's all right for now."

"Can he answer a few questions?"

The nurse screwed her mouth to one side. "Well…he's doing amazingly well. His GCS is up to 14, but his speech is still confused. You can try, but I doubt you'll get much sense out of him." The nurse finished her chart notations and set it aside.

"I'd like to try." She gave the caregiver a reassuring smile as if throttling the bastard was the last thing on her mind. "Definitely."

"If you need me, I'll be with the next patient." The nurse straightened her shoulders and left Tess alone with her suspect.

Taylor's face was bruised and swollen on the right. Too bad, so sad. Killing was too good for him. "Taylor. It's Detective O'Malley."

His eyes opened and his gazed fixed on her. "Bitch," he hissed.

"You don't sound so confused to me. Been playing possum for your pretty nurse?"

He cut his gaze around the room. "You again. Crazy-assed bitch, you nearly killed me."

"Wish I had, but no matter. Your last victim survived, big boy. He identified you which means you're going away for a very long time—that is, if you live long enough to get to prison."

"If I were you I'd be more concerned about your boyfriend. He might already be dead."

"Sorry to disappoint you, but you blew that one, too. Who did your dirty work? Someone local or have you always needed help with your nastiness?"

"Who says he's through? Maybe I gave him more than one assignment." He gave her a crafty grin, then shut his eyes.

She'd been threatened by worse, but his words sent a chill curving through her body. Finding his accomplice was crucial.

The nurse returned. "Get anything out of him?"

"Yeah, and you can give him another point on the GCS. His speech is completely oriented. Don't let him fool you. He's been playing possum and he's dangerous. I'm instructing the uniformed officer to stay in the unit with him. In case you don't know it, your patient's a serial killer and a flight risk."

The color leached from Barker's face. "Yes, ma'am."

Shuddering, Tess turned and left the ICU. Creepy bastard. The urge to take a shower and wash off the filth of his presence shook her. No doubt about it. His threats were real and not something to ignore. She pulled the cell from her pocket and saw she'd missed two calls from the same unfamiliar number.

Dammit.

She listened to the voice mail—from the gas company inspector it turned out—then quickly hit call-return and waited until he answered.

"Good call, Detective. There were fresh tool marks on the pipeline entering the house. Crawled under the house and found a leak. Good thing they got out when they did. A spark could've blown the whole place sky high."

A shaking shudder ran up her spine. She took a deep breath. "Has it been repaired? I don't want the family going back until it is."

"Working on it now. I'll let them know when it's safe to return. Someone knew what they were doing and just where to do it, too."

"When do you think it was done?"

"Considering the family lived through it, I'd say late Friday evening. Whoever did it meant business."

"Thank you," she told the inspector. She disconnected, then called the department and requested a uniformed officer to guard Scott, who was still in danger if she believed Taylor's threat. No way would she risk Scott's life on the slim chance Taylor was bluffing. The CO leak had come too close to ending Scott's life, not to mention his sister's.

Taylor was already in the hospital when the leak occurred, so his threats about an accomplice rang true. Who, and in what capacity, was this accomplice? A full partner in his crimes? Or just someone local for his dirty work?

It was a short drive back to PMC. Tess strode down the south eighth-floor hall where Scott's new room was located. A slender woman with strawberry blond hair was hovering over him. Maybe his sister—the one who was a nurse, but this one wasn't wearing a uniform.

Tess cleared her throat. "Excuse me. Am I interrupting?"

Scott glanced up and grinned. "Allie, meet Detective O'Malley."

"One of your sisters?"

"That's right, Detective." She gave Tess the evil eye, the one that said 'you're not exactly welcome on my turf.'

"Any news on who tried to wipe out our entire family?"

Snarky little thing wasn't she? "Who said it wasn't an accident? I just found out myself."

"Intuition. I don't appreciate nearly being murdered in my bed." Each word was imbued with an underlying sarcasm which was clearly discernible to a trained investigator, especially another woman.

This young woman was Scott's sister and discretion was the word of the day. "Understood. An officer is on his way to stand guard outside Scott's room." She kept her tone neutral and professional, refusing to respond to his sister's prickly barbs.

Scott sat up and swung his feet over the side of the bed. "Hold on, ladies. No throwing down while I'm still in the room."

She hid her grin at Scott's 'throw down' remark and continued her professional spiel. "Repairs are being made to your heating system as we speak, and I'll let you know when you can return home. We have reason to believe the suspect in custody has an accomplice. As soon as we retrace the first suspect's steps, we'll locate and bring him in for questioning."

"You have no clue who this accomplice is?" Allie asked, her attitude not improving one tiny bit.

"Hold on, sis. You've been here all day." He cut a quick glance toward the door. "Why don't you take a break? Tess and I need to talk about the case."

His sister's jaw clenched. "You're kicking me out?" Irritation took up what appeared to be permanent residence on her face. From Tess's vantage point, she noted the bounding pulse in his sister's throat. "She's the reason our family's in danger."

"Not even half right. Go on back to the hotel." He grabbed the tail of his hospital gown and shifted to a bedside chair, but not before Tess caught a nice shot of his firmly muscled ass. She hid the grin, knowing it would probably set off his sister even more.

Little sister folded her arms across her chest and arrowed her chin a notch higher. "It was *her* case."

"Nah, goes farther back than this one. That's where we need to look." He made shooing motions at his sister. "Go on. Get outta here."

His sister huffed and shot Tess a look of undiluted disdain. Her lips moved as if she had more to say but was counting to ten to keep from saying it. "Well, if you think you can protect him until the uniformed officer gets here…"

Tess pasted on a smile, knowing it was impossible to sound pissed-off when smiling. "I can manage."

His sister frowned, grabbed her purse and marched for the door. "Fine, but I'm coming back to spend the night."

Tess's face heated. Enough with the guard dog routine. "No need. I'll spend the night. I don't want anything to happen to him, either." There— she'd put her claim on the man.

Allie's brows rose a fraction, then her face relaxed and an honest-to-God grin replaced her former frown. "Okay. Just see you take good care of him, 'cause you'll answer to me if anything bad happens." With that statement, she swept from the room, like a queen, and shut the door behind her.

"I don't think your sister likes me." She eased into the other chair and sat close to Scott, covering his strong hand with her smaller one. His eyes widened as if surprised by her touch. She lowered her gaze, not quite ready to meet his. Too many emotions crowded her mind, and this was no time to let her emotions get the better of her.

He let out a low chuckle. "Sorry, she's in full nurse mode and protective of her big brother."

"No kidding." She waited, enjoying the everyday warmth of being alone with him.

Relief colored her thoughts. Relief, he was alive and well. "I saw Taylor. The bastard's awake and he definitely threatened you again." No need telling him about Taylor's vague threat against her. "Any idea who might be his accomplice?"

He shrugged. "Beats the hell out of me."

She leaned closer. "I keep going back to your four counselors. Could his accomplice be one of the others?"

A frown furrowed his brow for a second. "Possibly. Are you ruling me out this time?" The soft warmth in his tone let her know he understood her need to keep to the case.

Pulling a notepad and pen from her inner pocket, she nodded. "Tell me about them again—from the beginning."

Luxuriating in his presence, she listened and made notes while he rambled about the events of fourteen years ago. Somewhere in those memories was a clue, if she could only find it. Stymied, for the time being, she gave him a smile of gratitude when he finished. Yet, something nagged at the back of her mind.

"You left something out—I won't know what until I compare my earlier notes with what you've just told me." She rose and leaned over, planting a light kiss on his forehead.

"Thought you were aiming to spend the night."

A glimmer of desire flashed in his eyes, darkening them to black, but she did her best to ignore it. "Business before pleasure. I'll be back."

"Good. I was sort of looking forward to it." He leaned back and propped his feet on the side of the bed.

She blinked. "I wouldn't do that if I were you," she said with a wide grin. "The…uh, boys are getting a little too much air, if you know what I mean."

His face darkening with embarrassment, he jerked down his feet. "Damn hospital gowns."

She bit her bottom lip and tilted her head to the side, then grinned. "They have their advantages."

Still smiling, she waved and quickly left his room. She noted the uniform sitting beside the door and stopped.

The officer stood. He was at least six-feet tall, broad-shouldered, blond, still had peach fuzz on his baby cheeks, and some very nice biceps. "Ma'am?"

She updated him on the circumstances, adding, "There's a good chance our serial killer's accomplice was responsible for the gas leak. I was just over at Vandy where he made some vague threats against Mr. Holt. So, be on the lookout for anyone out of the ordinary. Don't let anyone in his room without a proper hospital ID."

He nodded. "Yes, ma'am."

"I mean anyone. No visitors. I'll be back in an hour or so."

All the way down the hall, Scott's omission troubled her. What had he forgotten?

Hell, she'd figure it out soon enough. All she needed were her notes—the ones she'd copied to a flash drive before the Feds played grabby hands with her case.

Chapter Thirty-Two

Tess entered the squad room, nodded at the A.A., headed to the coffee machine for a caffeine hit, then wove her way through the maze of desks to hers. She signed on her computer, then rummaged in the bottom of her purse for the flash drive, an act which took just enough time for her slow-as-summer-vacation computer to finish booting.

After loading the flash drive, she pulled up the case files for the cold case and reread each interview carefully. All the while she couldn't help but wonder what Scott was like before his parents died and the responsibility for his five younger siblings was thrust on him. He'd have made a damn good attorney.

Focus.

Drew Wilson and Dakota Taylor turned in at ten. When Scott and Tyler Jamison came to bed after eleven, they didn't turn on the lights so they can't prove Wilson and Taylor were actually in their beds. Scott's omission wasn't today; it was during the first interview. He hadn't mentioned staying up for the eclipse. But that was already resolved. What a waste of time. In her mind, he wasn't a suspect. Never—well, not after she got to know him. Maybe it was something else she'd picked up in her various interviews, but damned if she could spot it now.

Drew Wilson was a happily married man with a child. It wasn't likely he'd taken part in a rape/murder, then settled down to live a perfectly normal aboveboard life.

Tyler Jamison was also a married man, although he'd admitted he and his wife had separated more than once. Plus, his career path had taken him to all the cities where the single shoe killer had apparently set up shop. Perhaps they'd always worked together. Both were celebrities of a sort. A pro football player and a news anchor would have easy access to older male teens.

Jamison looked better and better for Taylor's accomplice. What was his alibi for the time of the Brennerman and Hurley abductions?

She picked up her cell phone, called Jamison and made an appointment to see him at his downtown apartment at seven. Smiling, she disconnected. Her call left Jamison sounding breathless and a little on the shaky side. How was that for rattling her suspect's cage?

Tess sat in Jamison's beige-on-beige downtown apartment, drank her mocha latte and watched the man pace until she figured he'd have to pay for replacing the carpet. The muscles in his face twitched as if a seizure was imminent, his jaw clenched, his hands fidgeted at his sides.

"Let's talk about the governor's grandson. Where were you when the Brennerman boy was kidnapped?"

He sidled over to the window and gazed for a moment. Still delaying the inevitable, he raised his left hand and tapped on the window, his manicured nails clicking like castanets.

"Enough, Jamison. You need to answer my questions now…or would you prefer to answer them downtown?" That threat usually loosened a suspect's tongue, if he was of a mind to talk at all.

He turned to face her, his eyes widening. His nostrils flared. His cheeks paled. "The Brennerman boy? That's your case, too? I thought Dakota was already in custody for that."

She took a sip of her latte, then set it on the dated brass and glass cocktail table. Caffeine she needed. Jamison's delaying tactics, not so much. "We haven't ruled out his having an accomplice. In fact, he's admitted he does, but he's a little stubborn when it comes to telling us who." She arched her brows. And waited.

Jamison sank into the nearest overstuffed chair. "You can't possibly think I had anything to do with any of this." He dug at his tie as if it were a noose and unbuttoned his shirt collar.

"I'm waiting for you to answer my question." Her foot tapped. "Where were you when—"

"I heard you the first time, Detective." Head in hands, he leaned forward as if he might upchuck. "When was that exactly? The date?" His voice cracked, ending with a rising inflection.

"July third. You said you've done career presentations for the campers. Were you there that day…presenting?" What a lily-livered prick this guy was.

He reached in his jacket pocket, his fingers scrabbling for something. "July third? I-I have to check my calendar." He pulled it out a smartphone and tapped on the screen. His shoulders straightened. Tess saw relief cross the news anchor's face.

"July third…" He smiled, showing his perfect white caps. "I was in Augusta, Georgia, teaching an undergrad seminar at the Paine College."

"The topic?"

"Professional Ethics and the Television News Journalist," he said, his words ending with a rising tone of elation and triumph.

She wanted to hate him, but how could she? Any man would be thrilled with providing an alibi which could clear him of murder." And you can substantiate your presence?"

"Detective O'Malley, I have time-stamped and dated footage." His face literally beamed. If she wasn't careful, she'd have to put on a pair of shades to keep from being blinded by his pearly whites.

Try as she could, she couldn't refrain from curling her lip and making a face. "I need it. The original."

Still shining like a new headlight, he nodded. "Gladly. The station taped my presentation and ran a clip of it on the four o'clock news. The original broadcast is in the station library."

About time. She rose from her spot on the sofa and took a step toward the door.

He sprang from his chair.

"I'll follow and pick it up now," she said. "Have to verify that alibi."

"Excellent. That's a superb idea."

Enough. Already. His ebullience was starting to chafe like sand in her bikini bottom. All the same, if he was cleared, he was cleared, and it was time to look in another direction.

***

"I'll need that back." As Jamison offered Tess the tape, his hand gave tiny backward jerks as if he wasn't as anxious to cooperate as he'd indicated.

"Sure." She deposited the digital recording in an evidence bag, labeled and sealed it. "Thank you for your cooperation." She kept her tone professional and headed for the car.

No point in pissing-off the media. Never knew when a media contact could be used to the department's advantage.

The sun was still high in the bright late August sky...and hot. The air was so stifling in her rental car it left her breathless. She switched on the AC, then raised the window as soon as the air started to circulate and cool.

Back at the CJC, she verified the recording which documented Jamison's alibi for the time of the Brennerman kidnapping/ murder. That left Drew Wilson as number one on the most likely accomplice list.

Not in his office on the weekend. Not at home, either. His wife wasn't very forthcoming, and to Tess's experienced ears, the woman sounded worried. Anxiety grew and built in her chest. She needed to find Wilson.

Scott hit the remote. The hospital's internal cable TV didn't exactly carry any of the better sports channels. Who wanted to sit in bed all day and watch TV anyway? He wasn't sick. According to his sister, his oxygen readings were fine or "within normal limits."

Where the heck was Tess? He'd already played a couple of hands of poker with his guard and was getting damn bored.

The sound of raised voices reached him. He hauled from the bed, padded to the door and peered into the hallway. The guard was arguing with Drew Wilson.

"Come on. Let 'im through," Scott said. "I know him."

The guard shook his head. "The detective said no visitors."

"He's okay. I can vouch for him." Maybe he was inviting trouble. And if he was, so be it.

Drew entered the hospital room, but this Drew was a stranger. Unlike his usual neatly pressed, well-tailored, and polished persona, the man in front of him was dressed in wrinkled khakis, a half-tucked, mis-buttoned shirt, and a pair of loafers with scuffed toes. His shoulders were hunched as if burdened by an unbearable weight. His gaze darted nervously around the room. "You're alone?"

"Yeah." Scott sat on the side of the bed and gestured to the straight-backed visitor's chair. "Take a load off. I'm in a private room with no one but the guard for company, so I'm dying for some real conversation. Nothing much on TV unless you're of a mind to watch a colonoscopy." He gave a theatrical shiver and waited for a response to his sophomoric humor.

The corner of Drew's mouth twitched, but the smile never happened. He sat, knees apart, his elbows resting on his thighs. His gaze darted toward the window; he rubbed his hands together in a washing motion. "Doctor say you're gonna be all right?"

"Yeah." What the hell was up with Drew? "How's your sister? TV said she was critical."

"She got the worst of it, but the docs think she'll be all right. She was in the den. Closest to the leak, y'know?"

"Ye-ah." Drew dragged out the word as if just saying it choked him. His handwashing intensified, then his hands clenched together in a single fist. He rose with a jerk and gave a sharp nod as if he'd decided something. "Gotta go."

For the first time since entering the room, Drew met Scott's gaze. "Glad you're okay."

"Thanks for stopping by, buddy. Appreciate it." Still puzzled by the man's behavior, Scott watched him leave the room, his shoulders back, his gait determined.

He reached for the bedside phone and punched in the number for Tess's cell. It rang, then rolled to her voice mail.

Dammit.

He left a quick message about his suspicions regarding Drew's odd appearance and behavior, then disconnected.

Was it possible Drew was Taylor's accomplice? With his early background, the guy knew his way around gas heating systems. Dammit. He could've engineered the gas leak, but it just didn't fit with the man he knew. Why on earth would Drew give any kind of assistance to a serial killer?

Blackmail?

Tess sped down Charlotte Avenue. The niggling anxiety had mushroomed into a mountain of dread. The hair on the back of her neck was playing tiddly-winks with her emotions. Ready to turn into the hospital complex, she slowed when the squawk box erupted with the code for "shots fired" with the location given as Centennial Park's duck pond.

She flipped the switch for the lights and siren and blasted through a red light until she reached Twenty-fifth. She whipped left and headed for the closest entrance which would put her at the location.

A park police car and a Metro cruiser were already on scene. A uniformed officer was marking the perimeter with crime scene tape while his sergeant was talking to a bystander on the far side of the cordoned-off area. She parked with a screech of tires, then jumped from the car and badged the redheaded uniform before ducking under the tape. She slowed her pace just long enough to ask, "What've we got?"

"Looks like the dude in the black Mercedes offed himself."

"Touch anything?"

The uniform flushed and hunched his shoulders, then wrinkled his brow, his attitude aggrieved. "O'Malley, I don't make mistakes like that twice." He clipped his words.

"Just checking." Her mouth twitched. Nelson was just a rookie when he'd made his 'mistake'.

"Any witnesses?"

"Couple of joggers." Nelson nodded toward a tall dark-haired man and one very pale woman who clung to his arm. "They were about ten feet behind the victim's vehicle when the gun went off. The guy—he hit the deck and jerked his girlfriend down with him. They didn't see anyone else near the car. The window was down. I looked inside. Gun's in his lap."

"How'd you get here so quickly?"

"Sarge and I had just grabbed a burger at the McD's next to the park when we heard the shot and a woman's screams."

"The witness?"

He nodded.

"Good job, Nelson." She glanced over her shoulder at the Mercedes. "Get me a read on that vehicle registration. Guess I'd better have a look. M.E. ought to be here soon."

The sporadic quacking of ducks and geese offered an absurd counterpoint to the thudding of her heart. She pulled on a pair of latex gloves, then strode over to the vehicle. Blood and brain matter were splattered as far as the rear window. She glanced inside, into the very dead face of Drew Wilson.

Chapter Thirty-Three

Dammit. Her case against Taylor was majorly screwed. That bastard wasn't about to talk, and now, her best bet for Taylor's accomplice had just eaten his gun and blown his brains all over his sleek Mercedes. She wiped sweat from her forehead with her forearm. Never a breeze when you needed one.

Or a break. Was it asking too much of fate to hope he'd left a suicide note? Just a teeny-weeny one?

She walked around the car, eased open the passenger side door and glanced inside.

No note.

However, there was an iPad in the passenger seat. It figured a financial guru would have one. Granted, it was splattered with a bit of blood and a speck or two of brain matter, but the contents—ah, the contents could be golden. More than anything, she wanted to retrieve that puppy and open it, but the chain of evidence ruled over everything. The forensics team would arrive soon enough and it needed to be photographed in situ before she could get her grubby hands on it.

"Hell of a mess, ain't it, O'Malley?"

She whirled and found herself facing Sergeant "Hank" Napier. Somehow, he'd managed to avoid the donut addiction so common to officers his age. In his late forties, he was tall, still muscular and wore his salt-and-pepper hair buzzed Marine short.

"Indeed it is, Sarge. Any of the witnesses see anyone near the vehicle?"

"Nope, two witnesses say he was alone when they heard the shot." He cast a skeptical glance at the car and its occupant. "His clothes don't fit with his fancy ride. Reckon he stole it?"

"No. I know him. He's the owner. Name's Drew Wilson. He's a financial counselor and…was a person of interest in my case."

"Like they say, 'Money don't buy happiness'."

"As a matter of fact, it seems like money attracts the opposite." Her cell phone rang. She tugged it off her belt and eyed the caller ID.

Scott. What was he doing using his cell phone in the hospital? He'd already tried to reach her several times, but she'd been so intent on finding Wilson she'd ignored his calls and let them go to voice mail. "Gotta take this."

Opening her phone, she answered, "Sorry."

"Dammit, Tess. Been trying to reach you for a good twenty minutes. Drew Wilson was—"

"How'd you know about Drew? I'm still at the scene. The video journalists are just now pulling up."

"What're you talking about? What scene?"

"Drew Wilson committed suicide in Centennial Park."

Silence. Then… "Fuck. I had a chance to stop him and I didn't even know it."

"Give me the condensed version. This scene is heating up with news crews and the M.E. and forensics."

She listened while Scott gave her the down and dirty of Wilson's visit to Scott's hospital room and his strange behavior. "There wasn't anything you could've done. You didn't know. Hell, he almost killed you and your family. I'd bet money on it."

"Still…"

His tentative tone told her he needed more reassurance, but there wasn't time. "Look, I'll call you later. We need to talk…just you and me."

Before he could object, she hit the disconnect button. Yeah, they needed to talk, but what was she going to say? She still hadn't figured that out. Not completely.

The man she loved came close to dying last night. Could she live without him? Did she even want to try? Even if it meant a major obstacle to her career plans? In spite of being the hero of the quarter-hour, with a formal reprimand in her jacket, her career path to captain was a little iffy at the moment.

Somehow before she talked to him again, she had to make a decision.

Scott set the handset back on the phone. Damn. She'd hung up on him. Sure, she was involved in a case. Sure, she said she'd call him later. But one thing he wasn't too damn sure about was the "we need to talk" part.

It could only go two ways. Either she'd reconsidered their having a future together or it was the final kiss-off.

She cared about him. Hell yes, she did. He'd even bet his prized Tennessee Titans season tickets on it. But was caring enough?

He kicked off the top sheet and set his feet on the cold tile floor. He wasn't spending another five minutes in this damned hospital bed, much less an entire night.

He snatched on his shirt and jeans, then headed to the door.

"Hold on. Detective O'Malley said you weren't going anywhere."

Dammit. He'd forgotten about the uniformed officer stationed at his door. "I'm just going up to see my sister in ICU. I just talked to O'Malley. Call her. She'll tell you all the bad guys are out of commission."

The guard reached for his comm. unit. Scott brushed by him and headed toward the back elevator.

The officer called after him, "Hold it."

What was the officer going to do? Shoot him in the hallway? Not likely.

He slipped through the elevator doors, smiled and hit the button for the fifth floor. "Back in a few," he said as the doors closed just in time.

He hadn't exactly lied. He was going to check on Carrie, but he wasn't going back to that hospital bed. He walked into the hall outside ICU. Luck was with him. It was visiting hours if you could call ten minutes every two hours visiting hours. He nodded to the unit assistant at the desk. "I want to check on my sister, Caroline Lackey."

The U.A. didn't even look up. "Number five."

"Thanks." He eased over to Carrie's glass-walled cubicle. He stopped for a minute and watched. She still had an oxygen mask, but her heart tracing looked regular, and the vital signs displayed seemed okay to his untrained eyes.

He tiptoed inside the cubicle. She appeared to be sleeping. He chewed his bottom lip, trying to decide whether or not to wake her. Better not. He turned to leave.

"Where do you think you're going?" Her voice was muffled by the mask, but her attitude rang through loud and clear.

Reassured by the knowledge she would be okay, he whipped around and gave her a quick salute. "I didn't want to disturb your beauty sleep."

"They say I'll live." She lifted a corner of the mask. "But I might have problems with my memory and stuff like that."

"Yeah, they told me that, too."

She scooted up in the bed and rested on her elbows. "Might be a problem at the office."

He shrugged. "Don't worry. We'll work it out."

"Everybody else came out okay. That's what they said."

"Right. Allison was here most of the afternoon bossing me and the staff around. Justin and Tam took a couple of double rooms at the hotel across from the park. I'm heading over there now. I'll bunk with Justin. Just until we get the go-ahead to move back in the house."

"They dismissed you?"

"I—uh, sorta dismissed myself."

"Allie will have a fit."

"Won't matter." He flashed a smile. "It'll be too late."

His sister grinned, then sighed and lay back against the pillow. "Getting tired." She repositioned the mask.

"I'll go. You take it easy and don't give the nurses a hard time. You're such a drama queen."

A muffled semi-snort was her response as she gave him a weak goodbye and good riddance wave.

After leaving the ICU, he headed back to the nurses' station. Guilt had gotten the better of him. It'd be better if he signed out AMA and absolve the hospital and physician of any responsibility for his headstrong actions. Allison would still be pissed-off when she heard he left against medical advice, but he'd have legally crossed the Ts and dotted the Is.

***

At the TBI forensics lab, Tess hung over her friend Dani's shoulder—make that her ticked friend Dani who'd apparently had enough.

Eyes blazing, she whirled on Tess. "I'm covering an extra shift. I don't need you dogging every move I make. You're gonna have to wait until the computer forensics guy comes in on Monday morning."

Tess stuffed her frustration into a hole somewhere between her stomach and throat and raised her hands in surrender. "All right. Crap. I need to know if our suicide victim left a note or anything on his iPad. A quick peek. That's all."

Dani's mouth twisted to the side and she gave a slow knowing nod. "How badly do you want it?"

Elation bubbled in place of frustration. Her friend was a pushover. "Damn bad. For my case."

"A day at the spa bad?"

Not a pushover, but workable. "Yeah, definitely a day at the spa bad."

"One condition."

"Okay, I'll bite." She hoisted her hip onto a high stool and perched. "As if a spa day isn't enough of a bribe by itself."

"You look like crap. You have to join me."

Tess's shoulders sagged. "Gee, thanks. I just came from a very messy suicide. How am I supposed to look?"

"Let's just say I've seen you looking better."

She eased off the stool and held out her hand. "Deal. Now hand it over."

"Gloves first. It hasn't been dusted yet."

"Sure. Whatever."

Dani unsealed the paper bag, made the appropriate notation, then handed it over to Tess who removed the pricy tablet and turned it on. "Now all I have to do is figure out his access code."

"Didn't I say you should wait for the computer forensics guy?"

"Wipe that smug expression off your face. I'll figure it out." She leaned her elbows on the counter and tapped the onscreen keyboard. "I guess I could take it to my office. I can check my files for his birthday.

Stuff like that."

"Hell, no, you can't. Don't bother trying."

"Fine. Just let me access one of the computers down here. Actually, I might just have a flash drive with the files on it in my pocket." She fished in her pocket, pulled out the small drive and waved it under Dani's nose. "Pretty please?"

"Should've said so in the first place." She nodded at an unused terminal. "Have at it. Sign in with your usual password and it'll bring up the MNPD system instead of the lab's."

Tess flashed Dani a thank-you smile and slid over to the keyboard. "Where's the USB port? Never mind, found it."

She inserted the drive, signed into her account, then pulled up and opened her files on the thumb drive. After spending a full ten minutes of trying Wilson's date of birth, his social security number, his phone number and finally his street address from five years earlier, the PDA finally allowed her access. "I'm in."

"Have fun." Dani's tone was a somewhat good-natured murmur.

Tess checked Wilson's texts—just a quick text to his wife saying he was sorry. And there it was—Wilson emailed his confession to himself. His last words before he sucked on his automatic and splashed his brains all over his fancy Mercedes.

A single lapse in judgment on Wilson's part fourteen years ago. He and Taylor took the Mason boy into the woods. To teach him to be a man. Taylor, the sick bastard, got carried away with their games and killed the boy. Wilson claimed he'd never touched another underage boy since then, but Taylor was back in town when the governor's grandson disappeared from the same camp. Wilson contacted Taylor and begged him to leave town. Instead, Taylor blackmailed Wilson into tinkering with the Holt-Lackey's heating system. He was supposed to do the same at Tyler Jamison's house and Tess's condo. Instead, wracked by guilt after his first botched job, he took the easy way out.

Everything she needed. The connection between Wilson and Dakota Taylor.

And more.

More than she ever imagined. Or wanted to.

***

Once Scott had signed the Against Medical Advice waiver, he called a cab and directed the driver to drop him at the hotel. It was a short trip, a matter of a couple of blocks. He paid the cabbie and hot-footed it into the lobby where he picked up the key card his family left for him. He headed up to the sixth floor where the rest of his family was staying in adjoining rooms.

At the door to his room with a key card in hand, he hesitated. Why had he ducked out of the hospital in such a rush? True, he was tired of the hospital bed, but the reality was he was running from Tess.

No, he was giving her time to decide. She could find him easily enough. Not like she didn't have his cell number.

Time to think—for him, too.

He opened the door with the key card. Justin was semi-reclining in a chair, his feet propped on the bed and a laptop positioned on his thighs. He shot a startled glance at the doorway. "Didn't think you were gonna be dismissed 'til tomorrow."

He walked over to the second of the double beds and sat on the side. "About that. Signed out AMA. Checked on Carrie before I left. She's better. Feisty even." He kicked off his shoes, adjusted the two pillows and leaned back against the headboard.

His brother shook his shaggy head, signaling his disapproval. "Ya left the hospital AMA? Allie's gonna be—"

He averted his gaze from Justin's. "She'll get over it. Just keep your voice down. She doesn't need to know I'm here until the morning. I'd like one good night's sleep before she has a genuine hissy fit."

"What's really going on, dude?"

"Nothin'." Scott shot a quick look at the blank TV screen. "Any games on?"

"Bound to be." Justin snatched the remote, pointed and clicked. The local news was on with footage promised from the suicide in the park. "How's it going with your detective?"

He gestured with a dismissive wave. "Hush. Want to see this."

"Not the game?"

"No. Tess was on the scene. Drew Wilson killed himself." He leaned forward intent on watching for her on the small screen, and maybe by a major happenstance, he could figure out her frame of mind and why they needed to talk.

"Holy crapola."

"Exactly. Now zip it."

His brother grumbled some trash about Scott's attitude, but he did his best to ignore it. Would the news story ever come on?

Finally. He caught a glimpse of Tess talking to an older uniformed officer. As soon as she ducked under the yellow tape, there was a video journalist in her face.

"Any idea who the victim is, Detective?"

An expression of irritation flashed across her face. If the reporter knew anything about her fiery temper, he'd be wise to tread lightly. "You know I can't say until his family's notified."

"Any idea why he killed himself?"

Her gaze fixed on the journalist, pinning him like a bug. Man should've cringed but didn't. "I know you have a job to do but so do I. Let me do it and stop asking questions you know I'm not going to answer." The words came with a sweet smile, but her tone was laced with pure saccharine.

The journalist cleared his throat. "That's all we have at the moment, and apparently, all we're going to get for now. Ray Hanson from News Channel Nine HD."

Justin let out a chuckle. "Whew-ee! She's a pistol. Sure you can handle her?"

"Sure." But would he have the chance? Odds were she was ready to boot him out of her life as easily as she laid waste to the video journalist?

It was after ten. More than likely she wouldn't call this late. She'd head back to the CJC. Hell. He'd call her. He snatched the cell phone from his belt and punched in her number.

"Hey," she answered. Her voice sounded tired and worn.

Probably not the best time to call her, but he'd been patient long enough. Time to take back control. "You said we needed to talk."

"We do but there's so much going on right now. The investigation is over. An arrest warrant for multiple counts of murder, kidnapping and attempted murder has already been issued for Taylor. Drew's last email spelled out the whole sickening story. And I mean that. I'm sickened by all of it."

All right. Backpedal. This wasn't the time to get in her face about their future. The woman needed a good night's rest.

"Wanna share details? If you don't or can't, I'll understand."

"Just not tonight. Meet me for coffee in the morning—say, ten?"

"At our place?" He held his breath and waited. Would she know where he meant?

Her delicious chuckle followed, and it tempered his mood. "Yeah. Our place...where I nearly kicked your butt onto the street. You were so obnoxious, all over a little indecision."

"A little? You took a full ten minutes to order your coffee."

"Did not...well, maybe."

As her tone grew playful, hope fizzed through his mind and sizzled through various body parts. He adjusted his position to allow room in his jeans. "Ten it is. Goodnight, babe."

"Night."

He disconnected and set the phone on the bedside table.

"Omigod." Justin let out a raucous cackle. "That's the closest I've ever come to witnessing phone sex."

Scott snatched a pillow and tossed it at his brother. "And that's the closest you'll probably ever come to any kind of sex, you pencil-necked geek."

"Harsh. Dude, that's just uncalled for." More cackles, then... "Just to show you who's mature and who's not, I won't retaliate."

"Cause you know I'll kick your ass."

"There's that." Justin picked up the remote and clicked over to ESPN, then flashed Scott a shit-eating grin. "Go to sleep. Don't you have a big date tomorrow morning?"

"I do. And that's more than I can say for you." Scott's phone rang again. An old friend was back in town, looking for a job. He quickly made an appointment for eleven-thirty the next day.

Across town a couple of hours later, Tess entered her condo and turned on the lights. A frozen margarita would hit the spot right now, but a light beer would have to do. She ambled over to the fridge, opened it and pulled out one of the long necks. Taking a long pull directly from the bottle, the icy cold liquid cooled her parched throat—it was damn near perfect.

A long day's weariness grinding her down, she kicked off her shoes and wandered over to the sofa. She plopped down and grabbed the remote for the MP3 player. Soon the mellow tones of a country-western song wafted through the late-night air.

She just needed to chill-out.

No more worrying about the future. Making captain by forty was a childhood fantasy. With one formal reprimand already in her jacket, she wasn't likely to achieve it. Her father and brothers were stand-up guys and good cops. She was too.

Basically.

Just one tiny little problem with following orders and playing by the rules.

Why shouldn't she have a personal life? All of her brothers were married, two with kids. One already divorced though.

If Scott had died…

She shook her head. No, losing him wasn't an option. As much as she hated to admit it, her mother was right. Living without Scott as a part of her life wasn't something she wanted to consider. He was sane and steady where she was—admit it—a rule breaker.

The man was anything but boring. He stepped up to cover her back after she'd kicked him to the curb and was barely speaking to him. Kicking him from her heart—now that was a little more difficult.

All right, so he made her pay him a retainer. Her mouth curved into a smile at the memory. Yes, he enjoyed taking her money and making her squirm.

And he had more than one way of making her squirm. His hands and lips played her body like a five-string banjo, then moved and finessed her emotions like a country love ballad.

What woman would willingly give up a man like that? Not this woman.

Chapter Thirty-Four

After picking up their coffee, Scott and Tess walked all the way down Church. She filled him in on the contents of Wilson's email. It included a full confession going all the way back to his participation in Rich Mason's death at Camp Einstein up to the point where Dakota Taylor blackmailed Drew into rigging the gas leak with threats toward his family.

When they reached River Front Park, gaily colored flags whipped in the breeze and the dank smell of the river penetrated his nostrils, but something was wrong. The life and spark which were such a part of Tess were missing. No doubt about it. She was ready to dump his ass. For good this time.

Together, they sat on one of the benches. He stiffened his resolve, reached over and grasped her hand. Somehow, he'd convince her they belonged together. "All I want to say is, if you're dumping me again, get it over with."

So much for his convincing words.

She set her cup aside and gazed into his eyes. He read uncertainty, then a flicker of mischief.

She emitted a very unladylike snort. "Why would I do something as stupid as that? I admit a lot of my choices have been rash—"

"Like meeting a serial killer with only yours truly as backup?"

"Anyway. Since my career's in the toilet..."

He sucked in a deep breath, stood, tossed the contents of his cup, then crushed it into a ball and threw it into a trash receptacle. "Second place never suited me, lady."

She grabbed his wrist. "You're wrong. That's not what—"

"Sure sounded like it to me." He freed his wrist and turned to walk away. Walk away from pain and utter stupidity. But he stopped and turned back to face her. "God. I'm such an idiot. All this time, you weren't playing hard to get. You were impossible to get. I don't get you at all."

"No, I guess you don't, but you cut me off. You didn't let me finish."

"Oh, we're finished." He took a couple of steps, still not wanting to believe they were well and truly over.

Her hand snaked out, grasped his wrist and twisted it up behind his back. "Ouch!"

"You have to listen to me. If I have to cuff and place you under arrest, I will." Her expression was tense; lines furrowed her brow and tightened her lips into a thin line.

The words 'crazy bitch' came to mind, but seeing as how she had him at a disadvantage, he wasn't about to piss her off even more. "Cuffs could be fun." He shot her a half-grin, hoping to defuse her urge to kick his ass and humiliate him further. Tess was his kind of crazy, after all.

"Sit down and shut up." Her facial muscles softened a bit. "You're going to let me finish what I was trying to tell you before your lawyer's side so rudely interrupted. Now I understand why cops hate lawyers."

"Yes, ma'am, Detective O'Malley." Wondering just how far she would take her routine, he nodded. "Just to refresh your memory, and if it makes any difference, I'm a law school dropout."

"Back to 'since my career's in the toilet...'" Lowering her tone, she loosened her grip on his wrist. "I don't intend to give up my career, but given the fact you almost died on me the other night, I took some time to think. I realized I didn't want to give you up either. My career being in the toilet really doesn't matter the way I initially thought it would. I realize that having you in my life is more important than making captain by forty. So what if it takes me 'til I'm fifty?"

He shut his eyes for a second, then faced her. "What if it never happens? Can you live with that or will you blame me for ruining your career?"

She gave a bark of laughter. "You give yourself too much credit." Her gaze softened and her eyes shone as if she might cry. "No one can ruin my career but me. I accept that responsibility."

She released her hold on his wrist and sat on the bench. "You're not second place in my life. Never will be."

He rubbed his wrist and sat beside her. Good. Even though he knew she'd never really try to hurt him, having his wrist broken on a Sunday morning wasn't his idea of a coffee date. "I don't know…" He let his words fade, just to tease her a bit.

"I admit I'm not easy to get along with. I'm hot-tempered. I jump to conclusions—"

"And you nearly broke my wrist. Damn. You don't play fair. I'm not about to hit a woman, even if she is off-duty."

Her luscious lips drew into a pout. "Haven't you heard? I always get my man."

That seductive pout and statement sent a rush of blood to his groin. "You don't have me yet."

"Now who's playing hard to get?" She rested her hand on his thigh and squeezed.

The pressure in his groin increased until it felt like his balls would burst. "Babe, I'm not so 'hard to get' as hard."

A surprisingly seductive giggle erupted from the woman of his dreams. "How inconvenient. Right here on a Sunday morning too." She snuggled closer. "How about we take this inside? Out of public view?"

"As much as I want—no need—to take you up on that spectacular offer, I have an appointment—"

Her mouth pulled into a disappointed pout. "On Sunday?"

"See, I'm not the only one who interrupts. This old friend of mine called me last night. Former cop. He just moved back from Atlanta and needs a job."

"Why doesn't he apply with Metro?"

"Seems like his ex-wife's new husband is your new Chief of Police."

"Yikes." She waved her hands. "New plan. Come over after your appointment."

He shook his head. "I have to check on Carrie, then see about getting us moved back into the house." He glanced at his watch. "How about dinner at seven-thirty? I'll pick you up. We'll go out, do it up right and then…"

"Major makeup sex?"

"Absolutely. The best we've ever had."

She leaned her head against his shoulder, the citrusy scent of her shampoo tickling his nose. He slipped his arm around her waist and hugged her closer. The woman in his arms, soft and pliant—for the moment anyway—was all he'd dreamed.

"Sounds like a plan." She gazed up at him with both regret and warmth in her gray eyes. Standing, she gave a wink. "I'll let you go. Remember, I'm just a block away from your office."

"Like I could I forget?" His heart lighter than an hour ago, he stood, pulled her into his arms and kissed the tip of her nose, then stopped with a low groan. "If this goes any further, I won't make my appointment."

He strode away, cursing his lack of foresight in making the Sunday appointment. Still business was business.

Besides, anticipation would make their evening all the sweeter.

Damn. He'd better get his ass in gear. First a ring. Then if she said yes, a new place to live and start their lives together as man and wife—sooner if he could talk her into it. Besides, the house on Richland belonged to the Lackey side of their blended family. He and Tamsyn had always planned to move out at some point and get their own places. Would Tess's mother want to do the wedding up big? Probably so. Personally, he'd prefer a small family ceremony.

Better yet, what would Tess want? Yeah, better get used to thinking that way.

After his eleven-thirty appointment left, Scott sat behind his desk and reviewed Nick Vitelli's résumé. Former Atlanta detective, narcotics division, divorced, thirty-five-years-old, former Nashville native, back home because ex-wife and son had moved back to town. And most importantly, an old high school friend.

The agency needed new blood. It was past time to take on someone who wasn't a part of the family. Allison had no interest beyond applying the occasional bandage. Carrie was more interested in management and being behind-the-scenes. Justin was joined at the hip and brain to the IT side of the business, which left Tamsyn and Scott for the investigative work. Since Tamsyn would be tied up doing Carrie's managerial duties while she recovered, that left only him and business had picked up recently.

Simple decision. Hire Nick—and be damn quick about it.

He picked up the phone and punched in Nick's cell number. After a bit of small talk, Scott offered him the job and quoted a generous starting salary, contingent on Nick's passing the obligatory background check. The offer was accepted without hesitation or negotiation.

Scott texted Tamsyn to let her know of the new hire, and she responded she'd have the paperwork ready for Nick to sign on Monday. Satisfied with her quick response, he crossed one more item off his to-do list. Covering office management duties didn't rate high on Tam's list, but she'd pitch in like everyone in the family.

Now all he had to do was get Tess to say, "Yes."

Chapter Thirty-Five

A million thoughts whirled through Tess' mind while she rushed around picking up the condo. A small wedding would be less disruptive to her work schedule. Frankly, she couldn't see herself as one of those bridezillas, obsessing over the color of bridesmaid dresses and place settings.

Sheesh. No need to get ahead of yourself.

This was another dinner with Scott. Just dinner. And sex.

As for dinner, she didn't want to go out; it was being delivered. She was entirely too crazed to cook and have any expectation whatsoever it wouldn't be burned to a crisp or raw and rife with a hint of salmonella.

The clock chimed six. She glanced around the condo. Everything clean and neat. Kitchen spotless. The fresh summer flowers she'd bought down on Market Street were an informal arrangement of red, yellow and orange in a cut-glass vase on the counter. Now for a quick shower.

All for Scott.

Yes, the man loved her in spite of her determination to have a career. Where it would go from here was anyone's guess. But he was a family kind of guy. Whether he asked her to marry him or not, she was his.

Tess raised her face and let the tepid water rinse the soap from her face and the lime-scented shampoo from her hair.

Buzz.

Was that the delivery guy already? If so, he was half an hour early. She reached and turned off the faucet, then grabbed a couple of towels. Wrapping one around her head and the other around her body, she tiptoed into the foyer and peeked through the peephole.

Scott. She let out a girlie screech then took a deep breath. The man had no right to show up this early. She unlocked the deadbolt and opened the door. There he was all right, over an hour early with a large bag of takeout food in each hand.

"You're early," she said, pulling and tucking the towel around her a little more securely. "I thought we were going out?"

He smiled down at her, then walked over to the counter and set down the food. "See how well I planned everything? I brought dinner, just in case you wanted to stay in...and I bet you have a tendency to burn things."

"If I do, I just call it Cajun cooking." Aspersions on her cooking abilities aside, a warm thrill coursed to her barely covered naughty bits as she closed the door behind him. "So this was your plan? Come early and find me naked?"

"Exactly." His dark eyes smoldered with heat and humor. "I'd say it worked pretty well."

"Obviously." More than a little disconcerted, she poked the end of the towel in again.

"Wish you wouldn't do that." He pulled her into his arms and insinuated his forefinger into her cleavage. "I'm just going to see everything anyway..." He loosened the edge of the towel with a nudge. "...when I do this." The towel fell, leaving her entirely naked.

Resisting the strong urge to cover, she straightened her shoulders and thrust out her breasts. "No fair."

"From where I'm standing, the view is very fair...beautiful, in fact."

Her body betrayed her with a hot flush that spread from her breasts, up her neck to her cheeks. To cover her confusion, and not to mention one very naked body, she gave in, bent over, snatched up the towel, and covered the front of her body. "Better watch it, bud. As of this very moment, you're on very thin ice."

While it was a given they'd end up in bed that evening, there was no point in making it easy for him.

"You're gonna make me sweat—hell! You've already got me so hot and bothered I don't know if I'm coming or going."

"Which would you prefer? Coming...or?"

A dark eyebrow arched and a deep laugh erupted. "You have to ask?"

She giggled. "Cute. Now you can cool your heels until I get dressed."

"But—"

"But nothing. I understand your plan, but I ordered food too," she admitted with a grin. "Being interrupted in the middle of making love isn't exactly my cup of latte."

He took a step closer. His proximity set her heart thrumming; she took a ragged breath, then stepped back—just one step. Somehow, she had to clear her mind and get focused. Dammit, she was naked and he was fully dressed. Vulnerable she didn't do so well.

"It was a little hurried. Not my usual style, either." Scott's oh-so-kissable lips curved into a smile. "But it sure was hot."

Her lower belly grew warm and her inner muscles clenched at the memory. "Can't deny that." She grinned and bit her bottom lip. "But July is always hot." Without waiting for his response, she spun around, raced for the bathroom and shut the door.

Through the door, she heard his somewhat agonized and frustrated, "Come on, Tess!"

Dammit. She fanned her cheeks. He had her so confused she didn't know her ass from a hole in the ground. He had no business showing up an hour early.

None whatsoever!

Twenty minutes later, Tess emerged, attired in a turquoise cotton dress with a full flirty skirt. Hair reasonably styled off her neck, a minimum of makeup…and no panties. Not even a thong. She smiled. Wouldn't he be surprised?

"Your food delivery came while you were hiding out in the bathroom." He motioned at the counter which now held four large sacks of take-out food. Heaven only knew if any of it would ever be eaten.

She posed, then gave a model-on-the-catwalk twirl. "I wasn't hiding. I was slipping into something more comfortable. You like?" she asked, giving him a coy glance over her shoulder.

His warm, lazy glance slid up and down her body. "You look good enough to eat."

"Is that a promise of things to come?" Casually, she walked within his reach—just—and smiled up at him, tempting him.

Scott rubbed his chin and swallowed hard. "Sure hope so."

She cut her gaze to the take-out. "Pity about all that food going to waste." Moving closer, she molded her body to his, feeling the jut of his firm hard-on.

"Is it?" He licked his lips. "Thought you'd be hungry."

"Oh, I am. Take-out's fine…" She dropped her tone until it was a bare whisper, "…but tonight I'd rather take you." Snaking her arms around his waist, she grasped his knit shirt and pulled it from his khaki pants and over his head.

"I can live with that," he gasped, then inclined his head and kissed her neck below one ear, then her throat. Each kiss like a point of fire, he worked his way down to the cleft between her breasts.

"So beautiful." He slid the tiny straps off her shoulders and unzipped the top of her sundress, exposing her breasts completely, then let it fall to the floor. "So fucking beautiful. Skin's so soft." Then he cupped her breasts, tweaking her nipples until they were exquisite points of sensation. He pulled her close, her hands splayed across his sculpted chest and down.

Down. Down.

For a moment, she struggled with his belt and zipper, but finally, his khakis fell to the floor. Jerking his briefs down and over his ass, she caressed his sac, gently weighing his balls in her hand, then moved to rub his jutting, hard cock. He shuddered against her body and moaned her name.

He backed her against the cool stainless fridge. She heard his sharp intake of breath as he pressed against her. "My God, woman, you bowl me over." He kneeled in front of her and licked her belly, left a trail of kisses through her thatch of curls and then licked her damp folds, centering on her clitoris.

The warmth from his tongue spread throughout her lower body. Her legs weakened and she grabbed his shoulders to steady herself.

One long finger probed her, then two. Her inner muscles contracted and she moved her hips against him. "Please, I need you," she murmured. God, he was driving her wild. She needed him—all of him— inside her. She needed to feel him deep inside, stretching and thrusting…filling her.

Like his love and acceptance filled her heart and mind, erasing the hurtful words she'd spit at him not so long ago.

"No, not yet." He rose and kissed her long and hard, his tongue probing and battling with hers, the taste of her musk still on his lips. He grasped her thighs and picked her up. She wrapped her legs around him as his penis nudged at her outer lips. Whimpering, she tried to capture him with her hand, but he moved her hand away, centered himself at her entrance and thrust deep and hard, emitting a primal groan.

He began to move, slowly and deeply. Her body stretched and accommodated his length as if she were made for him and him alone. Each thrust deeper and fiercer than the one before, she grasped and squeezed him with her inner muscles, until the telltale flush and sparks of her climax began. "Faster," she begged with what breath she could muster.

Her back slapped against the cool stainless steel of the fridge as she rode him fiercely until the unswerving pressure sent her spiraling over the edge. Her inner walls throbbed with wave after wave of glowing and fiery sensations while a kaleidoscope of color exploded behind her eyes and in her mind.

Her body shuddered as he hammered home, his strokes faster and deeper than ever. His exultant cry as he came rang in her ears. Their sweaty bodies slid weakly to the kitchen floor. She tried to breathe, but all she could do was cling to him.

"Damn!" Scott sucked a ragged breath. "That was fan-fucking-tastic."

"Believe me, I know."

"You know, this floor's kind of hard."

"Ditto." She smiled at him. "Counselor, I move we take this to the bedroom."

"Motion sustained."

Scott woke from his nap with Tess beside him, snuggled in the curve of his arm and shoulder. Totally female—soft and warm, but firm and strong as well. He kissed the back of her neck and she stirred. He brushed away her long tangle of lime-scented hair and kissed down her spine. "You know you smell like a margarita?" A scattering of light copper freckles adorned her shoulders and back and he intended to kiss each one.

"Mm. You don't have to stop." Her tone was low and sultry as she moved her head forward.

He hardened instantly. "Have no fear. I have no intention of stopping," he said with a growl, then pulled her on top of him. She straddled him on her knees and reached for him until his cock brushed her cleft, moving her hips sinuously back and forth teasing him. Her red hair fell forward in a mass of curls and tickled his chest.

"Easy, doll," he gasped. God, he wanted this to last all night, but if she kept up, he'd be lucky to last five seconds. He raised his knees to support her back, cupped her firm ass as she slid down over him, an inch at a time until he was fully sheathed by her silken walls. He levered up on an elbow and reached for one of her full rounded breasts, tweaked one pink nipple until it tightened into a bead, then the other.

Her gray gaze sparking with glints of silver, she smiled down at him and began to move. Oh, God how she moved. First circular motions, grinding into him, then back and forth, side to side, all while her inner muscles gripped him in rhythmic motions. Unable to control himself any longer, his balls contracted, his shaft pulsed, wave after wave, as he flew over the edge. His head went back and a groan ripped from his throat.

"Sorry. Couldn't hold it," he gasped, while her body milked his of seed.

"Oh, we're not done," she warned with a glimmer in her eyes. His woman kept moving up and down over his semi-erection. The warmth of her sweet body enveloped him and he grew rock hard again. She leaned closer to his chest and kept grinding her body onto his. Her soft round breasts bobbed in his face. He took a breast in each hand and squeezed them, until she whimpered with passion, then took a reddened nipple in his mouth and sucked. Her head went back and her thrusting hips met him, stroke for stroke.

A red flush spread over her chest and neck. She was close to coming. He increased the pace. "Come on, baby. Come for me."

Her sweet warmth tightened around him. The heat overwhelmed him as he took both of them over the brink in a fast flurry of deep thrusts to her very core.

Moaning with her release, perspiring and shaking, she collapsed on top of him. "Now I have to marry you," she said with a faint giggle, then nestled her head on his shoulder, molding her body to his.

Scott rolled Tess to his side, then levered up on an elbow and grinned down at her. "Hold on. You didn't give me a chance to ask. How come?"

"No one ever made me come in Technicolor before...and I'm not about to let you get away."

"Technicolor?"

She nodded. "Yeah, baby. As in fireworks, better than the Fourth of July."

"Sounds good." His tone was hesitant. Technicolor had to be a good thing, right?

"Better than good. So-o-o much better than good." She rolled over to check the time.

There it was again—those numbers tattooed on her ass. "You gonna tell me about those numbers on your ass?" He caressed her firm ass cheek.

She turned back and grinned. "Those silly numbers? So you want to know about 'em?"

"Yes, the numbers on your very gorgeous ass."

"They're my gold badge number. I was pretty excited when I got it— the gold badge, I mean. And I lost a bet."

"Must've." He threw his head back and laughed until he was weak. Then he remembered...the ring. He sat and threw his legs over the side of the bed. "Be right back."

"No, don't go." She patted the bed beside her and whined, but somehow, she made it sound very seductive. "Stay with me."

"I'll be right back, babe." Finding an engagement ring on a Sunday hadn't been easy. He padded into the kitchen and picked up his khakis, felt in the pocket and retrieved the small box which had held his mother's half-carat diamond ring ever since she passed away.

Back in the bedroom, Tess was levered up on one elbow, her red hair spilling across her wonderfully freckled shoulders. What a picture she made. Why couldn't he be a painter and capture her just like that, fresh from their lovemaking?

"Whatcha got, big guy?" she asked with a smile. He smiled down at her. "Something special."

"You've already given me something pretty special." She bit her bottom lip, stretching sensuously like a cat warming in the sun, her back arching. Her beautiful breasts begged him to touch her again.

"My turn." Then he did the last thing he'd ever pictured himself doing, proposing on one knee—naked to boot.

"This ring was my mother's. Will you wear it? Marry me, Tess? I know you already asked me, but being an old-fashioned guy, I need to hear the answer from you…to make it official."

A delicious giggle emitted from this woman he loved. She threw her arms around his neck. "Yes. YES!" Then she giggled again. "How will we ever tell our children about this moment?"

"Simple…we'll lie."

"You better believe we will!" She gazed at him, the absolute love shining in her eyes. He bent his lips to hers and was lost in the sweet warmth of her love.

The End

ABOUT THE AUTHOR

Award-winning romantic suspense author Marie-Nicole Ryan has had a life-long love affair with books, so one could say it was only natural for her to start writing some of her own. She was born in Kentucky but lived in Nashville, TN for more decades than she cares to admit.

When she has time, she loves to read murder mysteries, browse antique shops and meet her friends for lunch. She's also devoted to her Shetland Sheepdog Cassie who tries to help her write by walking on her laptop.

She loves to hear from her readers, and she's never too busy to respond. You can email Ms. Ryan at marie AT marienicoleryan DOT com.

LINKS

Web site: https://marienicoleryan.com

FaceBook: https://facebook.com/MarieNicoleRyan.author

Twitter: @marienicoleryan

BIBLIOGRAPHY

NOVELS

THREATENED

MEASURE OF A MAN

HUNTED

MASTERING THE MARSHAL

PLEASURING THE PINKERTON

SEDUCING THE SHERIFF

BECAUSE OF YOU

BROKEN PROMISES

LOVE ME IF YOU CAN

HOLDING HER OWN

ONE TOO MANY

LOVE ON THE RUN

TOO GOOD TO BE TRUE

THE MAN FOR THE JOB

SEE YOU IN MY DREAMS

HOLIDAY THEMED SHORT STORIES

VALENTINE'S GIFT

PILLOW TALK

MISTLETOE AND MARIO